HIGHER GROUND

Meredith Sue Willis

**HAMILTON
STONE
EDITIONS**

Library of Congress Cataloging-in-Publication Data
Willis, Meredith Sue.
  Higher ground.
    I. Title.
  PS 3573.I45655H5   813'.54   81-8912
  ISBN 0-9654043-0-7
  (Previously published by Charles Scribner's Sons with
              ISBN 0-684-17225-9)

The line, "Take me home, country roads," by Bill Danoff, Taffy
Nivert, and John Denver, copyright 1971 Cherry Lane Music Co.,
is reprinted by permission of Cherry Lane Music Co.

The author wishes to thank the National Endowment for the Arts
for a Fellowship in Creative Writing, which provided much of the
time for writing this book.

Author Photo by Andrew B. Weinberger
Cover design by Howard Gilman

HIGHER GROUND

I'm pressing on the upward way,
New heights I'm gaining ev'ry day;
Still praying as I onward bound,
"Lord, plant my feet on higher ground."

Johnson Oatman, Jr.

Again, if two lie together, then they have heat: but how can one be warm alone?
And though a man might prevail against one who is alone, two shall withstand him; and a threefold cord is not quickly broken.

Ecclesiastes 4 : 11–12

To my parents,
Glenn and Lucille,
and my sister Christine

HIGHER GROUND

PART
ONE

ALL FAMILIES, I THOUGHT AS A CHILD, SHOULD BE LIKE MINE: TWO sets of grown-ups for one little girl at dead center of the universe. Mother and Daddy were my everyday guardians; they poured the cereal in the morning and woke me in time for Sunday school. Aunt Pearl and Uncle Joe Stone, on the other hand, took me to county fairs and carnivals. They had two Irish setters who rode with me in the back seat of their tan and cream Pontiac, and we watched the hills unroll alongside the window, stopping often to look at things—horses, mill wheels, old stone fences —and Uncle Joe knew where to buy homemade ice cream and hot dogs with the best chili sauce. They had a summer house, too, named Stone Paradise, and it was built on the side of a hill with Aunt Pearl's flowers growing in miniature terraces, and it even had a wishing well. It was years before I figured out that the other people who lived on Coburn Creek were terribly poor. All I knew then was that there were woods and fields and Uncle Joe had promised to build a paddock and a barn with a saddle mare for Aunt Pearl and a pony for me.

Mother and Daddy were afraid I was getting spoiled. They discussed it at length over dinner, in the backyard, and in our old Ford, where I liked to sit with my chin on the back of the seat between them. Mother would search my face with her huge eyes, and Daddy made jokes. I never worried seriously that I would be

[3]

separated from Aunt Pearl and Uncle Joe. Mother and Daddy were just trying to make me the best girl I could possibly be. Their voices passed over and ruffled me gently like summer wind in hay, bending me a little for my own good. Sometimes Mother told stories about when her mother died and she had to raise Aunt Pearl practically by herself, and how she loved Pearl but knew her faults. Then Daddy would recount the discussions he had overheard at the lodge about whether Uncle Joe was the best dentist in town or only the most expensive one.

Once I started school, I became a little more critical of Aunt Pearl and Uncle Joe myself. School was the official beginning of work, Mother and Daddy's world. They dropped me at my school every day on their way to the high school, where they taught. And then, as soon as we all got home, we sat down at the table for coffee—before homework or going out to play or cooking dinner—and told about the school day. Exciting things always happened. A boy smarted off at Daddy in class and Daddy had to take him to the principal, and they called in the boy's father who said Daddy was in the right, and if the boy ever talked back again Daddy should smack him, and then Daddy and Mr. Thornton had to explain that it isn't right to hit boys in school. Mother was always interested in right and wrong, and sometimes I would ask questions like what I should do if a girl in my class curses. But usually I told funny things, or how much homework I had.

I still loved going out with Aunt Pearl and Uncle Joe, but there were lots of people in my life now: kids at school, girl scouts, my piano teacher. I didn't like it the time Uncle Joe made me lean over the seat and hold the wheel of the Pontiac, even after I said I didn't think I should. Then he made me promise not to tell Daddy.

"If he just paid more attention to his driving," said Daddy, and I froze, thinking he had somehow found out what Uncle Joe made me do, but it wasn't that; they were talking about whether to let me spend the whole summer at Stone Paradise while they taught summer school. "He waves his pipe," Daddy said. "He waves his pipe and talks all the time he's driving. I can never figure out if he's a good driver, or just plain lucky."

[4]

"What worries me," said Mother, "is the way they give her anything her eye lights on."

Daddy laughed. "She'll come back thinking ordinary people play golf on Thursday and go all over three states to dog shows."

To demonstrate my maturity, I said, "I bet Uncle Joe wouldn't spend so much if he had children of his own to put through college."

That made Daddy laugh too, but Mother's eyes roamed over me, the part in my hair, the posture of my shoulders, the mustard spot on my blouse. "Blair Ellen understands things very well," she said. "Sometimes she's a little too smart for her own good. What *I* worry about is whether they'll let her get in the habit of criticizing her elders."

"Maybe I shouldn't go," I said. I wasn't even so sure I wanted to; I'd have to miss day camp and the new swimming pool.

Daddy said, "There's this fellow at lodge who used to go to Joe Stone for his teeth, and he says Joe tried to cheat him."

"Joe has a lot of faults," said Mother, "but cheating isn't one of them."

"I'm not saying he did, I'm just saying what this man told me. This man told me he paid Joe an arm and a leg for some bridge work and the next thing he knew, he got a bill in the mail for the same bridge work. So he goes storming into Joe's office and says he already paid and he sure as heck isn't going to pay again, and he *says* that Joe chased him out of the office with a hammer."

"A hammer!" Mother jerked her head back. "That's stupid. I don't believe it."

Daddy just grinned. He liked to tease Mother. "The last I heard, Joe was still billing the guy, and the guy tears up the bills and puts the pieces in an envelope and sends them back."

That very night, at the end of my fifth grade of school, after we had been talking about Uncle Joe, and I was mad at him for making me have a secret from Daddy, the phone rang while we were asleep, and a neighbor of Aunt Pearl's told us they'd taken Uncle Joe to the hospital with a heart attack.

When I got up in the morning, Mother was still gone. Daddy was on the phone getting a substitute teacher for her and trying to pour milk in my cereal at the same time, as if I didn't know how to get my own breakfast. Half of the milk went on the table, and I sat there staring at the edge of the white puddle, ready to cry, thinking that it wouldn't have been there if Mother had been home. There were coffee grounds and a brown ring on the stove too, where Daddy had let the coffee boil over. I put a paper napkin over the milk and watched it soak through.

"Yes, yes," he said on the telephone, "we're sure he's going to be all right."

When he got off the phone, I said, "Can I miss school?"

"What for?" said Daddy. "He's going to be fine. They've got him in an oxygen tent."

They didn't take me out of school when he died either, and I thought it was a sign of disrespect and told Mother so.

"Yes," she said. "You are absolutely right. If I had been thinking straight, I would have come for you, but, honey, I had to be with Pearl. She's in bad shape."

After the funeral Mother and Daddy agreed that Aunt Pearl really needed me that summer. She had to have company at Stone Paradise, they said. Blair Ellen will keep her mind off it. Blair Ellen will cheer her up. I was just old enough to squash the voice inside me that shouted, don't make me, please don't make me go out there! I kept my mouth shut, but I couldn't stop seeing her as she was at the funeral, how she had looked just like Uncle Joe in his casket. Both of them white and smelling of flowers, the only difference, that Aunt Pearl was still moving, and Uncle Joe had moved into stillness. She isn't dead, I told myself, she's a widow. And I knew a plain widow was not the same as a black widow even though at the funeral she had worn a veil that speckled her face with black knots like spiders.

So I was calm and understanding and grown up and I knew perfectly well why I was going to Stone Paradise, and I packed my suitcase by myself, and was a wonder of maturity. I told my friends on Davis Street and in the Girl Scouts that I was going away for the summer, and everyone was impressed; kids didn't do that in our town, not even Gail Gordon, whose family owned the biggest house in town and went to a country club.

And then, the morning we drove out to Stone Paradise, something began freezing inside me. First it seemed like doors closing.

[6]

The car door sealing me in glass from our house with its big porch and elm trees front and back. My own window, which I watched as we drove away, getting smaller, my window with the tiny secret porch between two dormers where I wasn't allowed to go but did sometimes anyhow. Under the trees along Davis Street I saw some of the kids I knew, and I didn't even wave, they were so distant. We drove the quarter mile to Pike Street so Daddy could pick up a paper, and we passed the swimming pool where all the kids would go every day this summer, gather around that oblong of perfect blue water without me. My not being there caused another shudder of cold, and then another as I looked around town as if I would never be there again: the Greyhound sign on the front of the drugstore, the granite pillars of the bank, the dark-painted glass of the pool room, and up above, on the hill, the high school, and on the other side more hills and fields and the water tank.

Never again, I thought, as we drove up into the squat hills, into the country, past cows and barns. I didn't even try to fool myself about how I was a country girl at heart. The only thing true seemed to be that I was not where I belonged, and I felt that like a block of ice, and I couldn't tell anyone. Not being at the pool, not being on the Scout cookout, not in my room with my horse pictures, not having dinner with Mother and Daddy.

I saw an old red plowhorse standing by the creek and something went so tight inside me that I almost retched. We passed a crowd of tow-headed children on a porch, and I hated them so much I thought I would turn inside out. Mother looked back and said, "Are you all right, Blair Ellen?"

"I think I'm carsick," I said.

"Well, stop the car, Lloyd," she said.

"Not here," I said.

And Daddy said, "You can see the sign at the top of the hill— we're almost there!" But he pulled over anyhow, in full view of those children on the porch. One of them was a big fat red-headed girl stretched out on a glider, sucking a Dreamsicle, and she followed me with her face as I walked back and forth a couple of times. I got back in the car. "I'm fine, I'm okay, let's go."

At the top of the hill we pulled in behind the Pontiac, next to the heavy sign with the words burned in the wood, "J. E. Stone, Stone Paradise," swinging from an iron pipe fixed in concrete and fieldstone. Rocks and roses landscaped up the hill, the fieldstone house tucked in among evergreens above us. At once the dogs started barking and came loping and leaping down the stairs with their big tails waving. I felt better as soon as I saw them, and Stone Paradise looked the same too, all the terraces and rock gardens where I played and read. The dogs almost knocked me over, and I hugged them both, Pandora and Eppie, and received my licks and patted their black noses. Then Aunt Pearl herself started yoo-hooing. At first all I saw was her big Welcome-to-Puerto-Rico straw hat zigzagging back and forth with the steps. To my enormous relief she was not wearing black, but one of her ordinary dresses, small lavender and brown flowers with touches of pink, a thin lawn fabric. She never wore dungarees or shorts like Mother; she always gardened and did her housework in a worn-out good dress. Mother would say, "Jersey and lawn for gardening, Pearl?" And Aunt Pearl would say, "Oh, just the ones that I lost the belt."

She was flushed apricot pink and smelled of Pacquin's hand lotion when she hugged me, just like Mother, but with a cloud of perfume over the Pacquin's. She felt like Mother in the hug too, about the same size, a little less substantial, but familiar. Aunt Pearl and Mother hugged each other and cried a little. I moved near Daddy. Everyone agreed that I was more like the Morgans than the Blairs, compactly built and on the dark side. The Morgans weren't as gushy and full of hugs as the Blairs either. The dogs plunged into the weeds and came back stained with green and yellow pollen, and Aunt Pearl said how she just couldn't keep them clean, so I volunteered to brush them every day all summer. Because even though I was mostly Morgan, I was dog crazy like the Blairs. I thought maybe everything would be normal after all.

Mother had warned me that Aunt Pearl would be sad, but, instead, she seemed to giggle all the time. Anything set her off. If one of the dogs licked her hand when she wasn't expecting it, or if I mispronounced a word, she would go off like fireworks, giggling from her hair and fingertips. I was trying to talk like an adult, not asking to be excused from the table, standing around while she fooled with her roses. I used to spend most of my time playing by myself when I was at Stone Paradise, but I never felt lonely. Now, talking all the time, thinking up mature things to say, I felt as if I were standing on a thin, gray shell over a hole, and when she giggled suddenly, I thought I had broken through.

The third morning, as I dried the breakfast dishes, I said, "I'm so happy to be at Stone Paradise. Stone Paradise is the most beautiful place in the world. I bet you wouldn't want to change a single rock, would you?"

"I wish he hadn't put up that sign with the name on it," she said. The idea that Uncle Joe had done something she didn't like shocked me, and I couldn't think of anything to say. "All I ever wanted was an old farmhouse," she said. Swipe swipe on the saucepan. Running her finger along the inside rim to get the Cream of Wheat off. "I just wanted an old farmhouse in the country. I never asked to live in Paradise." That made her giggle a little; her throat trembled. "People around here are just plain folks, you know. They don't go around giving their houses names. They shoot at that sign too. Boys lean out the car windows and use it for target practice." She had passed me the last pan and was standing in the middle of the kitchen looking like she'd lost something. "What am I doing now?"

"You said you were going to make a pie."

She got out the ice water and flour and Crisco. Mother always said how she and Pearl were just alike, they had to be busy, but Pearl filled her days with useless things sometimes, Mother said, and that comes of having more money than you need. Mother always made cakes rather than pies because you get more helpings for the time you put in.

"Joe Stone and his big plans," said Aunt Pearl, cutting Crisco into the flour with the half circle of wires. She jerked it up and chunked it down again, each time getting the Crisco bits smaller. Making them and the flour into one kind of thing instead of two. "Well, I guess I should be thankful he didn't leave me with an airplane hangar too."

He had been talking about putting a landing strip down by the

[9]

creek, and I had been worrying if it would be instead of, or as well as, the paddock.

"He was making me take flying lessons," she said, beginning to roll out the crust, wider and wider, lots of flour. "Everytime I had to go up, I'd get sick."

She was using too much flour on her rolling pin, I knew she was. It would get tough. I began to wonder if I should do something, call Mother. Aunt Pearl was a gentle person, she never got angry, especially at Uncle Joe. She's crazy about Joe Stone, Mother always said. I went over to the wall and started tracing pictures in the water there. The kitchen was partly excavated out of the hillside, and the walls sweated so badly Aunt Pearl had to mop a couple of times a day. I drew disappearing horses in the water on the wall.

She said, "He was building airplane hangars and all the time we were living in a mildew cave, with no telephone."

I stopped painting, but it was too late. I liked the cave smell, the dark red walls, green cabinets and green table, and chairs with spool backs and Pennsylvania Dutch stenciling.

"I don't know what I'm going to do with this place," she said. "In the fall they shoot holes in the sign, in the spring they throw disgusting things in the wishing well."

"What do they throw in the wishing well?"

"I don't know. Joe always cleaned it out, but now I'll have to do it myself."

Why don't you love Uncle Joe anymore, I thought. Why have you changed? She was just like kids in the lunchroom at school talking about whoever went to the bathroom. Only Uncle Joe wasn't going to get a turn to talk back. Eppie and Pandora whined at the door and I let them in, searched their coats for ticks, waiting for Aunt Pearl to say something else disloyal. But she shut her mouth small and tight like Mother's when I'd been bad, and when she put the rhubarb and strawberry filling in the pie, I had to remind her to put in the three tablespoons of flour to thicken it. After the pie was in the oven, she said she was going upstairs to take a nap. It wasn't even lunchtime yet.

I sat in the living room and looked at *Life* magazines. The dogs were wagging their tails to go out, but I stayed, flipping through the magazines until I was stopped by one full page, black and white picture of the aftermath of some disaster, I never even found out what kind. There was a dark boy in shorts squatting by a long object wrapped in a blanket that was supposed to be some member of his family, dead. I kept looking at it more and more closely, trying to see a hand or foot sticking out, something to make me really believe it was a body, and at the same time imagining myself as an orphan and where would I go if I were hungry? Just when I was deepest in that picture, I heard sounds. At first the sounds were like rending fabric, or perhaps a mine blast far underground, or an earthquake beginning. They were upstairs, huge round sobs, whirling enormous then screwing down. There would be just one, then, a little later, farther down the line, another. The dogs lifted their heads and whined. Pandora started pacing, and then Eppie, and finally the two of them went trip trip trip up the stairs on their toenails. You would think that someone like Aunt Pearl who wept over sad movies and a dead kitten in the road would have cried a river instead of this hard-fruited cabbage row of sobs. After a while I heard her talking to the dogs, reminding them they weren't supposed to come up the stairs.

"Aunt Pearl?" I called. "Aunt Pearl? I'm going for a walk, okay?"

She didn't even ask where I was going, but just sort of sang down in a gay little voice to be careful and have fun, and I got out of there as fast as I could, trusting the dogs to take care of her.

I ran along the flagstone path past the wishing well and the little garden shed, then through the pine woods and down the side of the hill, toward the creek and open field. Losing my footing on some loose dirt, I let myself fall and slide on my bottom halfway down the hill, finally grabbing a root and clinging there a little while, dust in my face, catching my breath and looking up through the pines in the sky, then down below at the creek twisting its way through the field, then at the yellow, dusty root I was clutching, eroded from the soil. Out of the dust on my forearm welled a line of rich blood, and I was fascinated that I hadn't felt a thing. I touched the blood with my tongue and there was a rush of energy through me. I wouldn't be afraid to fly an airplane, I thought. I'll do it someday, fly and be heroic and loyal.

I felt more like myself after that, going down carefully, then following the path through the high grass along the creek. Before I knew it I was at the barbed wire fence that separated Aunt Pearl's property from the Odell farm. I was humming to myself and tossing grass in the water, and I looked up, and to my great embarrassment saw children on the other side staring at me. A tractor wagon full of little kids and one big one, a red-headed, fat girl my age. It was the one who'd been eating the Dreamsicle the day I arrived. She was sitting with her legs extended down the tongue of the wagon.

The red-headed girl said, "Do you live up there in that rock house?"

I crossed my arms; after all, I was on my family property. "My aunt does. I'm visiting."

Her hair amazed me; it was very fine and bushed out around and behind her. She said, "Do you know who I am?"

"You're an Odell."

"Carmell Odell. I bet you think these kids are my brothers."

I shrugged.

"Well, they're not. They're my nephews. Do you want to play with them?"

I shrugged again, but stepped through the barbed wire, doubling over and twisting to demonstrate how I could get through without touching the wire. But Carmell Odell didn't seem impressed. She was giving the boys orders. She had, it seemed, meant quite literally that I was being invited to play with the little boys. She sat in ruddy splendor on the wagon tongue and directed the game. "Okay," she said. "Play punch tag, but you can't punch as hard because you're bigger than they are."

"I don't want to hit them at all," I said, not intending to take orders from her.

"You have to punch or it's not punch tag."

"Well, let's play some other kind." The nephews had gathered around us. They made me nervous, scrawny, yellow-haired little boys, not even in school yet. Two of them started to scuffle and Carmell kicked them apart without getting off the tractor wagon. I said, "Can they play statue tag?"

"I guess they can learn."

"It's where you have to stand exactly the way you are when you get tagged, just like a statue."

"That's freeze tag."

"No, it's not, it's different. In statue tag the person who's It gets to move around you in funny positions."

She told the boys to do whatever I told them, but they kept falling on the ground instead of holding their positions. We played regular for a while, but when she said, "Okay, you can switch to hide-and-seek now," I went over and sat on the ground beside her.

She said, "If you don't like hide-and-seek, I'll make them play something else."

"No, I'd rather sit with you."

The nephew who was It peeked, so she had to shout a threat at him. Then she said, "your arm's bleeding."

I pretended not to have noticed it before. "What do you know! Stuff like that's always happening to me and I never remember how I did it."

She turned her right leg sideways. "See this scar?" There was a rectangle of shiny white skin down toward her ankle; it didn't show up very much because she was naturally white, except for freckles on her shoulders and thighs. The scar didn't interest me as much as the thickness of her leg, about twice the size of mine. "The rooster spurred me," she said. "I would have wrung his neck for it, but Ma would have wrung mine." She kept the leg turned for my inspection, and I kept looking. "They let me kill the chicken for Sunday dinner last week."

Her hands were resting at ease now on her big speckled thighs. There was a touch of pink and a dimple on each knuckle. "You wrung its neck yourself?"

"I had to use the hatchet."

I couldn't help myself. "Was it bloody?"

"Yeah, pretty messy. My ma is teaching me how to can beans and beets this year too. I learned how to make jelly years ago."

The little boys came back, bored with hide-and-seek. I thought I had better go home.

Carmell said, "I play dolls sometimes. You can come down if you want to."

I said sure, not that I liked dolls, but I didn't want to lose the chance to play with a girl who could kill chickens. Walking back through the field, I told myself that ranchers sometimes have to shoot horses with broken legs. How am I going to learn this stuff, I thought. You don't learn anything living in town or with Aunt Pearl either. All she knew about was roses and Irish setters. I wanted to be tough like the Odell girl, to kill my own food.

At dinner I asked Aunt Pearl if I could have Carmell over to play.

"Of course, honey," said Aunt Pearl. "Have her tomorrow. I'll make lunch. What do you suppose she would like for lunch?"

"Pie and ice cream," I said. "She's pretty fat."

The next morning I put Pandora and Eppie on their leashes to walk down the road to Odells'. There was very little shoulder, and coal trucks came tearing by every so often with their big, blunt cabs and enormous double wheels and rattling, empty truck beds. Full, they were slow and not nearly so threatening. "Good girls," I told the dogs, getting a grip on their collars when a truck came by. "Stay." I loved it when they obeyed me. I glared at the coal truck, and the driver waved.

Carmell was lying on the glider on her brick-pillared porch, balancing a bowl of cold cereal on her midriff and drinking orange pop through a straw. "Hot enough for you?" she asked as I came down the walk.

She was wearing a halter made of a single band of fabric held up top and bottom by elastic. There were folds of chubbiness lapping over it and a triple row of folds between it and her shorts. Her hair was voluminous too. I sat on the painted concrete floor at a little distance from the glider so I could see all of her at once.

"You didn't bring any dolls," she said.

"Hey, Carmell, I was thinking, can you come up to Stone Paradise and play? And eat lunch? Aunt Pearl said so."

Carmell didn't fool around. She finished the pop in one long suck and hurried inside. Mrs. Odell came back with her and stood in the dimness just behind the screen door. She was fat too, but not evenly fat like Carmell. She was skinny except for the belly pushing out her apron. I couldn't see her face in the shadows, but I gave her a big smile anyway. She didn't say anything. I was thinking of explaining that Aunt Pearl and I didn't like that sign that says Stone Paradise either. But Mrs. Odell suddenly clipped Carmell in the back of the head. "Go put your shoes on!"

I said, "Oh, Mrs. Odell, that's okay if Carmell doesn't want to put on shoes. Why, sometimes Aunt Pearl and I go around half the day barefoot."

I could see her face now that she had moved, and it was rough and square like a brick. "Carmell," she shouted, "put on socks, too. I don't want Mrs. Stone thinking you don't have manners."

I was wearing my last year's school loafers with no socks. They left oxblood leather stains on my feet every night. I didn't look down.

Mrs. Odell went back into the house and came back before Carmell with a brown paper bag. "Take this to Mrs. Stone."

"Yes ma'am," I said. "Yes, I will. Thanks a lot."

She stepped aside to let out Carmell, who was pushing a toy baby stroller with about five dolls in it.

I said, "There are nearly a hundred steps up to the house."

Mrs. Odell said, "Don't you take all those dolls up there."

Carmell took out a teddy bear and a rag doll, but left two big Dynel blondes. I strode on ahead of her up the hill, pretending that Pandora and Eppie were pulling me even though I knew Carmell was having trouble with the baby stroller on the gravel. When we got to Stone Paradise, I let the dogs go and forced myself to be a good hostess and help her carry it up. I stopped every twenty steps or so to point out the beauties of the land-scaping—I told her about the special stonemason from Pittsburgh who built the fireplaces and the barbeque pit and the wishing well.

"I hear that wishing well don't have water," said Carmell. "I want to see that."

That was the only thing outside she wanted to see. She didn't want to stay out and play but to go right inside. Aunt Pearl met us wearing a lavender nylon dress and an enormous black sunhat that embarrassed me almost as much as the well with no water. But Carmell was embarrassing too, standing around staring with her mouth open. The two of them. Aunt Pearl gushing over the bag of beautiful leaf lettuce Mrs. Odell had sent up. I felt a great desire to go sit by myself and read a Black Stallion book in utter solitude.

Instead, I had to show Carmell the upstairs den that was my room for the summer. I showed her my private fireplace and the window seat and my trundle bed. She wanted to see my clothes too, and she kept making remarks about Aunt Pearl's cedar chest, so I knew she would have loved to go through it too, but I played dumb. Then she got interested in the bathroom, and I asked her didn't they have an indoor toilet at her house, and she said of course they did, but not pink. She had to go, she said, and sat on the toilet seat the longest time, kicking her heels on the furry rug and batting the white pom-pom fringe on the curtain.

I suggested a game of Monopoly or Sorry or drawing or even cut-outs, but Carmell shook her head and peeked in Aunt Pearl's bedroom. Little by little she eased her way in and started touching things, the four-poster bed, the crocheted doilies on the vanity table, and especially a silver watch you wore like a necklace. She held it up to her ear and listened and listened. I showed her the framed picture of Aunt Pearl and Uncle Joe in the Alps. "That was the trip when they got the watch," I said.

But she didn't care about Switzerland. "I'm going to get me one of them someday," she said, "and one of them things over the bed too. Only I want it pink."

"Listen," I said, "I have maybe one or two dolls here. Do you want to play dolls?"

"No," said Carmell. "Let's tell what our house is going to be like when we get married."

I felt cruelly deceived by Carmell. I began to doubt that she had really killed the chicken. I said, "I probably won't get married."

"Ha," said Carmell.

"Look, Carmell, we have to play something."

She said, "I never saw the kitchen yet."

Aunt Pearl was wearing the sunhat and frying bacon. I knew she'd been running in and out of the house all morning, but I couldn't stand the idea of Carmell going home and telling Mrs. Odell. I said, "Aunt Pearl, your hat's on."

She squealed, and I thought she was going to collapse in giggles, but instead she just took the hat off, chattering about how some morning she was going to forget her head, and hung it on the mixer.

Carmell watched everything, and after a while asked to go to the bathroom again. As soon as she was out of the room, Aunt Pearl said, "I'm making egg salad sandwiches and bacon and tomato. And I'll use the lettuce. Do you think that will be okay?"

I shrugged. I didn't care anymore; I was hoping Carmell would steal something while she was upstairs and be disgraced forever.

Aunt Pearl said, "I should send something back to Carmell's mother, since she sent the lettuce."

"Send her a doily. Carmell has been playing with all your doilies."

"Tea towel!" said Aunt Pearl, and she ran upstairs. She was gone a long time, so I played with the dogs. Aunt Pearl and Carmell came back together, and Carmell was carrying one of Aunt Pearl's hand-embroidered Mexican tea towels, homespun, heavy with orange and green flowers.

Carmell said, "You have some real nice stuff in that cedar chest, Mrs. Stone."

"You come back another day, Carmell," said Aunt Pearl. "We'll look at the things we didn't have time for today."

Aunt Pearl was pink cheeked as she hurried around serving us lunch—relish plate, two sandwiches each, lemonade, and then the strawberry-rhubarb pie with ice cream. Aunt Pearl and Carmell did most of the talking. I tried to think up a way to get her to go home. Should I say I was sick and had to take a nap? Should I just sit down and start reading and ignore her and see if she'd take the hint? I had a feeling Carmell would stay as long as she felt like it. She accepted seconds on everything. Another half-sandwich, more carrot curls and radish flowers. Another slice of pie, more ice cream.

When she was finally finished, we left Aunt Pearl in the kitchen and Carmell said, "Well, I gotta go now."

"How come?"

"Garland and India are coming down. That's my cousins."

She folded up her stroller and stuck the dolls under her arms and headed right down the steps. I was insulted. "You didn't stay very long," I called after her. She didn't even turn around. "Maybe I'll come down later," I said, and I sat on the top step and watched her go, not understanding why I was mad at her for going.

Aunt Pearl came out. "Where's Carmell?"

"She left."

"Without the tea towel? Oh, Blair Ellen, can you take it down later?"

That made it easy for me. I could go and come right back if I still hated Carmell. I said, "Do you know she went to the bathroom four times just so she could sit on the pink toilet? And she opened up your bath powder to smell it."

"Well," said Aunt Pearl. "It's a good thing I cleaned the bathroom before she came, isn't it?"

I fell asleep in my room reading *The Return of the Black Stallion*, and I never even heard Aunt Pearl come up. The sobs woke me. My eyes flew open, and it seemed to be dark, and in the room next to me, louder than yesterday, were Aunt Pearl's sobs. "I can't," she said. "I can't, I can't."

I leaped up and ran downstairs. At the bottom of the stairs I shouted, "I'm taking the tea towel, Aunt Pearl! I'm going to take the tea towel to Mrs. Odell!"

"Watch out for coal trucks, honey," she called, then went on sobbing.

There were tall, purple storm clouds along the rim of the hills, and the air seemed to press at me. A voice in my head, Mother's, I guess, because it was too stern for Aunt Pearl, said I was going to get caught in the rain. Everything seemed to be holding still for the moment, the leaves poised silver side up, no bird sounds. I pretended I was mounted on the black stallion and galloped as far as the curve, but I walked when I was in sight of the Odells'.

Mrs. Odell was on the glider breaking peas into a pot situated between her knees, with her bare legs extended a long way out in front of her. There were bruises on her knees and flat, red bites all over her calves and ankles. "They're in the back fooling around," she said.

"My aunt sent you this." I stuck the bag at her, and got scared for a couple of seconds because she didn't take it right away. "Carmell forgot to bring it."

She reached under the hem of her dress and wiped her hands on her slip. Then she turned the opening so that more light fell inside, and she shook it around. "That's real pretty," she said. "Has your aunt got green peas yet?"

"I don't think so. I don't think she has anything but roses."

"I'm going to pick her a mess. Don't you leave till I give you the peas."

Oh, no, I thought. Now Aunt Pearl has to think up another gift for her. I was afraid Aunt Pearl would start sobbing I can't, I can't when I handed her the new present. I sidled toward the door.

Mrs. Odell said, "I used to know your aunt and your mother too. The Blair girls. We all lived out at Owings mine then."

I could hear voices inside and music. I peered down through several dark rooms that opened one into the other and at the end I could make out a pale rectangle of outdoors, and back porch.

"Sibyl and Pearl Blair," she said, folding the top of the paper bag down over itself. "Your mother taught every one of my grown children. Not Carmell yet."

I smiled as brightly as I could. What did she want? I could never figure out what adults wanted from me.

"Well," she said, "don't you go without those peas."

I was shy of looking at the Odell rooms as I passed through; I didn't want to be like Carmell, but I couldn't help noticing they each one had a big bed, even the one with a couch, and coal fire grates in each room, and yellow linoleum on the floor. There was something clear about those rooms: no smothering sobs. When I got to the back, I stopped at the door to get a look at what was happening. It was a screened porch with a washing machine and a table, and they had a light on so that the barn and hills were just bulky shadows. Carmell was sitting on a stool beside a sway-back old wooden table. On the table was a red and a yellow Mickey Mouse record player with Mickey's gloved thumb pressing the needle into the record. But the center of attention directly under the hanging bare bulb, was a red-headed boy and girl dancing together like teenagers. The boy wore glasses and a long-sleeved, white dress shirt, and his hair was greased back in a long, curved plume like Elvis Presley's. The girl was in black and white too, except she had a pink felt poodle appliquéd to her circle skirt. When she whirled you could see a solid disk of crinoline slips, charms jangling on two separate bracelets. Her hair was even redder than Carmell's and she wore it in many tiny red curls in a puff on her forehead and then another puff in the back. I didn't like the song; it was about parts of the body, a piece of bone, a hank of hair.

Carmell waved me out and shouted, "They're my cousins."

I shouted, "I can tell," meaning the red hair. I had never seen so much in one place; it made me feel like a little dark foreigner in a place where the rules were unfamiliar. I did not, for instance, know any boys my age who would admit they could dance. I knew boys who would clump around as if they had buckets on their feet and make fun of dancing, but they would never get wrapped up in it the way this boy was. He seemed to be concentrating even more than the girl. He stopped her once and held both of her hands and counted the beat and made her start over. I didn't care much for boys altogether, but I always thought that if I ever did end up liking one, it would be someone athletic who disdained indoor activities.

The record trailed off, and the boy said, "Start it again, Carmell," but the girl gave me a big smile and walked over. I decided she was pretty in spite of the poodle puffs of hair and teen-age clothes.

Carmell said, "This here's Blair Ellen. She's the one with the pink bathroom. That's my cousin India, and *his* name is Garland but he's a boy anyhow. I bet you thought he was a girl."

Garland sneered, just the way an ordinary boy would have, and put his hands in his pockets. He took a couple of short steps in my direction. "You like Elvis?"

"I hate him," I said.

India looked anxious. "Don't they play his records in town?"

I was embarrassed, I didn't know why I had been so vehement. I didn't really hate Elvis anyhow, I just didn't like the way he looked. "I suppose they do. I don't pay much attention to that stuff. I'd rather read."

"Blair Ellen's real smart," said Carmell. "Her daddy is a teacher and her mom too."

Now I felt like I should explain that reading was just one thing I liked to do; I also liked to swim and play chess and all kinds of normal things. But Carmell wanted to do the explaining.

"Garland and India live up Odell Hollow. They live so far up on top of the mountain they have to drop groceries in by parachute." Garland sneered some more and India did not smile. "And they don't have a radio or television, and they don't even have electricity."

"We're getting it," said Garland. "We'll be getting it soon. On top of a mountain you get the best television reception anyhow. Did you know that?"

Carmell said, "Whenever they get a new record, they have to come down here to play it."

India asked me, "Do you like to dance?"

"No. I'm more interested in outdoor things. Do you have horses?"

Carmell said, "They don't have horses up Odell Hollow! If they had horses up there they'd have two legs short and two legs long because it's so steep!"

I wondered why they let her get away with the teasing. I supposed it was because she had the record player. "You two come all the way down here just to practice dancing?"

"Our floor's no good," said India.

"And you don't have electricity!" Carmell hooted.

India said, "We have an old-time Victrola you can crank up."

"That old thing; it just plays moon-and-June songs. You have to have my record player." Carmell laid one hand on Mickey Mouse's arm. Garland was looking at her hand too. He had these yellow hazel eyes that kept moving all over the place most of the time, but for now they stayed on her hand.

"Boy, you have fat fingers, Carmell," he said. "You have just about the fattest fingers I ever saw. How do you pick things up with fingers that fat?"

Carmell rose. "I'm not going to break your record," she said. "But I'm telling Ma to send you home for calling me fat."

"I never," said Garland. I never said anything except about your fingers, and boy, Carmell, they are *sure* fat."

Carmell's mouth and nose and eyes all tightened up close together in the middle of her face and she stomped out of the room.

"She'll go lie on the bed and cry," said Garland. "That's all she ever does."

"You're too mean, Garland," said India.

"She started it. She always gets too big for her britches." He grinned. "And that is *big*."

"Would they send you home?"

"Naw," said Garland. "There's a storm coming. The bridge might wash out."

I was full of questions. Had it ever happened, had they ever been stuck up there with no food, or down here, or in a snowstorm? But India started asking questions first.

"If they don't dance to Elvis and Jerry Lee Lewis," she said, "who do they dance to?"

I was going to explain that I couldn't possibly know because I didn't waste my time watching "American Bandstand" and all that nonsense, but, instead, this pitiful little voice came out of me saying, "I don't know what they dance to because I never learned to dance yet. Nobody ever taught me."

"We'll teach you, won't we, Garland?"

"Sure. Want to dance?"

I said no, but India was already putting the Mickey Mouse arm down, and this time I heard the bizarre words more clearly, about a girl like honeycomb. A hank of hair, and a piece of bone, and a walking, talking, honeycomb. I stiffened at the strangeness of the song, and I got even more rigid when Garland's hands touched mine.

"Can't you just go with the music?" he said, and I stumbled.

I was accustomed to being good at things, too. I could swim, and jump off the high board at the pool, and I was intending to dive off it next summer. I had more badges than any other scout in my troop, and I could sew my own skirts with matching kerchiefs, and I was the only girl I knew who could play chess. But Garland shoved me into a spin that made me dizzy and lurching, and I had a vision of myself as the formless thing with gaping pores, oozing honey. I tried to outguess him and be ready, but I never knew where the next prod would come from. It seemed to me the lights were dimming, maybe it was the storm, and I jumped free and pulled the arm off the record player.

Garland finished a turn as if there were still music, one hand extended to an imaginary partner. It is going to storm, I thought, so I wouldn't cry, and I pressed my forehead on the screen and watched the wind blow against the barn. A purple tinge to the air, a rushing in the grass along the creek. It's going to storm and they're dumb hillbillies and on top of being a hillbilly Garland is a sissy.

"You made it hard for her, Garland," said India.

I said, "Oh, it isn't his fault, I simply don't have any interest in dancing. Unlike everyone else, I am not in training to be a teenager. I have better things to do with my time."

India said, "I think she needs to learn the steps first. You just stand here beside me, Blair Ellen, and I'll show you what to do with your feet."

"And the songs don't make any sense," I said. But India was moving me over a little so I couldn't see Garland, just her, and she was demonstrating a simple two-step business with no music, over and over. "Well, I can do *that*," I said, "I just never bothered."

After a while, Garland came and stood with us, making a little chorus line, only he kept elaborating on it, moving forward and back, turning and dipping. Once or twice he tried to get India to dance with him, but she stayed by me, holding my hand; how cool and patient her hand was, longer than mine, and the reassuring slow jingle of her charm bracelets keeping the time. Plenty of time for me to get the step right.

"If that's all there is to it," I said, "I just get confused about turning and all that stuff."

[23]

Garland put on the record and India turned to face me and held both my hands and we did our two-step for a long time to the music. The girl in the song was as sweet as honeycomb now, and in the stormy air India was as white as a glass of milk.

"Okay, Blair Ellen," she said. "Here we go!" and she turned me with both hands and when I came around again she was waiting for me. Ha, I thought, did you see that, Garland?

Carmell had come back and was sulking in the doorway sucking on a Sugar Daddy stick candy, and Garland danced over to her and took her free hand, and they danced together. She wasn't bad either, not as good as India, of course, and she didn't do anything very active, but she kept the beat, and Garland did all the fancy turns he wanted while she moved her feet sturdily and sucked her candy. The next time round India went back to Garland and I danced with Carmell, and that proved I was doing it myself, not just because of India. I was even beginning to like the song, and I was saying so to Carmell when there was a crack of lightning, half the sky crackled and crazed, and a loud thumping from inside the house as Mrs. Odell came running out and told us to shut off the record player.

It didn't matter anyhow because at the next crack of thunder all the lights went out. Carmell screamed, and I jumped up and down with excitement. Mrs. Odell told us to stop fooling around, but we couldn't help ourselves from running from one window to the other to see the rain coming like thick, gray curtains across the bottom, hitting the barn, spraying us through the screen. We took the record player inside and started talking about whether to play Chinese checkers or Parcheesi because, said Carmell, Garland and India didn't have any games up on the mountain. I was pushing for Parcheesi, which I thought was a more serious, chesslike game, when there was a voice on the porch, Mrs. Odell calling me, and Aunt Pearl had walked down in all that rain in her trench coat carrying a big black umbrella and my clear plastic raincoat. We all stood around on the front porch while Aunt Pearl smiled and laughed and waved her hands and the umbrella, and Mrs. Odell didn't move at all, but they remembered each other, and talked about all the people they used to know at Owings. Meanwhile, we played a miniature version of tag, trying not to run and let the adults know what we were doing. When Garland was It, he cornered me behind Aunt Pearl and whispered, "Sorry. I'm no good at teaching people." I got him back while he was whispering, and then he chased Carmell and called her Sugar Mama, and she squealed, and Mrs. Odell shut them both up and Aunt Pearl and I started leaving, and from the porch I shouted, "India! When are you coming down again?" But she couldn't hear for the rain, and just waved.

Aunt Pearl asked me how I liked Carmell's cousins, and I said they were all right, but I didn't much like boys who were sissies. "That's a sissy?" asked Aunt Pearl. "They don't make sissies like they used to."

"Well," I said, "He's okay, but he likes Elvis Presley."

I went down to Carmell's every day after that to look for India and Garland, and also to be out of the house when Aunt Pearl cried. I didn't forget she was crying, but it didn't seem so terrifying to me anymore. Poor Aunt Pearl, I would be thinking as I had a pop with Carmell. She's probably up there crying her eyes out right now. I got used to Carmell too, her laziness, just sitting on the glider behind the clematis ladder sucking a pop. She could talk forever, told me all about her family, her married sisters and how many kids they had and how one little boy had a hernia. She never said much about India and Garland though. I would ask, and she would just say, "Oh, them, they're a half brother and sister."

"Which half?" I'd say. "What do you mean? Are they in the same grade? Are they twins?"

"No, they're not twins," she'd say, shaking her head. "But they *are* the same age. They live with our grandma. Do you want some more pop?"

One day so deep into the heat of July that the dogs didn't go off into the woods, but stayed with me, heads low and tongues hanging, I tapped on Odells' door. I could hear talking in the back, but it seemed like a long time before Mrs. Odell's head appeared. "Who's that? Blair Ellen? Well, come in, don't just stand there."

India was in the kitchen with them. She was sitting on a stool chopping something. I knew it was India and I was pleased, and then I looked again and thought it was some other girl, a poor girl wearing a blouse and skirt of two faded cotton prints that didn't match. A quiet, scrawny girl.

"We're making cakes," said Carmell, who had a big bowl in her lap and was mashing a stick of butter with sugar. "From scratch. For the homecoming at church."

They talked about this big homecoming party, and I kept hoping to be invited, but they didn't even give me a cake-baking job. I just stood there watching them be busy, disappointed with how quiet and thin India was. After a while, I said, "Where's Garland?"

Carmell said, "Garland won't bake cakes."

"He had to work," said India. "Pop needed him."

The idea of someone needing a boy to work sounded strange to me. When Mother gave me tasks, she always explained that they were for my own good, so I would learn how to do them, and Aunt Pearl never let me lift a finger. I said, "What kind of work?"

"The garden.'

"They work hard," said Carmell. "Grandma and Pop work them like the dickens, don't they, Ma?"

Mrs. Odell was beating a batter by hand. Muscles in her forearm separated and constricted with powerful regularity. "Work never hurt a body," she said.

"Garland gets mad, though, don't he, India? He gets in big fights with Pop and Grandma. He's always in trouble, and sometimes he runs away. Right, India?"

India shrugged and bent her face over the walnuts she was chopping into painstakingly small bits. But Mrs. Odell said, "Watch the laundry, Carmell. Watch your dirty laundry."

I thought I got the general drift of what she meant: that Carmell was supposed to shut up her blabbing. That there were things I wasn't supposed to know because I wasn't an Odell and I didn't even go to their church.

Once the cakes were in the oven, Mrs. Odell passed out sixteen-ounce soda pops.

"I always drink Pepsi," Carmell said. "Except for breakfast, then I drink orange."

"You ought to drink orange juice," I said. "Not orange pop."
I didn't say it, though, until we were out on the back step with
the washing machine thumping and sloshing away on the porch
above us. I didn't want Mrs. Odell to hear me. Carmell sat down
heavily on the steps, and India sat down too, with her knees up
under her chin. Where were the crinolines, and why wasn't she
dancing? Why did people always change on me?

I stood, and started suggesting games.

"It's too hot," said Carmell. "Who wants to run around and
play tag?"

"Garland might come later," said India. As if that had anything
to do with anything. It bothered me that her knees were red, and
her ankle bones too.

"We could take a hike," I said. "I mean a walk, down by the
creek." Carmell yawned. "Have you got paper and crayons,
Carmell? We could draw."

Carmell gazed at the hills. "I suppose I could show you the
puppies. We've got seven baby puppies. But you have to tie up
those big dogs, Blair Ellen."

Pandora and Eppie had come around to the back when they
heard us, and they were lying in the bare dirt under the steps,
trying to keep cool.

"They would never hurt puppies," I said. "Pandora is Eppie's
mother, and Eppie had puppies once too."

"You can't tell with a dog. Besides, they're so big they might
step on the little ones by mistake."

"Listen, Carmell," I said. "These are purebred Irish setters and
they are the most graceful dogs in the world."

Carmell said, "Well, they can't come in my barn."

I said, "We don't have to tie them. They're trained to stay."
They had been trained to stay by Uncle Joe, but I had never
tested them myself. I went down under the steps to talk to them
while Carmell and India finished their pop. They wagged when I
explained, and Eppie rolled over on her back to have her belly
rubbed.

"Are they going to stay?" said Carmell.

"Stay," I said. "Stay Pandora, stay Eppie."

The dogs kept their heads up as we started for the barn, and
Eppie got to her feet.

"Stay, Eppie!" I scared myself with the mean sound of my voice, but she lay back down. They seemed glad not to have to get up.

The wide open front of the barn had a truck and a tractor parked in it, and it smelled like a garage too. On one side were tools and cans and nails, a couple of tires and tire rims leaning against the wall, but when we had passed beyond the vehicles, the real barn began. A pyramid of old hay bales reaching up through the deep yellow heat into the loft. Carmell led us to the bales and started climbing. India turned once and offered me a hand, but I was embarrassed to be helped. "I'm okay," I said, wishing my legs were as long as hers. There was one precariously balanced bale at the summit from which you leaped to the loft. When India offered me her hand this time, I took it, and let her guide my leap lightly to safety. We were so high, and there were spaces between the boards up there, and beams with ropes and pulleys crossing the abyss. I wanted to swing on the ropes and run at top speed all the way around the balcony. India looked good again to me, long-bodied and bright-eyed. A good companion for adventures. Poor but spunky, like Little Orphan Annie.

"Look at that bale wobble!" I said. "If we got attacked, we could kick it away and be as safe up here as the Pueblo Indians!"

"The who?" said India.

"The Pueblo Indians. You know, the ones that had their houses carved out of rock, and they could pull their ladders up behind them. They're my second favorite after the Northwest Indians. Well, maybe they're tied for second place with the Iroquois."

"You're real smart, aren't you?" said India. And she meant it not as an insult, but as admiration.

"I just like to read. I go to the library twice a week."

Carmell was all the way at the front of the barn. "Do you want to see these puppies, or not?"

They were in a cardboard box with two sides flattened down, yapping and crawling in pink blindness over their mother, a small part-beagle who beat her tail when she saw us. I couldn't stand the way the puppies squirmed and piled on top of her. I felt sorry for her and extended my fingers so she could smell Pandora and

Eppie. When I scratched her head, she got so excited she stood up, and the puppies fell off like a rain of leeches.

"Poor little things," said Carmell, picking up one of them, and making kissey-kissey noises at its muzzle.

India lay down on her side in some old hay and gathered an armful of the puppies to her. She said, "Do you want to hold one of these, Blair Ellen?"

"I'd rather pet *her*. I never did like babies."

Carmell giggled. "I bet you don't even know how you *get* babies."

"Oh, yes I do." I knew a little. Last year, almost every girl in my class at school had had a birthday party where one of the main activities after the cake and ice cream had been whispering about *that*.

Carmell said, "Did you ever see puppies come out? I didn't see these, but I saw the last bunch she had. It's like shelling peas for that old dog."

"I saw a goat," said India.

Carmell said, "Well, I saw a cow. And my oldest sister saw me."

"No she didn't!" I said.

"Yes she did. I was born at *home* and my oldest sister *saw* me."

"It's awfully hard to see things born when you live in town." I said it very firmly, and when they didn't answer I went on. "I was thinking these puppies need names."

Carmell thought it over. "There are seven of them, that's two for each of you and three for me."

"Of course, they're your puppies. Now what kind of names should they get? It can't just be any old thing. How about if it's something there are already seven of, like the seven dwarfs?" It seemed just right to me, seven ugly little names like Dopey and Sneezy.

"That's cute," said India. She was still lying on her side, as if she were a mother dog herself, enfolding the puppies.

"No," said Carmell. "That would be the same as Blair Ellen naming all of them."

"No, it wouldn't. I don't even know all the dwarfs' names."

Carmell pointed. "That one there is Spot."

"Spot! Just plain old Spot?"

"And that one's Pinky and that one's Ruff."

India said, "You go next, Blair Ellen."

I nodded, under pressure to choose well, not that I would have to be very original to better Carmell. I felt I had a tradition to uphold because Mother had named Aunt Pearl's dogs, first Pandora, and then the puppy Epimetheus because he was in the Greek myth with Pandora, but he turned out to be a girl dog so we called her Eppie. I knew more American Indians than myths, so I pointed to the most active looking of the puppies and said "That one's name is Apache."

"Apache!" cried Carmell. "You're not naming my dogs after cowboy movies!"

"I'm naming him after a Plains Indian tribe. And that one is named Algonquin." I turned to India. "I'll give you some tribe names too, if you want them. There's Comanche and Seminole and Crow—"

"Not Crow," said Carmell. India selected Comanche and Blackfoot for one with a spot on its foot, and then we all lay back on some hay and sacks of feed, and India and Carmell talked about what they would name their kids someday.

After a while I said what I always said when these discussions got boring. "I wouldn't mind having kids," I said. "I like kids all right. But I don't intend to have a husband."

India said, "Well, you have to, if you're going to have kids, Blair Ellen."

"Not necessarily," said Carmell, covering her mouth and rolling onto her side in a giggle.

"People have been known to adopt, Carmell," I said. "You don't have to be so dirty-minded."

"I'm not dirty-minded," said Carmell. "Are you dirty-minded, India?" India shook her head, and then they both started giggling, and I felt my cheeks turn red because I didn't know what was going on.

India was keeping two puppies penned between her legs. One of them tried to climb up and got caught between her thighs. She lifted the other one up against her chest. "Look," she said. "A by-kini."

Carmell really haw-hawed this time. Threw her fat legs up in the air. "That would be a good by-kini for winter, it's made out of fur!" India had spots of pink on her cheeks, and she put the puppies down on her belly, and they tumbled and wiggled until they were under the skirt. "What are they peeking at?" called Carmell. "Oh, those bad puppies."

I turned my face away, looked out the window and saw Garland crossing slowly from the house with his hands in his pockets. "Look," I said. "An enemy."

"It's just Garland," said India.

The feedsack Carmell was lounging on had a slit and some fine grain and powder had sifted out when she sat on it. She grabbed two handfuls of the stuff. "We'll bomb him."

I sprang to my feet and ran as fast as I could to the other end of the loft. I grabbed a piece of board from a pile and, lying on my stomach so I'd be less visible, poked the topmost bale until it toppled and fell with a resounding thud.

"Carmell?" Garland had heard it too. "India?"

I lay flat, the first line of defense of our pueblo, ready to die fighting for our women and children.

Garland appeared between the truck and tractor. To my left Carmell was dragging half a bag of chicken feed behind her. "We're up in the loft," she said, and, as Garland turned his face up to see, she dumped chicken feed on him. He had time to dodge most of it, but the grain spread through the air so much that he ended up coughing and spitting.

"Son of a bitch!" he shouted. "Son of a bitch!"

Carmell jumped up and down and laughed. "Now he's cursing! India, India, you have to tell Grandma that Garland cursed!"

She threw another handful of feed at him, and he stopped brushing himself and let it sift through the golden shaft of air all over him, closing only his eyes. Then, when the shower was over, he exploded into a run, not toward the pyramid of bales, but toward the other side of the loft where there was a staircase I hadn't even seen.

"Look out!" I yelled. "Here he comes!"

Carmell didn't run away. I had to admire her for standing there while he clattered up the ladder, thumped across the loft. "You have chicken feed in your hair!" she shrieked. "You have a mouthful of corn!"

She finally started backing away when he leaped over the box of puppies, but he caught her easily, snapped a knee behind her, knocked her to the floor and wrestled her head into the bag of grain. She squealed and kicked her legs, and then there was an increase of urgency in the squeals, and India and I ran over. He was stuffing her mouth with grain and she was making choking noises.

"Hey!" I said, "Stop it!" and I gave his shoulders a light punch. At the same time, Carmell shoved him off her chest and got to her feet with drool and feed coming out of her mouth, tears streaking the dust on her cheeks. She took a swing at him, and he leaped away easily.

"You're going to be sorry, Garland Odell," she said, and stomped off toward the stairs.

"Stick it in your mouth, pig!" shouted Garland at her back, grabbing another handful of feed and tossing it after her. "I ought to of done it to you too," he said.

"Me? I didn't throw anything at you."

"I saw you knock off that bale."

"Well, I wasn't throwing it at you."

India said, "You better hide, Garland, because Aunt Dora's going to be over here after you."

He slapped at his clothes. "I'm not afraid of Aunt Dora."

India pointed out the window. "Well, here she comes."

When I saw the length of her stride, I wondered if Carmell had taken the time to explain that India and I had been on her side in the game. She stopped at a bush along the driveway and bent a branch back and forth patiently till it broke, and then she stood there stripping it of leaves.

"Come on," said India. "We've got to hide him."

"Hide him from *her*?" She seemed to be staring through the walls of the barn as she stripped that switch. India jumped ten feet to the bales, and Garland went right after her and crouched where she pointed, in a crevice between two bales. She pulled a length of canvas over him and went down to the bare floor. While I was frozen in terror, they had done all this, without a word. I went down the ladder and went and stood with India in the square of sunlight in the center of the barn. Mrs. Odell came holding the green switch with one hand at either end, pressing its shaft crosswise into her belly. She seemed eight feet high, and India didn't say a word. Come on, India, I thought, say the magic words, get us out of here. But her head was lowered, the nape of her neck exposed to Mrs. Odell. I looked straight up and saw the underside of Mrs. Odell's jowls, and there were three flat moles growing there.

She said, "All right India, where is he?"

India said something at the floor.

"Speak up!"

"The back way, Aunt Dora. He ran out the back way when he saw you coming." The green switch pressed deeper into the belly. India looked up at last and her eyes seemed rabbit-poppy and terrified. "He said not to tell you."

I had an urge to shout out, oh no, Mrs. Odell, India is telling a story! The truth is that he's right in this room! And India is getting away with murder!

Mrs. Odell said, "India, that boy had better think twice before he lays a hand on Carmell again. That boy had better think twice before he comes down here again."

"Sometimes he's so bad, Aunt Dora," said India. "Sometimes we just don't know what to do with him."

"He had just better think twice before he comes down here telling me jokes and getting me to feed him dinner. You tell him, and you tell Ma Odell too. You hear?"

India heard, she heard and agreed with everything, she bit the thumbnail as she walked Mrs. Odell to the door. Her scrawny, sharp wingblades showed through her faded plaid blouse. India lied like anything, I thought, she lied to a grown-up, and got away with it. I expected her to leap and cackle in glee over her wickedness. But she came back walking rapidly and purposefully, looking older.

"Were you afraid?" I said. "Were you afraid lying to her?"

"She wouldn't hit me," said India, climbing the bales. I stuck with her. Was it so wicked after all? Hadn't Carmell started everything and wouldn't a beating for Garland be unfair?

"Would she have beat Garland?"

"Not much."

She pulled back the canvas. Garland was curled on his side with a beatific smile, snoring. She gave him a kick. He didn't move. She kicked him again. This time he rolled over and grabbed her leg and tried to pull her down beside him.

"Stop it, Garland!" she said. "You get out of here before Carmell comes back, right now!"

He got up, still grinning at India, who had made fists and was glaring at him. He shrugged, then lunged at me, gave me a smack in the shoulder. "Last tag!" he shouted and ran for the back door.

Every time we had fog in the morning Aunt Pearl made cocoa and cinnamon toast. The morning after the barn fight she put it on a tray and let me have mine on the lounge chair on the patio with an afghan over my legs. While I ate, she clipped roses. In the gray atmosphere her orange scarf seemed to give off the same glow as the pink and yellow tea roses. She looked so much like Mother, or the way I wanted Mother to look. I wanted to combine them: keep Aunt Pearl's long, supple back but add Mother's certainty about things. I closed my eyes, felt our stone patio and the tea roses moving through the fog, majestically slow and gentle, not hurting anything in our path.

Aunt Pearl said, with her back to me, "Do you suppose Joe watches us?"

My eyes flew open and I found myself trying to pierce the pale gray sky. I imagined him lying on his stomach up there to get a good look through some chink in the clouds. Wearing a short, white summer choir robe. "I don't know," I said. "Why would he want to watch us?"

She sniffed a rose, clipped it, then sniffed again. "Do you remember what he looked like?"

I saw a thick, tweedy, brown suit and vest but I couldn't see his face. "I don't know," I said, and then suddenly I did see his face, very clearly, on the tan satin pillow, all the flesh flowing from his nose down over his cheek toward his ear. His jaw powdery pink instead of dark with beard. I was ashamed to remember him dead, and I thought it was a bad subject for her to talk about with a child.

"I feel so bad," she said. "I try and try and his face slips away from me. Isn't that awful? My own husband? But I hear his voice. I hear his voice all the time, but especially at night. Sometimes I wake up hearing what he said—that night."

I was absolutely sure this was one of the things adults were supposed to keep secret from children. I had an impulse to remind her I wouldn't be eleven till next week.

"He sat up in bed," she said, "and grabbed me by the shoulder and said, 'Pearl! Pearl! It isn't my fault!'" She spoke this last part in a strange, scratchy voice that I was ready to believe had come from beyond the grave. "Right in the bed upstairs," she whispered.

If Mother were here, I thought, she would say, now Pearl, hold yourself together, Blair Ellen is here.

She said, "Do you know, those first two weeks, he told me what to do all the time. When I had to talk to the mortician and the lawyer, I'd start to cry, and then I'd hear Joe getting disgusted with me and he'd say right over my shoulder, 'Oh, come on, Pearl, don't *ask* them what you want, *tell* them. They're working for *you*.' Once I actually turned around and of course he wasn't there, at least not so I could see him, and I started crying even harder, and I could hear him telling me to straighten up. But it was better to hear him than the way he's fading now."

Where were the dogs? I thought, unable to move under my afghan. If the dogs would show up, we could talk about them. Aunt Pearl said, "Do you suppose we fade for him too?"

I saw Uncle Joe in the short choir robe again, overhead, rubbing at the little window in the clouds as if it had fogged over. Can't see a thing, he muttered. Where'd they go? Seeing him so clearly scared me, and I kicked off the afghan. "Where *are* those dogs?" I said, and whistled, "Pandora! Eppie! Where are they, Aunt Pearl?"

She smiled at me. "Do you know, the last thing he talked about, that very night at supper, was giving you a big birthday

[35]

party, with all the children from your class, like the other girls had last year. I know Sibyl and Lloyd didn't want you to have one, but it didn't seem right to Joe, after all the other girls did."

"Well, my birthday's in the summer."

"I know when your birthday is. It's next week. We could still have a party. We could bring some of your school friends from town, like that nice Gail Gordon, and I'd hang my Japanese lanterns out here on the patio—"

"Gail Gordon's not my friend. She's just always in the same class I am. I don't think I want a party."

"We have to do something."

"How about if we go to the fair?"

"We can have your friends out here for a cookout and then take them to the fair."

There was something funny. It was as if those kids, my school friends, the kids on my block, had faded for me just the way Uncle Joe had for Aunt Pearl, the way we probably did for Uncle Joe. "Can I have anyone I want, Aunt Pearl? Just exactly who I want and no one else?"

She said yes of course, because it was my birthday, and I smiled to myself and closed my eyes, holding what I wanted close to me as we cut forward through the fog. What I wanted for my birthday was India and Garland Odell with me in an exciting place, on the carnival rides at the fair would be fine. I had never exactly wanted a party before, although I felt a little bad when the other girls had theirs and I didn't, and the excitement I wanted was similar to the excitement at those parties, but more private, more individually mine.

Those other parties last year had been of equivocal pleasure for me. Gail Gordon's mother started them by inviting everyone in the class three months in advance to a big eleventh birthday party for Gail, so five other mothers got busy and threw parties for their daughters in the meantime. My official position to anyone who asked me was that the parties spoiled every Saturday all winter, but the truth was more complicated, and I knew it myself because I got excited the night before every one of them. I knew what I hated: crunchy dresses with sashes, and the way perfectly normal girls whispered and simpered in front of the boys who looked stupid with sports jackets on. I hated the first half hour with the games that the mothers foisted on us, button button who's got the button and pin-the-tail, but once everyone was loosened up, we played our own games, usually hide-and-seek so we could run through the strange house. I remember at Gail Gordon's party, the big one, the culmination and climax of the whole crazy season, we started out in Gail's playroom and spread through the enormous house. I hid in a bathtub in a guest room way up on the third floor waiting and waiting and making little sighs that echoed off the porcelain. No one found me, so I finally went down, just in time for the refreshments.

The refreshments were meant by the mothers to be the main event. Gail's mother knew exactly what all the other mothers served, and she served everything they did and more. Bowls of chips, Sloppy Joe sandwiches, and a cake in the shape of an old-time automobile with pink and lavender headlights and hubcaps. The ice cream came with bowls of toppings so we could make our own sundaes.

Then we all sat around in the living room holding our bellies while the presents were opened, and when Gail's mother went off to clean up, we drowsily began the final activities, the games the mothers didn't know about, the kissing games. At the first few parties it was just spin the bottle and post office. I played those games, for a little while. The element of chance was exciting, not knowing who was going to give you your peck on the cheek. But I wouldn't play movie star, which was the only game at Gail's. The game was simple and straightforward. A boy was chosen: Tommy Tucker usually because he was the tallest and blondest, and when he rolled up his shirt sleeves he had muscles. The girls pushed him into a closet and lined up outside the door to go in and get kissed. That was it, a kiss from Tommy Tucker in the closet. The girl would come out staggering and rolling her eyes, and when the others asked her how it was, she would just smack her lips and sigh. When someone said, come on, Blair Ellen, it's your turn, I made a sour face. Not me, I said, I don't want to get trenchmouth. I couldn't admit that I actually wanted to be kissed by one particular person.

At Gail Gordon's party that day, Tommy got tired of being in the closet and came out, holding Gail herself, and he kissed her right in front of us all, bending her over backwards. She had long sausage curls for her party, and they trailed on the floor. The boys who hadn't been picked for movie star went wild then and began to chase the rest of us girls and there was a thundering and screaming up and down stairs until Gail's mother and father and the maid began appearing in different doorways with our coats.

In the end, for my party, I had to invite Carmell as well as India and Garland. "What is wrong with Carmell?" said Aunt Pearl. "She's such a nice, mature girl." At least half the time I liked Carmell, but I couldn't explain that she was ordinary compared to Garland and India. What I kept thinking was that their hair was redder.

I said, "India and Garland are different. Even their names."

Aunt Pearl said, "Carmell is a pretty unusual name too."

"No it isn't, it's just an old candy."

Finally Aunt Pearl pointed out that we had no way of getting in touch with India and Garland except through Carmell and her mother, and I saw that I was going to have to take Carmell too, so I started muttering. "I thought I was supposed to be able to have exactly whoever I wanted for my birthday and nobody else," and Aunt Pearl wrung her hands and rubbed her forehead, and I began to feel like I was older than she was, and so I had to say it was okay, she didn't have to worry, I did like Carmell, it would be a better party with more guests anyhow, but could we go up to their house on the mountain to ask them?

Carmell went with us to ask them two mornings before my birthday. I rode in the back with the dogs and let Carmell sit in the front. The massive mahogany dashboard and steering wheel were so high that she couldn't even see out, but that was fine with Carmell. She touched the glove compartment button and the handle on the cigarette lighter. She pushed a button on the door, and down whirred the electric window. She sighed, and after a while said, "Can I raise it up and down again, Mrs. Stone?"

"Of course, honey," said Aunt Pearl.

Carmell lowered it, then laid her hands in her lap for several seconds before allowing herself the pleasure of raising it once more.

"I'm going to have a car like this someday," said Carmell.

Aunt Pearl said, "I'd like to trade this one in on something smaller. Joe and I went all the way across the country in this thing and I never drove one time because Joe said I couldn't handle it."

I got bored when people talked about material things like cars. "Where do we turn, Carmell? When do we start up the mountain?"

"Right up the road," said Carmell. "We should have got my daddy to bring us up here in the truck. He has four-wheel drive."

"We'll make it, won't we, Aunt Pearl?"

A coal truck came around the bend and Aunt Pearl hit the brakes and swerved onto the shoulder. "I hope so."

"Right here," said Carmell. "Turn right here."

It was a narrow, pulverized coal road, and I held my breath as we started up. This was Odell Hollow, and I knew we would see something special up here. Something exciting was sure to happen. Aunt Pearl said she heard that they still made illegal moonshine liquor up here, and I heard from someone else that there were little hollows off of Odell Hollow where people married their sisters and brothers and the children were all retarded monsters. I pushed Eppie out of the way so I could stick my face out the window and not miss anything.

The road opened into a clearing where there were some low buildings with rusting metal roofs and coal trucks. "That's Odell Mine," said Carmell. "The Odells never owned it, but so many of them worked there, they call it Odell Mine."

Beyond the mine the road narrowed and the pulverized coal faded away, leaving us with plain old rutted dirt. When she saw a bridge ahead, Aunt Pearl said, "Oh dear, oh dear," and slowed down as much as she could and still keep us running. She lined the wheels up carefully with the boards of the bridge. It creaked, and I looked back at it thinking, there are only a certain number of crossings on that old bridge, and we just used up one. We had to climb more seriously now, and there was a trickle of water running right down the center of the road. The woods had closed in on all sides and the car lurched. Aunt Pearl kept on talking and giggling nervously. "If Joe could see where I was taking his car! He had a special chamois skin for washing it and another one just to dry it off and another one for dust."

"It gets worse as you go along," said Carmell.

I saw a wonder in a clearing, a battered-looking old house on stilts with a sloping roof and a stone chimney. The front yard had no grass and was strewn with pieces of metal, two old cars without tires, chickens, skinny hound dogs who barked and set off Pandora and Eppie. Best of all were some ugly children who picked up sticks and clods of dirt and threw them.

Aunt Pearl said, "Those children are throwing things at us!"

"They're Crains," said Carmell. "They ain't all here in the head."

I settled back in my seat, thrilled by the way the Crains' hair seemed to have been snatched out of their scalps in irregular clumps, and how their legs were too short for their bodies.

"I can't drive all that much farther," said Aunt Pearl. "If I park, do you think those children would hurt the car?"

"Yes, ma'am," Carmell nodded. "They like to strip cars."

So we drove another quarter mile with Aunt Pearl gasping over every bump, and then we came to a place where the road took a dip and went under water for a few yards. "That's it," said Aunt Pearl. "We don't ford streams in this car."

"My daddy's four-wheel drive goes right through."

"Not me," said Aunt Pearl. "We're walking from here." She sat with her door open, taking off her shoes, slipping down her garters, and peeling off her hose.

I said, "Can I go on ahead with Pandora and Eppie?"

"You can't take those dogs," said Carmell. "Pop has big hunting dogs up there and they'll eat yours alive."

She made me mad, always wanting to leave Pandora and Eppie out of things, but Aunt Pearl thought maybe the dogs would keep the Crain children from destroying the car. I took off ahead, leaving them to walk as slowly as they wanted. I didn't bother with the stepping-stones but waded the water and walked fast up the hill to get out of their sight.

Carmell shouted after me, "You better watch out! It's just a little old path with a rope! You'll miss it!" But I had already got to the bend and was walking on as if I were completely alone.

The green bushes reached out from the banks, and sometimes insects burst out and buzzed me. Mud-clay caked my shoes and my feet became huge clomping things that slowed me down and I wondered what would happen if a Crain came out of the woods. Could I run? How far back were Aunt Pearl and Carmell? There were no birds or even flowers around me, just weeds and creepers going up the sides of trees. Leaves of all shapes. Like tulips, like blades; some with pinked edges, some with edges browning and curled. Ticks fall off of leaves, I'd heard, into your hair. Too many live things. At the top of another rise was a clearing with a bathtub rusting in the weeds, and an old Ford pickup that still had air in the tires backed into the bushes so its nose pointed downhill. I sat on the running board to wait for Carmell and Aunt Pearl, and I saw opposite me, up the side of the hill through itchy weeds, a hemp rope nailed to trees and posts.

I waited till Carmell and Aunt Pearl came into sight and then I pointed and shouted, "Up there?" and when Carmell nodded yes, I took a deep breath and leaped the ditch, plunged up the steps, mud reinforced with boards. I moved as fast as I could, lifting myself with my hands as well as my feet, wrenching myself up by main force. At the top of the stairs was a great swell of grass and sky. I moved forward cautiously, almost dizzy after being enclosed by hillside and weeds. There was a path through this unfolding of sky, and then I really was on top, with everything spread around me: fields, woods, roads, barns, and I didn't recognize a single place among all this doubling and corrugating of hills.

Ahead of me was a weather-gray house with a porch. On one side, like crosses with their tops knocked off, were two clothesline poles. Only the roof of the barn was visible as the hill started down again.

Dogs barked and a person came out on the porch and stood in the shadows, but before I had a good look, one of the dogs came baying over the grass, springing high to keep its eye on me. If you run, he'll chase you, I thought, and clasped my fist in my hand and pressed hard as panic came up out of my stomach. The dog stopped about fifteen feet away, a hound with a huge head and hackles up all along his back and down his tail. He gave a single, stiff-legged lurch in my direction, and everything seemed to fall away around me and the dog. The sun paled, the wind no longer touched me. There was no house, nothing human left in the world. He threw his head back and bayed so deeply that the sky vibrated. The sound seemed to shake Garland and India out of the air. They came from different directions, Garland nearer and walking directly to the dog. He slapped its head. "Shut up, Puny," he said, scowling at it and then at me. The dog melted down to about a third of its size and flopped wagging at his feet.

India had more dogs around her legs. "Don't be scared, he's just a pup." Her dogs were red like Puny, short haired and even bigger than Pandora and Eppie. They wagged but stayed with India.

Garland raised a fist at Puny, and the dog stopped wiggling. "Learn some sense, dumbbell," he said. "He's so chicken the rabbits hunt him."

"You don't have to hit him," I said. "He didn't attack."

Garland was bare chested. He pulled a tee shirt out of his jeans and wiped his face with it. "I hit my dogs if I want to. What are you doing up here anyways?"

For some reason, India was staying a little distance away from me and not smiling. At that moment Aunt Pearl and Carmell came over the horizon and Garland's face turned vicious. "Goddamn, here they all come!" he said and ran off toward the woods.

"He cursed again," I said to India.

She made a half smile and looked away. Puny came to me, crawling on his belly, and the other dogs came too. None of them smelled very good, but they were eager for petting and they nearly knocked me over.

India said, "Your aunt looks pretty."

She looked foolish to me coming through the field with her white pocketbook and the thin, plaid dress with puffy sleeves. I didn't mind her dressing that way most of the time, but it looked all wrong on Odell Mountain.

"Oh, the beautiful dogs!" cried Aunt Pearl. "What kind are they?" They leaped for her, sniffing frantically at her skirt and hands and their thick, long tails beat me as they kissed Aunt Pearl.

Carmell said, "Those are redbone hunting hounds. Pop and my daddy drove all the way to North Carolina to buy them."

Aunt Pearl squatted down and made her dog love noises, little clucks and lip smackings. One thing about Aunt Pearl, she never let her clothes get in her way.

India said, "Why don't you all come on over to the house. Grandma is waiting to see who it is."

Carmell said, "Don't you want to know what they came up here for?"

India dropped her head again and gave that tiny smile with her mouth closed. Her face for lying to grown-ups?

Aunt Pearl said, "Do you get water from a well, India? There's nothing as good as cool, deep well water."

"Yes, ma'am," said India. "We don't notice it one way or the other."

In front of the house were some broad, flat rocks and stubbly grass around them. Nearest the house was one spot worn to the dirt where some red hens were scratching. The grandmother sat in a hardback chair with her hands folded in her lap, a very old woman, I thought, but I think I was probably confused by her collapsed, toothless mouth. The skin over her cheekbones was still taut, and her center-parted hair more brown than gray.

Carmell gave her a kiss, and she snatched out and grabbed Carmell around the waist and held her close. "Look who's here," she said. "My big old fat granddaughter. India!" Only she pronounced it Injuh, "Go inside and make some Kool-aid for these folks."

"Oh, I'd be happy with a glass of well water," said Aunt Pearl. "A glass of well water would do just fine," but India was already gone.

Carmell said, "Grandma, this here's Mrs. Stone and Blair Ellen Morgan."

"Well, set down on the swing," said Grandma. "It ain't bad since we put the pad on it."

Aunt Pearl said some things as she sat down, she always had things to say. How beautiful the view was, how she really would be happy if they didn't go to any trouble and she would just have a drink of water.

Carmell was still squeezed up to her grandmother. "They're the ones that live at that house, Grandma. They're the ones that have that wishing well with no water."

Grandma Odell said, "Huhn. So that's why they want well water." She gave Aunt Pearl a glance, but she stared all over me with little eyes like mere glints of light behind the shiny tops of her cheeks. "Carmell, tell that girl to have a seat."

Aunt Pearl said, "Sit down, Blair Ellen."

I sank where I was, on the edge of the board porch with my back to a wooden pillar.

"What's the matter with that girl? We have chairs."

"She wants to pet the dogs," said Carmell. "She's animal crazy."

I was grateful to Carmell for explaining me to her grandmother, so I called Puny over.

"Well," said Grandma Odell, "when your sit-upon gets weary, you see the chairs."

Aunt Pearl crossed her ankles and spread out her skirt and took the scarf out of her hair. "Mrs. Odell, if I had a view like this I don't think I would ever get a thing done. I'd be out on this porch every minute."

"It's all right in the summer. But some winter they're going to come up here and find us frozen stiff."

I slipped off my shoe and scratched Puny's rib cage with my big toe.

Grandma said, "You like that smelly old thing? I'll give him to you."

I said, "We have Irish setters. I mean Aunt Pearl does."

Aunt Pearl laughed. "They're more yours than mine, honey. I don't know what I'll do with them when I go back to the apartment."

"If I had my way," said Grandma, "we'd never waste the slops on those dogs. But men are crazy to hunt. India!"

From way inside the dim house India answered, "Yes ma'am?" The windows had panes of a brilliantly wavy glass that made the air inside seem black.

"Hurry up in there!" Then, to Aunt Pearl, "That girl's dreamy. She ain't a bad girl, she does what she's told. But she takes a day and a night to do it."

I began to imagine that India was Cinderella. She and Garland were obviously orphans, and their grandmother kept making over Carmell. No wonder Garland was bad. I would never just say yes ma'am the way India did. I would rebel like Garland.

Aunt Pearl was explaining who we were. She told how she and my mother grew up around Short's Mine and Owings, and they used to know Carmell's mother. And my father was a teacher and my mother too.

"I wouldn't know," said Grandma Odell, letting Carmell go after one final smoothing of her hair. "I wouldn't know anything about who lives where because when you make the mistake of marrying an Odell you get stuck up on top of one mountain or another for the rest of your life." I was shocked, that an old woman would say such a thing like that about her life. Her voice changed too, thinned and shrilled. "Living with an Odell," she called. "Oh, what a cross to bear. I had two Odell sons, and they was tu-wins. Two boys, a bad one and a good one. The good one was Otis and he had Carmell, and the bad one was named Elroy Lee. I gave Elroy Lee the best name and all he ever gave me was trouble. Trouble and those two children, and the girl is dreamy and the boy is just like his daddy." She paused and looked at me and Aunt Pearl again. "If I was you, I'd keep that little girl away from Garland. Or she'll end up on some mountain herself."

Aunt Pearl bubbled out a giggle. "I don't think she's old enough to worry about boys yet."

"Odells start fast," said Grandma.

Down by the barn was a man in overalls and he started toward the house and then stopped and seemed to sniff the air.

"Watch him," said Grandma. "Watch him run away as soon as he sees we got guests up here."

He didn't exactly run, but he did turn on his heel and disappear behind the barn.

"Sometimes I wonder," said the old woman, shaking her head. "Sometimes I just wonder."

I was hoping Aunt Pearl would ask her what she wondered about, or maybe Carmell would translate, but here came India with a tray, and she had changed her clothes, put on an old party dress, too small for her, tight across the chest with pink puffs in the sleeves gone flat. She had her charm bracelets on again, one on each arm. "Changed clothes, did you?" said Grandma, taking the first glass of purple Kool-aid with no ice and tasting it. She made a face but waved India and her tray on to Aunt Pearl. Besides the Kool-aid on the tray there was a large plate of corn bread squares cut and spread with jam.

Carmell took hers and said, "I don't mind if I do even if there is no ice."

Grandma Odell pretended to reach over and spank her and said she was spoiled rotten. Aunt Pearl said how delicious everything was, and of course she really hated the Kool-aid. It didn't taste right to me either without ice.

After serving everyone, India sat on the step beside me, and I stared at her charm bracelets because the dress embarrassed me. I had never seen such full ones. Little sterling silver airplanes and Scottie dogs and rocking horses and a silver acorn. She saw me looking and turned her wrist slowly so I could see all of them. Her grandmother was still talking about weather and chickens and gardens and Aunt Pearl was exclaiming what do you know and is that so? India said, "Do you want to see something?"

Of course I did. I was hoping it would be something inside the house, but she pointed around the back.

"Where are you going?" said Grandma Odell.

"I want to show Blair Ellen you-know-what."

"Don't you want to go, Carmell, honey?" Everytime she spoke to Carmell her voice got tiny and silly as if Carmell were a baby.

"I don't want to go back there. *I* know what she's going to show Blair Ellen."

Aunt Pearl said, "Don't be long, Blair Ellen, we have to leave soon."

In the back was the roofed well platform. It had a crossbar with a long tin can tied to it, maybe a piece of stovepipe with the bottom closed off and a hole in the side. India let me untie the scoop and lower it slowly, clanging against the sides of the well. The hole was boarded over so you couldn't see the water, and it seemed like the scoop took a long time to get down. The depth of it gave me a shiver. A bottomless pit, I thought, just before the container hit water. The heaviness of it full was more than I had ever lifted, but I could crank it with the handle and it came up swinging and sloshing.

I drank three times from a speckled enamel dipper, looking out at the field each time, feeling that the sun and wind together were one powerful friendly animal that lapped at my ankles and lifted my bangs.

"Well," said India, "do you want to see my goat?"

"I didn't know you had a goat!"

"I always had a goat, but now she has a kid."

We ran together through the sun-wind, India loping ahead toward the farthest clothesline pole. The nanny goat trotted out to the end of her tether to meet us, dancing sideways with neat little steps. The baby came to me in two short dashes, pausing once to look me over. Fine brown hair along its back, white stockings, and tiny pink hooves. The end of its face was silky and it stretched its lips to suck my fingers. "Look, India!" I said, a shudder of pleasure running from my fingertips all through me. "Look!"

India lay down in the grass, smiling and smiling, and the light came from behind her red hair.

The mother goat shoved me, gently, and I scratched the coarse hair between her horn bumps. She bleated when I stroked her throat, and the vibration ran down her chest and along my arm. The kid seemed to realize suddenly that I wasn't what it thought I was, and it spat out my fingers and ran and butted the nanny and started to suckle. I sat back in the grass just like India, daring the gray jumping spiders and ticks to crawl under my clothes.

"We got Nanny to keep the grass short," said India, "and then we decided we might as well breed her. She's real smart with her baby. The dogs won't come on this side of the house at all. When Puny wants to go down to the woods, he makes a great big loop through the grass. I never saw her butt him or anything, but he sure knows better than to fool with her."

We didn't say anything for a while, and then my heart beat fast because I thought this was my chance, I wasn't sure for what. I said, "Why is Garland mad?"

"He's not mad. He ran off because he's shy."

"He acted mad. He cursed me."

"He wasn't cursing you. He was just surprised."

I tried some other questions. I was sure India knew what I wanted, if I could just figure out the question. "Hey, India, where does your daddy live?"

She sat up, and for a moment I was afraid she would run away too.

"Ohio," she said. "He's way off in Cincinnati, Ohio." She hesitated, seemed to settle a little. "He sends me bracelets all the time, but he don't claim Garland. Even so, everybody knows he's his father. They look alike."

I didn't understand. Could parents disclaim children any time they wanted? I didn't think so; I was pretty sure the meaning was more hidden than that. India's neck was long like a lady's, smooth. All of her that showed—arms, legs, neck—was long and smooth and secret, and I couldn't think of the right questions.

Aunt Pearl came around the edge of the house and waved her fingers. "Come on, India," I said. "I'm going to invite you somewhere."

Her eyes got large, and she ran ahead of me, never asking where I was inviting her. When we got to the porch, Grandma Odell said, "India, Mrs. Stone wants to take you children to the fair Thursday. What are you going to do about your chores?"

"Do 'em ahead of time!"

Grandma Odell said, "They'd have to sleep over down at Otis's."

"They do that all the time anyhow," said Carmell.

I wanted them to sleep at Stone Paradise with me, but of course I couldn't invite them, and I wouldn't be able to have Garland anyhow because he was a boy.

Grandma Odell sat for a few seconds perfectly still, and India stood rigid in front of her. "Well, I don't see any reason why they shouldn't. India anyhow. I don't know about Garland."

"He wants to go too," said India. "He'll do his chores early."

Grandma Odell called Carmell to her and stroked her hair. "I don't know how India knows, but she knows. Those two always know what the other one's thinking. She's just as good as gold, and that Garland is nothing but trouble, but they each know what the other one is thinking. It was the same way with my twin boys."

I worried about thundershowers, and Aunt Pearl worried about the food. Every time she asked me about Jell-O salad, or fried onions on the cheeseburgers, I would say, "But, Aunt Pearl, we just want to eat corn dogs at the fair." And she kept saying, "Yes, of course but we couldn't very well have a party without food, could we? And these people out here think it's an insult if you don't offer food in your house." We strung the Japanese lanterns across the kitchen and hung extras in the living room, and then I got dressed and went to watch the weather.

I had an outfit that Mother and Daddy had given me at my birthday dinner. Sunday was the first time I had been home since summer began, and Aunt Pearl and I had dressed up and met Mother and Daddy at church. I saw them all fresh-shaved, stockings on, ties tied, hats in place, and it was as if they were nice-looking strangers. I saw them in front of my eyes instead of feeling them all around me. Even at my house for the pork roast birthday dinner, it still wasn't like being home. I never took off my white tee straps and crinolines. I didn't go out looking for the kids at all, and up in my room I exchanged a couple of Black Stallion books for a couple of other ones, and I got a new load of comics from my collection and some different games, but it didn't smell right in the room. I was pleased, but also vaguely surprised that Mother and Daddy knew to get me *The Big Book of Indians*, and a poptop outfit—checked shorts and matching sleeveless blouse with rows of ruffles and rickrack. I was as amazed as if there had not been telephones and Aunt Pearl's trips into town to see her lawyer and buy groceries.

I didn't get homesick until I was back at Stone Paradise again, and then, suddenly, the house came back to me warmly, and Daddy's new redwood fence that he built himself to keep the rabbits out of the vegetable garden, and above all, my own mother, who didn't sob in the afternoon and never consulted me except out of politeness or for my own good. Not like Aunt Pearl who, when she asked where to hang the Japanese lanterns, really didn't know.

So I stood at the top of the steps at Stone Paradise, waiting for my Stone Paradise party, thinking I had missed my chance, that I should have begged to stay there, in town, at home. That this wasn't home, that there was nothing here but potential disaster. The sun went in and out behind clouds, but even when it was out and terraces and the road and the hills were golden, I found myself watching the next big cloud move ominously across the sky. What did I want from the red-headed Odells anyhow? Kids in town would laugh at them. The kids on my block would tease me about becoming a hillbilly. Even Aunt Pearl had whispered to Mother about their house on the mountain with no running water, and she whispered something even lower about their family. After a while, Mother told me she was proud of me for befriending those poor children and I felt guilty because it wasn't a good deed at all, it was because of something I wanted, and now I couldn't even remember what it was. I kept thinking of home, of our scout troop's autumn hike and camp-out, and the regular kids on my block who would be out with their bicycles and footballs and the girls would have to fight again to get to play sports with the stupid boys. It seemed to me that I had done something unnecessarily complicated by inviting the Odells for my birthday. That I had done something strange, even abnormal.

A coal truck came up the hill, and I looked directly down into its bed. For half a second, from this steep angle, I couldn't tell if the dead blackness was a mound of coal or something concave, a pit. The difficulty of perspective frightened me, and by the time the truck was gone, it didn't matter that I'd seen it was a heap of coal; I felt as if a vacuum cleaner were sucking my energy from the inside. I had often been afraid of things, of injections, of being caught at something, but I had never before had this fear of collapsing inward. I seemed to be in a place with high walls around me, and on the far rim of the pit were the Odells, scrawny, bouncing red demons.

I saw the real Odells coming, Carmell's mother too, and I was thankful to see them; nothing could be as lonely as that moment of collapsing into a hole. I ran and told Aunt Pearl they were here, and then ran back to watch them come up the steps, walking slowly and formally: Carmell first, wearing a poptop like mine only frillier and she looked a mile wide from above; India, wearing her black circle skirt; and Garland, with his hair slicked down. They were carrying things like a safari: presents, records, the Mickey Mouse phonograph. Carmell and India dumped gifts into my arms and Garland grimaced. Aunt Pearl swirled out in a chiffon dress like Loretta Young, and she and Mrs. Odell spent the next ten minutes lining us kids up in front of the wishing well for snapshots, and Aunt Pearl had to ask everyone's advice about how to use Uncle Joe's Leica with the f-stop. We stood in a row, the four of us, me caught between Carmell's bulk and India's crinolines with Garland muttering under his breath in the back.

When they finally let us move, I stayed close to Carmell because she seemed more normal to me, nothing unusual about her except fat, and I knew lots of fat kids. Garland and India looked all wrong again. She was too quiet, and he was wearing white socks with black shoes. And his hair looked like it had been painted on with shoe polish; it lay flat to his head except for one section toward the front that was uncurling like an inverted comma. What kind of boy, I thought, would go someplace with three girls and a woman anyhow.

Carmell said, "Well, aren't you going to open the presents?"

It wasn't the right time, but at least it was the right thing, so I led them inside and we sat around in the bamboo bentwood furniture and Aunt Pearl made me show the things Mother and Daddy had given me first, my outfit and the *Big Book of Indians* with the gorgeous full-page, color pictures. Aunt Pearl had bought me a knife-pleated skirt for school, and now there were the two boxes from the Odells, wrapped in the same pink and blue party-hat paper that was creased in the wrong places as if it had been used before.

"Open mine first," said Carmell, and she reassured me by seeming to know all about birthdays, and her gift was a real birthday party gift, a pink plastic vanity set: hand mirror, comb, and brush. I knew exactly how to handle each object and say how pretty and pass them around and tell how much I liked them.

But I touched the box from India and Garland gingerly, sure it wouldn't be right. Aunt Pearl and I had discussed the problem of their poverty, and we even thought of not telling them that this

[51]

was a birthday party, but we wanted a cake and candles, and Carmell already knew. So I opened their present, expecting something cheap, a bottle of twenty-nine-cent perfume or a couple of candy bars. Instead, it was a charm bracelet, one of India's, I realized at once, recognizing the acorn, the antique car, the rocking horse. Much too expensive for a birthday present, charms were a couple of dollars apiece, sometimes more. I held it toward Aunt Pearl, and Carmell exclaimed, "You gave her a charm bracelet? You gave her one of your—"

India broke in. "It's from me and Garland both. It's from the two of us."

"Why, I should think so," said Aunt Pearl, examining the bracelet and then passing it to Mrs. Odell. "It is an absolutely beautiful present. Blair Ellen, stick out your hand and I'll fasten it on for you."

"She never gave *me* a charm bracelet for *my* birthday," said Carmell.

I was so thankful for Aunt Pearl's and Carmell's big mouths. I kept wanting to say she shouldn't have given me this one either. I kept thinking, you aren't supposed to, you aren't supposed to make sacrifices for a birthday party. You aren't supposed to give the only thing you ever get from your father. I knew I should make over it at least as much as I made over the pink plastic stuff from Carmell, but I couldn't even smile. The bracelet seemed so heavy. I just stuck my arm out and let Aunt Pearl name each charm on the bracelet. After that India stayed close to Aunt Pearl, and I stuck with Carmell. Garland looked out the door.

"Well, let's dance now," said Carmell. She seemed to have put herself in charge of the party, and that was fine with me. Mrs. Odell and Aunt Pearl went out to the kitchen and I danced with Carmell to the hank-of-hair song, and Garland and India danced together and none of us made any effort to change partners. Garland and India seemed content, though, dancing with their faces still, doing amazing things and always knowing each where the other one was going to be. Carmell and I just went along, one foot two foot, more or less marking time till they called us in to eat.

"Garland!" said Mrs. Odell. "Get in here and help Mrs. Stone carry things to the table!"

To my amazement he stopped dancing and went in, not even making a face. "Why, thank you, Garland," said Aunt Pearl. Then he picked up a napkin she dropped, and she said, "Why, thank you, Garland," again. And when we all sat down, he actually pulled the chair out for her and got it back under her in plenty of time for her to land on it as she sat. "Why, Garland!" said Aunt Pearl.

"He knows how to get around a person when he wants to," said Mrs. Odell.

It was getting late and we were still eating, and Aunt Pearl and Mrs. Odell kept talking, and I imagined that we would be riding through the dark, and, just as we arrived at the fair with the colored lights of the carnival ahead of us, some unseen hand would pull the plug and it would all go out. I finally said, "Aunt Pearl, what if it rains?"

She was in the middle of talking to Mrs. Odell, but she stopped long enough to look me in the face. One thing about Aunt Pearl, if you could catch her right, she would really listen to you. She said, "Mrs. Odell, I think we better leave the pans," and within five minutes she had her scarf and pocketbook and Mrs. Odell had the records and phonograph to take home, and we were climbing in the car, me in the back with Carmell and Garland; India and Mrs. Odell in the front with Aunt Pearl. It was darkening too early because of the clouds and we had to drive all the way across the county, but once we had dropped Mrs. Odell and were moving, I was hopeful again. Even if it did rain, Aunt Pearl would make something good happen.

She said, "We have to play something since we didn't have any time for any party games. What's that car game you like, Blair Ellen?"

"Graveyard!" I said. "You count the cows on your side of the road."

"I know that game," said Carmell. "You have to bury them if you pass a graveyard."

Carmell and I discussed how to count sheep and horses and dogs, and Garland said, "That's a game? Counting cows?"

"It's a car game," I said. "It's a special game for long car trips and vacations."

"I go on vacations," said Garland, and then, in a low voice so that Aunt Pearl couldn't hear, "And I don't have to play dumb games either." His hair had come completely unstuck, and it looked like wet feathers. Something about the way it looked made me mean.

I said, also softly, "Where do you go for vacations, Garland? Last year Mother and Daddy and I went to Blackwater Falls. Where did you go?"

The hills were sidelit just now with a strange, almost horizontal light that had slipped out between two bands of cloud. Garland's mouth got tight and he didn't say anything. You could see how badly he wanted to run away, and for an instant I thought he would break a window and jump. I hadn't meant for them to hear me in the front seat, but India's voice came drifting over the seat. "We visited our daddy in Cincinnati, Ohio," she said. "We went on the train to Cincinnati."

Carmell said, "The main kind of trip Garland takes is hitchhiking. Right, India? He runs off and hitchhikes to town all the time. He almost didn't get to come tonight because he ran off and hitchhiked to town yesterday, right, India?"

"Two or three times a week," said India, sounding proud. "He can get rides anywhere."

"But it's dangerous," said Aunt Pearl.

Garland was staring out the window, but I saw the side of his face grinning. "Don't like to be tied down," he said. "Never did."

As if to prove his point, Garland disappeared as soon as we got to the fair, and I was disgusted with Carmell and India because they wanted to see the exhibits, paper plate loads of tomatoes and green peppers, shelves of fruits and jellies in mason jars, hangers with homemade aprons and baby dresses. I yawned and spoke of candy apples, hoping to lure Carmell out, at least. Finally we went toward the baby rides, the merry-go-round, and little boats in a pond. All the time I was watching the big rides, deeper into the carnival, the ones that took some courage to ride.

We were buying candy apples when Garland burst out of the crowd with his cheeks red. There was a stage, he said, and they had little dogs jumping through fire; we had to hurry or we'd miss it! We went rushing through the crowd after him, and it was a good show. The dogs climbed ladders and leaped off into the arms of their trainer. Aunt Pearl said that those dogs loved that man, that they had been trained with kindness; they liked leaping for him. Next Garland took us to a place where you could pitch pennies, and he won a blue glass and Carmell won an ash tray, and I suddenly realized that it hadn't rained and no one had pulled the plug, that I was having a good time even if Garland had discovered all the best things while we were in Agricultural Arts. I asked Aunt Pearl how long we had to go, and she said we could stay as long as we wanted. She was drinking coffee from a cardboard container and holding a fistful of tickets for our rides. "It's your birthday, honey," she said. But I could tell by her face that, kind as she was, there was a limit.

I decided not to waste any more tickets on baby rides. I was ready for the Octopus, the Whip, and the Great Ferris Wheel. The Octopus was fun, but after three times on it, Carmell said she wanted to try to win a plush dog, and Garland said he thought the Whip was a baby ride, so only India and I went on the Whip. We were just settling back in our cart, feeling for a comfortable place against the protective mesh hood, when Garland leaped over the barrier fence and up on the platform. "Move over," he said, slipping under the bar, crowding me to the middle.

"You didn't pay!"

"I'm out of tickets."

"Aunt Pearl has more." I glanced at India to see what she thought of him sneaking on, but she was looking at me.

"It's not like I was stealing," said Garland. "It doesn't cost them anything for me to be in here with you." His hair was thoroughly messed up now, and less greasy. He grinned, and I had never seen so many big white teeth.

The music started, the big belt in the middle moved, and our cart took its first, gentle, whirl, and the platform began to tilt. We accelerated then and I slid into India, and a few seconds later I was sliding into Garland. It was a good ride; sometimes you thought you were going to be cut in two by a sudden lurch forward into the restraining bar, and sometimes your head snapped back against the mesh, but mostly it was the sideways swoop and slide that felt like a mountainside looks. Once, for an instant, I saw our six forearms braced on the bar, like different animals; Garland's were red weasels, India's were swans, and mine were two little sea lions. "Look out!" I yelled. "Here I come again!"

"I can't breathe!" screamed India. But I didn't mind her screaming, she was so wide awake laughing. "You're on top of me!"

"Get on top of me!" said Garland. His grin looked a mile wide, but I managed to stop myself from rolling onto him by leaning forward and letting my hair get jerked in the wind.

"I think I'm sick," giggled India.

Garland reached behind me and punched her and told her she better not throw up, and then he left his arm back there, and when we spun again, I was swept against him. He seemed to have about a dozen knees and elbows, and he tried to keep his arm around me.

"Let go!" I yelled, "I'm slipping!" and I wrenched myself back into the center with my cheeks burning and braced both feet as widely as possible. You might as well play spin the bottle, I thought, as ride with Garland. When we stood around after the ride, India said she wasn't going on any more. "But what about the big Ferris wheel?" I said. "I don't want to ride it alone!"

"I'll go on with you," said Garland, and Aunt Pearl yawned and said she thought it might be the last ride. India knew what was going on, and I knew what was going on, but I wanted to ride the big Ferris wheel, so it was me and Garland, at the opposite ends of the swing.

They rolled us up a few feet at a time as the operator filled the next swing. I leaned over and waved, and India shouted, "Have fun, you two! Don't do anything I wouldn't do!"

I pretended Garland wasn't with me, and in fact he slumped down in his corner as if he didn't want to be. We kept rising bit by bit until we were at the outermost bulge of the wheel and I couldn't see any of the other swings or Aunt Pearl and India either. A breeze came up and we tossed gently, suspended over the pink and yellow chasm. I thought; the trouble with this ride is that there's too much time to think about it. I scowled at Garland, and he scowled back. I didn't intend him to spoil my last ride.

We began to roll, steadily but slowly, and I was gulping to myself that it wasn't going to be so bad, but as we crossed the top, going backwards, the wheel accelerated. Too fast! I thought. It felt as if the bottom were dropping out, and the blood drained from my cheeks and hands and feet. There was only one other thing as tall as we were, and that was the Red Rocket that shot down faster than we did and shrieked terribly as it went. I tried to look down and get my bearings by seeing the lights on the alleys and aisles between the stalls and rides, but I never could quite tell what I was seeing, and the loudspeaker never quite made sense. Once we seemed to be slowing down a little and all I needed was a couple of seconds to rest from the motion, but just when I could see the beaten-down grass under the wheel and the operator standing there in his railroad engineer's cap wiggling his chin as he chewed tobacco, just when I was actually leaping distance from the ground, he reversed a long lever and we climbed again so rapidly toward the low clouds glowing with reflected carnival light that I thought we were broken and hurtling off into space. I opened my mouth to scream and was filled by the wind.

"Whooeee!" called Garland, and I had completely forgotten I wasn't alone up there. He had his glasses off and waved both hands and yelled, "Looky here," at nobody in particular.

"You just keep on laughing, Garland Odell," I said. "You just keep on laughing."

Without his glasses he may not have been able to see the seriousness of my face, but at any rate he did keep on hooting and laughing. Then they stopped us at the absolute apex of the whole wheel, and turned the machine off. Perfect stillness. The music was off, and there was nothing to hear but the creak of our swing, and the passing screams of the Red Rocket.

"What's the matter?" I said.

Garland was slouched back, arms on the back of the swing, legs spraddled. "They always do this. It's part of the ride."

"You're making us move. Stop swinging us."

"Are you afraid? I thought you weren't afraid because you didn't scream."

"I don't scream," I said, not mentioning that I had tried and failed.

[57]

Garland began to pump us back and forth again.

"You'd be afraid too," I said, "if you had your glasses on and could see anything."

He sat straight up, put them on and leaned way over the front bar. "You see those struts over there?" he said. "If this swing started to give, I'd catch hold right there and work my way down hand over hand. I'd take you down too."

"No you wouldn't. I'd climb down myself. But you'd have a better chance because you're on the inside. There's nothing on my side but air. When do you think he's going to start us up again?"

"I've been on these things where you sat for fifteen minutes or a half hour and didn't move because some guy paid the man off so he could sit and hug his honey."

My only hope was that at least Garland had a little experience at these things. I looked down again cautiously, as through black ice, clear to the bottom where the lights made precise little points, and I remained terrified, but at the same time glad to be here. I said, "I don't know about climbing down. There are wires all over this place. We'd probably get electrocuted."

"I'd rather get electrocuted," said Garland. "You just can't sit around. You know? You have to do something." He was leaning toward me suddenly very serious, suddenly like a different boy. "So listen, Blair Ellen, what I wanted to tell you was, that present India gave you? It was only from her. She just said it was from both of us because she thought I didn't get you anything. But I really did get you something."

He extended a fist. Stretched across the swing to me. "How nice," I said, afraid to take it. His fist hung there in midair until I had no choice but to reach out palm upwards to receive it. His dry knuckles touched my hand first, then his fingernails, as he opened his hand. The thing stuck briefly to his skin before it fell into my hand.

It was a diamond ring. That is, it was the kind of dime-store glass stone set in a gold-colored claw that we called a diamond ring. I wanted to say, what does it mean? Because if it's an engagement ring, I don't want it, I don't want to be engaged. But the Ferris wheel had started moving again. "Put it in your pocket," he said. "Nobody has to see it. It's private." They took us around twice more, and I let Garland put his arm around my waist and my face turned red from wind and embarrassment because my poptop slipped up a little and two of his fingers burnt my skin.

"Whooey," said Garland, and he gave me a squeeze. But he didn't ask me to wear the ring, only to receive it, so it didn't have to mean anything in particular, I decided. Or rather, what it meant was up to me.

When we were on the ground again, he ran away backwards, hooting again. India said, as if she knew all about it, "That was the best ride yet, right, Blair Ellen?"

Going back in the car, I sat in the back between her and Garland, just the way I wanted to be. Garland was very quiet, like a little boy. No more trying to put his arm around me. He half lay with his cheek against the window, and a big moon came out for a little while. Aunt Pearl said, "Is everybody asleep back there?" And I sighed and pretended I was so I wouldn't have to talk. I watched the hilltops walking along under the moon, and India seemed to have fallen asleep too, because she slowly spread out, taking up more and more space, and I could feel the heat of her leg through her slips and mine.

I thought, this is the end of my birthday, the birthday when India gave me a bracelet and Garland gave me a ring and they will always be my special friends who mean exactly what I want them to mean.

PART
TWO

AFTER THAT SUMMER I DIDN'T SEE INDIA AND GARLAND UNTIL WE
all started high school four years later. In those four years, things
happened to me that were as if I had changed species, and I felt
every change as a terrible loss. Aunt Pearl and Stone Paradise
went first. She sold the house when she decided to marry a man
from New Jersey she met on a Caribbean cruise. I might have
been forced to see the reason in selling out, but she also sold
Pandora and Eppie to a breeder in Pennsylvania. "How could she
do it?" I said bitterly to Mother. "How could she do it to them?"

Mother said, "Well, Blair Ellen, when your husband has an
allergy, you have to make certain sacrifices."

"Sacrifices?" I said. "Sacrifices? That isn't a sacrifice, it's white
slavery!"

I wasn't absolutely sure of the ramifications of that phrase,
especially since Pandora and Eppie were both a deep red color,
but for once I didn't care if I sounded like a fool. I couldn't free
myself of an image of the dogs, sometimes looking like themselves, sometimes like sad, red-haired sisters of India Odell,
crowded into a pen or boxcar, taken out only rarely, and then to
be used—I would usually press my fists against my eyeballs at
that point to smear the rest of the vision.

"They're only dogs," mother said. "After all. And I know
Pearl visited the breeder."

But I wasn't so sure I trusted Mother anymore either since she had made us move. Out of several years of teaching flunkers in summer school she and Daddy had got together enough money to build a ranch house in the backyard. The idea was that we would live in the small, efficient, new house and get the income from renting the big, old house. The new house had no eaves, no dormer windows, no old-fashioned clothes press or pantry. My room was next to the bathroom, and the walls were so thin that I heard every sound in there, and I would sometimes lie on my bed trying not to breathe until they stopped rustling and flushing and clearing their throats.

The other problem was that Mother chose bad tenants. They were a family named Hoover, a mother with a couple of noisy little boys and two girls around my age, who shared my old room with the secret balcony. There was no father, and they weren't very clean. Mrs. Hoover would hang out sheets and leave them for days on end, through rainstorms and children playing hide-and-seek. Once I saw a passing dog lift his leg and aim at them.

"They'll sleep on it anyhow," I told Mother. When she only shook her head, I added, "Those little boys are the kind who wipe their snot on the walls."

After a while Mother said, "I saw a tampon box in the garbage yesterday."

"Mrs. Hoover, I suppose."

"No, I don't think so. She had a hysterectomy. She told me all about it. I think it's one of the girls, the big one I expect. You have to wonder about a teen-age girl who uses tampons."

I caught my breath. What exactly did she mean? She was always hinting at things. Did she mean that tampons wouldn't fit in if you were a virgin?

I started paying attention to Bunny, the Hoover my age. I would watch from behind the drapes when she came outside to sneak a smoke. She would sit on one of the little kids' rusty tricycles with her legs stretched out, crossed at the ankles. She wore a lot of eye make-up and she teased her hair. As soon as she went in, I would run to the bathroom and lock the door and compare myself in the full-length mirror to the image of tall, probably not-nice Bunny Hoover. From the side I didn't mind the way my back curved into my buttocks, but from the front I thought my hips were too wide. I would stand far away and up close. Sometimes I stripped down to my underwear and sucked in my gut and tightened the straps on my bra to get my bosom up higher. I thought it would all look better stretched out another three inches. Especially the legs. Bunny had such long straight legs, and mine were short. My hair was in my favor, though. I wore bangs and a pageboy, and I admired the reddish highlights in the dark brown. My hair, in fact my whole face, not to brag, would look more appropriate on the cover of *Seventeen* magazine than Bunny's with the black around her eyes and that teased haystack of hair. Sometimes I turned away from the mirror and then whirled back quickly to flash myself a great big smile, slightly off-center, just like Daddy's, with dimples that lifted the cheeks high and crinkled the eyes a little. For that half a second, grinning at myself appealingly, I would like my face, like myself, and then I'd start to notice things. That the bangs were crooked, that a row of whiteheads was forming where my lower lip met my chin bone. The left incisor was crooked, and the neck was too short, and right on down to the ridiculously low-slung butt.

Bunny Hoover would never have these searching sessions in the bathroom that ended with a flushed toilet to hide what she was doing from her mother. When Bunny spent time in front of a mirror she would be doing something practical like trying out a new lipstick brush. *She* had boyfriends. *She* went out on dates on Saturday nights, in cars. I thought she was too young to go out in a car, but I would surely have liked a boyfriend. I would have liked not to spend Saturday night watching *Gunsmoke* with Daddy.

The fact was, I had no idea if I was going to make it as a teenager. All I was sure of was how not to be. Sitting home Saturday night was unacceptable. Being overweight was unacceptable, unless you had clothes as expensive as Gail Gordon's. Being poor was okay, but only if you were handsome and athletic like the Bardolines. But gathered cotton skirts set my teeth on edge. Boys with their hair in long shocks on top who wore their pants up at their waists instead of low on their hips were absolutely wrong. In fact, most things associated with the people who started riding the buses down from Coburn Creek to our high school were wrong. I never made fun of them the way some people did, but I didn't expect to start up any friendships, either, not with the Crains or the Critches or the Tuckers or the Odells.

I saw Garland and India on the very first day of high school. I had made a point of calling up Gail the night before so I would have someone to walk with. She and I weren't friends exactly, but we had always been in things together. We were always president and vice-president of the Scout troop, and of our homerooms in junior high, and officers of the Youth Fellowship at church. She gave me a lot of confidence, especially that morning, telling me I would no doubt make National Honor Society my second year, and I was certainly good looking enough to be a homecoming princess. I said, very pleased, that I doubted it, and she said, well, who else is there in class? We know everyone already except the new ones from Coburn Creek. So I told her she should be class president, hoping she would say no, I would be, but instead she said she thought it should be a boy, maybe Johnny Bardoline.

I was feeling pretty good that morning, until we stepped into the auditorium, hot and damp and echoing with a thick arc of voices. Three-hundred-odd students in that room, and the first individuals I picked out of all those people were up in the balcony in a row with the plaid shirts and gathered cotton skirts: three redheads—Garland, India, and Carmell.

I jerked my head down, terrified they'd wave, terrified they'd see me and want to make friends again. I slid in after Gail, and on the other side of her was dark-eyed, bouncy Linda Bardoline, cousin of Johnny's, the girl I'd most like to be. It must be easy, I thought bitterly, if you're a Bardoline, when you have all those brothers and cousins. It must be easy to get along with people. Fifteen years of experience being around boys while I was drinking coffee with a couple of schoolteachers. I wanted to be dark and athletic like Johnny and Linda. I would gladly have been Johnny, and if not Johnny, Linda, and if I couldn't *be* one or the other of them, why I wanted to go steady with Johnny, and until that happened it was best to sit close to Linda.

After the assembly, Gail and I went to our homeroom for our schedules and book lists.

Just at the door to the classroom someone called my name.

[66]

Even before I saw the hair, I recognized the secret closed-lip smile spreading across her face, so glad to see me. Gail leaned against the door jamb to watch, and I felt a flush of embarrassment for India's gray suit, something from the nineteen fifties with a straight skirt, too long, and a fitted jacket. I wanted to shout, but India, suits have braid trim nowadays! And A-line skirts! At the very least A-line skirts! I suppose I should have been glad it wasn't one of the homemade gathered skirts, but somehow this suit was worse. She hadn't just thrown on whatever old rag was lying across the bed: she had chosen this of all her clothes because she thought it was right for the first day of school. I wanted to throw my body over her and hide her shame.

When we were face to face, a voice came out of me like an elderly church lady, something in the rhythm of my, my, how you've grown: "Well, well, India Odell," I said.

It might have been less impossible if she had spoken, or if Gail hadn't been watching. Inside me a bubble swelled containing questions—the charm bracelet, her grandmother, what happened to the little goat? Did she and Garland still live up there in the wind and sun, and had they ever got TV? It would have been easier, too, if she had looked a little more pitiful, instead of content with herself. A particular, peculiar blend of beautiful parts and awkward parts, and I was so confused I couldn't bear to look at her.

I found another voice, the one the preacher uses when he shakes hands with all the people after church. "India," I said, "it's so good to see you. We have to sit down together and talk really soon."

She parted her lips, almost lost her smile, and her forehead puzzled up a little. She glanced at Gail, and to my horror I saw that she understood that I wasn't going to introduce her to Gail. You don't want to meet Gail anyhow, I thought. How can I be expected to help you when I can't even help myself? All the time that balloon was collapsing inside me at the same rate as her smile faded.

"Well, who on earth was *that*?" said Gail.

"Someone I used to play with when I was little. She had a goat."

"I'll bet she did," said Gail. I smiled in her face and thought, that's it for you and me, Gail, I may betray people, but I don't make fun of them. I'd rather walk home alone every day than walk with you.

India wasn't the kind of person to make a pest of herself or hold a grudge either. She always spoke when I ran into her in the hall but didn't try to make friends anymore. She had her own friends, two girls from Coburn Creek who went everywhere with her. One, the skinny daughter of a fundamentalist preacher, wasn't allowed to wear shorts for gym. She had a white cotton skirt that she safety pinned between her legs. The other girl was a big, quiet miner's daughter, who was never heard to speak aloud.

She'll do fine, I thought, and Garland too. They don't need me. I had too much on my mind to worry about them. One of the things on my mind was Johnny Bardoline. There was a two-week period at the end of October when I was sure he had a crush on me too. He was flirting with a lot of girls then, and already having lunch sometimes with Gail Gordon, but for one week he followed me at lunch hour. He sat behind me in French class, and several times a period he would tap me on the shoulder or shove at my seat with his foot, and then, when I turned around, give me a tiny wave. It took me a long time to believe Johnny Bardoline, who ran sixty-yard touchdowns, could do anything childish. I was slow to conclude anything from his waving. All I knew was that when it happened, warmth would flood me from the shoulder, cross the pulse in my neck, through my cheeks, down over my chest and arms. When he smiled, his eyes disappeared in creases and I would look at his soft, short hair and his large forearms. Later, I thought about strategies, how I should have sent him notes or told people I liked him. But at the time I kept waiting to be sure. He showed up in the vicinity of wherever I was eating lunch too, and I would go for walks alone outside the building, giving him a chance to join me.

The school site had been cut out of the side of a hill overlooking town, and I went and sat on the boulder they hadn't moved, giving my profile to the school and, I hoped, Johnny. I thought my face was too round seen full front, but I liked the line of my forehead and nose. Pretty soon he did come out and scooped up some gravel and scattered it in my general direction. I pretended not to see him right away and, while I was pretending, a bunch of boys came running out with a football and asked him to toss a few. The next day, before he even got to the gravel, Linda and some friends of hers started teasing him, and on the third and fourth days it rained.

The fifth day was the coldest of the year so far. The rain had stopped, but the raw wind was still whipping down the leaves and driving big silver and charcoal piles of cloud over the hills. There was nothing beautiful down in town and no color in the trees. The world looked rough to me, and I tried to keep from shivering as I stood on the boulder. My legs ached from the strain of not slipping down the damp face of the rock. I was trying for a look of tragic nobility, thinking that since Johnny was a hero, he would want to see the hero in me. I gazed down at the river and thought, how ironic that Daddy used to swim there. How ironic that the river once had fish.

"You look like you lost your best friend," said a voice. I turned slowly, expecting Johnny, and found Garland Odell standing by my rock with his hands in the pockets of pants that were too high waisted. His old argyle sweater had turned gray and there was a big moth hole in the shoulder. "What are you going to do, jump?"

Garland had turned into a real smart aleck. He was in my geometry class and drove the teacher crazy, always calling out and getting the boys laughing. I made a sour mouth, and was about to say something smart in return when Johnny came out the fire exit.

"Leave me alone, Garland," I said. "Go away."

Johnny was walking straight toward the boulder, not pausing for gravel this time. Indistinctly it occurred to me that it might be easier for Johnny to come and talk to me with Garland there.

"Oh," said Garland, backing away. "I get it. Excuse me for living."

I had already forgotten Garland; the miracle was about to happen. Johnny broke into a cheerful trot, and I stood poised to drop lightly from my rock to meet him, and at that moment there was a clang, the fire door opened again, and another voice squalling, "Johnny! Johnny!" Out came Gail Gordon herself,

[69]

running hard. She ran badly too. I suppose Gail weighed at least as much as Johnny, and her big jaw and breasts stuck out in front of her. She laid her hand on Johnny's arm, and he stopped. I couldn't believe he would let her stop him. "I have to tell you something," she said. He glanced at me sheepishly, and let himself be led away. I couldn't believe that Johnny Bardoline, who easily outran tackles like bears and linebackers like lions would let Gail Gordon take him away so easily.

I stared around wildly, saw that Garland was still there, witnessing my humiliation. I wanted to kick him, but instead I lost my footing, couldn't get moving enough in the cold to catch myself, and I slid off the boulder, breaking the fall with my hands and knees, rolling when I struck the ground. I started to cry; I hadn't cried in front of anyone since I was a kid, but something about the bloody plaid of scratches on my knee made me feel so damaged.

Garland squatted down beside me, and at least he was blocking me from anyone else's view. "You're bleeding," he said, with his hands hanging between his knees.

"I see it, I see it." I took a big snivel and wiped my eyes and tried to get up, and my knee gave on me with pain, and Garland stuck his arm out and I grabbed him.

For just an instant his face was close to mine and very serious. He said, "Listen, Blair Ellen, do you like him?"

"Who? Johnny Bardoline?" I had my balance now, all I needed was my pride. Everything was over, no one was going to know anything. "Johnny Bardoline? Of course not. I'm not interested in boyfriends. It takes too much energy, dating and all that. I have things to do." The pain in my knee shot me up with something sustaining. "I intend to do things someday. I intend to do things for other people." Garland, at an increased distance, looked skinny and peculiar again. But I said, "Thank you. Thank you very much for your kindness."

Something in the way I said it set him off. He seemed to twist up and do a stomping dance like Rumpelstiltskin. He did an imitation of me in a hoity-toity voice. "Thank*ew*! Thank*ew*! And drop dead!"

"I didn't mean it that way. I really meant thank you. For helping me up."

"What do you care," he said. "What do you know. Bull. Bullshit!" He spat on the grass just in front of my feet, a big translucent glob, and then he snapped his body like a whip and went off.

That same afternoon they posted the results of the elections for junior varsity cheerleader and my name was crossed out. Linda Bardoline got it, of course, and Teresa Spinett, and, to my devastating surprise, so did our tenant, Bunny Hoover. Bunny Hoover who had dates every night and wore her skirts too tight and her hair in a big teasepile.

When I got home, Mother and Daddy were having coffee in the dining area. Behind them was the glass sliding door to the patio, and in the distance, looking grim today, the hills. We always had coffee together after school. All the times I heard them talk about the high school, I thought, and nothing they said then was of any use to me now. The plate in the middle of the table had a slice of yesterday's apple pie and a stack of chocolate-covered graham crackers. I reached over and took a cookie, but I didn't sit down. They waited in silence. They had seen the cheerleader lists; they knew how much I had wanted it. "Well," I said. "That's one thing I failed. It's all over for cheerleading."

"They have tryouts again in the spring," said Daddy.

"Oh, come on, Daddy. You know they pick the varsity cheerleaders from the junior varsity."

"Aren't you sitting down?" said mother.

I didn't think I could keep grinning long. "No, I'll go start my homework."

"What's the big hurry?" said Daddy.

"Let her go, Lloyd," said Mother.

I couldn't stand them when they were worried about me. If they were going to be so sensitive, why hadn't they prepared me better for the real high school?

I lay on my bed watching the air turn gray, watching the colors drain from my room. I waited for the phone to ring. Johnny was going to call and say, listen, Blair Ellen, there's been a terrible mistake. Gail found my wallet, that's what she had to tell me. It wasn't what you thought.

No, I thought, it isn't going to happen. I have to rise above it. I have to find something big enough to crowd out cheerleading tryouts and Johnny Bardoline. Some great service I am called to do. My ears rang from the silence, and I listened for a call. A voice that would speak my name and everything would be lit with new color, the world changed. I remembered the boy Samuel in the Bible, who grew in favor with both God and Man. He thought the old man he lived with was yelling for him, but it turned out to be the Lord. Samuel! Samuel! out of the dark and Samuel said, "Lord thy servant heareth." That was what I needed: a loudspeaker in the night, the heavens opening. Sound and light.

Garland Odell pointed me toward it. Geometry class met after lunch in a first floor room that seemed to get twice as much heat as anyplace else in the building. Everything in that room was dull except Garland. The teacher, Mrs. Atha, also the girls' phys. ed. teacher, didn't like geometry any better than we did. Sometimes she would get so caught up in the dullness that she would talk sports and never get to a new theorem. "But don't think you're getting away with anything," she would say. "You'll get double homework tomorrow." But instead she gave us little vacations. Three afternoons in October listening to the World Series. No homework for Columbus Day, no homework for homecoming. That particular day Garland came in late, after Mrs. Atha had already drawn some triangles on the board. She was leaning on a window sill gesturing lazily with a long wooden chalk holder.

"Sorry I'm late, Mrs. Atha. I got caught smoking in the bathroom and I had to go talk to Mr. Thornton."

Mrs. Atha liked Garland. She didn't stop us from laughing, and she didn't make the effort to go up to her desk and mark him late. She just told him to sit down. The only empty seat in the room happened to be beside Evalina, one of the retarded Crains from Coburn Creek. All the Crains had big round heads and pear-shaped bodies with short skinny legs. I remember the skirt Evalina was wearing that day was a summery pale yellow with a napped pattern like a chenille bedspread, and the zipper was broken, so some skin and slip bulged out. Garland walked by the empty seat and leaned against a back wall. Mrs. Atha pointed at the empty seat, and Garland grinned and shook his head. Everyone tittered. "All right, Garland, take a seat."

The radiators fizzed. Garland said, "Hey, Mrs. Atha, can I go to the board and do the next problem? Look, I did my homework!"

Evalina Crain's deep laugh lasted longer than anyone else's.

"Garland," said Mrs. Atha, "take a load off your feet. In that seat. Now." She tapped it with the chalk end of the long pointer, and Garland sat, and then she had to tell Evalina to shut up because she kept guffawing out of her big moon face. We all turned reluctantly back to the board. "Let's go on to a new theorem," said Mrs. Atha. "We'll skip the homework if it was so easy that Garland got it." We rustled and muttered, passed up the homework, found the new page in the book. When the room was still, a deep, agonized moan rose from the back of the room.

"Arrghh," it said, like a comic book.

"Who is that? Who's moaning and groaning?"

All I could see from the front was Garland's long arm snake up in the air. "It's me, Mrs. Atha. I'm sorry, but I'd like to have permission to move my seat."

Laughs from the hillbilly boys in the back row.

"You may not. Garland, I'm getting a stomachful of you today."

"May I scoot over a little bit?" Mrs. Atha made a move in his direction. "But this is serious, Mrs. Atha. This is an *odor*."

Oh, they loved that. The country boys haw-hawed and the town boys snickered and we girls in the front who were too far away to tell exactly what was going on giggled nervously. Mrs. Atha strode back at Garland, powerful tendons rising out of her sneakers, carrying her chalk stick point forward like a lance. Abruptly she changed directions and leaned over Evalina. We could hear Evalina saying "Yes, ma'am" and "No, ma'am" and then another "Yes, ma'am" and she got up and lurched toward the door, seeming to have trouble balancing her body on those pinskinny legs. She turned around and grinned at the class several times on the way, and everyone was laughing, except some girls who gasped.

"Shut up, class," said Mrs. Atha.

Up until that point I hadn't understood what was going on. I didn't see the back of her skirt until she was almost to the door, and when I did see it, it exploded in my eyes like a fireball. At the door she put a hand on her hip and gave her butt a shake, and the blood was like a bullseye, a red afterimage on my eyes, centering the whole class's attention. For an instant I was ashamed to be the same sex, and then the flood of white light fell on Evalina and me. I recognized it at once as the call, and got to my feet. "Mrs. Atha," I said, "may I go help her?"

"Please," said Mrs. Atha. "Please do. And, Blair Ellen, bring back some wet paper towels when you come."

I touched Evalina's elbow when we were out in the hall and didn't speak. It was so simple when you came down to it. The retarded, the poverty-stricken, the spat upon. Just what I needed.

Dreamily I saw them spread about me, on street corners, cowering in rundown buildings, hiding in attics.

Evalina kept slowing down to try and look at the back of her skirt. "I made a mess, huh, Blair Ellen? I shouldn't let boys see, huh?"

No one else was in the bathroom; the grayness and emptiness seemed just right for what I was doing. Diffuse light through glass bricks, and no shadows, a flat equality of gray enamel on locker baskets, concrete floor, and asbestos-wrapped steam pipes.

"All right, Evalina," I said. "We'll take care of you now."

She leaned on the wash basin and looked at herself in the mirror. "Hey, Blair Ellen, do you like boys? Have you got a boyfriend?"

I couldn't understand why she didn't realize that she had been humiliated. She *is* retarded, I thought. She really is.

"Take your skirt off, Evalina, we have to rinse it out." I ran the cold water as hard as I could. "Have you ever had a period before?"

"Sure, lots of them. Hey, Blair Ellen, what color lipstick do you use?"

"Take off the skirt. Why don't you wear a Kotex, Evalina?"

She dropped the skirt around her ankles and pretended to lose her balance, trying to get me to laugh at her. I kept my face still. Just because she deserved pity didn't mean I should indulge her.

She said, "I wear Kotex. Miss Ross gives them to me in the office. She has lots of them. My ma said use rags, but I come to school and get Kotex from Miss Ross. *I* ain't washing out no rags."

I picked up the skirt, wondering if I had courage to touch the blood, but decided it wasn't necessary.

"I have to take off my slip too," she said. She had on a thin little pale blouse and she laid that on the bench and peeled out of the slip and a pair of old nylon underpants with most of the elastic gone. Everything puddled around her ankles. She giggled and crossed her arms over her crotch, wobbling like a pink rubber piggy. "Hey, Blair Ellen, what if some boys come in here?"

"Put your blouse back on, Evalina, you'll catch cold."

The blouse didn't cover her buttocks. "There had still better not be any boys coming in here."

"Evalina," I said, "I think you think too much about boys."

She nodded her head yes, and big dimples I had never noticed came out on her cheeks. I picked up the bloody things by a finger and thumb and dropped them in the sink. But she's going to wash them out herself, I thought. She has to learn.

I said, "Look Evalina, I'm going to lend you my sweater so you won't freeze to death. You can wrap it around your behind, but you have to wash yourself first. Now take some paper towels in the toilet and get good and clean and then I'll lend you the sweater."

"Can I have the diamond thing too so it will stay up?"

"Yes, I'll lend you the clip too. But go clean up."

Her head appeared up in the air, above the cubicle. "Hey Blair Ellen, I'm standing on the seat."

I was going to have to throw away my good old regulation green Girl Scout sweater, I knew. It would end its life stretched into Evalina Crain rear-end humps. But giving it—an old friend like that sweater—was proof of my seriousness. I'm not fooling around, I thought prayerfully. I am serious about this.

When she got out, I arranged it with the opening on the side like a loin cloth and snapped it in place with my rhinestone sweater guard.

"Hey, Blair Ellen, have you got a lipstick? Can I borrow your lipstick?"

Now I pretended I was Mother, disciplining her for her own

good. "Evalina, I'm going upstairs to get you a Kotex, and, boy, when I come back, these clothes had better be washed out. I mean it, Evalina."

She said, "Hey, Blair Ellen, when you come back, can I borrow your lipstick?"

The office was on the second floor: Mr. Thornton on one side, Miss Alice Ross and the file cabinets on the other, and a waiting room in the middle with a vinyl couch and a water machine with a blue-tinted bottle. Mr. Thornton's door was closed, to my relief. He liked to invite students in and give them advice. I could see his back through the glass, though, so I made a quick dodge into Miss Alice Ross's room. Too quick, because she jumped.

"Blair Ellen! It's you! You scared me to death." She went to our church, and we sang in the choir together, but I avoided her at school, just as I avoided Mother and Daddy. Alice said, "Your father is in there shooting the breeze with Mr. Thornton. Are you going to go say hello?"

I shook my head hard. "Please, Alice, I'm in a hurry. Evalina Crain had an accident."

"Not again." She leaned under the typewriter and came up with a tin file box. She winked at me and opened it. Inside was a stack of brown paper lunch bags, each one plump and bulging. She whispered, "I keep them ready like this because we have a lot of accidents, and with these glass walls you never know who's looking in." She handed it to me, this lunch bag of Kotex. "Don't you have your notebook? A pocket? Where are we going to put it? That Evalina. You tell her—oh, never mind. It doesn't do any good to tell her anything. The best thing will be when she quits school."

"I think she likes school."

"I'd like school too if I got everything free. Free lunch, free sanitary supplies. She thinks it's welfare. That family, they think the whole world is welfare. What they don't get from the government, they beg, and what they don't beg, they steal."

At that instant, out of the corner of my eye, I saw a movement in the other office; Mr. Thornton was tapping on his window, gesturing to me. He opened his door, "Hey! Young Morgan! Come on over here."

"Oh dear," said Alice, and then, before I could protest, stuck the bag into the waistband of my skirt, tugged my sweater down over it and winked again. It felt pudgy and fat. I clasped my hands in front of me like a singer and went into Mr. Thornton's office with my cheeks burning.

"Well, well," said Mr. Thornton, closing the door behind me. "So this is the young Morgan."

They were having a smoke together, Mr. Thornton and Daddy, and Daddy was supposed to have given up cigarettes. He relaxed on the couch, grinning at me, his hair pushed off his forehead, eyes hidden by the reflection of his glasses. I was always surprised when I saw him in school by how young he looked. His good white teeth, his wide chest. He and Mr. Thornton used to play football in high school. Mr. Thornton had been in the Marines, too, and still wore his hair in a crew cut. He was famous for yelling at some boy so loud that a crowd would gather in the hall, and then, when the crowd was big enough, he would spring out and yell to make the students scatter. Daddy raised his voice less often, but was known as a teacher you didn't fool around with.

The two of them, Daddy sitting with one fist in his pocket, Mr. Thornton with his arms crossed, leaning against his desk, stared at me. They both nodded cheerfully. I clenched my hands together and pressed the bag of Kotex tight into my middle. They grinned, and I sweated and smiled. Evalina would have stood here in perfect comfort, enjoying the attention. She doesn't know what's going on, I thought. My sweater stuck under my arms. My antiperspirant was failing. I wanted to scratch; a fine sunburn torture of itching was passing in waves over my whole body.

"Fine looking girl, Morgan," said Mr. Thornton.

Daddy chuckled, "We decided to keep her."

I didn't look at Daddy; I looked at the small embroidered things on Mr. Thornton's tie. Symbols. Masons or Odd Fellows, something that couldn't be explained by reason. You had to be one of them and memorize things. You had to be a Mason; you had to be a man. The back of my mind was working on a lie, what errand had Mrs. Atha sent me up here to do?

"Well, young Morgan," said Mr. Thornton, and it finally occurred to me that he didn't know my name, "how do you like being in school with your parents?"

"I don't have them yet," I said. "I'll have Mother for English next year, but I won't ever have Daddy."

Mr. Thornton rolled his eyes. "We could arrange for you to take shop if you wanted to." A wide guffaw.

I had a small flash of light, not like the one downstairs, but a little flashbulb of a revelation. "I wouldn't want to take shop, but there are some girls in this school who could use a trade." He hadn't stopped smiling, but his smile got a little smaller. I still ignored Daddy. He was on Mr. Thornton's side, that was obvious. I crunched the Kotex bag again. "I'm thinking of people like Evalina Crain. She doesn't do so well in school, and I think it would be good if she knew how to do something with her hands."

Mr. Thornton snickered, just the way the boys in geometry had. "How about it, Morgan?" said Mr. Thornton. "How would you like Evalina Crain working on your car? How would you like Evalina Crain in machine shop?"

Daddy shook his head and ground out the butt of his cigarette. "Lord spare me any more Crains."

I glanced at Daddy finally, but he missed my look. You'll go along with anything Mr. Thornton does, I thought. He's the principal, so he's okay. I wanted to make a speech. Just because Evalina's a girl and dumb. There is still right and wrong.

The bell was ringing, Daddy getting up and stretching. Mr. Thornton gave my shoulder a quick pat. "Young Morgan is a good girl," he said, and they walked me to the door, one on either side, as if I were a defendant and they two burly bailiffs.

I let Evalina keep the sweater, and she wore it all winter instead of a blouse, perilously buttoned over her bobbling chest. She always dressed next to me for gym and asked to borrow my lipstick. I took her to town for lunch one day and bought her a hot dog in Woolworth's and a lipstick of her own. She chose a stunningly bright one called Red Hots and then asked me to buy her hair spray and scarves and candy and to give her a dollar or fifty cents and a nickel. I was firm. "Evalina, it's bad manners to ask for things. Especially when someone already bought you lunch and a lipstick."

"A Mars bar?"

"Evalina, when people give you things, you say thank you and you go about your business and if you're good they'll buy you something again *maybe*."

Sometimes she embarrassed me by shouting from way down at the end of the hall, "He-ey, Bla-air El-len!" But it wasn't a bad embarrassment. I was a little proud. One day at the Future Teachers of America meeting one of the seniors said, "Oh, you're the one who helps Evalina Crain," and she asked me if I wanted to head the committee for the Christmas party at the nursing home. I was the only sophomore with my own committee, and my party for the old people was a big success. After that, at the spring elections in March, the F.T.A. elected me secretary of the whole organization.

I told Mother and Daddy at supper, and Daddy said, not enthusiastic enough to suit me, "Well, well, what do you know. Very nice, Blair Ellen. What's for dinner?"

It looked boring to me; creamed lima beans and pork chops fried black to be sure to kill the trichinosis. Darkness had fallen and the glow of election was fading fast. The only thing left in light was this dining area.

Mother sat down. "You'll have to work hard to uphold the honor, won't you?"

"I already worked hard. That's how I got elected."

The two of them didn't say anything. "I'm not boasting; it's a fact. They told me so. And I got nominated for vice-president of the class too."

"Just don't let it get in the way of your schoolwork," said Daddy.

"My school work! What do you want? I only got a B+ in gym. I'll work harder in gym."

Mother sighted me along her impressive straight nose. "Don't raise your voice, Blair Ellen."

I gulped air and turned my face down to my plate. This happened every once in a while; my gestures became too broad, my delivery too melodramatic. Mother and Daddy would speak more and more softly until I got myself under control. I concentrated so hard on the food that the flavors separated, the flour in the lima beans, powdery and dry, from the starchy inside of the beans. The black outer skin of the pork chops divorced from the stringy white inside. In the back of my head a voice went on rising to a squeal. What do you want from me? What do you want? After a while they had said so little that it occurred to me they had something important on their minds. I thought maybe one of them was sick. A lump in Mother's breast. Heart trouble for Daddy.

He said, "How's your friend Evalina?"

"She's okay. She's been missing a lot of school."

"She never had any business in high school in the first place."

"She has a right to an education."

Mother said, "She has a right to be trained for something useful."

"She learns useful things at school."

Daddy said, "Blair Ellen's trying to housebreak her. I think I'd rather try to housebreak a skunk than a Crain."

I said, "She's happy. She thinks the teachers and the kids like her."

"Well," said mother, "being happy isn't exactly the object of high school, is it?"

A frame of mind dropped over me. A door sprang shut. Something was going on. "I don't know. Sometimes I wish I was as happy as Evalina."

Daddy said, "Well, the real truth is that she doesn't belong in high school. She's disruptive. She takes the other students' minds off their work."

"She does not! Sometimes she laughs too loud, but that's all."

"The boys talk about her," said Daddy. "I hear them making jokes in shop. She disrupts the boys."

"Well, that's not her fault!" I braced for the next round. "That's their dirty minds."

"She's going to get hurt," said Daddy, "if something isn't done."

"She doesn't wear a brassiere," said Mother.

"Well, maybe somebody should buy her one."

[80]

"Yes," said Mother. "That's what we were thinking. Alice Ross and Mrs. Atha and I are going to make up a little gift box for her. A brassiere, some deodorant, a little traveling toothbrush. We want to have a talk with her too. She hasn't been coming around to Alice for Kotex lately, Blair Ellen."

Daddy looked at the ceiling.

My heart started to pound. I said, "Maybe she bought some herself."

"Maybe," said Mother.

"Maybe," said Daddy.

"Maybe *I* bought her some."

"Did you?" said Mother.

"No, but somebody might have. Just because somebody doesn't wear a bra doesn't mean—"

"Blair Ellen, she's stopped using sanitary napkins."

"All you know is who she isn't getting them from! That's all you know!" I felt my big colorful gestures extruding again. I couldn't help myself. I wanted to stand on a chair and wave a banner. "It really is disgusting of you. Haven't you ever heard of innocent till proven guilty?"

Mother said in her gentlest voice, "We all appreciate how you've tried to help her, Blair Ellen. We think it is very fine of you." But, her voice said, that part is over. You failed, and now the real stuff begins.

"You're going to try and trick her, aren't you? You're going to give her presents, and you know how she falls for presents. I told you that myself."

"Now take it easy," said Daddy, and Mother's lips were beginning to get a little tight.

"I'm the Judas goat!" I said. "You're using what I told you in confidence to trap Evalina." But even as I spoke I was thinking of how she'd been looking extra fat lately.

The next day Evalina sashayed into geometry class late, mouth painted halfway across her face, wearing a short-sleeved lime-green pullover and a white bleached streak in her hair. Garland whistled and she put a hand on her hip and made an elaborate silly turn like a model on a walkway. In profile I was sure her belly had the outline of a hard egg. It's true, I thought, the whole thing is true. Evalina didn't sit by me that day; she went to her old seat in the back, near the boys, and I spent all of geometry thinking that one way or the other, I was a fool. Either I was wrong all along, or I was wrong now. I can't even stick to my guns, I thought.

After class Mrs. Atha asked me to take her key and let the girls into gym. Coach was going to take the class till she got back. I made one paltry effort to save Evalina. "Okay, Mrs. Atha," I said. "Let's go get dressed for gym, Evalina."

"Not Evalina, Blair Ellen. I thought you knew. Evalina is coming upstairs with me. We're having a meeting with her."

A grin slowly crossed Evalina's face. "Who's having a meeting with me?"

"Oh, just some of us," said Mrs. Atha. "Miss Ross and Blair Ellen's mother and me."

Evalina made a Red Hots rosette and said, "Those teachers want to have a meeting with me? Hey, Blair Ellen, those teachers want to have a meeting with me."

I saw India when I got to the dressing room, and I was going to talk to her, vaguely hoping she could reassure me about Evalina, but she didn't seem to see my wave; she was busy as usual whispering to her two buddies. They always dressed for gym in the most isolated corner of the whole dressing room, stripping to full-length cotton slips that seemed to have been freshly ironed that morning. They always hung their clothes from the steam pipes so they could finish dressing behind a curtain of skirts and blouses. India went behind the clothes now, and I thought, oh, well, I didn't wave very hard anyhow.

Bunny Hoover was already dressed, and she kicked at the locked door to the gym. "Where's Atha? Why isn't the door open?"

"I have the key," I said. "Wait till I tie my shoes."

"What's Atha doing, having herself a smoke?"

Bunny was sitting on the steps down to the gym door with her legs stretched out, blocking anyone else who wanted to go down. She had wonderful legs, very long and straight and without a hair on them. I could never figure out if she had no hair to start with, or if she just knew how to shave better than the rest of us.

"There's a meeting," I said, unlocking the door. "Coach is teaching us today."

"Coach! That'll be good." Her mouth went the slightest bit sour; Bunny didn't move her face muscles more than she had to.

I walked along beside her to the equipment closet. I hadn't hated her so much lately, not since she'd been eliminated from the varsity cheerleaders. I needed to tell someone. "The teachers are having a meeting with Evalina Crain," I said. "They think she's pregnant." Bunny grunted. I felt better already. "They make me sick, so suspicious. All they want is to throw Evalina out of school."

Bunny bounced a basketball gently in front of her. "You can't have pregnant girls in school."

"Why not?"

"People get ideas."

"The only idea I get is to make sure as heck it never happens to me!"

Bunny grinned. It only lasted a fraction of a second, a little flash of a grin, and then she was down the stairs and out on the floor practicing foul shots. I really liked the grin. It had been as if she thought I was crazy, but not a fool. Crazy wild. I would like to have people say of me, that Blair Ellen, she's such a nut.

Coach came in late shrugging on his sports jacket, smelling of tobacco. "Okay," he yelled, clapping his hands, "Let's shoot foul shots and the first ten to make their shots form teams." When the game started, he screamed at the guards for hanging back, and we laughed and tried to explain girls' rules to him. "Forget that," said the Coach. "We're playing real basketball today." The whole class cheered, but pretty soon it developed that no one was going to get to play except the ten people who had made their baskets. At least Mrs. Atha saw to it that everyone had a turn.

Bunny was the best player in our class. She always dribbled and always shot. She moved down the floor with her back straight and her teased hair towering above everything else.

"You!" shouted Coach. "What's your name? Bugs Bunny! Get that dribble lower and pass off to someone. Come on, pass off!"

Bunny passed, and the others passed it right back to her because if Bunny was on your team, you always let her take the shots. Bunny made a jump shot, and Teresa Spinett dribbled the ball back for her team, and the coach made her pass off too, only the girl she passed to tried to shoot and missed. Bunny rebounded and brought the ball back down the floor, but this time Teresa started guarding her. Teresa's head only came to Bunny's shoulder, but she leaned around and waved her arms and generally made a nuisance of herself and Bunny, without any change of expression, as Coach sneezed, smashed Teresa in the chest with an elbow. Teresa stomped on Bunny's foot, and Bunny chunked the ball in Teresa's face and Teresa grabbed it and they both ended up on the floor.

"Jump ball!" we all shouted from the bench. "Jump ball!"

"What's Shorty doing guarding Bugs Bunny anyhow?" said Coach. "No jump ball. You don't know enough for a jump ball. I need somebody tall. You! Red!" He waved at India to come in. India never played if she didn't have to. She and her two friends always sat in the corner with their heads together chatting and hoping no one would notice them. But Coach moved Teresa to guard and put India on Bunny.

"Now Red," said Coach. "Stay with her, but don't touch her. No hands. Got that?"

India ran along beside Bunny until Bunny stopped and made her neat little jump shot. We all clapped for Bunny, but Coach yelled. "Can't you do a layup, Bugs Bunny? That was the stupidest jump shot I ever saw. All of you! Set up like you were before, and lay it up this time!" Bunny dribbled around India and made a perfect layup. "All right," said Coach. "That was better, but what the Hay are you doing, Red? You're supposed to try and stop the ball from going in the basket. You're on the other side from Bugs Bunny, understand?"

Everyone sat up, alert now, wondering if India would cry. Something was frail about her, maybe her long neck. But she just pursed her lips and nodded. Back at the other end of the court Teresa powered her way through a crowd just like her brother and made a layup at least as good as Bunny's.

This time down the floor India stayed between Bunny and the basket. She even ran backwards a little. And Bunny, out of boredom or disdain, tried her easy little jump shot again, only this time India went up with her, without any apparent effort, no twisting of muscles or sweat, but suddenly there was India up in the air snatching the ball out of its intended trajectory, and then down on the floor, face to face with Bunny, holding the ball.

"All right!" shouted Teresa. "Let's go!"

"Wake up, Red!" shouted Coach. "Pass it off!"

Pretty soon all of us on the bench were cheering all the time, for Bunny or India or Teresa. We had never cared very much before. Bunny and Teresa went after a loose ball once, and Bunny came up with most of her hair loose, but she just brushed it out of her face and took off. India's cheeks and the fronts of her thighs turned pink. Teresa had a floor burn. My joints ached, as if they would burst open if I didn't get into the game.

I was a terrible shot, but I figured I could be energetic and at least guard someone. Maybe Teresa, we were about the same size. I went and stood close beside Coach, giving him time to notice me, to remember who I was. I said, "Gee, Coach, this is the best game we've ever had."

"You want to go in, Morgan? Go guard Spinett, she's running away with everything."

I rushed in, I waved my arms, I stomped at her.

"Take it easy, Blair Ellen," said Teresa, passing the ball to India, who gave a sort of surprised look around the room and then lifted herself up in the air in that strange effortless way and got so high that she tossed the ball through the hoop easily.

"I won't ask what kind of shot that was," said Coach. "But where were you, Bugs Bunny, fixing your make-up?"

All I wanted was to run up and down the floor with the others. If Coach would just forget about me and let me be there. But the period was almost over, and Mrs. Atha and Evalina were back, Evalina carrying a foil-covered box that I recognized from Mother's Christmas collection. I played harder; I didn't want to think about Evalina. Out of the corner of my eye I saw her lay her things out on the bench. Evalina was waving at me, Coach telling us to call it quits, we hadn't been half bad, and then everyone gathering around Evalina while she showed off her presents: lotion-style underarm deodorant, bath powder, a pink satin Kotex belt.

Bunny said, "Hey, Evalina, did the teachers ask if you got one in the oven?"

Evalina giggled, "Your hair's messed up, Bunny."

Going upstairs to dress Bunny said to me, "Evalina's so dumb she doesn't know if she's got one in there or not. She's so dumb I bet those teachers never found out a thing."

Probably right, I thought, taking my time dressing, sitting on the bench in my underwear letting the sweat dry. No one could find out anything from Evalina. *She* didn't care. I didn't care so much either. I was feeling good because Teresa hadn't scored during the time I was in the game. Feeling good because Bunny had said "those teachers" to me as if she'd completely forgotten I was the daughter of two of them. I watched her leaning her flat belly into the wash basin. She had a small butt and long thighs, and she had her arms raised to retease her hair that spread up and out like tongues of flame.

She saw me looking at her. "Are you going home? We walk the same way, in case you never noticed."

I could have had someone to walk with this whole year, I thought. "I have an F.T.A. meeting. But listen, Bunny, in the morning, I could knock for you. If that'd be all right."

She shrugged one shoulder, "Sure, why not?"

I was delighted with her. I had had enough of Evalina begging for this and begging for that and saying hey, Blair Ellen, you're my friend, right? I sat there smiling to myself and feeling my tired muscles. I was going to make friends with Bunny Hoover. Mother would not be pleased.

India and her friends came past. I said, "Hey, India, you're really some basketball player."

As if she had been waiting for me to speak, she swung out of the path she was on, almost knocking over the skinny little preacher's daughter, and dropped on the bench beside me. The friends looked surprised and waited a yard and a half away, clutching their school books to their bosoms. She sat and smiled, still pink cheeked, but she didn't say anything. So I said, "I was afraid you'd feel bad when Coach started yelling but I guess you didn't mind."

"I've always been a pretty good jumper," she said. Still her eyes were fixed on me, and the smile with the mouth closed. She had come swooping at me as if she wanted to talk, but she seemed to be waiting for me.

I said, "I wish we always played boys' rules."

Her cheeks rose up, crowding her bay brown eyes. "Listen," she leaned close. "My brother Garland thinks you're sexy."

It was the last thing I was expecting to hear. I wasn't even thinking about boys. All the sweat that had been drying up started to pour again, armpits, palms of hands. "Garland said that?"

Her eyes seemed to be peeling me. I was thinking that I liked her better than Garland. "I'm not the sexy type, India."

"Garland thinks so." She was suddenly up again. "I thought you'd want to know."

I guess I did. Of course I did. All girls wanted to hear that someone thought they were sexy. Garland wasn't my ideal man, but on the other hand aeons had passed for me since September when I turned my face away from the two of them. They had become so much more normal looking lately, too, faster than the other kids from Coburn Creek. First Garland had figured out about hair cuts, and he now wore his parted on the side and the same length all over, no more long shocks on top. And he wore his jeans low-slung. India still wore the straight skirts from those old gabardine suits, but she had a couple of nice sweater sets now, green and blue to set off her hair, and velvet collars. I wasn't interested in having Garland for a boyfriend exactly, although I did need a boyfriend, but it seemed desirable to exist in his mind as a sexy person.

After my meeting I came out alone into the bright, chilly March afternoon, and took a deep breath. The hills were still mustard brown and leafless, but the low-lying sun gave a richness to their outline. Past a couple of houses, through some trees, the pavement like a small river came up the hill to the high school, past Buddy's Body Shop and Used Cars. Behind me were the football field and the bus garage, where I heard the last bus of the day warming up and voices of students trying to talk the driver into letting them on early. I was feeling pretty good. I didn't have a boyfriend, but I was running for class vice-president and the church was sending me to the statewide leadership conference in June. I could wait for a boyfriend, I thought; there's more to this world.

At the end of the walk were the steep steps down to the street, and I saw two people at the bottom waiting for the bus at its proper stop. I recognized Garland by his hair. He bent toward the other person, a girl, I figured, who was obscured by the concrete pillar. He likes all the girls, I thought. He probably sends India around to two or three a day telling them he thinks they're sexy. The girl he was teasing threw a hand out in an awkward play-slap, and then stepped from behind the pillar. Evalina. Garland was teasing Evalina. He whispered something to her, and she took a step back, grinning and shaking her head no. Then a voice, as sure of itself as a public-address system, spoke in my head. Garland, it said. Garland is the one who did it to her. He lives up there on that same mountain. I could see it, too, as clearly as I'd heard the voice, a place on their mountain, a field of yellow grass growing up around an abandoned truck that rested on its brake drums. Dusk falling and Garland and Evalina come from different directions to the truck bed and Garland gives Evalina a lipstick and a green sweater, and the next thing I see is moonlight and Evalina lying on some old quilts, as quiet as the dead, and Garland sneering and tucking his shirt into his pants. My cheeks started to burn, as if I had in fact been a witness. People said they were all like that up on Odell Mountain, no morals. Not Garland or India either. At the corners of my eyes the light seemed to diminish and I was going to go down over the bank to avoid them, but Evalina saw me and started waving, and I had to go down the steps after all, slowly and carefully, looking only at Evalina, not at him. I said, "See you tomorrow, Evalina."

"Can I come home with you, Blair Ellen?"

"You'd miss your bus, Evalina. How would you get home?"

She giggled. "I'd stay at your house all night."

Garland said, "Yeah, Blair Ellen, I'll stay at your house too." He looked like a fox, the redness of his hair, the brown red of his face and the way his chin narrowed and teeth filled his smile. The nosepiece of his glasses had been broken and repaired with adhesive tape.

I said, "Why are you still here? India left hours ago."

"I don't go when India goes. I go down to Buddy's. I'm getting a job down there."

I thought, maybe Evalina begged him to do it. Maybe she said, hey Garland, be my boyfriend? Maybe he doesn't even know about the baby. Maybe he did it to be nice to her, as a favor. He flickered with energy, danced a little in the cold. Up on the hill they were loading the bus, and someone yelled at him and Evalina.

He said, "I'm getting a motorcycle."

"How are you getting a motorcycle?"

"Don't worry about that, I'm getting one."

"I won't worry until I actually see you driving on the road with one. Then I'll worry."

The bus eased down the hill. Garland ran out into the middle of the street and put his palm out toward it, pretending to force it to a halt. The driver opened the door. "All right, Odell, let's go. Last call."

Evalina hurried in, but Garland leaned an elbow on the fender and grinned at the driver. "Hey, Blair Ellen," he said, "will you go for a ride when I get my motorcycle?"

I shrugged. All the people on the bus were looking at me.

"Will you go for a ride?"

The bus driver hit the horn, and Garland jumped up on the fender. The driver let the bus coast a yard down the hill. People inside all ran to where they could watch Garland sitting on the wide yellow fender. They cheered. The driver stopped and said, "Much as I'd like to see how long you could hang on, Odell."

Garland slid off and backpedaled toward the door. "Will you ride with me, Blair Ellen?" He pounded both fists on the side of the bus. "Will you go with me for one ride?"

I gave a very small nod, not wanting anyone else to see, and Garland whooped and sprang in, and the bus rolled away, off to Coburn Creek and Odell Hollow.

Bunny was right about Evalina being too dumb to give herself away. By the time there was no question at all, it was late May and the teachers decided she might as well finish out the school year. I had a vague, secret envy of Evalina. Evalina never tried to please anyone, never seemed to make plans, was in a fix, and didn't care. She *said* she was getting married, but the school made arrangements with the county: there would soon be another Crain on their hands. Evalina missed a lot of school, but when she did come, she was wearing skirts with functional zippers and new blouses. Since I'd been elected vice-president of the class, I had a plan to take up a collection and buy a layette for her baby. I had a picture in my mind of entering her hospital room and making it overflow with flowers and crocheted and quilted baby garments in pastel colors. But she didn't have the baby until way into the summer, and I didn't exactly forget about it, but I got very involved with other things.

Garland never showed up at my house on the motorcycle either, and that was probably just as well because Daddy was trying to have him thrown out of school. One afternoon soon after class elections I came into the house as Mother and Daddy were sitting down to coffee, and all the humor was gone from Daddy's face, all the comfortable jowliness stretched out of shape by a long thrust of chin. His whole face the color of dull metal.

"As big as life," said Daddy, as if he'd been waiting for me. "That boy stood there as big as life and said, 'Hello, Mr. Morgan, nice afternoon, isn't it?' Just as cool as a cucumber."

Garland had been cutting machine shop classes. I knew it was because of his half-job at Buddy's Body Shop where he was getting paid with the hulk of an old Harley Davidson that had been pulled from under a tractor-trailer on Route 73.

"Well," said Daddy, "he can be as cool as he wants. He can smile and be cool for the rest of his life while he tries to get a job with no high school diploma, because he's through at that high school. I mean it. I'm talking to Thornton first thing in the morning and out he goes. 'Hello, Mr. Morgan, nice afternoon' with that slick smile of his."

Mother clicked her tongue on her teeth.

I said, very softly because of the thrust of Daddy's jaw, "He's probably learning a lot though. You always complain about how the county's too cheap to provide you with real motors."

Daddy fixed me with my own reflection in his glasses. "The

way I look at it, what I see is a greasy, defiant teen-age punk. I don't see any motors in it at all."

Mother said, "Every year there is some student who wants to challenge everything. One who thinks he knows more about his education than the school does."

Daddy said, "Well, Blair Ellen's friend Flowerpot, or whatever his name is, is about to get a real lesson. You don't cut my class and stand across the street from school smirking about it."

But, I thought, Garland isn't really a punk. He doesn't hate school; he just loves his motorcycle.

Daddy had a sour stomach for three days. He couldn't stand it that Garland was invariably polite. "The only thing I hate as bad as insolence," said Daddy, "is hypocrisy."

After two days' suspension, Garland showed up in geometry class. I ducked my head down and checked my homework until Mrs. Atha came in and started class. I thought that in Garland's mind now I must be an ugly thing, not sexy; a squatting lump. And, at the same time, I was humiliated because Daddy had been made to go back on his professed intentions. I half wished Garland were really gone, permanently. Then I could forget about him. Daddy didn't look humiliated, though. They watched me lay down my books after school, then Daddy said, "Well, we reinstated your friend Bouquet."

"I saw him."

Mother said, "It was so near the end of the school year."

I said, to get over the worst possibility first, "Mr. Thornton refused to do what you wanted?"

"Oh, Thornton would have done what I wanted. He would have thrown him out permanently. But I didn't insist. No, it was the girl. Thornton asked me to talk to the girl."

Mother said, "It's hard to believe those two are from the same family."

"Well, if he makes it through high school, he'll have her to thank and no one else. There he stands, smirking at me, so slick you could fry him in his own grease, and there she is, neat as a new pin, and just as soft-spoken as you could ask. A real lady."

Distrust ruffled me. India could lie. India could handle people so slickly you never knew it. "You mean to tell me you changed your mind because of something India Odell said?"

Daddy bit into a store-bought hermit bar. "I really like these things, Sibyl," he said. "They're spicy. I always give a kid a second chance."

I glanced at Mother to see if she was as shocked as I was that Daddy had changed his decision. Every once in a while her face would fail me this way, give no hint of what she expected me to think about something. I said, "What did India say?"

"It was the way she said it. She said none of their family had ever made it through high school. I said I doubted this boy was going to be the one to do it, but I'd give him the chance. I looked him in the eye and said, 'Odell, if you miss one single class for any reason whatsoever between now and the end of school, I won't wait for excuses. I'll write out the expulsion slip. And you're luckier than you'll ever know to have her for a sister.' And do you know what he said to that?" Daddy's eyebrows went way above his glasses, and he did a high voice for Garland that didn't sound at all like him. "He said, 'Yessir, Mr. Morgan, and I appreciate it too, but I do know how lucky I am to have her.' "

I said, "He doesn't talk like that, he's not a sissy."

"He's some kind of oddball, I'll tell you that."

Mother said, "Don't you think it's a good sign, though, that he appreciates his sister?"

"No, I think that makes him look even more queer. Boys love their sisters, but they don't make speeches about it. Anyway you look at him, he's a little askew. He's a screwball. He should change his name too; it's embarrassing to have to say it."

Mother's face finally showed something. "You didn't say that to him, did you?"

"No, but I should have. It would be the best piece of advice I could ever give him, to change that fool name."

I said, "Somebody thought that was a beautiful name."

"Then they're a screwball too," said Daddy.

I wished I had been the one to save Garland. It never occurred to me that I might have any influence on Daddy. I watched India more carefully after that, how she sat demurely in class, how she played kickball and brushed that short hair Daddy thought was so neat. "Why don't you cut off your hair?" he said one day when I was putting curlers in. "Wear it like what's his name, Rosebud's sister." He was teasing me, but criticizing too. I thought bitterly that there were a lot of things he didn't like about me, the way I got carried away and made speeches. India knew how to make people like her; she just walked around smiling mysteriously. I figured by now India and Garland must both hate me. When India looked across the dressing room in my direction, I looked down quickly, and when Garland was at the body shop after school, I went down the hill on the other side of the street unless I was walking with Bunny.

Yet, on warm evenings at the end of May, and into June, evenings that were blue at twilight, I would sit on our little aluminum-roofed front porch and listen for motorcycles. If I heard a car with a bad muffler a few streets away, I would twist its direction and imagine Garland was coming to see me. I made a drama of it. Oh, I would say to myself, one of Bunny's boyfriends. And then the motorcycle turns in our quiet, dead-end street, and then into our driveway, on down to our garage, and Garland is sitting like a statue on a big black machine, a cruel expression on his mouth, daring me to come to him. Sometimes slowly, through the blue dusk, I go.

But once school was out I didn't see Garland and India every day, and I had a lot to do. First I earned my Red Cross Senior Lifesaving, and then Mother and Daddy and I went to New Jersey to visit Aunt Pearl. Aunt Pearl and Mother and I took a bus into New York City for a whole day. Daddy refused to go, saying he had always been a big frog in a little pond and he had no intention of feeling like a tadpole at this late date. So he sat in Aunt Pearl's backyard with a pitcher of lemonade and a portable television with an extra long cord. We shopped at Bergdorf Goodman's and walked in Tiffany's, and through the Plaza Hotel, and made a short foray into Central Park where we saw ducks and toy sailboats and one bum with sores on his ankles sleeping on a bench, but not a single mugging or gang fight. We got back to West Virginia just in time to wash and iron my clothes for the teen leadership conference, which I thought would have to be a letdown after my visit to the city, but I was wrong, because the teen leadership conference was where I finally, at long last, got myself a boyfriend.

His name was Thad, and he was from South Hills, Charleston, the state capital. He went to a high school so large it had its own swimming team, and he was a varsity swimmer. Handsome, with a deep tan and soft, golden hair on his forearms, he had well-shaped legs, was on the short side but looked taller because of his swimmer's muscles, and—on top of all this—he intended to be a medical missionary. My whole two weeks were illuminated with religion and dedication and necking. Every evening after vespers we sat together on a blanket in the woods for a whole hour. It was by far the best entertainment I had ever had. We were scrupulous, of course, to keep his hands off my chest and both our hands off anything below our waists, but we did all kinds of things to one another's mouths. At the last evening of the conference we dedicated ourselves together to lives of Christian service at a candlelight service, all of us in a vast spiraled order of white candle flames and three hundred voices singing "Just As I Am." That night we agreed to date other people, but never more than three times, and to write one another on alternate days, and to apply to the same colleges.

And then, suddenly, almost brutally, I was home with half the summer ahead, wide and flat and bland, and everything had already happened. I tried to keep the excitement by holding Thad's presence around me like the Holy Spirit, but I kept forgetting his face. I slept a lot for a couple of days, and then went down to the pool, but I was too late for a job. Stubby Bart, pool manager and band director, told me he might let me substitute sometimes, maybe. So I went to the library and took out a stack of books and bought an economy-size supply of pale green ripple-weave stationery and went home. I put on my bathing suit and dragged a lounge chair to our front yard, Hoover's backyard, and settled myself in the sun with the stationery, the books, and a bottle of Diet-Rite. After I'd been out there half an hour, Mother came and stood at the screen door. "Why do you want to sit there?" she said. "We've got the whole patio in back, why do you want to put your chair in the grass with all the bugs jumping on you?"

From the patio you couldn't see a single house, just the garden, and the redwood fence, and the fifteen acres of abutting farmland that Daddy had bought to protect us from having a trailer court stuck up our necks. "It's too quiet back there," I said. "I like a little activity."

She didn't approve of my two-piece madras bathing suit either. It was very decent, with boy-legs and my brand new Red Cross Senior Lifesaving patch sewed on. She said, "You never used to lie in the sun doing nothing."

"I'm reading," I said, although I really wasn't so much reading as feeling the sun seep into me, and dozing, and thinking of Thad. I had told her about Thad, about the medical-missionary-swimming-team side of him. I even said he was handsome, and she knew we were corresponding, and that I wanted him to come up for a weekend in the fall, maybe for homecoming. I would talk about him to her, and all the time be thinking of those post-vespers visits to the woods. She knew something had happened, and she was trying to figure it out. I got satisfaction from her puzzlement and my secret. I lay there feeling the sun on my shoulder, a delicate thing that moved along the surface of my back and then would dig in, burrow inside of me until I found myself unexpectedly breathing heavily. Once or twice I opened my eyes to see her watching me from inside the door, and I had an instant of terror, that she had heard my breathing. "Why don't you call up a friend," she said. "Why don't you call up Gail Gordon and go down to the swimming pool?"

"Gail Gordon! She never goes anywhere with girls, Mother. She's got Johnny Bardoline. He practically lives over at her house." I said it that way just to disturb her further, to make her think of sex. I looked at her over my legs, wonderful brown shiny legs. She was in the shadows, so nervous. "I'll maybe call somebody up this afternoon if it would make you feel better. Maybe Bunny will come over and talk."

"What do you and Bunny have to talk about?"

On the one hand I wanted to hint that it was boys and sex we talked about, but at the same time I didn't want her to think badly of Bunny. "Oh, nothing in particular. Sometimes we just read."

"What does Bunny read, love magazines?"

That was very cutting from Mother who prided herself on never backbiting. On being the kind of neighbor who provides casseroles in time of bereavement, but refuses to listen to gossip. Very softly I said, "How come you don't like Bunny, Mother?"

"I never said I didn't like her. I never said that at all." She waited for me to agree, but I didn't. "I've been very good to the Hoovers. They're two months behind on their rent right now."

"But you don't like them."

Mother regrouped a little. She got her voice lower, better modulated. She couldn't bear shrillness in a woman, she always said. "Like or dislike doesn't have a thing to do with it. They're irresponsible as tenants, that's all. To tell the truth, I don't think you're as crazy about Bunny as you pretend to be. It's just that you're too lazy to get off that lounge."

"That's not true!" I said. "Mother!" There was a faint swish, and I had to take off my sunglasses to be sure, but she had slipped back inside and left me with my anger, jumping up and down, pounding myself into the ground.

I moved the lounge chair farther out into the yard so that if Bunny did come over Mother wouldn't be able to hear what we were saying. As I was moving, a breeze scattered my letter paper, and I had to run around and pick it up. When I finally got settled, I couldn't seem to sink back into my body. I picked up the Bible from the bottom of the stack of books and all the others tipped and slid over and spread out in the grass. Thad and I had been in a study group at the conference that pledged to read all the letters of St. Paul this summer, but every time I picked up the Bible I started yawning and gazing at cloud formations. Sooner or later I would lay down the Bible and go back to reading *Gone With the Wind* for the third time, or one of the popular histories of the Civil War like *The Day Lincoln Died* or *Stillness at Appomattox*. It was the hundredth anniversary of West Virginia's secession from Virginia and the Confederacy, and the Civil War was in the air. There were pageants and articles in the papers and advertising displays in the grocery stores. But that day none of it kept my interest, not even the gory prison camp passages in *Andersonville*.

After a while Bunny came out and hung some nylons on the line. "Hey, Blair Ellen!" she shouted. "Want a bottle of pop?"

Mother couldn't abide shouting. "Sure!" I hollered back. "Thanks a lot! Please!"

Bunny came over with her lounge chair, two Cokes, and a lovely blue brocade make-up box that was one of her chief treasures. It was shaped like a train case with a long shoulder strap, embroidered with pink and green ladies who looked like Marie Antoinette. The inside was quilted and had trays of carefully arranged lipsticks and fingernail polishes. Bunny was very organized about beauty aids. She had separate nylon bags for her giant rollers and her small ones. She laid out her brush and comb in front of her and started taking down her rollers. "Reading again?" she said. "No wonder you're so smart, you don't do anything but read." She gestured with her chin at the book lying open over my midriff. "What's it about?"

"Civil War." I went back a few pages and found a passage about gangrene. "Read this."

I had to hold it open in front of her face because she had started brushing. She read about three lines and then her eyes popped between liner and mascara, and she shoved the book away with the handle of her hairbrush. "You *read* stuff like that? *That's* what you read?"

"I read everything. But this really happened."

She twisted her nose to one side and bared her front teeth.

"It's the real world," I said. "You should have seen what I saw in New York this summer. I saw a bum lying on a bench in Central Park. He was either asleep or dead, you couldn't tell which. People just walked by."

"You wouldn't catch me living in a place like that," she said.

I went on. "He didn't have any socks, and his ankles were swollen and purple."

"Blair Ellen, if you're trying to gross me out, I'll go back in the house."

"I feel sympathy for people like that."

Bunny made a sour mouth again, and I thought she was being a little prissy for someone who had a boyfriend at her house last night until after the late movie went off. I knew who it was too,

Don Hagen, who was at least twenty-two years old, and worked as a policeman part-time.

She said, "I bet Mrs. Morgan wouldn't like it if she knew you were reading books like that."

"I can read what I want to read."

"There are other things they don't let you do."

"Like what?"

"Like you don't date."

I smiled, mysteriously. I had a feeling I was going to tell Bunny what I wouldn't tell Mother. She might not like gangrene, but she knew about sex. At least I was pretty sure she did.

She stopped teasing her hair. "I didn't think Mr. and Mrs. Morgan let you go out. I would have asked you to double with us instead of Teresa Spinett. I can't be with her five minutes before she starts something. There's this guy I know in the navy who's coming in on leave, and he's bringing a friend home with him and he wants me to fix him up. I would have asked you if I knew you went out."

I was somewhere between flattered and relieved. "Thanks, Bunny, but I couldn't have anyhow."

"You're going steady?"

"Well, there's no class ring or anything like that, but there sure is something." I skipped the medical missionary part with Bunny, but I did tell her about the swimming team, and then got on to the good part. "And one night," I said, "we held hands for an hour, just held hands, nothing else, and it was the most exciting thing I've ever done."

Bunny patted her hair back over its French roll. "You have it bad!"

I liked that, it was just right, to have it bad. I watched her open out her fingers on her knee and spread thick, pink nail polish. There seemed to be no end to the tasks she had to do to herself. The sun beat on the nape of my neck, and I wondered if I should paint my nails.

"Well," she said, "when can I meet him?"

It wasn't exactly what I wanted from her, but I was relieved that she wasn't laughing. "It's a terrible problem. He hasn't got a car. I have to talk Mother into letting him come up and stay overnight here."

"Go down there. No joke. I'd find a way to go down there and make sure some girl doesn't beat me to him." She had lifted her hand to check the nails at an angle, and over the hand her eyes came at me, small and greenish with the thinnest rim of black around the iris and a few gold flecks. She rarely moved the rest of her face, but her eyes would open wide and flick around you. "I think you should double with me. I'll get rid of Teresa. If you wait around, everything just dries up."

I wanted to know what dries up, the relationship or something in your body. But it seemed impossible to ask; I didn't know how to form the sentence.

Bunny's sister came out of the house and started twirling a baton. "*She* wants to double date with me," said Bunny. "The little creep."

Kim was only two years younger than we were, but she was still flat and bony, a slightly elongated kid. She scowled when she saw us looking but drifted over and sat on the end of Bunny's lounge chair. No one said anything, and she picked up Bunny's Coke and took a drink. Bunny extended one impeccably smooth leg and touched the center of Kim's chest with her big toe. They froze like that for a second, Kim scowling with her chin tucked low, and Bunny staring from her distant eyes. Then she gave a precise little push and bumped Kim off the lounge. Immediately Kim started to whine. "You kicked me in the breast."

"In the what?" said Bunny. "In the *what?*"

Kim muttered something too low to be heard, and then muttered it again louder. "At least I don't have hickey bites."

Bunny was wearing a sleeveless black pullover, but it had a high turtle neck. Bunny set her nail polish on the ground and grabbed Kim's baton out of her hand. "Get out of here, Kim."

Kim scrambled off backwards. "Don't you throw that at me!" She started to run then, glancing back every few steps, and Bunny tossed the baton in a high, easy arc after her. "She's been such a little piss-ant lately," she said.

I was glad to see Kim go; I wanted to know if Bunny did have sucker bites, and did it hurt to get them but I never found a way to ask and she had to go inside to do some housework. But that night Don Hagen's pickup truck left early, and there was a screaming fight at Hoover's. When it started, Daddy filled a pipe and took a chair all the way down to the garden where he couldn't hear it; Mother paced in the darkened living room watching the lights pop on from room to room at the Hoovers'.

"This is no way to live," she said. "I can't live with this going on every night."

"It doesn't go on every night," I said. "Smoke a cigarette, Mother. You know how nervous you've been since you stopped smoking." I felt her turn toward me in the dark, but I was safe because I couldn't see her gaze. I had been giving her trouble lately, and I was proud of it. "Daddy sneaks cigarettes at school. You might as well too." She said nothing, so I went on. "At least there's some excitement at Hoovers'."

"Excitement!" She took two steps in my direction, then stopped. I sat up quickly. "Where did you get your values, Blair Ellen Morgan? Just where did you get your values?"

Her voice trembled; the darkness trembled around her, and that wasn't what I wanted. I would have liked to slip over and watch the Hoovers through the windows, but I didn't want Mother exploding. "I didn't mean anything," I said. "I just feel so stupid sitting here with the lights out. I'm putting on a lamp." I turned on the television too, and Daddy came back in time for "Maverick," and Mother went to the kitchen and made fruit salad, and after a while things died down at the Hoovers, and then their house was dark and ours was the one gently percolating with a kind of life.

In the morning, Kim came out first. She usually seemed to have more work to do than Bunny, or else she was just very slow doing her share, but this day she came out in a red and white checked bathing suit, the top simply two bands of elastic in a casing, red barrettes in her hair, and white plastic sunglasses. She was dragging the lounge in one hand and Bunny's blue brocade make-up case in the other. She put the lounge in exactly the position it had been in yesterday, lining it up with mine, aluminum bolt to aluminum bolt. She settled the make-up case on her lap, drawing her knees up to cradle it and popped the mirror and got out the Cover Girl base.

I said, "I wouldn't get too comfortable on Bunny's chair with Bunny's make-up if I were you."

"She's going to be inside for a long time. She has to clean the whole kitchen. Oven, floor, everything. She has to."

Pretending to yawn, I said, "How come?"

"She's in trouble, that's why."

"I bet she doesn't know you have her make-up out here."

"I'm not hurting it. I know how to put on make-up as well as she does." She slid lipstick around her mouth quickly and started working on her eyes. "Bunny's not so sweet when *you're* not around. She's always acting so *nice* around you and your mother."

I wasn't going to be able to do it. I was trying to be loyal to Bunny, but I wanted to know what happened. And I was sure Kim wanted to tell. I said, "What kind of trouble is she in?"

At that moment there was a slam, and Bunny herself pushed through the drying sheets. Kim started tossing make-up tubes back into the case. One of her eyes was finished, mascara and curled eyelash, the other one bare and frightened. "I don't care," she muttered, "I didn't do anything wrong. Mom said it's my make-up just the same as hers. Everything we have is both of ours."

Bunny whipped through the last sheet, and paused there looking tall, legs and arms stiff. There was something wrong with her face, too much cheek, too flat and blank.

"I don't care," said Kim, clutching the make-up case to her chest, curling herself around it. "I don't care, I don't care."

I closed my stationery box, laid it on the ground. Thad had never been more ethereal. I got my feet on the ground too.

Bunny took the bag first, thrust two hands down into Kim's lap and ripped it out brutally, nearly pulling Kim out of the chair with it. The strap broke, but Bunny didn't notice, she slung it over her shoulder without looking where it fell and there was a shower of little tubes and brushes. I was immediately and completely convinced of Bunny's desperation. She slapped Kim with her left hand and punched her arm with her right. Kim screamed, and Bunny dragged her off the chair by the elasticized bathing suit top. I think she wanted to fling her as she'd thrown the make-up case, but Kim stayed at her feet, flat nipples exposed, trying to get up and pull up her top all at once. But she changed her mind suddenly and pulled Bunny down on top of her, and Bunny started punching her in the chest and hips.

"Saturday night!" screamed Kim. "You came in bowlegged!"

Bunny slapped her in the mouth.

"He humped you bowlegged!"

She slapped her again, and Kim's nose started to bleed. It was the thick bubble of red that frightened me. "Mother!" I shouted. *Mother!*" Trusting her to come, I ran for the Hoovers'. Hot wind tossed the sheets as I broke through, burst into their kitchen yelling for Mrs. Hoover and found her standing at the window, looking out as if she had seen everything, would have been perfectly satisfied with the way things were going if I hadn't disturbed her. "Mrs. Hoover, Kim's bleeding!"

Mrs. Hoover wasn't wearing anything that morning but a ruffle-bosomed night gown and pin curls, and she pulled a tree branch club from behind the stove and headed out the door. She said, "You know how those gangs of dogs go at it sometimes? Well, I keep this around to break up dog fights."

My mother had come out too by the time we got back, and she was already dragging Bunny off Kim, saying in her sternest classroom voice, "Bunny Hoover, get off your sister. Kim, pull up that blouse, cover yourself!" Bunny seemed to have run out of anger, or maybe it was something about my mother's voice and hands. She let Mother pull her away, but Kim immediately butted her in the belly, and Bunny brought a knee up into her chest.

"Step aside, Mrs. Morgan." Mrs. Hoover waved her club in the air.

"Mrs. Hoover!" said Mother. "I can't let you use a stick!" I had a flush of pride: Mother's eyes so gray, wide, and noble.

Mrs. Hoover smiled as if she'd been waiting for Mother to say that. "I don't believe—" she gave Bunny a little poke in the belly with the stick, "I don't believe—you have the right—to stand between me and my children." Suddenly she moved sideways, grabbed Kim by one arm and began whacking her. Kim shrieked so loud the little boys came running from the front of the house with several kids from around the block. Eyeliner ran down one of Kim's cheeks, and smeared blood formed a moustache. Mrs.

Hoover kept whacking her backside, all the time grinning and talking to Mother. "I know how to handle these children. These children aren't delicate; these are your garden variety children, Mrs. Morgan. You have to strop these children every once in a while."

Mother let go of Bunny and was covering her throat with both hands; she made a noise, and then ran at the children in the driveway flapping her apron. "Go home," she said. "This is private business, go home."

"They don't bother me," said Mrs. Hoover, but she started for the house dragging the sobbing Kim by one arm. "Let them stay and learn something. Bunny, you pick up all that stuff you spilled. I paid good money for that stuff."

Bunny nodded, knelt, and began picking up tubes and brushes, examining each one for spills, tightening caps, laying them out, arranging them in rows like a battlefield hospital.

Mother said, "Come in, Blair Ellen."

I had a great reluctance to go in. The house seemed too heavy. Out here, slivers of light flashed, and the high haze seemed to threaten a storm. A strange, silver, morning storm.

"Blair Ellen!" Mother already behind the screen door.

I said, "Bunny, she won't hurt you, will she?"

"She better not. She better never try."

She didn't look at me, so I couldn't tell if she was bluffing or telling the truth. "See you later, Bunny?" I said. She shrugged and worked her way methodically across the grass.

I stepped inside and peered around, half blinded, trying to locate Mother, and found her leaning against the wall with one hand on her throat and one on her forehead. The shadows made her sooty and skinny, and the lower half of her face seemed to have developed deep hollows. Is she sick? I thought. Is she gravely ill? "That woman," she whispered, "should never have been allowed to bring children into the world."

She had just had a headache clamp into her; I saw it in the way she was holding her head; I heard it in that wavering whisper. I wanted to tell her to stay noble and strong, but instead I asked if I could do anything for her.

She said, "I want you to stay away from those people."

"Stay away from them! How can I stay away from them? They live forty feet away!"

"I won't have you spending time with people who hit each other. My sister and I grew up just as poor as those people, and we never raised a fist at each other. We would have thrown ourselves under a train before we would have hit and pulled each other's clothes off."

I loved references to the old days, when she raised Aunt Pearl single-handedly. They were like the bravest of the poor orphan children. I waited for the story: a time when she got so mad she almost hit Pearl? But she seemed to be collapsing, closing her eyes.

She whispered, "I won't have my daughter under their influence."

"Their influence! I'm not under their influence! Don't you think I know enough not to hit somebody? Just because Bunny and Kim fight doesn't mean I will. Mother!"

The bricks had hit; she was staggering toward the bedroom, feeling her way along the wall. Why did her headaches have to fell her so completely?

I yelled, "You can be friends with someone and know their faults!" She disappeared into the bedroom, and I stopped making sense even to myself. "You always do this! You always get sick when I need you!"

I ran out the sliding door onto the patio, back into the heat of the day, down the slope to the garden, where Daddy was calmly staking tomato plants. He had missed the whole thing, of course; he would miss everything if he could.

"Daddy! I don't care, she's the one who's out of line this time. Even if the Hoovers do give her a headache she hasn't got the right to say they should never have been born!"

Tan soil and dust on his hands, green plants to his knees, face in the shadow of his hat. "Your mother's got a headache?"

I would have been mad at him too, but he looked so calm and earth-bound in his wide-legged work pants and tee shirt. He was never knocked flat by passions or headaches.

"There was a big fight, Bunny and Kim Hoover, and Mother

broke it up, and Mrs. Hoover started hitting Kim with a stick. It was a big mess."

Daddy glanced sadly around his garden, out at his field where he let a farmer graze cattle. "Well," he said, "I better go see what she needs."

We walked up the slope together. I became calm in his presence, more clever. "Mother told me I couldn't see the Hoover girls anymore, but I think she was carried away with her headache."

Daddy said, "Well, if we had my way, you wouldn't see them because they wouldn't live here anymore. I told her, people who give her headaches should be evicted. As simple as that."

"Daddy!" I stopped where I was, Bunny suddenly of vast importance to my life. Glittering phantoms of Bunny up in the air, just out of my reach. Bunny lightly going up for a layup, Bunny in bikini underpants and uplift bra. Kneeling over the make-up as over dead children. "They don't have anyplace to go. Bunny is my friend."

"If I had my way, they would have been gone the first time they were late with the rent. They gave her a headache then. She's too softhearted."

I said, "All I ask, Daddy, is not to have to stop seeing Bunny. I want to be able to get along with all kinds of people. If I stopped walking to school with her, you know what people would say."

"No," said Daddy. "I don't."

"It's Mrs. Hoover who's the problem anyhow. Bunny admires Mother, she wishes she had you two for parents."

"Lord help us!" said Daddy. "Listen, Blair Ellen, let me go see what she needs. You know how she is; you know this will blow over. So just play it smart and keep your mouth shut for a while, okay?"

I lay flat on my back on the hot flagstones of the patio, burning the back of my thighs and shoulderblades. I held myself as stiffly as I could, concentrating on the points that were in pain. I was a magnifying glass, burning holes in the stone. I would never go inside the house again. Inside, something happened to me, I became dark and confused. You could catch headaches in the house.

Outside I spoke convincingly, I knew how to play it smart. I lay and watched the sunball through my eyelids.

Bunny wanted me to try out for the majorettes. I liked better lying around and talking about Thad but ever since she failed to make varsity cheerleader she had been working on marching and twirling. "Come on, Blair Ellen," she'd say. "You'll look good in front of the band."

"I don't know, Bunny, my legs are kind of short."

"But they've got a *good* shape, a nice curve. You've got good legs."

I thought so, too, but I liked having her say it. I let her talk me into it. Every evening around dusk, between the heat of sunset and the cool August fogs, we went out in the yard to practice. They took the sheets down so we'd have room, and we stood in a line, Bunny, Kim, and me. Kim wasn't eligible to try out till next year, but she was the best twirler of us three. She practiced every day; I wasn't very good at it at all; I couldn't even hold the position for the national anthem: right knee and elbow cocked, batons making a line from our hearts to an imaginary Old Glory. Bunny's idea was to stand this way for the length of the national anthem just like when the band plays it for football games, but I kept getting a cramp. I dropped out and lay on my back and sang, "And the ho-ome of the brave!"

Bunny and Kim stayed cocked, not a muscle moving until Bunny murmured "And one—and two, and one—and two!" and they marched off a few paces toward the fence. Bunny turned back to me with her mouth tight. "You like to mess that up, don't you?"

"I can't help it, I got a leg cramp."

If it had been Kim acting up, she would have hit her with the baton. I said, "If we had the music, I could do it. Or even if you'd let me hum, but I just can't stand there not knowing when it's going to end." I rolled over on my stomach in the dampening grass. "I'm no good at it, Bunny. I don't know why I'm even trying. I never particularly wanted to be a majorette."

She sat down beside me. "This is our last chance. If we don't make it this year, that's it. It's all over for us. They won't train seniors."

I didn't feel like anything was all over for me. I had plenty of things coming up. Homecoming weekend, with a visit from Thad. Piano recital. Committees I would head as junior class vice-president. All kinds of things. But, I thought with a certain sentimental condescension, this might very well be the end of the road for Bunny. College was never spoken of in their house, and she didn't get elected to things. Poor old Bunny, I thought. Even her good looks. That type of looks never lasts, Mother said; the stomach muscles loosen up, the face gets jowly. Poor old Bunny.

I said, "Why don't I just go along with you to the tryouts for moral support?"

She pursed her mouth. "You'll make it. You just have to practice more. You don't practice enough."

"Daddy was talking to Stubby Bart, and he said they're looking for people who can play instruments, and not just march."

"Stubby Bart!" she snorted. Everyone snorted over Stubby. He wasn't much older than we were, and he was already divorced and paying alimony and managing the pool and selling insurance as well as directing the band. He wasn't supposed to have held the band job this long, but somehow he always did just enough to keep from getting fired. "Stubby is so dumb. What does he want them to do, play a tuba?"

"Look!" shouted Kim. "Look, Bunny, I got it." Her baton went up and came down as if it were in no hurry, and she snagged it easily and continued to twirl.

"Good, now all you have to do is learn to play the tuba."

"I'm just telling you what Daddy told me. Mr. Thornton started it, anyhow, not Stubby. Mr. Thornton said this isn't Las Vegas, he doesn't want show girls. He wants Stubby to try out girls in the band first."

"Who in the band could they take? That's the fattest, hairiest bunch of legs I ever saw. I mean, I couldn't believe they took Gail Gordon, that tank on stilts. What you want marching in front of the band is good legs, pretty much of a size, not heavy."

"Gail's got good legs."

"As far up as her knees. Her thighs are going to look awful in the new uniforms."

"Daddy saw the uniforms," I said. "But all he could remember was that they were purple."

"Blue violet. With white piping and six-gore skirts and an old-gold lining. The skirts are stiff, so the lining shows. But that's why you have to have good legs, because skirts like that make everyone look at the legs. I've been planning some routines that feature legs."

"I thought up a routine too," said Kim. "And Bunny says if she makes the majorettes she's going to teach it to them."

Sometimes it all seemed like such a waste to me, making up routines. Hand claps, shuffles, marking time and crossovers. I said, "You two are really talented at that stuff."

Bunny bounced her baton on its rubber plug, just dropped it from six inches and caught it as it came up. "I made up all the cheers the j.v. cheerleaders did last year, and you know what, they're going to go ahead and use them on the varsity and no one will give me any credit, that's for sure."

"They cheated you out of being varsity cheerleader, didn't they?" asked Kim.

"Who did?"

Bunny spoke softly, almost nostalgically: "Oh, I couldn't get along with some of those girls, and the teachers never have liked me."

"Yeah," said Kim, "and who knows what those teachers and cheerleaders did in there when they were counting votes, right, Bunny?"

I said, "Well, I don't think they'd cheat."

Bunny threw her baton up into the dark. It flashed a couple of times, catching light from the windows at my house, finally thudding in the distance.

Kim said, "You oughtn't to throw it like that. You always told me not to."

"It doesn't matter. This is going to be just like the cheerleaders. Some people have everyone on their side and some people don't. Teresa Spinett's got her brothers, and Blair Ellen's got the teachers."

"That's no help, that's a hindrance!"

Bunny said, "There's no one on my side. People look for a chance to dump on me."

Kim said, "I'll find your baton for you, Bunny."

"Well, that's the biggest nonsense *I* ever heard," I said, and, even as I said it, thought of the glaze over Mother's eyes when Bunny was mentioned, recalled voices at the cheerleader tryouts in the spring, before I was friends with her. Bunny Hoover, said this voice behind me. They say *she* does her best routines on her *back*. And I remembered my pencil hanging over the ballot, and then passing on to another name. Not wanting to vote for someone people talked about like that.

I said, "You'll get majorette, Bunny, you're built more like a majorette than a cheerleader, anyhow. Even Stubby Bart will have to see how good you look up in front of the band."

"If they don't pick me, I won't tell them a single one of my routines, and they're so good, Blair Ellen."

The softness in her voice in the darkness disturbed me; I had never heard her voice that way; I didn't know the face that went with it. I liked Bunny tough, not soft. Sitting there by her in the night, I had a vision of something that was not impossible. That the two of us would try out, and in spite of how good she was and how mediocre I was, I would be chosen. Because of Mother and Daddy, or because I played the piano, or because they needed a pair of short legs for the end of the line. They could easily choose me and not Bunny. Even in my imagination, I thought, I betray people.

The morning of the tryouts I ate the biggest breakfast I'd had all summer. I didn't exactly intend to eat so much, but while the egg was boiling I ate some cold cereal and then fried two slices of bacon and made some toast. When it was all eaten, I sat a while at the table with the heavy mass of food pressing my black elastic cinch belt. Bunny and I had decided to wear identical outfits for the tryouts: black shorts, white blouses, and black cinch belts. She thought that it would help our chances if Stubby saw us as a matched pair. But my shorts didn't have loops big enough for the cinch belt, so it kept hiking up in the back, and now my stomach was popping out over it in the front. And I was sweating.

It looked like a thoroughly nasty morning. The sky was as greasy and gray as a nickel. Mother came out of the bedroom in her nightgown without a housecoat. I said, "You look like Mrs.

Hoover. I thought you couldn't do anything till you got dressed."

"Your father's in the bathroom and I'm waiting to take a shower. We're going shopping, don't you remember?"

I did. There was a new shopping mall outside of Graysburg, and they had decided to go this morning, hoping I would go with them instead of to the tryouts. Daddy kept saying maybe we'd even go to a movie, a nice, indoor, air-conditioned movie, how about that.

She glanced at my outfit as she scooped coffee into the pot. I went to the mirror beside the phone and tried to settle the belt in one place. "Those shorts are too tight," she said. "Do you intend to walk through town like that?"

I controlled myself and didn't say no, we're hoping somebody will pick us up. I shrugged and started puffing my hair, and of course the belt slipped when I raised my arms.

"If you want to know what *I* think and I'm sure you don't because you haven't listened to a thing I've said in months, *I* think you'll be a lot better off if you don't get chosen."

"Thanks for your support. It's always nice to know your family's behind you."

"I absolutely mean it. With school starting and busy as you are, I don't know why you'd want to take on another activity anyhow."

Daddy came in damp and pink cheeked, wearing a thin, plaid sports shirt. "Well, well." He rubbed his hands and moved toward the coffeepot. "Have you decided if you're coming with us today?"

"She's decided all right," said Mother.

Daddy's voice curled around, all hurt. "Are you going to try out for those majorettes, Blair Ellen?"

"I told you I was. I never considered not trying out. Yes, I'm trying out."

"We were going to have lunch at Clark's Family Style Oak Room. They're supposed to have good butterscotch pie." He made it sound like I was spoiling a good time for the three of us just out of meanness.

"I told you weeks ago I was trying out. You didn't have to go to the mall today. You just want to stop me from becoming a majorette."

Mother said, "I wish I could stop you. I don't want you to be a majorette. They have one single function in this world, and that is to wiggle their behinds."

"Well, Sibyl," said Daddy, who didn't like extremism in defense of anything, "I don't know if I would go that far. The band always has had them."

"I'm not saying we should abolish the majorettes, I just think Blair Ellen can do better. She wouldn't be involved in all this nonsense if it wasn't for Bunny Hoover. She does anything Bunny Hoover wants now. She doesn't have a mind of her own anymore."

I managed to keep my voice gentle. "I like to be a part of the show. I like to participate and learn things. I figure if I'm a majorette and go to all the games I'll get some exercise and learn a lot about marching music, and I'll also learn to watch football intelligently."

Daddy burst out laughing, and anger flushed me, spread out in ripples and waves, making Mother tall and rigid and Daddy's mouth rubbery.

"I have to go now," I said, walking out, not seeing anything as I passed through our yard into theirs. Blind and deaf until from a distance I heard Kim telling me to come in.

She was bent over the kitchen sink with a huge accumulation of pots and pans. "Hi, Blair Ellen," she said. "I can't come and watch you and Bunny."

"Couldn't you wash them later?"

She shook her lowered head. "I already got beat one time for not doing them."

The kitchen felt dirty; it had always been old, but Mother never left things to crunch under foot on the linoleum. The ridges of Kim's backbone exposed between her halter and shorts seemed gray and scaly. I sat down at the table and felt crumbs under my thighs too, and there was a big glob of jelly beside my elbow.

One of the little brothers, Robbie, came in then, wearing gray underpants and nothing else. He climbed up on a chair and started eating curds of scrambled eggs directly off the table. I had thought the eggs were garbage. I said, "You should train *him* to do the dishes."

He squished a piece of egg through his lips at me.

Kim said, "They never have to do anything they don't want to and they don't want to do anything ever."

I wasn't liking Kim very well either. I wanted to get out of this house almost as much as I'd wanted to get out of ours. The whole trouble, I thought, is being closed in. People want to lock up girls. People like Mother. I tried to think of where I would like to be, and decided on the pool, swimming underwater at the deep end. Totality of blue. Blue coolness. Blue poolness. Tons of water between me and all houses.

Steps came down, Mrs. Hoover in a flower-printed short peignoir. She was carrying an ash tray in the shape of a little ceramic turtle. "Where's my coffee cup? Where's Robbie's plate? He's eating off the table. Don't eat off the table, dumbo." She gave him a cuff that caused ash to bounce out of her ash tray onto the table.

"He always eats off the table," muttered Kim. "Besides, I thought he wasn't coming back."

"He always comes back and he better stop eating off the table." She made a noise down in her throat, and I cringed for more hitting, but instead she twisted her mouth into a strange grin that wrinkled her forehead and bared her teeth. "Be smart, Blair Ellen, don't have kids."

Kim brought a plate, and Mrs. Hoover swept the curds onto it. I never knew how to act around her. She was always yelling at someone when I was around, or giving a smack, but she pretended to be nice to me. "Don't you look cute," she said. "All dressed up for your tryouts. Do you want something to eat while you wait on Bunny? She's never on time. Bun-ny! Blair Ellen's waiting!"

"I'm early," I said. "Honest, I'm early, it's okay. I just had breakfast."

"Want a smoke? My girls both smoke cigarettes, but they pretend like they don't and they never let me catch them either. You don't smoke? I figured you wouldn't."

Robbie stood up on his chair and wiggled his hips back and forth until she gave him a light slap, and he slid back down and played with his eggs some more. I looked away from him and had

[1 1 2]

a choice of Kim's sad, bent back or Mrs. Hoover with her bony knees spread and her arms crossed and resting on her abdomen. The funny thing was that I had seen her dressed up once or twice, with a girdle and her hair done, and she had been recognizable only because she came out of Hoovers' house, said goodbye to the Hoover children.

Bunny came down, head held high above the squalor. *She* was not sweating. She was wearing her black sleeveless Helenca turtleneck and a red patent leather belt. I didn't say anything until we were out of the trees on our block and walking in the unshaded concrete streets of town.

"I see you decided not to dress alike after all. I wish you'd told me, I might have decided to wear something different."

She rotated her head and tipped her face down toward me. She was walking on her toes, already marching. In her mind it was crisp October, and around her the radiant green of the football field at half time. She said, "You better relax, Blair Ellen. You sound a-way too tight."

"I am! My shorts ride up and I ate too much breakfast and this stupid belt is killing me and I never would have worn it except you said we had to dress alike."

She gave me a distant glance. "It makes your waist look tiny. You should wear it all the time."

"And your brother about made me throw up, sticking food out of his mouth at me."

"They're little pigs. They always have been little pigs."

Nothing perturbed her. We tromped on, or rather, I tromped and she went over the rhythms, did dance steps to a beat in her head, across the creek bridge, up High School Hill, past Buddy's Body Shop. It was so hot not even one guy was standing around the Coke machine there. I could feel humiliation coming. My whole body had turned awkward and ugly. I only got involved in this to be with Bunny, and now Bunny was off in another world. Mother and Daddy were right this time, I thought bitterly, and their rightness was a metallic taste in my mouth like dentist's hardware, the clamp over my tongue.

Bunny paused at the bottom of the steps. From here you couldn't quite see the building itself, only the three flights of stairs and the concrete balls on pillars at each level. She clicked her heels in a salute and marched up with one hand on her hip, baton over her shoulder. I began to get cynical. Bad luck, Bunny, I thought. Bad luck to make it so obvious that you care.

Something about being there, in the auditorium, maybe the high school itself, calmed me down. Gail Gordon came and sat on the other side of me, ignoring Bunny. She started talking about the picnic the Youth Fellowship at church was having. She had been in the band since grade school and last spring had been chosen majorette when somebody moved, or got pregnant, as one rumor had it. Gail made scathing remarks about every girl who marched across the stage. I said, "Wait till you see me, you'll be laughing from here to kingdom come."

"Are you really going to try out?"

"What do you think I brought the baton for?"

She shrugged. "Well, it can't hurt."

"What do you mean by that?"

She shrugged again. They had just called Bunny up on the stage, so we had to be quiet, but I was suspicious.

Bunny was as good as I'd ever seen her, marking time as soon as the drummer gave the roll, face blank, those straight, perfectly smooth legs lifting just enough, and her routine with its quick turns and twirls coolly better than anyone else's. I clapped as loud as I could.

Gail said, "Are you really friends with Bunny Hoover?"

"Yeah," I said, "Bunny and I are pretty good friends." I felt proud of my loyalty and somehow cleaner than ever before.

It was my turn, and Gail moved back to sit with the other majorettes and Stubby Bart. I looked at Stubby with Mother's eyes as I went up on stage, disapproving of his shorts and hairy ankles in loafers. He was snickering with those girls over something too, and not paying very much attention, it seemed to me, to what was happening on stage. Something was definitely not right, and I was so preoccupied with figuring it out, that I marched without forethought, quite easily, and better than I ever had before.

Bunny was waiting for me, sweating at last, whispering that she had known all along I could do it. Stubby and the majorettes whispered a little while, and Stubby got up. Bunny grabbed my wrist.

"Hey," said Stubby, "I want to thank you all for coming out, I mean it." But, he said, and the *but* was about some other factors, some things he had to work out before he would make his final decision. We would be notified.

Bunny wanted to go out to the football field and watch the majorettes practice. "If we get picked," she said, "we'll want to know what they're planning for the first game."

"Not me," I said. "I'm not going to stand around with my tongue hanging out."

"Oh come on, Blair Ellen."

"No, really. I have something I have to do."

"I know," said Bunny. "Love letters."

She was more faithful than I was, I thought sadly. I was having trouble keeping up the correspondence with Thad, although the arrival of his letters still thrilled me. Something about my address written in his dark black, sharp-topped sloping handwriting. But the letters didn't satisfy me. No one around me seemed to satisfy me anymore, not Thad, not Bunny. I avoided her for the next couple of days because she kept practicing and talking about the majorettes and the majorettes' uniform, and the brand of twirling baton the majorettes used. I said my piano teacher was coming back from vacation, and I had to spend my free time catching up on my music.

On Thursday Daddy came home for lunch after a school meeting and glanced at me several times in quick succession. "Well," he said, "I talked to Stubby Bart today." Mother put sandwiches in front of us. "Old Stubby comes up to me and says, 'Well, Mr. Morgan, we've made the decision about the majorettes and I want you to know your daughter was excellent. But—'" He took a bite and looked at the ceiling, "But he's decided to move three girls out of the wind section into the majorette line because you can't hear all the flutes anyhow when they're marching. He's not taking any of the girls who tried out."

"The open tryouts were a farce?"

"Stubby didn't say that, and I didn't say that."

"I knew from the beginning. He never meant to choose anyone from the open tryouts."

Mother said, "You'll be glad, honey."

"I've been expecting this," I said. "But I feel bad for Bunny. She really had her heart set on it."

I only ate half a sandwich I was so eager to go and tell her. I almost missed her too because she and Don Hagen were putting a cooler in the back of his old Ford pickup truck. Since Don was the municipal night policeman he was available to take Bunny on picnics to Valley Falls. He kept beer in the cooler, and I wondered if Bunny drank it. I had met Jimmy Minard, her sailor boy friend, and liked him better. Don sneaked up behind people and gave them bear hugs.

"Bunny!" I shouted, "I've got to talk to you."

She seemed exceptionally grown-up, wearing her two-piece bathing suit, yellow and aqua, with aqua thongs to match, and a man's yellow shirt floating over it. She said, "Want to go? Don would be glad to have you, right, Don?"

"Sure, come with us, Blair Ellen."

"Bunny, Daddy talked to Stubby Bart today and Stubby says he decided to move three girls from the flutes to the majorettes. I don't think he ever seriously considered taking anybody from open tryouts."

First there was a complete shutdown of her face, blankness and flatness, and then the mouth open just enough for some words to come out, a thin bile spill of words. "The dirty little dago," she said. "The filthy stinking little dago pimp." She kicked the truck's hubcap. "What a cheap guinea trick," she said.

Those words shocked me. There were words at my house that we never used in any circumstances, words about things that people had no choice about.

"What's going on?" said Don, coming from the back of the truck.

Bunny said, "He has an apartment, you know, in Graysburg. He keeps a little apartment, just for him and the majorettes. They say he picks one out after every game and they go there and get drunk. They get drunk on dago red wine."

Don wasn't taking it very seriously. "Hey," he said, "that sounds like a real party."

She said, "He tried to ask me out once, but I wouldn't go."

"Bunny!" I wanted her to shut up; all my affection and sympathy were fading. I had always thought the wronged were beautiful.

"I'll go up there," she said. "I want to see if he'll tell me to my face. I want to see if he's got guts to tell me to my face."

"Well, let's go," said Don. "Hop in. I want to see old Stubby run. Are you coming?" He winked at me, and I hated his chubby cheeks; I wanted to slap him for taking us lightly. Didn't he think Bunny would do anything? She was already in the cab, face turned away from me so I couldn't tell if she wanted me to go. I shook my head and watched them drive off. I wondered if I should try to beat them to school and warn Stubby. Everything seemed impossible and embarrassingly stupid. I went and sat on the lounge and waited for something to happen.

The day drifted on quietly. No sign of Bunny. Mother and I went for groceries; we had dinner; Daddy left for the lodge; and Mother went to prayer meeting. I sat at the table, watching dusk come over the hills, thinking about writing a letter to Thad, but not sure I could find anything to say except that Life was smothering me with stillness.

There was a tapping at the plate glass sliding door behind my back, and I jumped, because no one came to the house that way. There was nothing out there but garden and fields, and now, Bunny, wearing jeans and that same yellow man's shirt, with the sleeves rolled down, clutching an unopened pack of Lucky Strikes.

"You scared me to death," I said, opening the sliding door and letting in some damp night air with her. "Why did you come that way?"

She was peering into the kitchen, around the darkened living room. "I wanted to be sure your parents were gone. Can I have a light?"

Something had happened after all, there were circles under her eyes. She had a look of surfeit, as if she had gone too far with something. Violence, I thought, or sex. I thought that if I had gone with her today, I might have saved her.

She finally sat down at the table, holding her hand cupped under the tip of the cigarette. I went and got the biggest ash tray,

Daddy's heavy green glass one, and put it in front of her. She didn't thank me but did stroke it with her fingertips before dropping her ash in it. I was afraid she had been damaged during the day, but her voice was full of energy, even decision. "Well," she said, "I was ready to punch Stubby Bart's fat face, and, if not that, I was going to curse him so bad I'd burn his ears out. Don knew it too. He kept making jokes, but he knew I was mad. I was going to mess up anybody who got in my way." I waited. She tapped ashes into the green glass with care, as if she hated to soil it.

"Did you? Did you curse him out?"

"He wasn't there. Nobody was there but the majorettes. The tuba legs. Gail Gordon parading around in short-shorts. I talked to them for a while, and then some of the football boys started showing up for practice and we talked to them, and then we left. It was too late to go to Valley Falls, so we got pizza and came home."

"You just came home? You've been here all this time? You didn't curse out anybody?"

"I told the majorettes to tell Stubby to keep out of my way. He will too, he's such a greaseball coward."

"I've been worried all day. You could have come over and told me."

"I didn't want your mother to hear. She hates me already."

I was too disgusted with the lack of climax even to say my mother didn't hate her. I stared at the ash in the ash tray. Is this all? I thought. Nothing really does happen. I had the aching in my joints again—elbows, hips, knees—as if they were making one last outcry before freezing up forever.

"But then I had an idea," said Bunny. "I was just sitting there thinking how unfair the whole thing is, not just the majorette tryouts, but everything. How there are all these girls who can march better than the majorettes can and think up better routines, and how the cheerleaders pick their friends, and the majorettes get picked because they can lift a tuba. And I thought up this plan, Blair Ellen. You and I are going to start a drill team."

"Who's going to start a drill team? What's a drill team?"

"And once we've done a show at half time we'll have so many

girls wanting to get in that there'll be nothing to it. We'll take anyone who can march, even junior high girls like Kim if they're good enough." She leaned forward, and the night light from the kitchen stove cast a blue aura over the side of her face. Those marks under her eyes were gone, and her long eyelids rose word by word, drawing me in. "Listen, Blair Ellen, I've been thinking for hours. I've even designed the uniforms in my mind. Black shorts, some kind of full white blouse, everyone has a white blouse, and the only thing we have to buy is sashes. Old gold, so we blend in with the school colors."

"What's a drill team?"

"A drill team. You know. All the schools have them except jerky ones like here. You do routines. You march, with or without batons. Like pom-pom girls only better. You do formation marching and routines."

"But for who?"

"What do you mean for who? You do it for football games. It's for girls like us, anybody who can march."

I was flabbergasted. She was talking about just casually starting up an organization because we wanted it. "People would say we did it because we didn't make the majorettes."

"Listen, once we march, the majorettes will be quitting to join us."

"But you just can't walk out on the football field at half time you know. You have to have a sponsor to be a school activity."

"I thought about that too, but all you have to do is ask. The teachers will figure it must be a real nice activity if Blair Ellen Morgan is in it."

"Thanks a lot. I knew you'd want me for something."

"I want you to be co-captain. You're a good marcher."

"I am not a good marcher. I'm not good at anything but getting teachers to like me."

"What are you mad about?"

I told her it was embarrassing to have to start an activity for ourselves, but I think what really bothered me was that I, class vice-president and church representative to leadership training camp, had never even remotely considered setting up an activity to suit me and my talents. I had always wished we had a singing group, or a drama club, but I only wished. Bunny, with her Lucky Strikes and bleached hair was calmly rising from the ashes of disappointment to create what she wanted. I made us tea and crackers and cheese, and Bunny described the marching routines that had been filling her head all afternoon. The longer she talked, the more her face moved, the more she satisfied me again, the more I wanted to have the drill team too.

I talked Mrs. Atha into being our sponsor. I biked out to her house all alone and caught her just as she was going out to play golf and promised she wouldn't have to do a thing; we would even put on the assembly she was responsible for this year. We wanted to run the Hi-Steppers ourselves, I explained, that's part of the project. My case seemed airtight, and Mrs. Atha said sure why not and would I like to come along and learn to play golf? I said, no thanks, and went home dissatisfied by how easy it had been. Bunny wasn't impressed either. "You know how to talk to teachers," she said. "You're good at that."

But the two I lived with were more difficult. I asked if we could use our wide backyard for practice, until we could schedule time at the football field, and Daddy's eyes got wide behind his glasses. "No! I don't want twenty teen-age girls tromping the grass. The end of August is the worst time for the grass."

"We'll rotate," I said. "Besides, we don't need it every day, just a couple of times. Just till we can show them what we can do, and then we'll start using the football field like the band."

Daddy said, "I have little enough privacy as it is, with Hoovers in the front yard, and Hoovers using my ash tray and in a week and a half I'll have teen-agers all day long at school and I don't want them in my garden."

"We won't step in the garden. I promise not to ask once school starts."

In my family we had an unspoken agreement that the person who appeared most reasonable always won arguments. In this case Daddy was so panicked over the idea of girls in his garden that he waved his fingers and refused too soon, so I eventually got permission. Mother, however, was most rational of all, watching the discussion and analyzing it, and when she finally spoke she used a mournful, gentle voice.

"But why, Blair Ellen? I am having a difficult time understanding. It seems to me there is something cheap about it. There are so many organized activities."

"This *is* organized. Mrs. Atha is our sponsor—"

"Mrs. Atha." She almost waved her hand to dismiss Mrs. Atha, but caught herself in time. "I'm not trying to stop you, Blair Ellen. I can see you're determined to do this, and no doubt you'll learn from it, but I'm trying to get you to explain *why*."

I had a sheaf of reasons I had been saving for this moment. A speech in my mind especially for Mother: because we want an organization all our own; because the school needs us. But when I looked at her face, the wide gray eyes, the gently folded forehead and pursed lips, I realized the true reason, one I could never come out and say. I was using the Hi-Steppers for balance. I saw myself on a balance board with her and Daddy at one end and Bunny and the Hi-Steppers at the other. I didn't want to be Bunny. I liked my good grades and having Mrs. Atha invite me to play golf with her, and I liked planning for college and piano lessons and church choir, and I liked sitting around while Mother and Daddy discussed everything under the sun. All of that weighed heavily in my life, so heavily that I tended to slide in that direction. I wanted to add weight in the desperate and exciting direction where there was more open air and out-of-doors. Even if it meant marching and practicing to boring excess.

I think it was because of the Hi-Steppers that Mother assigned us a composition the first week of school. "You're the advanced class," she said. "This will be good practice for college." She wanted us to think very carefully about the topic, "What Is Really Important."

"Advanced English," said Gail Gordon after class. "Some advanced English. Nathan Critch and half of Coburn Creek." Then she twisted her mouth at me. "I thought we'd have it easy with *you* in the class."

I gave her a big smile. "Oh, no, she said she'd be especially hard on whichever class I was in, and she'd give us lots of compositions." None of that was true, but I thought Gail deserved it. Sometimes I liked Gail, and sometimes I didn't. Her father had given her a red Barracuda for her sixteenth birthday, and Mother, Daddy, and I all agreed it was a gross indulgence. But I did admire the way she stood up to her parents when they didn't want her to date Johnny Bardoline. She looked them right in the eye, the way she told it, anyhow, and said, "I can do it in front of you or I can do it behind your back, but I am going to go steady with Johnny." When her Dad gave her the Barracuda, she said, he handed her two sets of keys in leather cases, one monogrammed G.G., and the other J.B.

I considered beginning my essay with reference to a red Barracuda as an example of unimportant worldly possessions, but finally decided it would be meanspirited to use a real person's car. I never worked so hard on a composition in my life; I told Mother I had algebra every night for a week, but in my room I was rewriting the essay word by word, thinking in despair that I would never make it through college where they say you have a paper every week. But I was determined that there would be no question in Mother's mind that I deserved the best grade.

I got my A, and I also received a note and a number indicating that I would read my essay aloud. Since I had number eight, I figured I would be the final reader, and that therefore my paper was the best. The more people who read ahead of me, the more certain I was, because all the papers were boring repetitions of Love and Democracy. Gail Gordon's was the most pompous thing I ever heard, and India Odell didn't even get to read. *My* essay began boldly with what is *not* really important: Clothes and other material possessions, teen-age crushes and winning ball games. These things, I wrote, will be forgotten. These things will pass away. What will not be forgotten is what is important, and among the important things are civil rights and missiles in Cuba. I guess it was still Love and Democracy, but it sounded more interesting, and three people raised their hands in the comment period to say they thought it was the best one. Only Gail had any criticism: "I think Blair Ellen is wrong about one thing. Winning games *is* important. I mean school spirit is like patriotism for your country, and also the ending was too depressing."

"That's a point," said Mother, sitting on her desk with her ankles crossed. She wore shirt dresses in the fall, or matching skirt and blouse sets. Looking at her an hour a day, I couldn't get over how fresh and young she seemed up there perched on the desk. Sometimes, when she got very excited, she would bang her heels lightly against the desk. She and Daddy seemed incredibly attractive to me at school, desirable people, full of force. I understood perfectly the students who told me they wished they had one or the other of them for a parent. At school Mother shed light; even her criticism failed to darken the corners of my eyes: "Yes, Blair Ellen," she said. "I think Gail may be right. You want to stir the reader to action, not make him crawl in bed and pull the covers over his head." That got a laugh, and people tried to catch my eye. They still hadn't got over the novelty of a daughter in the classroom. I was pleased to have caused a little controversy; in school all diversions are welcome. I closed my binder and stacked my books to wait for the bell, but Mother said, "Let's see, I think there's one more essay."

I heard footsteps before I saw who it was because he came from the very last seat in my row. I was amazed that Garland Odell had even done the assignment, let alone been chosen to read. He had transferred into our class a couple of days after school started under mysterious circumstances. It must have been a fight with the other Junior English teacher, but even Mother didn't seem to know the details. Mr. Thornton had just asked her one day if she would take Garland, and she said yes. Garland had been on good behavior, too; he sat in back with the country boys, but cracked no jokes, made no silly noises.

He had dressed up in a red cowboy shirt with black shoulders and blue and white trim, and cowboy boots too. Nobody dressed that way in our town. Maybe for the homecoming parade if you had a horse, but not for school. I wondered if he'd done it in honor of the reading, and the idea made me uncomfortable. He slouched against the chalk ledge and grinned and someone in the back whistled.

Mother was immediately off the desk and pacing the front of the room, scanning for the source of the disturbance. Squinting, stretching her neck and flaring her nostrils, she seemed dangerous. We were all still until she relaxed again on the desk. "Now, Garland," she said, "let's consider this a lesson in public speaking. Stand up straight so your voice will carry all the way to your friends in the back. Take three steps forward and balance your weight on both feet and don't slouch. Thank you." Just the instructions she'd given me when I was six and recited in church for the first time.

His essay was about motorcycles. It began with: "What is really important is a solid engine that you can take apart and repair yourself. What is not important is a lot of chrome junk stuck all over it."

People laughed at the way he curled his lip on the word junk. Mother said, "Be professional, Garland, and if they laugh, wait till it's quiet before you go ahead."

Garland read: "People think loud engines are for troublemakers. I think it is important to hear your engine. Then you can tell if something is wrong. A loud engine is important, but not to scare livestock and old people." That brought down the house, and Garland grinned too, but he didn't make any faces, he just stood quietly balanced on both feet, the way she'd told him. "The most important thing of all," he read, "is to be sure your motorcycle is a Harley Davidson."

The class clapped. They hadn't clapped for anyone else, but then no one else had been funny. Only a boy, I thought with a special bitterness I reserved for things closed to me by sex, only a boy could write something that would get those guys in the back to clap. Only Garland was crazy enough to write an English essay about motorcycles. About what really *was* important to him. I would have died before I wrote about what I really wanted. I wanted peace and toleration of course, but I probably would have traded them in an instant for the chance to be homecoming princess.

Hands went up for comments. "Well, well," said Mother. "Nathan Critch. I haven't seen your hand yet this year. What's the question, Nathan?"

Nathan was a tall, heavyset, country boy who never played sports or carried home books, but Garland said he had shot a deer every season since he was eight years old. He said, "Garland's the best.

"Yes?" said Mother. "You have to say why, Nathan."

He looked puzzled. "Because it was about motorcycles."

Laughter: everyone in the class wide awake, hands waving. The boys making their desks creak with their weight as they leaned forward to be recognized. Mother had a sort of innocent, surprised look on her face as she gazed out at the enthusiasm. "I think Nathan is saying that Garland's essay was interesting to him because of the content. We may not have emphasized content enough, but I believe it is one of the main things on the good composition checklist."

I had my hand up in the air too, waiting to be called on. She always called on me last, so I had plenty of time to plan something intelligent to say. This time I used my left hand to flip through the grammar book to the unit on composition. There it was: number five, "Be sure your content will hold the reader's interest."

Meanwhile she had called on Gail, who was saying she thought it was funny and all, but shouldn't it have been more serious?

"No!" shouted the boys in the back. "No, no, more motorcycles."

"Raise your hands," said Mother, too mildly in my opinion. She was being indulgent. Another boy asked how big was the engine in Garland's Harley Davidson. Finally she got around to me, and I had thought up something better than the page reference for the composition checklist.

"First of all," I said, "I think it was a good essay because it got people involved. Second, I thought it would make a good advertisement for Harley Davidson."

"Well," said Mother. "Now there's an idea. You did end it with a sort of slogan, didn't you, Garland? 'The most important thing is to be sure you buy a Harley Davidson.' You should send a copy of your essay to the company. Who knows, they might pay you. I'm serious, Garland. It will be for extra credit. But it should be typed."

"Gee whiz, Mrs. Morgan," grinned Garland. "That's a great idea, but I can't type."

India said, "I'll type it, Mrs. Morgan. I have typing next period."

"Good," said Mother. "Fine. Now here's an assignment for all of you, and you have the whole weekend to do it. I want you all to write a sample business letter for Garland, explaining how you wrote an essay in school, and asking them if they would be interested in using it. I want proper business form, and I'll give extra credit to the ones who find the address of the Harley Davidson company."

"But Mrs. Morgan!" Gail didn't even raise her hand. "How are we supposed to find the address?" Her chin was all wrinkled as if she were about to cry.

"It isn't required, Gail." The warning bell sounded. "Try the library. Or that body shop across the street where the boys stand around all the time. They must have some brochures."

"But Mrs. Morgan! That makes it easy for the boys to get the address. Or somebody like India, who has a brother."

"Why, you're absolutely right, Gail," said Mother. "This assignment gives an advantage to anyone who knows a little about motorcycles." She smiled, and Gail waited for an explanation, but the second bell rang, and Mother picked up her rollbook and walked out.

Immediately Gail's face switched from tearful to baleful, and she stared at me.

"I didn't do anything," I said. "And I don't intend to look up the stupid address either."

She said, "I suppose Johnny can get it for me somewhere. But *I* need the extra credit. *I'm* not as sure of getting an A in English as some people."

I let Gail go out ahead of me, and when I got to the door Garland was partly blocking my way. His face was redder than usual and he was showing his mouthful of long teeth. "Hey, Blair Ellen," he said. "Do you want the address? I'm getting it from Buddy's shop manual. I'd give it to you."

There was too much red in his shirt and face. Something went icy blue inside me. "Oh, I don't think so, Garland," I said. "I'll just go to the library and look it up. Thanks anyway."

He made a short backwards jump out of the doorway so I could pass. "You're not going to find it in any library."

I answered him with only my pale blue smile, as if that were the only trick I knew.

Harley Davidson didn't buy Garland's essay, but they did send him a hood ornament in the shape of an early, classic motorcycle.

He brought the letter from the company to school, and we had a big discussion about how it differed from the business letter paradigm in our textbook. Gail was particularly offended by the absence of paragraph indentation. "Mrs. Morgan! Look at this! They skip a space instead of indenting. That's just plain wrong."

"How can it be wrong?" said Garland. "It's a business letter and they're a business."

"What does a motorcycle company know about grammar?"

"What does a grammar book know about business?" And the boys in the back clapped and cheered for Garland. They seemed to have grown taller and more colorful during the argument. In the end Mother ruled that both forms would be hereafter acceptable, and the boys shook one another's hands as if they'd won some kind of victory.

To tell the truth, I thought they had. That night Mother told Daddy all about how she had the boys writing letters to gun manufacturers and car companies. "You should have seen them, Lloyd," she said. "Garland Odell and that big Nathan Critch discussing whether to sign a business letter 'Sincerely' or 'Yours truly.'"

"That must have been real edifying," said Daddy, who didn't very much like her having a success with boys he'd written off as troublemakers.

"What gets me," I said, "is that the girls study hard all the time, but the minute some boy does his homework you teachers run out and kill the fatted calf." Daddy chuckled, so I went on. "Nobody gives the girls credit for doing their homework night after night, year in and year out—"

"I believe," said Mother, "that the credit for doing homework is to earn a satisfactory grade. I believe that is generally considered credit enough for most people."

"It isn't just grades I'm talking about. It's the way you all get excited about the boys and try harder for them. It's just like the prodigal son; that parable always sounded to me like a recommendation to sow wild oats."

"Hear, hear," said Daddy. "Get that girl a soapbox."

By this time I knew he was making fun of me, but I plunged ahead. "It's always like that. Mrs. Atha would draw baseball diamonds and have us find the angle of the baselines at home plate. Anything to attract the boys' attention."

"Equal time for girls!" called Daddy. "Assign them to write recipes."

"I just don't like special treatment for boys, that's all," I said.

"Well, what do you expect?" said Daddy. "It's natural for the women teachers to like the boys. You don't want queers for teachers, do you?"

"Lloyd!" Mother fixed him with her most far-reaching squint, but Daddy was having too much fun laughing at both of us to be affected. I had a vision of him as the kind of kid who snickered with his friends over women and others who took things seriously. He would have put a mouse in Mother's desk, I thought, or chased me with a worm. The kind of boy who would certainly never vote for a class vice-president for homecoming princess.

This is silly, I thought. I asked to be excused, though, because I felt a crevasse opening up under my feet. I went to my room and lay in the center of my bed, trying to keep the crack from spreading, trying to hold everything still. The violet walls turned murky, losing their color. I had gone around to the English classes that day distributing ballots for the homecoming princess elections. Usually I liked standing up in front of people and giving instructions, but my name was on the list of nominees, and I felt every word I spoke was an explosive hammer blow nailing up my chances to be selected. I felt their eyes on me, all the boys who would never vote for a girl who told them to draw their circles in ink. I should have got someone else to do it, I thought, a boy, any boy. Then when they saw my name they might have thought of me in my Hi-Stepper shorts, maybe, instead of me giving instructions.

Talk about what is not important! I thought. Who wants to stand around in a skimpy evening gown on a cold Saturday night? But of course I wanted to. *I* wanted to be in the light, to be Beauty. Mother had given me permission to invite Thad for homecoming, and what I wanted was to stand there in the gown with him beside me, out on the awesomely green football field, in a golden aura shed by the high-power night lights. I knew how the lights felt from being out there with the Hi-Steppers, but that wasn't what I wanted. I wanted the moment when I was drawn out from among all the others, made special. I would be myself, but tall and willowy, less physical. Thad would be beside me, representing large towns, even cities. The eyes of the world approving me. I said to myself, This is junk. But I wanted it, and I couldn't hide from myself that I wanted it, and the wanting made me ugly. Suddenly I was at the bottom of the pit. I never exactly had the sensation of falling, but I was there, staked out at the bottom, prone, looking up at a princess on the rim, who shone and sang to me, and I couldn't tell if she were encouraging or mocking.

In order to get to the bulletin board before anyone else on the day of the announcement, I told Mrs. Atha that I had to leave gym early to get things ready for Hi-Stepper practice, and then I went and sat in the dressing room with my coat in my lap. The pressure behind my eyes was like a headache, but it wasn't pain, just a terrible fullness, and I thought maybe something was wrong with me, that I would collapse on the painted concrete floor. There had been a boyfriend of Aunt Pearl's when she was young, a boy who died like that, in the misty days before Uncle Joe. This lovely college boy in a letter sweater, the best of Aunt Pearl's many boyfriends, at home during the Christmas holidays and just going upstairs to his room. Suddenly he called to his father, Dad? I feel so funny, like something popped in my head. And fell down dead with a burst blood vessel. In perfect health, like me. I stared at the shininess of the painted concrete, and the fullness seemed to increase. I tried not to breathe.

The door from the outside hall opened, and Bunny came in. She leaned over the sink to roll off some excess mascara from one eyelash. She said, "Are you coming today?"

"I guess I have to, don't I, if I want to stay in Hi-Steppers? I missed two rehearsals already."

She shrugged. "I don't care. You're the co-captain."

I had a flash of righteous indignation. "You can't change the rules, Bunny, you cannot change the rules. Not even for co-captains. We don't have many rules, but they're important." She had made up the marching routines, but I invented the rules: few, simple, and ironclad. Three practices to become a marching member, three missed practices and you were out, even if you were one of the original members. I typed up four dozen three-by-five cards with the rules and a long blank for the signature.

Bunny said, "We have too many girls in there now, that's the trouble. I knew it would happen. One good half time and every girl in the school wants to join up. Half of them don't even have sashes." She sat on the bench with me and pulled up the collar of her varsity jacket. It was old style, yellow and purple, but without a boy's name on the back. I always thought that once, years ago, before I knew her, when she was even younger than Kim, she had stolen that jacket and kept it in the bottom of a drawer somewhere until she was old enough to wear it to school. That would be like her, I thought. She lit a cigarette, and said, "You should have been there yesterday. You should have seen what Spinett was trying to pull."

"Oh, don't start in on Teresa."

"*I'm* not starting in, *she's* starting in. I told you what would happen if we let her in. First she whines. The minute I tell her to do the simplest thing, she whines how it's too hard. 'Don't go so fast.' That's what she says to my face. Behind my back she's telling them that my routines are no good. So I go over and say, 'Listen, if you don't like my routines, give me something better, I'm listening, I'm all ears.' And she whines in that sneery little voice of hers, 'I'm not the drill sergeant, you're the drill sergeant.'"

I wondered what time it was. I had to go upstairs before the bell rang.

Bunny said, loud, as if she were hoping someone would overhear and report to Teresa, "The trouble with those Spinetts when you come right down to it is that they're dumb. Just plain out-and-out dumb. Her brother asked me out once, and I laughed in his face. He was so dumb he didn't know I was laughing at him."

"You just keep on talking that way, Bunny, and there sure will be trouble."

"I'll fight her, I'm not afraid to fight."

"Oh, great, that's what we need. A couple of fights and you'll see how long the Hi-Steppers last."

"Well, what do you care? Some co-captain. You don't even come to practice."

"When did I get to be co-captain? I don't remember anybody electing me."

"*I* elected you. What's the matter with you anyhow? Are you on the rag? Oh, I get it, no letters from *Charleston*."

I was mean enough to fight myself. All day long I had been skidding along the surface, smiling thinly when people like Linda Bardoline, glistening with good humor, asked me if I could do the algebra. But what did she care, she always won her elections. At least Bunny had noticed there was something wrong with me. "I've got to go to the office," I said.

"Well, I hope you get off the rag before rehearsal. One Teresa Spinett is enough."

The whole second floor was empty, not a student in sight on the oiled, wide-board floors, no one at the olive drab lockers. I was careful in my approach to the bulletin board because I didn't want Mr. Thornton pulling me into the office to hear about the good old days when the football players had to wash their own uniforms and everyone studied debating. I could hear his voice as I came up the hall, but it was distant and muffled, his door closed, and Alice Ross not in sight. I made a right turn, directly to the water fountain and bulletin board, and I took a long drink first, as if that were my purpose. Oh, a deep, thirsty drink. And then, by the by, I scanned the bulletin board, just looking for any interesting announcements. Flyers, an organization chart of which teacher had which homeroom, a lost scarf; I thought it wasn't posted yet, but I was looking off center. In the middle of the bulletin board was half a sheet of paper, typed, Queen, First Runner-up, Junior Princesses: Linda Bardoline, India Odell. The Linda Bardoline was to be expected, of course, but the other name was too short. The shape wasn't right. I kept reading it over and over to make sure I had it right, and then, when I realized I'd lost track of time and someone might have seen me, I said in a pert little voice, "Well, my goodness, what do you know!" and gave my head a shake. As fast as possible I got off the second floor, down to the side entrance. I couldn't quite imagine how I was going to make it through Hi-Stepper practice, marching and talking to people, but I would have to see even more people if I went home through town. I gazed through the glass of the side door, out over the teachers' cars, at the back of the bleachers, and beyond them, the side of a hill, dun-colored. I seemed to have missed the glory of autumn, or maybe there had been none this year. I wished for a heavier coat that would hide me more completely. India, I kept thinking. Of all people, India Odell. I had never expected her to win; I had thought it was sweet that she had been nominated at all, and that was why I had voted for her myself. Something appealed to me about the combination of Linda, popular and vivacious and dark, and India with her red hair and quiet ways. I had imagined them, Linda in a yellow gown and India in pale blue. Only in my imagination I had been there too, in pink, not my favorite color, but it brought out my rosiness. That'll teach you, I thought, you have to vote for yourself around here.

The bell rang, and I pushed through the door, intending to get to the field before anyone saw me, but someone called when I was just past the hedges and into the parking lot. It was Carmell Odell, waddling a little in her hurry to catch my attention. "Hey, Blair Ellen," she shouted, "you didn't win it for princess!"

Carmell didn't seem to have a jaw anymore, although there was a sort of chin in the middle of her vast, white throat like a little cream puff.

"Oh, hi, Carmell," I said. "I never expected to get it. Why, I voted for India and Linda Bardoline myself. Listen, when you see India on the bus, congratulate her for me, okay?"

People burst out behind us, hooting boys, shriek-laughing girls, all the happy people who had not hoped and were not disappointed. Carmell yelled after me, "Well, *I* voted for you! I voted for you and India!"

And I wondered, why on earth did she? It only added to the whole mystery. I don't think she and I had exchanged three sentences since we were eleven years old. The mystery made me angry, the impossibility of penetrating. Who else had voted for me? Bunny? Maybe no one except Carmell. I imagined Mr. Thornton and Alice Ross counting votes. Isn't that odd, only one vote for Blair Ellen Morgan. Probably voted for herself.

I sat in the bleachers shivering, dreading the moment when the others would come and ask how come I didn't get it for princess.

After a little while, Teresa Spinett and Tommy Tucker came in through the gap under the announcer's booth, and I waved to make sure they saw me and didn't think they were alone. I hadn't even known they were going together. Something inside me woke up, an inevitable curiosity about who went with whom. They leaned at one another, as if Teresa's little dark head were going to support Tommy in his long curve around and over her. She gave me the coolest possible nod, to make sure I didn't come trotting down to talk to them, and then she shifted around until Tommy had his back to me. I could see her face staring up at him in her suspicious, intense way, and they seemed to be speaking at the same time. I didn't know Tommy could talk that much. Teresa doesn't care, I thought, elections and princesses, she couldn't care less. All she wants is a good-looking, tall boyfriend. That's all there is to some people's lives. In grade school Tommy used to be everyone's heart throb. Gail Gordon used to write him love letters and buy him these twelve-inch-tall valentine cards. He was the best we had on our football team except for Johnny Bardoline, but his grades were so bad there was a big doubt right now about whether he would get to play the rest of the season. He used to go with Linda Bardoline, and she helped him with his homework, but since they broke up, he just seemed to fall apart. They said he drank a lot of beer after they broke up, so I figured it must help him to have a girl friend again. The Spinetts were built like anchors, anyhow, low to the ground, and they had a way of standing with their legs wide and dug in.

Some other girls came in, and my trouble hit me again, my sense that people were looking at me and seeing a sign: Did Not Get It For Princess. Bunny made an elaborately wide circuit around Teresa and Tommy and climbed the bleachers to sit by me. "Sorry," she said sidelong.

"What for?"

"You know what. You would have made a better princess than either of those two."

I almost said my goodness *I* don't care, but instead shrugged and muttered, "I'll live." I was so pleased with the way it sounded, I said it again. "Yeah, I'll live."

"Where is everybody?" shouted Bunny. "How come everyone's late? Where are the little kids?" Meaning Kim and her friends who came over from the junior high school. "Let's get started! Good-bye, Tommy Tucker, unless you want to practice with us."

Tommy gave one of his slow, blushing grins, but Teresa's face clouded over. "There aren't enough here to practice anyhow," she said.

"We're starting," said Bunny. "You can stay or you can go, but we're starting."

Teresa said a word that I couldn't hear, but it must have been pretty pungent because the girls in the front row all went Uh-oh and Ooo, Teresa. Teresa said, "Let's go for a walk, Tommy."

Bunny grinned, the biggest grin I think I'd ever seen from her. She called after them, "Have a good time, you two. Don't do anything I wouldn't do!" Then, when they were out of earshot, "He better watch himself, I hear she bites."

I laughed with the others, glad that Bunny and I were on the same side. Amazed that I wasn't in a deep depression. Glad to be marching and working up a sweat and hearing them gossip about Teresa and a lot of other people who weren't there.

But Bunny was right that the Hi-Steppers were looking ragged. Teresa and a couple of tough friends kept giving Bunny trouble, and Bunny and I kept arguing over whether or not she could throw somebody out. Then Thad wrote that he would come for homecoming weekend, and I couldn't think about marches and routines and whether or not Teresa Spinett was insulting Bunny every time she rolled her eyes. I had decided not to march at homecoming, but I hadn't told Bunny so I couldn't ask her things I needed to know, like how to talk to a boy you haven't seen in three months.

I tried not to think about his coming, or about not marching. But the closer we got to the weekend, the more Mother began to talk about it all the time. You'd think Thad was coming to see her instead of me. "He'll want to go to church," she said, "if he plans to be a minister. I would think he visits as many churches as he can, to get ideas, don't you think? And that way there won't be any question."

"There won't be any question about what?"

"About a boy spending the night here. If people can meet him, shake his hand, see he's a nice boy, they won't talk so much."

"Mother! I mean, he's sleeping on the *couch*, isn't he?"

"I've been thinking maybe Lloyd and I should give him the bed in our room, since he's the guest."

"Oh, no, please, that's awful, Mother, he would feel terrible if you did that. If you do that, I'll ask Hoovers if he can sleep over there."

The idea of Thad in their bed panicked me. The idea of Thad in the house panicked me.

Mother said, "I suppose he'll bring a dressing gown of some kind. I expect his mother will make sure he does that."

The dressing gown gave me an even more vivid impression of Thad in the flesh. A person sleeping on the couch Mother would make up with tightly stretched sheets. A body whose face I couldn't remember using our shower and toilet. Did he shave, and would he leave little hairs in the sink when he cleaned out his shaver the way Daddy did? And what kind of robe? Wasn't a robe faintly sissified? I like my men roughhewn, I thought, not sure what that had to do with a robe. I hadn't been comfortable about the stationery his last letter came on. It had been masculine enough, tan, faintly printed with a sort of wood-grain pattern, but I kept thinking a boy shouldn't bother with things like that. I hoped his robe would be an old plaid one, not something that matched his pajamas.

Then I began to wonder if there might be something wrong with him anyhow, a boy from a big town like Charleston, a real city, the state capital. Why would he want to drive ninety miles north through the mountains to spend a few hours with someone who couldn't even get herself elected princess in a tiny little town like this? Maybe he thought I was easy, since I had French kissed so early in our relationship. Or maybe he really was a sissy.

He was supposed to arrive around 4:00 Saturday afternoon, in time for dinner, and then the game and dance. I ran the vacuum and cleaned the bathroom, and Mother said I was doing a terrible job and kept snatching the vacuum and the Ajax away from me. She got out the furniture tool and went in the cracks between couch pillows, and she polished the fixtures on the sink. I had meant to cook dinner, too, but when she found out I was going to throw together a regular hamburger meatloaf, she had said, "How about ham loaf with pineapple slices?"

"I don't want to go to all that trouble," I said.

Her eyes started flashing and she reared back her head. "When I was dating your father, it was a pleasure to go to trouble for him."

"I'm not marrying Thad! You act like I wanted to get married."

"You never know," she said. "I thought Pearl was an innocent baby and one day she up and married." I knew all about Aunt Pearl, and how Mother had had to raise her. They lived in a little mining camp and Mother was doing everything for Pearl and then one day Pearl ran off and married her first husband. It was a long time before I found out that Uncle Joe wasn't even Aunt Pearl's first husband. And after that husband died in the war, Mother had tried to put Pearl through college, but Pearl dropped out to marry Uncle Joe. Finally Mother just went ahead and put herself through college.

In the end she made the special ham loaf, while Daddy wandered around making jokes about the Prince of Wales coming to visit. I couldn't stand either one of them, so I went over to Bunny's to tell her I wasn't going to march. I should have told her a long time ago, but surely she would understand that a person had to choose a boy over the Hi-Steppers.

It was a gray, rough day. There had been cold rain in the morning, but the clouds seemed higher now, and some wispy lower ones encircled the tops of the hills. I knocked and went on in. Their kitchen was dim, and the television was the only light in the living room. Even the blinds were down. Bunny had the ironing board set up in the pantry area where she could watch the television while she ironed. Cartoons made the walls flicker and she frowned when she saw me. "Look, I'm ironing their blue jeans."

I sat down on the staircase.

"I never ironed their blue jeans before."

A commercial came on and the littlest brother, Robbie, leaned backwards over the couch, dangling his head, and his whole naked top half seeming about to slip out of his pants. "Hi, Blair Ellen," he said.

"Hi, Robbie. Where's Rusty?"

The other one appeared, rightside up. "Hi, Blair Ellen."

Bunny said, "Why don't you two put on your shirts and go outside. I'm tired of that TV."

To my amazement they turned it off and ran past me up the stairs, without any whooping or pounding or fistfighting. I said, "What's the matter with them, do they think Christmas is coming?"

She shrugged. "Mom got a job at the Heritage Nursing Home. She even got the day shift."

I waited for the explanation of how that made the boys tractable and Bunny so mild-humored, but she didn't think anything was unusual. Maybe nothing was unusual, I thought, maybe I had the Hoovers all wrong. I was feeling strangely ignorant. Thad driving north at this moment. All things a mystery.

Bunny said, "You've got your hair in curlers. I bet you've got a big date for the dance. Who is it, Garland Odell?"

"Garland Odell! Why on earth do you think Garland Odell?"

"Because you've been eating lunch with him."

"I have not. I talked to him a couple of times with a whole bunch of people." It had been girls, mostly, India was there, and Garland just sort of showed up and started saying one thing and another, we were all making fun of something. I couldn't even remember what we talked about, it was as if I hadn't really been paying attention. "That must be how rumors get started. I've known Garland since we were little kids."

"Who is it then?"

"Thad. Thad is coming."

"Thad! Thad from this summer? I finally get to meet Thad?"

"He's on his way right now, and he's staying over. Mother's letting him sleep on the couch."

"Mrs. Morgan's letting him stay at your house! Oh, wow. Wait till he sees you in your marching outfit."

"I was thinking I might not march. I was thinking Thad and I might get all dressed up and I'd sit with him."

"You can change before the dance. Boys love those short-shorts in cold weather."

"I don't want to get all sweaty."

"Oh, don't be dumb, Blair Ellen."

"No," I said, not very loud, but I think I must have looked guilty enough that she finally believed me. "I don't think I'll be marching tonight."

I thought for a second I was finally going to feel what it was like to receive Bunny's anger. She cocked her head, her eyes like little black marbles. But she spoke calmly, at a distance almost. "You've been trying to get out for a long time, haven't you? You've always been too good for the Hi-Steppers; I don't know why you joined up in the first place. You never really wanted to. We don't need you, you know. We've got plenty of girls."

I almost changed my mind. I had a sudden vision of sitting here around the kitchen table with her and Kim and the little boys making all their noise in the other room and Mrs. Hoover coming in sometimes and smoking a cigarette and telling us what she thought of our plans. I would miss that a lot. I hadn't thought about losing that. I said, "I'll march next time, I'm proud to be a Hi-Stepper, Bunny, but I want to sit with Thad tonight."

"We can do *without* you. Don't do us any *favors*."

"He's my boyfriend, Bunny."

"I said we can do without you."

It left me so empty; what did she expect of me? I thought I was doing what she would do in my place. I got up to go. "I hope everything goes great."

"Baby stuff," she said with her head down, and I couldn't figure out if she meant me and Thad or the Hi-Steppers or something else.

I was thinking of wearing some old outfit to homecoming instead of my new desert-rose wool ensemble, which had been so expensive even on sale that Mother said I had better like it because it was going to be my last suit for years. I had no doubts about *it*, but I was afraid someone would think I had bought it expecting to be a princess. What if Thad thought so too? What if he was expecting a princess instead of me? I had to keep the conversation off princesses and all honors that might lead to princesses. To tell him I was vice-president of the junior class and the pep club would be to get us both thinking of what else I might have won or not won.

I had other things not to talk about with him. I never finished reading the Epistles of St. Paul. What *had* we talked about all those easy hours in the summer when I had the feeling we could say anything at all to one another, far more than I had ever said to my mother or any girl friend? I couldn't remember the topics. I thought of the woods, and Thad's knees. He always wore khaki hiking shorts, and they showed off his wide, golden-haired knees. I remembered just opening my mouth and things poured out, fascinating, musical things. I was so free then, and so bound up now, by school and the Hi-Steppers and Mother acting like it was her boyfriend not mine, and even by the new outfit hanging stiffly in its own shape.

"Blair Ellen! Blair Ellen!" Mother called and I heard her feet hurrying around. "Blair Ellen, he's here!"

Our Father, who art in heaven, I prayed, please don't let it be too awful. But not my will but thine be done forever and ever and this too will pass away amen.

I thought he was at the door, but he had just pulled into the driveway in a boat-length white Impala convertible. I hadn't expected such a car. I hoped Bunny was looking out the window at this moment. It would be too cold to put the top down, but that was okay because I didn't have a head scarf to match my ensemble.

Thad was closing the door, pulling a small suitcase out of his back seat. I waved and ran out, and all the time I was waving and running I was thinking why does he have his suit on already? Why does he have a suit with a vest? He seemed short and pale, not golden like last summer. We stopped short of embracing, but he grabbed my forearm and for a couple of seconds I gripped back. Then I started talking, asking how the trip was, thinking how silly I must sound and wondering if he could see that I'd picked up two pounds since last summer. And why had he cut his hair when he used to look so cute as a blond Beatle.

Mother was waiting at the door, asking the same stupid questions I had, and Daddy came behind her, pipe in one hand, newspaper in the other, getting them both in his left hand long enough to shake with Thad. I suppose I should have been thankful to Mother and Daddy for being there because in my mind I started criticizing them instead of Thad: Daddy's discomfort, Mother's real Blair giggle that bounced off the ceiling like a spider monkey. She took over, of course, insisted on getting the suitcase out of Thad's hands into Daddy's, made him take off his suit jacket and wrestled with him politely about who was going to put it on a hanger. Did Thad want to go wash up? Was he hungry? No, he'd had lunch on the way, but after Mother had shooed us into the living room, she brought a tray of brownies and glasses of milk. She filled the air with words and action, while Daddy muttered something about how he had never been any good at balancing food on his knees. He kept casting glances toward the table where we usually sat for our coffee. In the distance, behind Mother's voice, I could see Thad and me in the driveway at the moment we clutched one another's forearms, but it seemed incredibly dim, almost as far away as the summer. Meanwhile this other young man was thanking Mother for one small service and another, and every word from him, and the ones that came out of me, too, echoed in a sort of empty gray room where I seemed to have retired for a while. A hard-walled, reflective room, and no one noticed I was there. Or maybe they did notice and I couldn't tell; I couldn't tell much about them at all; they were flat, cut out of low-luster sheet metal, with the light behind them.

By the time we sat down to dinner, Daddy and Mother and Thad had made friends and were chattering about the school system in Charleston and the differences in organization of a big high school like Thad's and our little one. Mother whispered in the kitchen that Thad seemed like such a nice boy, and I had that sensation again that I was an observer at her date. By the end of the dinner Daddy was so cheerful that he was threatening to bring out the baby pictures of me with no clothes on, and I was thankful to be alone in my room to dress. I took my time, thirty seconds to curl each set of eyelashes, brushing my hair, pink lipstick but not too pale. No eye make-up. The girl in my mirror was the natural type, and she had eaten so little dinner that her dress fastened with no trouble at all. That caused a happy calmness deep inside me. I was slim tonight, with perfectly straight long shiny bangs, a stylish A-line dress and A-line coat to match. Black leather bag and low pumps. And no white gloves. Mother pleaded for white gloves, but I thought they looked like Minnie Mouse and I abhorred scrubbing the grimy little fingers. I stayed longer than necessary in my room looking in the mirror. I would have liked to send that nice reflection out on the date while I stayed home in blue jeans.

And at last there was the cold front seat of the Impala, only Thad and me, getting settled, starting the car. The gravel crackled, and we backed out onto John W. Davis Street, named for the only West Virginian ever to run for the Presidency. A dead-end street, very quiet, with big houses, most of them broken up into apartments now, but still graced with front lawns and heavy maple and elm trees that met overhead. Halfway down a street lamp had been knocked out, and Thad pulled over. I was just about to say that the light had probably been smashed by our neighbor's kids, but Thad leaned over and, using both hands, drew my head to him and we kissed. It was an iron kiss; we both kept our lips closed and I could feel his teeth behind the flesh, and my own teeth pressing into the back of my lips. I waited for the ocean to roll over me the way it had last summer, but everything stayed chilly. I hadn't wanted to kiss yet anyhow. I hadn't been ready. We separated and I gave a little sigh so he wouldn't know I hadn't liked it and he said, "Hello, Blair Ellen, I've missed you."

I had a feeling he had been planning to say that all along, and probably planning the kiss too, as soon as he got me alone. No one planned anything last summer. Our kisses had come inevitably, one moment looking at one another, and the next become a kiss with no distance between us at all.

"I'll never forget," said Thad, touching my hair, "how amazed I was that someone who said vesper prayers could kiss like that."

My garterbelt fasteners hurt, and I wanted us to get a good seat for the game. "It seems like a different world," I said.

He wanted to kiss again, but I said we should hurry along to be sure to get parking. As we drove, though, I was glad the first kiss was over, and I started talking. I told him about Bunny and the Hi-Steppers, even how I had quit them, although I didn't mention that I had only done it an hour before he arrived. He said Bunny sounded like a real character, and then I got suspicious and wondered if Thad might be up here slumming, checking out the little town, the miners, and the hillbillies. The funny little small-town girl who prayed in public and tongue-kissed.

We were playing Buckhannon that night, and since they were number one in the state that year, a lot of their people had come, and others from Graysburg to see them, so the parking lot was filling up fast. Thad was worried about scratches on the Impala, which belonged to his uncle, so after pulling up on the grass where we were directed, after we were actually out and starting to walk, he decided he wanted to repark. I waited for him in the alley between the cars with the dark high school looming above, the high-power stadium lights behind. A constant broken stream of people passed among the cars, across the teachers' parking lot. A motorcycle came in low gear up the aisle, glittering from the lights. It was Garland Odell, wearing a suit and a thin tie that had whipped back around his neck, leaving an expanse of white shirt and the reflection of his glasses.

I said, "I never knew you owned a suit, Garland."

He grinned and raced his motor, leaned back enough to pull one leg up on the gas tank and show off a tooled leather cowboy boot. "Well, you know, I'm an escort tonight. For the crowning." He moved his body forward a little, toward me. "But she's got someone else taking her to the after-dance." In the background I heard the Impala door slam at last, and I wondered what Thad was going to think of the cowboy boots. Garland said, "How about you, are you going to the dance?"

Then Thad was there beside me, thick and soft compared to Garland. I introduced them, and Garland took his time extending his hand to meet Thad's, and pulled it away immediately. He gave us a nod and growled away. I said to Thad, "His sister is one of the princesses and he's her escort. I've known them since I was little. They live way up on top of a mountain with no electricity or running water or anything."

I didn't know myself why I told him that, especially when I knew very well that they had moved off the mountain and taken over Carmell's house when Carmell's family built their new one.

It was a kind of test of Thad, but mostly I disgusted myself. They had an old windup Victrola, I told him, and they used to play Elvis Presley songs on it.

Thad said, "Does he play a gui-tar too?"

I was furious with him, and with Garland for the cowboy boots. Thad's shoes, I noticed, had thick crepe soles that I hated almost as much as cowboy boots.

The girls I knew, though, didn't seem put off by Thad's shoes. There was a regular parade of them, some who hardly ever spoke to me, coming up to meet him. Even Teresa Spinett came by in her Hi-Stepper shorts and gold cummerbund. "Have you seen Tommy?" she asked, looking at Thad all the time.

"Isn't he playing?"

She made a little face. "Coach doesn't care whether we win or not. None of those teachers do either. Tommy says he's playing whatever they say, but I haven't been able to find him. Where's your uniform? Aren't you marching?"

A little later I saw Tommy down by the fifty yard line in regular clothes. He was shouting and stumbling and red faced. Without Tommy, all the team had left was Johnny Bardoline, and against Buckhannon that year he wasn't nearly enough. By half time we were down forty points, having scored exactly one touchdown on a freak punt return by Johnny. We didn't even get the extra point. Thad seemed to be getting a tremendous kick out of the slaughter. "This is gruesome," he said, "just gruesome. This will probably even make the papers in Charleston."

The queen and her court came out at half time not wearing wool suits at all to my relief, but velvet gowns in deep gem shades. All except India. When they announced her, Thad asked if she were the queen because she was wearing white. Not white velvet, but a strapless white net evening gown with a wide skirt, the kind of dress girls wore to proms ten years ago. Thad answered his own question, "No, that's the cowboy and his sister, isn't it?"

India and Garland walked a little slower than the others, and she didn't smile. They seemed to be concentrating entirely on their passage over the field of rough divots, paying attention to neither the crowd nor their own clothes. I think I would have

[143]

done anything rather than wear that net dress when the other girls were wearing velvet. I would have found the money somehow. If Garland could afford leather cowboy boots, surely India could have a velvet dress. A few rows behind me someone said, "What does she think this is, her wedding?" And while the chairman of the school board was crowning the queen in her sapphire blue, I kept looking at India and wondering how she could be so calm when she was different from the others, when people were whispering about her in the audience. She seemed untroubled by those sifting flakes of worry that fell like dandruff on my whole life. But the longer I watched her, the less grotesque the dress appeared, the more it seemed that a special light fell on her, more than on anyone else.

I was so preoccupied with India and her white evening gown that it wasn't until the football players had streamed back onto the field that I realized the Hi-Steppers hadn't marched. Something had gone wrong all right. I felt a small thud of satisfaction. Kim Hoover came walking along the sidelines. I thought it was Bunny at first because she had teased her hair back over a clasp just like Bunny, but her scrawny legs gave her away, and her coat, outgrown and red with fake fur pom-pom buttons. I waved to get her attention, and when she saw me, she came dashing right up. "Blair Ellen! Blair Ellen! We didn't march!" Then she saw Thad with me and pulled her chin down and frowned.

I said, "This is Thad. This is my next door neighbor, Kim Hoover."

Thad extended that ready right hand of his. "Hello, Kim, nice to meet you."

She kept her brows together but gave him her hand and pulled it away quickly. "We saw your car." Then she remembered what she had come running to tell. "Blair Ellen, did you hear what happened? Bunny beat up Teresa."

"Teresa?" said Thad. "The one I met?" He is going to run back and tell his big city friends all about us, I thought.

Kim said, "She beat her to a pulp. Bunny wouldn't have had a mark on her if Teresa wasn't such a short little shrimp and butted Bunny in the eye, and now Bunny's eye is purple. It got Bunny so mad she ripped old Teresa's blouse off." She stopped there and took a second to see our reactions. "So Teresa ran off screaming for Tommy Tucker and her brothers and her mother and I don't know who else. She said she'd get her brothers to fix Bunny and me too. Do you think they will?"

"No one's going to hurt you, Kim."

She pulled out her lower lip. "You didn't see the shape Teresa was in when Bunny got through with her."

So that's the end of the Hi-Steppers, I thought. All those gold satin cummerbunds we'd made, and the excitement of being out on the field where usually only the band and the football players got to go.

"And that's not all," said Kim. "Bunny went off in a car with some boy she doesn't hardly know. She said she was going to get some fun out of tonight one way or the other." Her face had become still more like Bunny's, rigid in the cheeks and mouth with the eyes flickering around, checking out the situation. "I don't have anyone to go home with."

"You never go home with Bunny," I said, but it was too late.

"We'll give you a lift," Thad said. "It's the least we can do to save you from Teresa's brothers."

Kim said, "The only car Bunny and I like better than a white Impala convertible is a red Corvette Sting Ray."

She went off then to tell more people about the fight, and after the start of the fourth quarter came back with her five best eighth-grade friends and asked if we could give them all a lift down to the dance instead of home. At this point our team was down by sixty points and a rumor was going around that Buckhannon intended to win by one hundred points in honor of the state centennial. Thad was still worried about the finish on the car, so we decided to leave early and avoid the crowd. The eighth graders were happy, and all insisted on crowding in the back seat together. The girls rolled down their windows and looked for people who might recognize them, and we drove them through town twice before dropping them at the Women's Club.

Thad and I went to the Brazier Burger. He suggested going someplace to talk, and I think he meant park, but something in me was like the eighth graders and wanted to be seen in public with him and his uncle's Impala. The Brazier Burger was situated along the highway to Graysburg in the middle of a big parking lot. It used to be part of a three-store shopping center, but the other stores shut down and the Brazier expanded into the laundromat, using the extra space for some redwood picnic tables up on the platforms where the washing machines used to sit. I chose the table next to the window because I wanted to see every car that passed, those that pulled into the lot, and those that rolled on south and north.

A school bus full of students from Buckhannon went by, so we knew the game was over. They leaned out and screamed cheers, and other people began arriving, almost more than I could watch all at once. A half a dozen motorcycles pulled in, and I looked for Garland, but it was some older guys, friends of his. One great big one, about thirty years old, called Nuts, because, Garland said, he was stone crazy, for one reason, and he couldn't tell the other reason in mixed company. Nuts had shaved off all his hair lately and it was growing back in patches and he had rolls of fat on the back of his neck. He was supposed to live with some woman in a shack up on Coburn Creek and they had four or five kids, but they never got married so she could stay on welfare and he spent her checks on chrome decorations for his bike. Thad thought he was real interesting.

Another car pulled up close to our window, and a crowd got out, people I only knew by sight, mostly married couples, but Bunny was with them. She still had her marching shorts on, and her leg make-up and varsity jacket. A long, pale section of her hair had come loose from the French roll and was waving up and down. "Look," I said, "that's Bunny we've been talking about. Kim's sister." The people she was with didn't seem to be paying much attention to her, the women especially were laughing and talking with each other and walking ahead of her.

Thad said, "She doesn't look like she's having a very good time."

At the counter they picked up coffee and Cokes and headed back to the car. Bunny stayed a little behind them, fooling around in her change purse. It was strange, how young she looked. I was used to thinking of her as knowledgeable and tall. I said, "I'm going to ask her if she wants to sit with us."

Bunny saw me come through the interior door, and I noticed right away the clotted blood in her brow, and a puffy redness around her eye and the top of her cheek. "Hey, Bunny," I said. "Thad wants to meet you."

"I'm with some people," she said, but the people had already filed out without her, except for one thickset guy I had seen around with Don Hagen.

He held the door open. "Hey, Bunny, are you coming?"

She glanced through the inside door at Thad, from this distance looking like a man in the background of a fashion photo, three-piece suit, sharp profile. She said, "So that's the Thad I've been hearing about. Thad with the Impala." She glanced at Don Hagen's friend and shrugged. "I think I'll stay around here a while," she said. "If you see Don cruising around, tell him I'm being good, okay?"

I felt a surge of pride. I had changed Bunny's mind.

She said, "They're going drinking. That's all that bunch ever does. Don used to go drinking with them all the time too, until he met me. That's why they don't like me, 'cause I keep Don from drinking with them."

So I had not only changed her mind, I'd saved her from temptation. I was pretty sure she drank beer sometimes. I said, "You don't want to run around with those people. Come and meet Thad."

"What about my eye? I haven't had the guts to look in a mirror. Do you think it'll leave a scar?"

"No, there's just a lot of dried blood is all."

"I've seen scars like this. They leave a big bare spot right in the middle of your eyebrow. It won't even take pencil."

"Are you coming in or not?"

"Who else is inside?"

"Nobody. Nuts Davis."

"Well, it's too wet to plough."

Thad stood when we came in, and Bunny walked around him the long way, keeping her bad side away from him. I sat next to Bunny so she wouldn't feel like a fifth wheel, and Thad gave her an enormous grin. "I hear you won the fight."

"He just comes out and says it, doesn't he?"

I shrugged, not knowing for sure if she were pleased or insulted.

She took a look at her reflection in the window and saw her

hair and started fastening it down. "You could have told me about my hair," she said. "None of this would have happened anyhow if you had marched with us like you were supposed to instead of sitting with him."

Thad smiled at me so sweetly. "You didn't march with your Hi-Steppers because of me?"

I couldn't remember anymore; I had a feeling I had wanted not to march first. I said, "I couldn't have stopped you and Teresa."

Bunny said, "But I wouldn't have been in such a bad mood. I guess it had to happen one of these days, though. She's been asking for it for weeks."

"Kim said you pulled off her blouse."

"Kim's got a big mouth. I only pulled off her cummerbund; her blouse sort of came open on its own. I told her she couldn't march, and she said I couldn't stop her, so I pulled off her cummerbund. That's all. Then she got lucky and butted me like a billy goat. And gave me this." Bunny cupped a hand over the side of her face.

"Let me see it," said Thad. "I'm going to be a doctor."

She leaned across the table on her elbows and closed her eyes. He touched the wounded cheek with one finger, pressing just enough for traction, and pulled the face a little closer to him. He said, "That cut won't amount to anything, but your face is going to turn yellow when the blood drains out of the bruise." Bunny made a little grimace and shudder but didn't hurry away from his examination.

I had a fantasy that Thad and Bunny would fall in love. I imagined a whole new life for her, with a better type of people. She would stop teasing her hair and let it fall down shiny, a natural honey color, the same color as Thad's. She'd come to me one day and say, my happiness, Blair Ellen, I owe it all to you.

There was another motorcycle outside, and Bunny twisted out of her seat to see. "She's still got on that evening gown," she said. "Do you believe that? On a motorcycle?"

It was India on the back of Garland's bike with a length of white net tossed around her shoulders and neck. As we watched, she slid off and ran across the lot toward a car in the shadows by the garbage barrels.

"Whose car is that?" said Bunny. "Who's she meeting?" She rapped on the plate glass to get Garland's attention and he hesitated and then decided to come in.

"Ask Garland," I said.

"Sure I will. Fat chance he'd tell." Garland had come in and was standing just inside the door, taking a pack of cigarettes out of his pocket and running a hand through his hair. The thin black tie was still wind tossed back over one shoulder. "Hey Garland!" Bunny beckoned with more animation than usual. "Come and see my shiner!"

Garland stopped by Nuts Davis's table to share out cigarettes, then he came on to us, walking with a slouch, his pointed cowboy boots preceding his body. He ignored me and stood facing Thad and smoking. "How's that car holding up?"

"Well, sit down, Garland," said Bunny. "Take a load off."

The question was, who would sit where. Garland looked reluctant to sit beside Thad, and there was space by me, but that would put three on one side. Thad jumped up and took charge. "Bunny, stay where you are. Blair Ellen, you move over here with me."

There was something humiliating about being shifted around in this open way. Garland sneered a little as he slid in beside Bunny and he put his foot up on the bench and clasped his knee, so that his back was to Bunny and his profile to me and Thad.

Thad hopped up again. "I'm buying everyone something to drink," he said. "What'll you have?" He was being too hearty. I wished he would just sit down and hold still. In the fluorescent light his skin looked thin. I could see the veins in the back of his hands. Garland had red cheeks from the wind. Thad had a pimple developing at his hairline.

Garland said, "I can pay."

"No, I want to, I want to buy a Coke for everyone. Stay where you are."

As soon as he was gone, Bunny said, "He's really cute, Blair Ellen, and polite too. But in a masculine way. You know what I mean?"

"Do you two want to be alone?" said Garland. "I'll be glad to take a walk."

But Bunny obviously didn't want to be left without a boy

[149]

again, so she put her arm around his shoulder. "What happened, Garland, did India stand you up?"

He gave a further twist to his wide mouth. "I'm meeting her at the dance. The court has to be *presented*." Something funny was happening to me. Something about Bunny putting her arm around him. Something about his sulky face. Every little shrug and gesture he made was causing a ripple in me. A vibration through heavy fluid. That's just Garland Odell over there, I told myself. You've known him since he was a little, scrawny boy. He's still a little, scrawny boy, most of the time. Cowboy boots and the stuff he puts in his hair. Motorcycle grease most likely. *Thad* is here, I told myself. But Thad was the one who seemed ordinary and stale.

Bunny had a hand in Garland's hair, she was all over him. "But you're not India's date. Who's her date?"

He slumped low and sneered at me. My heart leaped. Was he jealous? Would he like to switch partners too? Bunny would be perfectly happy to. He said, "Bunny, what the hell happened to you? You're a real mess."

She pulled away from him. "She doesn't look so bad," I said.

"Oh yeah she does. She looks Godawful. But I'd lay money the other one looks worse. She looks Godawful, don't she, Mr. Impala?"

Thad was passing out Cokes. I wondered what he thought of Garland.

Bunny said, "Well, I'll tell you one thing, it wouldn't take much to look better than old Spinett." She pulled her knee up now and clasped it. Garland had a knee up too, and one arm laid out in front of us with his long nervous fingers moving from Coke cup to cigarette pack. The fingers were dusky on the sides, dirt, or shadows, or nicotine stains. Thad and I sat primly shoulder to shoulder sipping through straws. Garland balanced his straw on the tip of his finger.

Bunny said, "My face is starting to hurt."

"Get drunk," said Garland. "Then you won't feel it."

I giggled. I didn't mean to; I detested gigglers, but one slipped out. Bunny glanced at me defiantly, and said, "I don't know about getting drunk, but a beer would sure taste good. Of course Blair Ellen wouldn't approve."

Garland was looking at me too. "I don't have any beer, but I have something better. If anybody wants to go someplace, we can drink it."

Bunny said, "Come on, Blair Ellen, don't look like that. You get as big-eyed as—a cow or something. What the hell anyhow. Nothing worse can happen to me tonight."

I couldn't bear looking like a cow to Bunny, and I couldn't bear the way her face had gone flat and harsh and distant again. Garland had become distant too, but it wasn't just his face, it was his whole figure, as he stood up, small and slight, like a goblin. "Well, let's go," he said. "What are we waiting for?"

"Why don't we all go?" said Bunny.

But Thad was there too, a deep voice at my right side. "I think we'll pass it up this time, right, Blair Ellen?"

I said, as suddenly as I'd giggled, "Don't go, Bunny." Meaning, don't do it. Don't do the things that Mother says you'll do when you drink and lose control of yourself, and above all please don't do those things with Garland.

"Don't go?" said Bunny. "Don't go where? Where don't you want me to go?"

Garland was showing lots of teeth now, and he was touching Bunny. He put his whole hand flat on her back between her shoulders. "She means don't have fun."

"Do you want me to just sit and not do anything? I'm not interested in being bored."

"Let's go," said Garland.

"Shoot," said Bunny, shaking her head. The hair had come loose again, the bruised quadrant of her face was redder than before. She shook her whole self like a dog and walked out ahead of Garland. He went sideways, saying something to Nuts Davis as he passed, and I thought they were laughing at Bunny for her bruise and flying hair and for what she was going out to do with Garland.

I didn't move until the motorcycle had started and they were really gone. Then there was a dull weight on my hand, the one down on the seat beside me. "I was proud of you for trying to stop her."

I held very still again, braced now against a wave of anger at Thad. For touching me. And how dare he judge Bunny, and when he went ahead and said something about Garland, I thought, how dare he judge Garland either. Thad broke into irritating chunks around me, the hand on my hand, the voice.

"I think we'd better go to the dance," I said.

Garland showed up at the dance later without Bunny and escorted India and made a lot of jokes with people, and then he and India left. Lots more people wanted to be introduced to Thad, and we danced all the slow dances, and by the time we went home, I wasn't irritated anymore. I was ready to park under the elm tree at the head of Davis Street near the big apartments and we kissed a long time and passionately kneaded one another's backs. It wasn't like the summer, but it was interesting. It was perhaps more purely sexual than before because I didn't feel in love, and religion had nothing to do with it. When we got back to the house, Mother was waiting up with cocoa and melted cheese and crackers, and Thad talked easily, just as if we had not been kissing moments before. The next morning in church we sat shoulder to shoulder singing and I mixed up our voices and the warmth of our shoulders with the kissing the night before, and he asked me if I would come down to his prom in the spring and I said would he write more regularly, and yet, as soon as he'd driven away, I started thinking there was something wrong with him, and something even more wrong with me.

I rode to school with Mother and Daddy because I couldn't bear the sight of Bunny. I think I was afraid there would be hickeys like cigarette burns on her throat. I sat behind Mother with my face pressed to the glass, away from Hoovers' so I wouldn't even chance a glimpse of Bunny's umbrella. Daddy said, "Where's your friend Bunny Rabbit? Doesn't she want a ride out of the rain?" Mother rotated her head toward me. As far in the corner as I was, she still found me, turning slowly like a ruffled owl, fixing me with her eyes magnified by the glasses I hated her to wear in public. I shrank further, but felt her coming in through my cheekbones, penetrating to the hollows under my eyeballs with her wide, gray irises. Daddy saying, "What happened, did you and Bunny Rabbit have a fight?"

"No," I said, "of course not. I have a meeting. I have to get to school early."

The worst times that week were the hours I usually spent with Bunny, walking home after school, lunch period. I had the great good fortune, however, to be chosen by Gail Gordon for a lunch hour friend since Johnny Bardoline was officiating at the junior high intermural basketball tournaments. There were still horrible moments when I might run into Bunny, or Garland, in the hall. He wasn't as horrible to meet as she was. He was pretty much what he always had been, skinny, red, dangerous, and always changing. But the sight of Bunny at the end of the hall hurt me, made me feel broken open, the way she looked at me: like a fruit that seems intact but is soft and rotten on the inside. A couple of times I even spoke to Daddy or Mother in the hall so that, when Bunny passed, I could legitimately not notice her.

She had gym the period before I did, and I told Mrs. Atha that I had some class officer business to attend to and would she mind if I were late to gym from time to time. Sure, said Mrs. Atha, who was one of our class sponsors and glad to think things were being taken care of by the students, which meant less work for her. Take your time, she said. One day I dashed into the dressing room five minutes after class had already started and saw hanging over the door of one dressing cubicle a brassiere, lacy, and as full and uplifted in its emptiness as if Bunny herself were in it. I was sure it was one of hers, and I darted into a cubicle to wait for her to finish dressing. There was utter silence in the broad concrete room, and I finally got down on the floor and saw no feet anywhere down the line and went on to gym thinking that somewhere Bunny was walking around the school with her breasts sloshing under a sweater, her nipples drifting from side to side.

It was still on my mind that afternoon when I saw her hair coming up the stairwell, the tower of blonde with a patent leather clasp. I made a desperate left turn to a small landing with a few lockers and an entrance to the auditorium. "India?" I called. "India Odell! I've got to talk to you."

My assault was so sudden and unexpected that India jumped. I never had business with India, but she smiled when she saw who it was, as if she were pleased as always to see me.

[153]

"India," I said, "I've been meaning to ask you for the longest time. Have you heard anything about Evalina Crain? I mean, is she okay?"

Bunny passed. I felt the fullness behind me; I heard her feet hesitate, then go on. I leaned close to India, nodding encouragingly.

"Oh, sure," said India. "Evalina's fine. She's got a great big baby boy."

"Has she! What do you know?" Guilt washed over me. India thought I was really talking to her. She thought I really cared about Evalina. "I've been so bad. I had all these big plans to go visit her in the hospital and everything."

"She lives right near us," said India. "If you came up to our house, we could take you over."

"Would you really? That's really nice of you."

India was opening up before me. "You could come this weekend," she said. "You could even stay over at our house if you wanted to."

She opened up, and there was something squirming inside her too, I thought: she wants me for Garland. He had Bunny, and now he wants me. I never had been sure they were two separate people; I used to want them both, together, India and Garland. Her face was so bland, just a noncommittal smile that could mean anything. I believed anything of her, that she was pathetic and needy, that she would procure me for her brother.

"I couldn't go this weekend," I said. "But I'd really like to some other time."

The auditorium door opened, and Gail Gordon was shouting in her big voice, "Blair Ellen, Blair Ellen, we're doing it! Come in here! We're going to do it!"

"Some other time," I told India. "Really."

And she smiled back, just as sincere, just as phony as I was. "Okay," she said. "Whenever you want to."

A relief to run to Gail who was always clear, contemptible in some things, admirable in a few others. Always sure to call me on the phone only if Johnny weren't available, or if she needed a girl for some particular purpose. This time it was H.M.S. *Pinafore*. Mrs. Ellis, the chorus teacher, had been fluttering around talking about putting it on, and she finally decided to go ahead. Tryouts right away, rehearsals beginning after Christmas. I was elated; forget Bunny, I thought. Forget weird India and Garland. I had already been picking out songs on the piano, and I knew I wanted the part of Buttercup. Gail and I and the others made plans. The best costumes, terrific sets. The whole spring given over to this exciting thing. This important thing.

I was still thinking about it as I walked home alone. It was drizzling again, and suddenly I saw that I had walked too fast, I was catching up with Bunny. I saw her at the bottom of the hill, no umbrella, a tan raincoat, black flats, and stockings with seams. A sort of dreamy idea came to me: I would combine everything at once, make up with Bunny, do good. I would save her by having her try out for *Pinafore*, and she would discover a great talent, dancing or singing, and go on and become a star of musical comedy in New York City. We'd meet there one day and she would say, Blair Ellen, this is thanks to you.

Bunny turned off to walk through the alley. Usually I was the one who liked to take the alley and Bunny wanted to go through town and see the windows at the Clothes Horse and who was hanging out at the poolroom. I had to decide whether to go after her, because she would be sure to hear me in the empty alley. I thought, well why not? and started running. "Bunny! Wait up! Don't you want to share an umbrella?"

She spun around and I stopped. She was carrying *Modern Literature* pressed to her chest, and a thin line of mascara was trickling from the outer corner of each eye. I said, "Your mascara's running down your face."

"Where?" She rooted in her pocket for a Kleenex, and I pointed while she rubbed. "Did I get it all?"

"You're still a little gray in the cheeks."

She scrubbed some more, squinting and frowning in my face as if I were a mirror. Meanwhile, the rain picked up and I tried to hold the umbrella over us both, and the angle hurt my arm. She said, "Oh, let me carry it, Shorty." We bumped a few times because the alley was rough with its old brick paving, and maybe we'd lost the rhythm of walking together. She said, "Well, what decided you to lower yourself to walk with me?"

I was a little disappointed that she was so willing to make up. I said, "I've had a lot of meetings. Before school and after school and at lunch time—"

"I waited at the house Monday morning and you never showed. I was late."

A giddy rush of guilt, blood draining from my head, my feet growing heavy. Whatever she did with Garland, I didn't know anything for sure—I had no right to leave her hanging like that. I said, "We've been planning the H.M.S. *Pinafore*. You know, the musical." My voice sounded small and whiny. She said nothing. I said, "I wasn't *mad*, Bunny."

"Ha!"

It seemed vitally important that she not know how confused and hurt I'd been. I really wasn't angry! I thought. Why would I have been angry? I said, "I just didn't understand why you went off with Garland that night."

She gave me a full face stare. "So it *is* that. I can't believe you. You were sitting there with Thad having the time of your life, and you wanted Garland too! You want everything and everybody, don't you? How was I supposed to know? You never said so. You told me you didn't care a thing about Garland. Well, my Lord, Blair Ellen. How was I supposed to know you wanted him too?"

"I didn't! I didn't want Garland. I wanted you to—I didn't want you to—get in trouble."

We were just at the end of the alley. You have to walk along the highway for a block to get to Davis Street. There were a lot of cars passing and little kids in slickers waiting for the crossing guard. Bunny stopped right where we were and faced off again, and, since she had the umbrella, I was left standing in the rain.

"Listen, Blair Ellen, what I do is none of your goddamn business. And I don't care if I do curse. What do you think I am anyhow? And what do you think you are, the Virgin Mary?"

"I didn't mean that. I didn't mean I thought you did *that*." Rain was flattening my bangs and water running down my forehead into my eyes. Didn't she see I was practically drowning? And I was lying of course, I did mean exactly that, although now I was thinking it was all my suspicious guilty mind, and it became important to convince her that I had not meant that. "I was worried about driving and drinking."

She shook her head. "You and Don Hagen should get together. All I did was go for a ride with Garland Odell. It's none of your business or Don's either. He came looking for me that night, you know. He was going to beat up Garland, only I was already at home in my robe watching television." She made a sour little mouth. "I don't know why I'm telling you anything. You go around calling me a whore—"

"I do not! I never!" I could be righteous about that because I certainly didn't use the word. I almost never even *thought* the word. "I never said that and you know it."

"Well, you meant it."

"I did not!"

She looked at me, and then rolled her eyes away. "What are you doing out there getting wet in the rain, stupid." So I went back under and we walked on across the highway and turned slowly down Davis Street where the oak trees were dripping black. She said, "Garland tried to get me to drink some awful homemade rotgut liquor his friends make. I wouldn't touch that stuff for anything. You couldn't pay me to drink that stuff. He's really wild; he's not your type, you know."

It warmed my insides that Bunny was taking care of me. "I never said he was. I used to play with him, that's all."

"Well, don't change your mind. Stick with Thad."

Guilt again; I felt a million miles distant from Thad. I was glad he was gone. More interested in the sullen look in Bunny's mouth. "Did Don get over being mad?"

She shrugged. "I'm getting tired of that nonsense," she said.

We were passing an old mansion that had once been bigger and finer than anything on the street where Gail Gordon lived now, but it had been broken up into apartments. People's washing hung across the upstairs porch, and a tricycle and a toy wagon were rusting in the rain. Several little kids ran into the mansion ahead of us, and a mother met her little boy on the downstairs porch and seized his shoulders. "Where's your slicker?" she shouted. "What did you do with your coat you little dummy?" He started to cry, and she shook him. "Stop whimpering; I'll give you something to cry about." Then she noticed us, and dragged him inside.

"You know what I'm going to do?" said Bunny. "I've had it with that school, and all those girls whispering, and those teachers treating you like dirt. I've had it with this town. I'm going to get married."

"Oh, that's a great idea. Who's the lucky man? Don Hagen?"

She shrugged, as if she didn't care one way or the other. "Not Don. I don't think."

"You'd have ten kids and end up sitting around all day watching television."

"You don't have to have kids if you don't want them."

"I know. Birth control." Actually I didn't know the details at all, and I tried to think of a way to work the conversation around to where she would explain it without my showing ignorance, but we were already home, crunching gravel, splashing. I didn't believe the stuff about her getting married—I mean we were only *teen-agers*—but there was still no telling what she would do in a mood like this. I decided I had better go over after dinner and talk her into trying out for *Pinafore*.

But Bunny refused to have anything to do with the musical. She couldn't sing, she said, and she thought the whole thing was stupid. Besides, she once had a run-in with Mrs. Ellis. It was in her study hall, said Bunny, and she hates the sight of me. I'd known Mrs. Ellis for years because she went to our church too, and Mother's always said she was one of the funniest people she knew. I couldn't believe she hated anyone. People took chorus to get their grade point raised and her English classes were supposed to be the easiest in the school. I said, but Bunny even if you did have a run-in with her, if you're good enough, she'll have to put you in the play. Ha, said Bunny, what century were you born in?

The day before the preliminary tryouts, I was still trying to convince her. We stood around the driveway talking so long that I was later than usual getting into the house, and to my surprise Mother and Daddy were still at the table, sloshing a little cold coffee in the bottom of their cups. Mother never stayed at the table; she always hopped up to do something about dinner.

"Oh," I said, "I missed coffee. You didn't have to wait."

"We saw you standing out there talking to Bunny," said Mother. "There's a piece of pound cake left. Daddy ate Oreos so you could have it."

I wasn't hungry, but Daddy had made a sacrifice, so I sat down to the slice of pound cake, and Mother made me a cup of half-milk half-coffee, something she hadn't done in a long time, and Daddy pushed his chair back enough to put one ankle on the other knee and get out his pipe for a smoke. He never smoked at the table either. They had something to talk to me about. My stomach took a little half-screw of a churn.

After they had sat in their chairs quietly watching me for a while, Mother said, "I hear Francie Ellis wants you to play the piano for the play."

"She asked me to, but I said I was going to try out for a part. There are lots of parts. I'll even take a sailor if I have to. The sailors get to do great dances."

Mother looked into her coffee cup, and Daddy blew some smoke toward the ceiling and watched it rise. Was the bad news about them or me? I must be the victim, judging from the respectful way they were listening to whatever I said. Mother said, "Playing the piano is awfully important for a musical. though. I guess it's an honor for her to ask you."

"Not really. She just wants someone dependable."

"Sometimes," said Mother, looking at the ceiling along with Daddy, "sometimes there is a responsibility for the greater good."

He said, "If it was up to me, we wouldn't be wasting all this energy on plays. I mean, they have the senior class play already. Why does Francie Ellis want to stir everything up anyhow?" Mother's eyes became enormous. Daddy said, "If I were you, Blair Ellen, I'd just play the piano and be done with it and not cause a fuss."

It began to come through then, like a greasy glare of sunlight through fog. "But I don't want to play the piano. I already told Mrs. Ellis. We're having open tryouts, and I'm going to try out. If I'm not good enough for a big part, I'll be a sailor."

Mother said, "Mrs. Ellis told me to tell you she isn't going to give you a singing part. She wants you to play the piano. She asked me to explain."

The two of them seemed to grow enormous, like huge primitive statues. I had to stand up and put my chair between me and them. "That isn't fair," I said. "She's having open tryouts. If she's having open tryouts they have to be open to me too."

"Now, Blair Ellen," said Daddy. "High school is not a democracy; high school is a benevolent dictatorship. And when the kids get too smart, it gets less benevolent."

Mother said, "Think of it as a compliment to your musical abilities."

I said, "I'm not the only one who can play the piano. She just figures I'm the kind of person who'll sit there and go over and over the same old piece till doomsday." I couldn't begin to express how cramped it would be. Worse than practicing. I saw darkness in the auditorium; I saw myself connected by a neck noose to Mrs. Ellis. I had imagined the play as a great burst of dance movement and voice freedom. They all wanted to shackle me off to one side, in the shadows. "It's an extracurricular activity," I said. "I don't have to do it. I don't have to be in it at all."

"Oh, that's smart," said Daddy. "That will fix your reputation with the teachers all right. You have to have recommendations, you know. You can't apply to college and use your mother and father for references."

Mother said, "The point is whether or not she's willing to cooperate."

"You don't care about me," I said. "You both just care about what Francine Ellis thinks of your daughter. This is worse than a dictatorship. This is blackmail." I could feel myself looking foolish again, going too far. I started for my bedroom. "Will you all take away my A in English? Will I get kept back this year?" I hurried away before I went any further, before they had to discipline me.

I heard Daddy say, "There she goes off the deep end again. Why can't she stay calm for fifteen minutes?"

And Mother said, "Shhh."

For once I didn't fall asleep and wake up free of fury. This time I stayed awake and righteous. I might have gone too far; I might be overreacting; but Mrs. Ellis had no right. I did my algebra homework in double quick time with my mind not wandering at all, and every once in a while I would look up and stare at the wall and think how right Bunny had been. She's always known, I thought bitterly. She's always known how the world is.

They called me to dinner; we three back at the table again. Mother said, "I was going to boil the potatoes but I had a little bacon fat, so I fried them for you, Blair Ellen."

"Thank you," I said with my voice low and musical.

"Me too," said Daddy. "Thank you for me. I love fried potatoes. I guess Blair Ellen inherited it from me all right."

Mother passed the cube steak and the green beans and said, "Gail Gordon plays piano doesn't she? It seems like a lot of music for one person to learn."

"That Gilbert and Sullivan music," Daddy said, as if I might not know what she meant.

"Blair Ellen does have her Rachmaninoff to work on for the recital."

There was a small ray, a little hope. I said, "Not to mention the Christmas music at church. And they asked me to play for the junior choir too. Of course that music is pretty simple."

"Still," said Mother. "You have a lot, when you add up everything."

I started watching for a flicker in her cheek, for a raised eyebrow.

"What time are those tryouts tomorrow? After school? I guess there'll be a lot of rehearsals after school too, won't there? We wouldn't want her school work suffering, would we, Lloyd?"

He dumped the rest of the fried potatoes on my plate without asking if I wanted them. "Absolutely not. That's the one thing you can't fool around with on college applications."

I almost didn't breathe. It was as if this time they thought I was right. No, they really *did* think I was right. Mother was going to take care of everything. She was going to talk to Francie Ellis, she said, and get her to divide up the music so it wouldn't be too much for me. Daddy even came up with the idea of having the piano onstage so that Gail and I, or whoever did the piano playing, could be musicians and sailors too. I couldn't believe he had thought of that himself, and that was actually how we did do it, in the end, with the singers sometimes leaning their elbows on the back of the piano like nightclub performers, and once someone even sat on it for a little while.

But most of the excitement with the play was after Christmas; before Christmas it was just talk, trying to talk Bunny into trying out, and Bunny brushing me off, and me finding out why: that she had something underway that she thought was more exciting than the "H.M.S. *Pinafore*."

That Christmas holiday began with my complete absorption in a book I pulled off the shelf at the Women's Club Library, a grim, dusty-magenta old volume that had been checked out many times, but not once since 1958. This gave me the sense that I had discovered the book, even though it must have been at least vaguely famous to have been translated from the Russian. The name of the book was *Crime and Punishment*, and I took it out thinking it was a prison novel, perhaps on the lines of *Andersonville*, but the horrors would have to be even worse, I thought, if it took place in Russia. Almost as soon as I started reading it, the name Dostoyevsky seemed to be popping up everywhere, in *Time* magazine, in other books, even once on the "Tonight Show." The name was often linked with Tolstoy's, although for several months, until I discovered *War and Peace*, I thought Tolstoy was a revolutionary with glasses and a goatee.

Between total immersions in the book, I accused Mother of not having prepared me properly, of not having the right books in the home for my education. I've heard of Dostoyevsky, she said; and Tolstoy too. But I went to a teacher's college during the Depression. I was supposed to learn American literature and techniques for teaching grammar. We were lucky to get Shakespeare.

Still, I blamed her whenever I lost the thread of the prose. Sometimes I wouldn't know what was going on for two or three pages, and I would go into a blind rage at my ignorance, at how she had taught me nothing I really needed. Finally I would sink in again, under the surface, and only come up again when Mother called me to come and chop eggs for the tunafish salad, or when Daddy tapped on my door wanting a hand installing the new bathroom heater. Then I would walk through the house carefully, touching the walls with my fingertips for balance, because they seemed to curve in toward the ceiling, and the shadows to grow deeper as I passed, hastily concealing crevices packed with enemies hunting for me.

The few other things I did before Christmas were colored by that book: a party at Gail Gordon's where Gail, Johnny, and I were the only local people, and everyone else was a country club friend of hers from Graysburg. I sat in a corner sneering cynically at the bustle and color, but I spoke easily to anyone who came up to me, because I despised them so much. One short boy told me nasty stories about how all of his teachers were queers, and Gail called me over and said this little guy had an enormous crush on me and wanted to ask me out and have my phone number and buy me a Christmas present. I laughed in her face. I had a wonderful time at that party, and even, on the following days, enjoyed tree trimming and cookie baking, but all the while, like a miracle, my true self was Raskolnikov, peering out through sooty lavender-ringed eyes.

On Christmas Eve we got back from church and I stood around in my blue wool princess waiting for something to happen. Daddy changed clothes right away and went out to his workshop to get colored bulbs to replace the burnt out ones on the evergreens, and Mother went to the kitchen to make pies to take to Buckhannon tomorrow where we were going to have dinner with Aunt Pearl. She and her husband had come down from New Jersey for the holiday, but they were spending it with *his* family in Buckhannon instead of with us.

Their activities surrounded me: the sound of the garage door opening, Mother singing "Hark! the Herald Angels" in the kitchen. The furnace went on with a gentle puff of warm air on my ankles. Here at the center was darkness, a disembodied place; the breath of the pine tree, the colored lights and reflecting Christmas balls seemed strung across space and emptiness. What was I doing here? I thought. Mother and Daddy always so busy and content here in the house, but for me this strange dark emptiness, a waiting, as if what was real would start later. I wanted something: a call from Thad or even from Gail's friend with the crush on me. Something evil or something good.

Someone knocked on the door, and I filled with breath, convinced it would be Thad; that he had hitchhiked up to be with me at this moment. I pulled the door wide open, let in a big bubble of cold air, and there stood Bunny with her head wrapped in a pink wool scarf. "I brought your present," she said, thrusting it at me, something medium-sized with a stiff department store ribbon top. "I have to get back and roll my hair."

"Well, you can come in for a minute and let me give you yours." She wasn't Thad, but she always brought a little excitement. Besides, I felt bad because she'd been trying to get me to go shopping with her all week, and I had preferred to stay home and read.

Mother called through the breakfast bar, "Who is it? Come on in, Bunny, I just put on some cocoa. You and Blair Ellen go sit by the tree."

We had a huge, wide-spreading tree that year. Mother and I always chose a big one, and Daddy always complained that it was too big for a ranch house, and then he would spend a couple of hours shortening and shaping it until it was just the way he wanted it. This one had seemed to get bigger and bigger as the branches settled and spread out. It hid most of the window and had begun to envelop the piano. Bunny squatted in front of it and tipped her head to one side like a chubby little toddler girl. She sighed, and I noticed the pine scent again, as if her breath had caused it to move.

She said, "You always get the best trees. We buy these little old scrawny things with the needles falling off, but not you. You get trees that could last forever."

"This one's too big," I said. "We had to buy an extra string of lights." I hoped Bunny wasn't going to turn sentimental just because it was Christmas.

Mother came in then with a tray. She planned Christmas for weeks in advance. She made things to hang from the ceiling out of lampshade frames and tinsel, and she made edible molasses and popcorn centerpieces in the shape of trees or reindeer. She brought out her special Christmas cups and dessert plates with a holly pattern all over, three sugar cookies for each of us, individually decorated with food coloring and silver bits: a bell, a

Santa, a star. Bunny put the plate on her knee and sighed again.

"I'm glad you dropped over, Bunny," said Mother. "People have lost the tradition of Christmas visiting, and I think it's a dirty shame. People do nothing anymore but watch television."

"Yes, ma'am," said Bunny. "That's all those kids in my house ever do."

Mother sat beside Bunny on the couch and poured cocoa from the silver pot. "Poor Blair Ellen," she said. "Poor Blair Ellen doesn't have any brothers or sisters. I often think we should have had one for her. I don't know what I would have done without my sister Pearl when I was growing up."

I decided to sit on the floor at the coffee table in order to look up at them. Bunny was admiring Mother's plates and cookies and decorations.

Mother started telling about the wonderful homemade fun she and Pearl used to have, how they had strung popcorn because that was all they had to decorate the tree, and of course they had to cut their own tree in those days, just the two of them, because Grandpa Blair had had to go way down to Tennessee to find work.

I said, "Tell about the Christmas when you got coal and sticks in your stocking instead of gifts."

"Well," said Mother. "It *was* hard times. It was the Depression. It wasn't like now. We had almost nothing to eat that whole year but buttermilk and potatoes. We had plenty of that, but no variety. I still dream of the taste of that buttermilk. It wasn't like the stuff they sell in the containers now."

"But tell about the Christmas when Grandpa Blair had to go away and you and Aunt Pearl lived with the witch."

"She wasn't a witch," said Mother, "and I won't say her name because she still lives here in town. That was the year my father got a job with a logging company in Tennessee, and Pearl and I moved in with the lady. We had to break up housekeeping. That lady was good and clean, and she did the best she could for us, but she was as poor as we were, and she said from the very beginning that if we weren't good we'd get lumps of coal in our stockings."

Mother wasn't really in the mood to tell the story, I could tell.

It was a Christmas story, but not a happy one. She kept smiling at Bunny, who nibbled around the edges of the cookies. She left out all the witchy parts, about how half the time they got sent to bed with no supper at all, and how they kept each other's spirits up by saying Papa Blair'd be back for Christmas with all the toys they could ask.

"Well," said Mother, "as it turned out, there was a whole box of presents coming for us on the B & O, but the car they were in got sidetracked for a couple of days so they were late."

She really had spoiled it, I thought. Nothing about how horrible it was to feel your stocking from the outside and tell yourself it only *felt* like coal in there, and it was really presents, and then to dump out the stocking and there was nothing but lumps of slag and coal dust on your fingers.

"You may have got your presents," I said, "but you know Christmas presents aren't the same if they don't come by Christmas."

Mother shrugged. "We lived through it. I expect we're better people now for having suffered and struggled."

Bunny said, "I'm always going to have a big tree. Wherever I am, I am going to have a big tree like yours." There was something strange about Bunny; her eyes were wide, and she seemed to be impressed by everything; Bunny, who was never surprised. She had a pink glow, and her shadows were blue and green. What's the matter with her, I thought.

Mother got up to make Daddy's coffee and finish the pies, her face all alight with holiday happiness. "Now you stay awhile, Bunny," she said. "You stay as long as you can. I just like knowing there are visitors here."

Bunny kept her face toward the kitchen for a long time. "I never knew how nice your mother was. I used to think she was strict all the time just because she's a teacher. I used to think—"

She paused, and I nodded. Yes? Yes? I loved Bunny's elaborations. It didn't matter whether she was describing a dress she'd seen or telling something stupid one of her enemies had done, she could talk on and on in a peculiarly uninflected tone, amassing details that never bored me. Finally I said, "Used to think what?"

"Oh, never mind. You know. Live and learn."

"Live and learn!" I said. "What is that supposed to mean?"

She was sunk in this strange quietude, low on the couch, smaller and softer than I'd ever seen her. She stirred and set down her cup and plate on the table. "Open your present," she said.

"If you'll open yours." I handed it to her, and she held it on her lap. I had done hers up in green foil with three foil snowflakes I had cut out of scraps, one green, one red, and one gold, all overlapping.

She said, "You are so good at things, just like your mother. You can make something pretty out of nothing. And you have good taste."

In fact, the present inside the foil and snowflakes was in rather poor taste. I had chosen it as the kind of thing I thought Bunny would like: a cologne and bath powder set called Thousands of Roses with the powder cover and cologne bottle molded in the shape of a pile of blowsy pink roses. I had thought it was just right for Bunny.

She said, "I don't want to mess up the package yet. Open yours first."

She had bought me a compact and mirror with different colors of metal, brass and copper and a little silver, impressed in a pattern of branches and leaves, very delicate, very expensive. I would have had to guess ten dollars or better. "But Bunny," I said, "you talk about good taste—this is about as pretty as anything I've ever seen. But what I got you—it's so cheap in comparison."

"That's okay. I wanted to get you something to remember." She leaned over and took the compact from me and touched its incised surface and nodded at it. "You won't forget this, will you?" And while I was saying how great it was, and how awful mine to her was, and would she please open it and get it over with, she looked at herself in the compact mirror and made a face. "No, I don't think I'm going to open yours yet. It'll be okay, Blair Ellen, I love the way you wrapped it. I've got to do my hair."

At the door I asked her who was coming over tonight, Don Hagen or Jimmy Minard. It had been pretty lively over at Hoovers' the last few days, with Jimmy on leave from the Navy, and either his Chevrolet or Don Hagen's pickup or even both together parked in the driveway all the time.

"Jimmy," she said, glancing toward the kitchen where Mother was singing again.

I said, "Don't go till I show Mother the compact."

"No, show her later. And tell her thank you for the cocoa and cookies." She opened the door, hesitated, seemed to be thinking. "Tell her I really appreciated the cocoa and cookies. And thank you for the present." She was out the door now. "And please wish Mr. Morgan Merry Christmas for me. And you and your mother too. Okay?"

A large-flaked wet snow had been falling since she came over. It was sticking high on top of the old dried grass, and Bunny made black footprints across the yard. Even though her hair was wet and she hadn't worn a coat, she didn't hurry and didn't huddle against the cold. I wished I had a boyfriend coming tonight. Anyone. The creepy little guy from Graysburg. Don Hagen, if Bunny didn't need him. I imagined sneaking into Bunny's house and hiding behind her couch tonight to watch her neck with Jimmy Minard.

We had a tradition at our house of eating fruitcake and coffee on Christmas morning. When I was little I used to wake up before dawn to see what Santa Claus had brought me, and I always got the adults up too, Mother and Daddy and, for many Christmases, Aunt Pearl and Uncle Joe as well. Mother always made coffee and cut everyone a little piece of fruitcake to keep them awake until I was finished, and then they would all go back to sleep while I played alone with my new toys. Later they got up again and we had a real breakfast. Christmas used to be exciting, so endlessly exciting. I would have been happy with a real breakfast now, to get the presents over and get on to whatever boring things we were doing, but Mother still cut the fruitcake and she and Daddy nibbled and said remember when Blair Ellen got up before sunrise. Remember when Blair Ellen was afraid Santa had forgotten her. We chewed nuts and candied pineapple at eight-thirty in the morning, and I looked out the window at the snow that had turned gray and was washing away in a mean rain.

There was a movement at Hoovers', and Kim came out, running, wearing that maroon winter coat of hers that I hated so much, too short, with the fake fur collar and buttons. Her legs were getting longer and longer, and her cheeks and forehead were breaking out. I hadn't bought her anything for Christmas. I just hadn't thought of it. I tried to think of what present of mine I could rewrap quickly and give her.

But it didn't matter; she wasn't bringing me anything either. She walked right past me, without an invitation, and went toward Mother and Daddy. "Hello, Mrs. Morgan, hello, Mr. Morgan. My mother wants to know if we can borrow your big electric coffeepot and can Blair Ellen come over and talk to Mom because Bunny ran off last night." She looked at each one of us in turn, to see what effect she'd made. Daddy pulled his robe more tightly over his crossed legs and sucked on his dead pipe. Mother sprang to her feet and wrinkled her forehead.

"Oh, no," she said, putting on her death-in-the-family face. "Sit down, Kim. Take her coat, Blair Ellen. I'll have to rinse out the coffeepot. Give her a piece of fruitcake."

I said, "She ran off with Jimmy Minard? Bunny's getting married?"

Kim nodded. "That's the best we can hope for, Mom says. They had it all planned, she had her suitcase packed and we never even knew it."

"I'll bet Don Hagen is going to throw a fit."

"They're probably halfway to Virginia by now. She waited till 12:00 midnight so Mom would just be starting home from the nursing home. I was sitting watching television with Jimmy, and I thought Bunny had gone to the bathroom or something, and all of a sudden she comes down the stairs with two big suitcases and her make-up case. She was wearing her new pink sweater and slacks set that Jimmy got her, and she stood there as big as life and said, "Well, Kim, this is it, I'm going.""

"Poor Mrs. Hoover," said Mother, rinsing out the coffeepot. "Bunny was just here last night."

"She never said a *word*," I said.

"Nobody knew. She even invited Don for Christmas dinner."

Mother cut one of the mince pies for Buckhannon and gave Kim a piece on top of the fruitcake and a glass of milk.

"Thanks," said Kim. "Things are pretty crazy over there. Nobody got breakfast. Mom's in bed with a sick headache, but she figures people will start coming over pretty soon to find out what happened, and that's what we need the coffeepot for." Daddy sucked and shook his head, and Mother made more sympathetic noises, so Kim went on as she ate. "Bunny was supposed to cook dinner so Mom could sleep in after working the late shift, but it turns out Bunny used the money for the turkey to buy some extra clothes and stuff, so now we don't even have Christmas dinner."

Bit by bit I was beginning to think it over. My compact was their turkey, I thought, and why hadn't I noticed a thing last night. Maybe Bunny had even wanted to tell me, and I had been too insensitive. Bunny was just about the best friend I ever had, and she couldn't even tell me she was getting married.

"Now, Kim," said Mother, "I'm getting a bag here and putting the coffeepot in, and I'm going to stick in a picnic ham we have in the refrigerator, and some pineapple, just to make it a little festive."

"You're giving them a ham?" said Daddy.

Mother gave him a look. "And here's a can of sweet potatoes and you may as well take this box of scalloped potatoes too. I'd give you one of the pies, but we promised them to Pearl's in-laws. Blair Ellen, put on some clothes and go over and talk to Mrs. Hoover."

Mother kept stopping us at the door with more things, little packages of homemade fudge for the boys, a can of green beans. When we got outside I said, "She acts like it's a funeral."

Kim said, "You think it isn't? Wait till Don catches up to them."

To my surprise, their kitchen was clean, as if Bunny had done everything one last time before she left. On the table, an open loaf of bread, and a jar of peanut butter. Otherwise the kitchen was cold and dark. No cooking going on here, I thought. In the living room the unlit tree seemed to have curled up in the corner. Robbie and Rusty were watching cartoons as if it were an ordinary Saturday morning. Robbie was holding a big fire engine in his arms, Rusty a plastic machine gun.

Robbie saw me first. "Hey, Blair Ellen, Bunny eloped!"

"So I hear."

"She joined the navy," said Rusty, and he began to sing. "She joined the na-vy to see the world! and what'd she see, she saw the sea!"

"She did not," said Robbie, kicking Rusty. "She eloped!"

Kim shook her head and pursed her lips. "We don't know what we're going to do with these two. Only Bunny can handle them."

Mrs. Hoover used the old sunporch on the main floor for her bedroom. It had always been the best room in the house when we lived there, and it was the room I always remembered, along with my bedroom. Daddy's pipe rack had been there, and Mother and I used to spend all our days there, especially when I was really little, before she went back to teaching. I used to play in the middle of the floor, while she did a dozen things around. It was the room where we kept the Christmas tree, I thought with a deep sense of things that had slipped away. We all ate our Christmas fruitcake there. Mrs. Hoover hadn't done anything so awful to the room; she'd let a Venetian blind just hang crooked after its tape tore, and the maple floor was scuffed, but mostly it was just the room was full of Mrs. Hoover instead of us. She had three bureaus sitting around, with a portable television on one of them and in the center of the room was her four-poster bed in which she was lying, propped up on pillows, wearing a peach satin bed jacket, of the kind they used to buy ladies when they were going to the hospital to have a baby. She was just lying there with her hands folded, listening to a choir on television sing Christmas music. Actually, she looked better than usual with her stomach hidden and a ribbon in her hair.

"It's in the kitchen," said Kim.

"Well, start it perking," said Mrs. Hoover.

"We don't have any coffee."

"You mean to tell me you went all the way over there and borrowed the coffeepot and didn't borrow any coffee?"

Kim started to whine. "You didn't say to, and she sent all this other stuff—"

I said, "For your Christmas dinner. A picnic ham and beans and potatoes—"

Mrs. Hoover stared at me for a long time. "Well, that was awfully nice of Mrs. Morgan. Put the oven on and then run back and borrow some coffee while I talk to Blair Ellen." She kept her face still the way Bunny used to, and then, all of a sudden, she would flash something, a big grin this time.

"That will be all the Christmas dinner we get," she said. "Hand me that emery board, will you, Blair Ellen?" she said. "My nails get so beat up in that nursing home. You have to wash your hands every five minutes." She spread a Kleenex over her covers to catch the fingernail dust and started sawing away. I leaned against the door jamb. "Well, Blair Ellen, the only one of my kids with sense to come in out of the rain, and she just ran away. I guess she didn't have as much sense as I thought."

I had no idea what she wanted from me. "Bunny'll be all right, Mrs. Hoover. She's very adult for her age."

"Seventeen years of living with a child, and then she up and runs out on you."

"She can finish high school some other way. She can take high school equivalency."

"She never will. She's just like me. I did the same thing to my mother, walked off and left her with a houseful of kids, and one morning I woke up and here I was, with a houseful of my own."

I almost told her that Bunny knew about birth control, but I wanted to be careful. I said, "You still have Kim."

"Kim's as bad as those boys three-quarters of the time. All she does from morning till night is twirl a baton. I'll have to hire someone to watch all three of them, and it's all I can do to buy them shoes."

Maybe it was the rent, I thought. Maybe she wants me to feel sorry and talk Mother into reducing the rent, and then I said, Blair Ellen, what a terrible, suspicious thing to think when she just lost her favorite daughter. And then I thought of what I had lost, and I saw it as places she wouldn't be: not lying on the lounge in a bathing suit all summer; not coming out her back door miraculously just at the moment I came out our front door so we could walk to school together; not in the girls' room at school leaning her bare belly on the sink after gym so she could see herself up close in the mirror and stroke on mascara.

But she'll be back, I thought. It's not like she's dead. She'll be smoking a cigarette and telling me all about the navy, and the details of birth control maybe, now that she was married and supposed to know. I could ask her directly: could you show me one? She might even invite me down for a weekend and I'd have a date with a sailor. I had refused last summer, but I was braver now. I wanted real experiences too. Maybe not to run away and get married, but I wanted something outside my house. What would it be without Bunny?

Suddenly Mrs. Hoover leaned toward me. "Why did she do it, Blair Ellen?" I was going to say for real life, for her own experience, but Mrs. Hoover added, "Was she pregnant? Did she say she was pregnant?"

I stood tall. "Mrs. Hoover, I am sure Bunny wasn't pregnant. Absolutely sure."

She dropped back against the pillows. "She better not be. She better not show up here in six months and dump a baby on me."

I was about to say in a ringing voice that Bunny was not pregnant and furthermore she would never dump a baby on someone, when there was a bellowing and stomping in the front of the house, and in ran Rusty and Robbie in their print flannel pajamas. They ran to the bed and threw themselves at their mother, one on either side. Then came Kim screaming, "He knocked the ham on the floor! Ma—the ham's on the floor!" And behind her, Don Hagen in his blue policeman pants and a high school sweat shirt with cut off sleeves.

His gun was still strapped low, down below his beer belly, no metal in sight, but the bulky leather pack caused an effect in me, caused my head to get very clear, then very distant, and I edged along the wall.

Don's face was twisted into balls, and the cheek-balls had squeezed his eyes shut. He screamed, "Goddam it, Betty, you didn't call me, why didn't you goddam call me when you knew it?" and he kicked the foot of the bed.

Mrs. Hoover, in her peach bed jacket, laid one hand each on the head of Robbie and Rusty and lifted her chin so high it didn't look double at all. She looked more like Bunny than ever. "Because you would of done something stupid," she said. "You would of done something stupid like coming into my bedroom and scaring my children."

He kicked the bed again, but not so hard. "I would have stopped her from running off with that goddam tightpants sailor, that's what I would of done, goddam it, why didn't you *tell* me?"

I felt the door jamb behind me and felt safer, able to escape if anything worse happened, but Don seemed to be softening up, getting blubbery. He grabbed hold of a bedpost and pressed his forehead into it.

Kim, hanging onto a post at the opposite end, said, "That ham was all we had for Christmas dinner."

Don banged his head once on the post. "I'll wash the ham. I'll take you out to Christmas dinner. *She* invited me."

"Well," I said, somehow more alarmed by his maudlin-muffled voice than by the bed kicking. "I must be going. Merry Christmas, Mrs. Hoover, Merry Christmas, Kim. And Robbie and Rusty." I was going to ignore Don, but I said, "You too," and ran away without knowing if he had heard or not.

At the kitchen door I stopped running. No need to scare Mother and Daddy. I didn't want to lose all the Hoovers.

In the spring, as soon as *Pinafore* was over, we started planning the junior senior prom. Ordinarily the class president would have done the organizing along with the sponsors, but Johnny Bardoline had baseball practice, and Mrs. Atha didn't want to do anything she didn't have to, so the responsibility fell on me. I was delighted; I was going to show the class they should have elected me president in the first place. I set up meetings and called committee members out of class to confer, and I phoned hotels with ballrooms for price lists. I never went to gym anymore, and rarely to American history, which Coach taught straight from the book. I did go to English, because I didn't want to have to give Mother my prepared speech about the educational value of organizing a prom. I'm ambitious, I thought, but I'm doing it for the good of the class. I want our class to have the best prom ever. Sometimes I wrote myself little moral essays: "Work hard for the good of All," I told myself, "But keep up your grades. Don't lose your perspective. It's only a prom, not one of the Really Important Things. Don't worry about things like elections and having a boyfriend. There's plenty of time for boyfriends later in life."

I had to include that, because I hadn't heard from Thad in weeks. Our relationship had shrunk to a tiny pencil beam of light, and that was wavering. I was somewhat comforted by nightly phone calls from Gail's friend Wray. He wanted to take me out, and I explained it was impossible, I had this guy in Charleston, and also I was too busy with school just now to date. Wray's wonderful persistence kept me from getting depressed on Saturday nights at home with my parents. I didn't scream that I was suffocating, because I knew I could have been on a date with Wray. Sometimes I imagined Wray at his house, grinding his teeth over the quietness, over the soft-lit cotton waddedness of home, where nothing ever happens. Sometimes I would slip above my body, and peer into all the houses and I'd see people who went steady like Gail and Johnny sitting on a couch looking bored and watching "Gunsmoke," just like Daddy.

So I had my sense of perspective pretty well in hand, all things considered, until one day at the end of April when Mrs. Atha came into the dressing room after gym. As a rule we were safe from teachers in there unless someone was smoking, and no one had done that since Bunny left. I was sitting on a bench in my underwear, letting my sweat dry and enjoying being quiet, just listening to the voices gossip about who had a fight with her boyfriend and who might be pregnant. I smiled to myself, because there had been a time when I would have felt sick to hear that, but it was just mildly interesting now. I even closed my eyes for a couple of seconds, and that was when the violation occurred.

There was a brief silence near the sinks and the door, and when I looked, Mrs. Atha was charging up the steps, whistle bouncing on the Florida-tanned V of chest. "Where's Blair Ellen?" she said, and I jumped up, pulling my blouse in front of me. "Blair Ellen, listen, I almost forgot. What about the prom queen? Don't we have to set up some kind of class meeting so you can get yourself a prom queen and court?"

"Sure, Mrs. Atha," I said. "We should have already done that. I'll get on it right away."

Mrs. Atha was a nice lady, and she was just doing her job as class advisor, but my whole perspective failed. I seemed to go shooting off into space, where there was so much perspective, it scared me to death. The other girls in the dressing room seemed miles away, pink marshmallows scattered randomly on a field of hard gray. I had pretended it wasn't coming. I had tried to ignore it, the election for queen: I had pretended that all my meetings and work were the main thing, not the nominations and elections for queen.

I finished dressing slowly enough to be the last one out, and I walked down the hall alone, turned into a little alcove where they had the biology display that hadn't been changed in fifteen years, and I stared at the dusty bird mounts and crumbling models of habitats. Leaning on the case I thought, are you really going to go through all this again? For a rhinestone coronet and a white evening gown? For What Is Not Important? Oh no, said a voice, I don't have to be queen. It will be perfectly okay to be in the court. I could see a salmon-colored dress, a blue carpet and a pink aura. I fixed myself on the amber bead in the cardinal's flat head. They used to have a taxidermy club at school, and whoever did this one seemed to have thought it was a fish with feathers. I was determined to straighten myself up here and now, right here at the bird case. Being chosen does not matter, I said to myself severely. Be satisfied. You're lucky, you're young, you're smart, you've got your health.

In the back of my head a soft voice said, that's the way; all you have to do is not want it, and then you'll get it. Reverse magic. The rule of opposites. I may not even go to the prom, I thought.

At the class meeting, since Johnny was up front presiding, Gail sat next to me and talked about Wray. I glanced around the auditorium and thought that if Wray had gone to our school, at least he might have done some good by nominating me for the prom court. Sitting in the front were the National Honor Society and Key Club types with assorted girls and couples behind us, and the athletes who weren't leaders behind them, and way in the back, so far you couldn't see their features because of the white daylight pouring in through the eighteen-foot windows, the boys from Coburn Creek, with their feet up on the back of the seats in front of them. All those people, and no one I could count on to nominate me: some friend of Johnny's would nominate Gail, and Tommy Tucker would nominate Teresa Spinett. Nathan Critch or Garland would do it for India. Someone would nominate everyone except me. Girls nominated too from time to time, but usually it would be two girls who nominated each other, and that was a big joke. Mainly girls sat and hoped, although at one time I had planned to nominate Bunny because I thought she deserved some of the good high school has to offer. But that was all over. I had no act of righteousness; I was back to hoping.

Mrs. Atha wanted to get started. It was lunch hour, and she was missing her time down in the gym knocking tennis balls off the wall, so she gave Johnny a wave and he crossed his thick arms over his chest and started talking, much too quietly at first, staring at the floor. Gradually he regained the rhythm of public speaking as he always did; that was Johnny, he was so good at so many things that he always caught on, or remembered how. He just gave himself time.

I tried to pretend we were here to get information about buying class rings. Or for the yearly citizenship and patriotism speech by the VFW representative. Something I could ignore and just gaze around the auditorium. I liked it best when the blackout curtains were drawn and the spotlights lit, but even on a day like this when its great age and dinginess showed, I liked the high ceiling space, the creaking seats, the dark cave under the balcony. Many levels, many echoes, and secret corners.

Gail got her nomination first. She gave a hint of a smile and looked straight ahead with her chin tucked in smugly. I examined how her cheek spread into her neck with no jawline when she relaxed like this. She'll be in the court, I thought, because of Johnny, but they'll never elect her queen. From the back row Nathan nominated India, and then, causing a high sea of murmurs, Tommy Tucker nominated Linda Bardoline instead of

Teresa Spinett. So they were fighting again. Linda looked embarrassed, and Teresa's brother, who should have graduated a year ago, nominated Teresa himself.

The next name called was mine. It came from the back, projected in a long parabola that reached as high as the balconies and was almost lost in the darkness up there. It caused a creaking and groaning of wood as everyone turned to see. "That was Garland Odell," said Gail. "I thought you didn't like Garland. Did you know he was going to nominate you?"

"Garland Odell?" I said. "Are you sure it was Garland? I couldn't see who Johnny called on."

She cranked her neck around again. "It was Garland all right."

"Temporary insanity." I was soaring on the heat rising from my cheeks and shoulders. Nominated! By Garland! When I least expected it!

Gail peered into my face with one eyelid slightly low. Her measuring look. "He's not bad looking, if he'd ever stop cutting up."

"Knowing him," I said, "he nominated me for a joke."

Johnny was talking again, but Gail still leaned over and whispered, "Wait till Wray hears he's got more competition."

There were a few more nominations, and then I had to get up and give my report and get volunteers for the decorations committee. I couldn't see Garland, but I did find India smiling up at me. She had cut her hair even shorter, just now when the rest of us were trying to make long flips and French twists. What's the matter with those Odells anyhow, I thought. Garland had better not think I owe him anything because he nominated me for stupid prom queen.

Mother and Daddy had a teachers' meeting that day, so I had the unusual experience of being home alone for a while. I left my shoes in the middle of the living room and took a long drink of milk directly from the container the way I imagined a teen-aged boy would do, and I sat down at the table with a bag of vanilla cream Vienna sandwiches, and the mail.

On top was a letter for Mother, and under it, one for me from Thad. I looked again at Mother's and realized it came from

Thad's address too. He wanted me to come down to Charleston for his prom, he wrote, and his mother was writing to my mother to make the invitation official and convincing. I reread the letter, chomping cookies, feeling smug. A regular raft of boyfriends: Thad inviting me, Garland nominating me, and Wray dying of unrequited passion. The next cookie made my belly distended, and I wondered why Thad was inviting me, after all this time. Homecoming hadn't been exactly a disaster, but, somehow, it was after that visit that our letters became less and less frequent. An idea came to me, that I wasn't Thad's first choice, that he had a girlfriend down there, and something had happened, she had spurned him, they'd had a fight. In that case my going would do Thad a favor, and at the same time I would be free, maybe meet someone better than Thad.

I reread the letter. His prom was the same Saturday night as our prom. I put the letter down and straightened the mess I'd made: put away the milk, even wiping my germs off the spout; put away the cookies; swept up the crumbs; took my books and shoes to my room. When people asked me, I could say, I decided to go down to Charleston to be with my boyfriend.

I had coffee ready for Mother and Daddy when they got in from their meeting. Daddy wiped his mouth when I told them. "Let me get this straight. You decided to go to Charleston without consulting us. Is that right?"

"No, I'm consulting you. Right this minute, I'm consulting." He frowned. "I mean I'm asking for permission." It was hard to tell what Mother thought because she was rereading the letter from Thad's mother. I added, "And I've decided that even if you don't let me go, I'm not going to run for prom court anyhow."

"Well, that's dumb," said Daddy. "That's cutting off your nose to spite your face."

"No, I've come to the conclusion that all this queen and princess stuff is foolishness, and I don't want any part of it."

That was when Mother looked up, sliding her glasses low on her nose so she could see me over the frames. She seemed to be drilling through to the meat, to my meat. "Blair Ellen, do you mean to tell us that the reason you want to go to this boy's prom is that you're afraid of not being elected to the prom court?"

At moments like this everything about my mother maddened me. Her drilling gray eyes and her long fingers with slightly oversized knuckles, her thick hair with sprigs of gray running across the surface like cracks in a stone. Like tiny frozen lightnings. She would come to within a hairsbreadth of understanding, so close that sometimes I thought she *did* understand, and then I realized that she had it all wrong. That she understood my shaking moral foundation, but not my pain. So I lied as fast as I could.

"Oh, come on, Mother, it isn't that, it's what I said: I'm sick of the princess hoopla. It all seems so childish. Not important. Bunny always said that you reach a certain point, and high school doesn't seem to have anything to do with real life."

Daddy stirred. "Are you planning to get married while you're down in Charleston?"

Mother said, "Of course not. She doesn't even like Thad. She's using him."

"I'm not! You think that just because he's far away I can't care about him! I can't believe you think so little of me!" If anything, I thought in my self-righteousness, Thad is using me. I was absolutely sure that there was some other girl, that I was a replacement.

"Now, Blair Ellen." Daddy glanced out the sliding door toward the backyard, wishing he was down at the garden, or else worried that some neighbor would hear me shout. I sometimes thought we might as well live in an apartment in a city because he never felt private enough. "Now, Blair Ellen," he said. "You know we trust you."

I took a deep breath and glanced at Mother. Her eyebrows were elaborately curved, her lips blanched, because she hadn't quite caught me. I said, "You don't trust me very far."

"You're only sixteen years old!" said Mother.

"If we were to let you go," said Daddy, "you've got to admit it would be an unusual privilege for a junior in high school."

I did my best to keep my voice calm. "I know that, Daddy. It would be a really big privilege. I know it would."

He nodded, and I knew I had done it right; I had got my anger under control before Mother. They were going to let me go. I thought with a defiant pleasure of how I would walk into Alice

Ross's office and say, "Listen, Alice, you haven't already typed the stencil for the princess election, have you? Well, I'll be glad to retype it for you—but I have to make a change. I'm withdrawing my name. I don't believe in that foolishness."

No, I thought, I'll be more honest. "I'm withdrawing my name, Alice. I have something else I have to do that night."

The Wednesday before the prom I didn't come out of school until after the last bus had gone. I had been staying late every day that week making decorations, checking with the band, calling the caterer. I sat in Mr. Thornton's office after he'd gone and toyed with the photograph of his wife while I used his phone. I told the florist the colors for the members of the court: white roses and lilies of the valley for India, the queen. Everything had to be taken care of before I left for Charleston.

I had been bustling so much with the prom, that I had apparently missed the beginning of spring. Rain clouds were clearing away, and the giant weeping willow behind the body shop was completely green, a green as brilliant as a flower, picking up the late afternoon sun that broke through the shreds of passing clouds. There were other trees too, throughout town, half-transparent balls of green, surrounding the church bell towers. The breeze carrying the clouds away lifted my open raincoat, and the skirt of my dress, my favorite oxford cloth shirtwaist. I was sorry now to be going away, gently homesick in advance, for my hometown, for my prom.

A motorcycle started up at the body shop, snapping the quiet, so I went down the steps, watching my feet, humming. The motorcycle came up the hill, made a loop and pulled in front of me, barring me from crossing the street. It was Garland Odell with all the hair blown back off his face so that he seemed to have more forehead than usual. He just sat there blocking my way, and since he didn't say anything, I pointed at the hood ornament bolted to the frame of his motorcycle. "I see you changed your mind about decorating your motorcycle."

He shrugged. He had his shirt sleeves rolled up, and tendons moved under his thin, freckled skin as he adjusted the rear view mirror. I could have walked around him, I wasn't afraid. I could still feel Mr. Thornton's desk spread out before me. Garland rubbed at a speck on his rear view window. I started wondering if I should thank him for nominating me for princess. It seemed so long ago now, and I was afraid it would make me seem like a fool, that it would turn out after all to have been a joke, or he would say it was.

He said, "Can I give you a lift?"

"Oh, I don't think so, Garland. Thanks anyway."

"That's right, Mr. and Mrs. Morgan wouldn't approve of their daughter on a motorcycle."

"Don't be obnoxious. I don't trust those things myself. I'd never get on one unless I could drive it myself."

He didn't even hesitate the length of time it would have taken to crack a joke; he whipped his leg off the motorcycle and was standing beside it, offering it to me. "Go ahead."

I started to walk around. "You know I don't know how."

Pushing it heavily, he came with me. "I'll teach you. I'd like to. I'll teach you." I shook my head. "Seriously. Listen, Blair Ellen, I've been sitting over at Buddy's waiting for you to come out. I want you to go somewhere with me." Safely on the other sidewalk, with the way home open to me, I stopped to listen. "There's someone who wants to talk to you. Seriously."

"Seriously who?"

"Somebody. I'll drive you the back way. Nobody will know. It won't take more than half an hour."

"Who is it? Where?" Something with India, I thought, flattered to be the one who was needed. Something I was the only person who could help her with. A dress? Maybe she hadn't been able to afford a gown for the prom and she refused to wear that ratty old one of Carmell's sister's again. "Is it India?" I said.

"Just a little ways up Coburn Creek. Not far."

"My hair will blow." Garland snapped open a saddlebag under the back of the seat and took out a nylon scarf with blue roses. I felt like making a joke, something about how he certainly seemed prepared to pick up girls, but I was suddenly scared. Had I said I would go with him? "What about my books?" I said. He shoved them into the same saddlebag leaving me with nothing to clutch to my chest. The motorcycle seemed so enormous and heavy there between us that I hardly believed it would ever move. After taking longer than necessary to tie the scarf, I threw a leg over the seat and tucked my raincoat under my thighs.

He sprang on in front of me, and before I had time to think, the thing was vibrating and roaring. I half expected a crowd to come out of the houses to see what the commotion was about. Garland said, "Well, take hold of something."

"Take hold of what?"

"Me! You have to hold onto me. Anything but my neck."

"I've never done this before," I said. I hadn't realized I had to touch him. I was going to grab his belt, but somehow that seemed more suggestive than simply grabbing, so I put a hand on either side, gripped his rib cage. I was surprised by his skinniness. They yelled something at us from the body shop, but Garland just waved, and I hardly noticed because I was developing a cramp in my forearms from holding my body away from him going downhill.

He took a left at the bottom of the hill, drove past Gordons' and other large homes, and I kept my face turned away for fear of being seen by Gail. By the time we got to the highway I had some confidence that I could stay on the motorcycle, although I was glad we took the slower, dirt road that ran behind the mine supply warehouse and came out on Coburn Creek. We were soon in the real country, and I wondered if we would be going as far as Stone Paradise. At Christmas, Aunt Pearl and Mother drove out and reported that someone had dug up all the terraces and made a driveway, which was clogged with old cars and engine blocks. Aunt Pearl's rose garden had a trailer on it, and there were at least three separate clotheslines full of diapers and overalls. Oh, I hate to see all that, Mother had said. But Aunt Pearl said, let it go, Sibyl; you can't go back, and I would hate for it to look so good I'd want to.

It was a different world up here, climbing the hills. Garland hadn't spoken a word and I hadn't either, and it seemed natural not to. Even when we were in a shadowed bottom, the hilltops were in the sun, touched with green, and Garland's body protected me from the wind. "Hang on!" he shouted suddenly, cutting down a gear and making a breathtaking turn to the left where I never even knew there was a road. We seemed to spring over a corrugated drain pipe, and the motorcycle skidded slightly on the crushed coal surface. I lost my breath, and laced my fingers in front of him, clasped my chin on his shoulder too. I had glimpses of clay banks striped with veins of coal. A little wooden bridge, a muddy widening in the road, and then the road got even worse, rutted and muddy without the crushed coal. We skidded so badly once that Garland had to drag his foot to keep us upright. I might have screamed, but the air kept getting thwacked out of me.

The road flattened, although it was still slippery with mud, and then the mud widened to a place with two pickup trucks and I thought for a second it was a mine, but there was a house being built back in the woods. The sides were unfinished tar paper and there were a lot of boards stacked around the sides. One long row of single boards led over the mud from the house to the trucks.

Garland stopped the motorcycle, and I jumped off at once, deciding to take my chances on foot, and immediately lost a loafer in the mud and had to hop back to get it and then hop to a tree with wide, dry roots. "What do you think you're doing, Garland Odell?" I scraped the shoe on the roots.

He crossed a leg over the gas tank. "Were you scared? Why didn't you yell or something if you were scared? I'd of slowed down."

"Because I didn't want to give you the pleasure, that's why."

There was some activity at the house, a peeping at a window, a door opening and someone running out. I could hear the board walk suck and splash. A heavyset woman in bright green stretch pants carrying a baby. She started to wave, but the baby was so big she almost dropped it and had to take a big awkward stride to keep her balance. That was when I realized it was Evalina, and the baby I had made the big plan to buy a layette for. It came back to me shamefully, how I had congratulated myself on my idea and then done nothing. And all the while Evalina was here, not so far out in the country, living with this enormous baby. She reached the end of the boards and slogged on through the mud to us, stopping just short of my island of roots, grinning and holding the baby proudly in front of her. I noticed clip-on earrings, and her hair looked clean.

"Evalina," I said, "gee, you look good."

Garland said, "Everytime I see her she starts in, 'Where's Blair Ellen; when are you going to bring Blair Ellen to see me?' so I thought it was just about time."

She seemed to have lost weight or at least firmed up. Her clothes had proper fasteners and there was a certain brightness in her face, I thought. Less moon, more cheeks and chin.

"You want to hold my baby, Blair Ellen?"

I thought of myself as notoriously bad with babies, but I took him. He didn't struggle, but I had to brace a leg on the root and set him on my knee. He stared up as if he knew a lot more than he was saying. Something about babies made me nervous, even decent ones like Evalina's. Some odor that rose directly from their flesh. "He's so nice and clean," I said, and Evalina kept grinning.

"See them boots?" she said. "See them boots on him?" He was wearing a tee shirt and a diaper, and miniature yellow leather clodhoppers. "That's a present from India and Garland." Garland blew a smoke ring into the sky. "I got lots of nice presents when he came."

"I never brought you anything," I said. "I was going to."

"You had a present, Blair Ellen?"

I nodded, the least sort of a lie. I certainly intended to get something. "I never knew where you lived or anything. I still don't know your name—" I panicked; in fact, no one had said anything about a husband; maybe I was assuming things because she had started washing her hair.

"You don't know my name? How come you don't ask him? He knows." She stuck a thumb toward Garland. "It's the same as his now."

For an instant my stomach surged and plunged and I thought it was Garland, but he said, "She's married to Joe Odell. They're so many Odells up here I don't know the half of them."

"You know Joe," said Evalina.

"Sure, Evalina, I was just saying there are a lot of Odells. They named the kid Joe too. This kid's my cousin."

"Joe William Odell Junior," she said.

The baby started to smile. He did it extremely slowly. Every-thing about him seemed good-humored and slow, but the smile

[185]

surprised me. There was no reason for it; I wasn't particularly delighted to be holding him and I hadn't made any funny faces to entertain him, but this smile started and seemed to go on forever. I smiled back, of course, but I was a little frightened because he seemed to be sinking into my leg, maybe getting stuck.

"Hey, Blair Ellen," said Evalina. "You come back tomorrow, okay? You can't come in the house today 'cause I have to fix Big Joe's supper. But you come tomorrow and I'll show you my house and you can give little Joe a bath."

"Joe's building the house himself," said Garland.

"He ain't run in the electric yet, but the house is all wired up and I got a Mixmaster and a Motorola TV and a Frigidaire, and the gas for the cookstove is already in there. He's going to make a concrete parking lot out here. But I got to fix supper now."

"I can't come for a couple of days, Evalina, but soon. And I'll bring his present." I started lifting little Joe, and he did come off my leg, but his smile kept clinging. I passed him to her. "Maybe Mother will drive me up."

"You think Mrs. Morgan will come?"

"Sure. She'd love to see Little Joe."

The door opened at the house, and a man stood there in an undershirt and shouted for Evalina. She started backing away, grinning like anything. "The day after tomorrow, Blair Ellen?"

"Soon," I said, waving. Plans rose up in my head, how after I got back from Charleston, I was going to devote the whole summer to fulfilling my promise to Evalina. I would take her and the baby on picnics this summer. Swimming at Valley Falls. Big Joe yelled again and Garland halloed and he halloed back. I had a desperate desire to give her something now, just in case I failed her again. "Hey, Evalina," I called. "Guess who got married? Bunny Hoover! Bunny Hoover ran off and got married!"

"Bunny Hoover got married?"

"To Jimmy Minard. In the navy. They moved to Norfolk."

She started to run, but paused to yell back, "Hey, Blair Ellen, when are you getting married?"

Garland tossed his cigarette in Evalina's mud and said, "Ready?"

"Maybe I'll walk down."

"I was going on up and take the back way. It ends up on Black

Run somewhere. There's a view I was going to show you. I figured you're the type who likes views."

I stepped on the exhaust pipe and climbed back on, distrusting him, something bothering me, that Evalina hadn't been expecting me. This time I talked, as we started up the road, through the woods. "Does he treat Evalina okay?"

"Who, Joe Odell? Odells are always good to their women."

"He yelled at her!"

"He wasn't yelling at her, he just wanted her to get back in the house and finish his dinner. She probably left something burning on the stove, knowing Evalina. She's not real bright."

Well, I know that, I thought.

For five minutes we climbed with the bank on our right side getting higher and higher, and then we came out in the open and there was a quarter mile of flat road. The hill still rose, but this seemed to be as high as the road went, and on the left was a wide, cleared field, a cow pasture. Garland pulled over and pointed. "That's the view I was telling you about."

I got off and climbed through the barbed wire, walked a little way down the slope, hoping Garland would stay with his motor-cycle. There were no cows, but there was a concrete watering trough with water trickling out of a pipe stuck in the hillside, and a broad river of bright new grass in the path of its overflow. A couple of steps farther was a flat rock I hadn't seen from above. Some of it was wet, but there was a sun-warmed, dry area, and I sat down there to have a good look.

The pasture went steeply downhill to a crowd of trees, prob-ably around Coburn Creek Road. A rounded, clear hill rose be-yond that, then a hillside that was all wooded, and behind it another and another as far as you could see. From the roads, which followed the runs, and certainly from the town, which huddled around the river, you never saw so many hills. I suppose if I could have had my way I would have erased an oil derrick and the band the electric company had shaved for their high voltage wires, and at that time in my life I might even have got rid of the barns as unwelcome indications of human habitation, but in spite of those things, my heart leaped outward as from one hilltop to the next and higher.

Garland had meandered down the pasture after me, and stood off to my left, hands in his pockets. I hoped he would keep his mouth shut. It was one thing to talk about a view with someone like Thad, but even with Thad I would have preferred silence. Garland didn't speak, but he was there, and moment by moment he distracted me more. The person reorganizing the landscape by his very presence. I strained my eyes to see what he was doing without turning my head. Perhaps it was eyestrain, or the heat of the sun behind him, but he kept changing. He started out with his sneering country-boy stance, but got skinnier, more cave-chested as I watched, became some kind of Dickens city clerk, and then seemed to go on to no flesh at all, the light from two sides meeting in the middle till he caught fire, turned to a thing of light and red energy.

To fix him, to stop the changes, I said, "Garland! Can you see your old house from here? Where you used to live?"

He squatted down beside me on the rock, and I was relieved. He was wiry with tendons again, big knees, dirty nails. "You mean that old shanty up on Odell Mountain? We haven't lived there for years."

"I know. I know where you live. But I liked that place."

"You can see it from here if you want to. Count back one, two, three hills. It's a little chip on the rim. Do you see it?"

I thought I did. "I don't know why you ever moved."

"It was an old-timey place. Pop was old-fashioned and that's the way he liked it, but as soon as he died, Grandma wanted to get down where she could see things happening. She always said people are more interesting than hawks. Nobody's lived up there for years."

"That's too bad. *I'd* like to live up there."

"Yeah, I figured you were the kind who'd like views." Garland dropped off his haunches onto his back, with his hands cupping his head. He said, "I'll take you up there sometime. You could bring us a picnic."

"Oh, thanks a lot! *I* could bring a picnic. Why don't *you* bring the picnic?"

"I'd be providing the transportation. And the place. It's still

[188]

Odell property up there. All you'd be doing would be slapping some baloney on bread."

"Transportation! You don't think that motorcycle would climb that mountain?" I glanced at him sidelong again, and he had his eyes closed, his back arched slightly, sharp chin up in that air, bones pressing out on the top of his cheeks. His name suddenly sat in my mind like an unvoiced sob. Garland. I said, "Evalina didn't know I was coming today. She didn't have to talk to me."

He opened his eyes, rolled on his side, and scratched a piece of lichen on the rock. His fingernails were very short, and I was pretty sure it was motorcycle grease in a line under each of them. "I was thinking," he said. "I was thinking about that time for your birthday. Do you remember? When you came up on top of Odell Mountain to ask me and India to go to the carnival with you?"

"You didn't stick around to get invited. You went running off."

"I was just thinking about that. I wanted to know, would you go to the prom with me?"

I couldn't believe he didn't know I was going to Charleston. I had told everyone, the whole point was for everyone to know. "Garland, it's three nights before the prom. You're asking me to go with you three nights before the prom? Don't you know that's an insult? Besides, I thought you were going to be India's escort."

He slapped his knuckles lightly on the stone. "Her boyfriend's coming to the after-dance. We can get someone to stand up beside her while she gets crowned. Nathan or someone. She knows I'm asking you. She told me to."

I was going to make some remark about how I should thank India then for asking me, but he looked so down at the mouth. "Garland, did you really think I'd be sitting around waiting this long for you to ask me? It's late! I appreciated you nominating me for princess, I really did, but I made other plans."

"Who are you going with?"

"I'm not going to our prom. I'm going to Thad's in Charleston."

He jerked his body in anger, and landed on his back again, with the sneer aimed at the sky. "Oh, the Impala. I should have known the Impala would do it. Impala convertibles do it with girls every time."

"It has nothing to do with cars. I don't care about cars, not that you'd ever understand that. He wrote to me first. He wrote weeks ago."

"Guys with Impalas know how to plan ahead." He was rolling and tossing and turning beside me on the rock like something on a pin. Back on his side again, scratching fiercely at the lichen with all his nails at once. "You wouldn't have gone with me anyhow, you and him are so tight. Even if I *had* asked first."

I wished he would hold still; I couldn't say myself what I would have done if he'd asked in time. He twisted and thrashed, and liked me for no reason I could figure out, unless it was because India told him to.

I said, "Thad and I are not so tight. In fact, I was surprised he invited me down. I thought we were breaking up."

"Then don't go."

"Garland! You don't just back out. You don't just say, oh, I changed my mind. That's not right."

He turned his whole face to me, no sneer, and a flatness in his voice, but his eyes didn't give up; they flickered red bay all over me. He said, "It doesn't matter anyhow. You're not the type who would have anything to do with a guy who rides motorcycles."

"You don't have any idea what type I am. I'm not any special type at all."

His body and face had become still, and his eyes swam behind the lenses, there was a challenge: something that needed doing if I was the right kind of person. I leaned forward slowly giving myself plenty of time to draw back if I wanted to, to pretend I had only been swaying, if he didn't come to meet me. But he did come to me, at once, closing his eyes, a dry, muscular, lips-only kiss.

He pulled back, took off his glasses and laid them folded in the grass at our heads. He started the next kiss, open mouthed this time, but I didn't mind, not even the taste of cigarette smoke. He put his hand on my side and I could feel each of the five fingers. My eyes popped open, half expecting him to try something, but the fingers only touched my side, and his other hand touched my face. After a while I discovered that our breath smelled the same, and I lifted my head to look down at him, the thin vertical grin lines on either side of his mouth, the soft skin of his eyelids. I touched his ear lobe, and he caught my wrist and kissed it, and then kissed the hand in a dozen different places, along the underside of my knuckles, along the hard heel and fat thumb root, and in the very center where it started a tickle that ran up my arm and over my back, and I could feel my eyes getting wide and dry, too much light coming in, and Garland wasn't lying back anymore. He took my lower lip between his teeth, smiling at the same time and rolled us over so that I was the one on my back and he was hovering over me, with the late sun burning our two temples, our two cheeks. There was some terrible change in my body. My body wanting, and I was saying but this is too soon. I don't want to want. Garland's hand on my stomach, pressing down, and the downward spread my skin and caused my breasts to rise a little and join in the general wanting, and I kept staring past Garland at the deep blue overhead and thinking some rule had been broken, that Garland was doing something to me. He was supposed to be doing things that I could gently but firmly say no to, but he didn't seem to be doing anything; it was my leg that was trying something, pressing itself against his leg.

One of my voices said, have a good old time, Blair Ellen. And name it after me.

And I thought, it's not my fault, this is bigger than both of us, isn't it? There were a few clouds, silver and black stripes. I got hold of the cord that was vibrating in me, and I made it move in shorter, tighter periods until it didn't include Garland anymore, and then I said, "Garland, Garland, I have to tell you something."

He sighed, and slowly stopped pressing, lay on his side slightly curled, protecting me from the evening breeze. I felt old and sorrowful. Something I hadn't intended to learn so soon. His hand on my stomach, his eyes closed. His face had gone rounded, shaped more like India's than I'd ever noticed before.

"Garland, do you remember that ring that you gave me that time at the carnival? Do you believe it? I still have it, in my jewelry box."

He smiled and snuggled his face into my shoulder as if we'd

been sleeping in the same bed for years. He said, "I always used to think there was nobody I could talk to except India, and then for a little while I thought maybe you too, not since we've been in high school, but back then." I wanted to defend myself, how I'd been these years, but he went on, talking with his eyes closed, curled around me. "India and I have always been pretty much all there is to each other."

A different sadness passed through me. At least you had each other, I thought. I never even had one person. I used to hear Mother and Daddy talking to each other, at dinner, in the car, on the way to school, after school sometimes their voices from the bedroom no end of what they had to say to each other, private and enclosing, and no matter how much of their subject matter was me and plans for me, I was left out of some essential part of it.

After a while Garland rolled away, and the breeze made me shiver. He had his eyes open now, started fumbling over his head for his glasses. "My Dad's coming back," he said. "Everytime they take on five guys at the mines he decides to come back and cause trouble." He glanced at me. "Me and my dad don't get along. He's got a wife in Cincinnati, four little kids I never saw. India went out last summer and stayed with them, but I can't be in the same house with him. If he comes back to stay, I'll have to leave. Join the army or something."

"If I left every time my mother and I didn't get along!"

"It's not the same. Him and me," he showed his teeth, "we could kill each other if it was let go. I'd be leaving soon anyhow, I'm not hanging around here. A person wants to enjoy their youth, you know? You get stuck soon enough. I want to go all around, down south, out west. On the bike. I went to Pittsburgh two weeks ago; I met some pretty nice people up there. I might go to New York. Want to come?"

"I've been to New York."

"Not on a Harley Davidson."

We laughed; I was thinking of pulling up at Aunt Pearl's house in Tenafly on his bike; and I sat up again, and he suddenly grabbed my ankle, completely shackling it with his long fingers, the only time he ever grabbed me. "Blair Ellen, go with me to the prom. We'll have a real good time. You and me, and India and

Nathan or whoever we get to take her. We'll have a *good* time."

I had a premonition that I would have a much better time with Garland than in Charleston, that there would be pleasure here and some kind of nervous excitement down there, but I told him he couldn't think much of me if he thought I was the kind of girl who would go back on her word, and he shrugged over that, as if the people who lived in Charleston weren't worth keeping your word to, and I said could I take a raincheck and make a date for next year's prom.

"Next year's prom!" said Garland. "Hell, Blair Ellen, we may not be alive next year!"

"Then later this summer," I said.

"Okay," said Garland, and we kissed a few more times, but they were ordinary kisses, and we drove back to town through Black Run. I walked home from the head of Davis Street, clutching my books to my chest, trembly-legged after all that vibration, half hoping Mother and Daddy would have found out where I'd been, so I could say: look, there are parts of me that you know nothing about. There are parts of me that wouldn't think twice about going off with Garland to New York on his motorcycle, you know? We would just keep on moving, Garland and I.

But Daddy was in the workshop and Mother was breading fish. She said, "That prom certainly is keeping you late after school," and I said, "Yes, it sure is."

Everyone at Thad's prom was beautiful; there were no ranges of acne across foreheads and cheeks, no cowboy boots or stockings with seams. The girls flipped their hair, but didn't tease, and the boys wore theirs long like British rockers, not like Elvis imitations. No one obese or retarded to feel sorry for. You could have taken a color photograph at any time during the weekend and used it to advertise something sweet-smelling in *Seventeen* magazine, and furthermore there would have been no reason to pick me out as the hick-town girl. I discovered I could talk with these beautiful people; I talked all the time. I was on a high plane, I ran on a fast track. I was less interested in Thad than I ever had been, but I loved his friends.

On Sunday Thad and his mother put me on the bus home. I

sank back at once as the bus stirred up stale smoke and sloshed gasoline, ground through its lower gears down the deserted Sunday streets of Charleston. I waved without caring if they saw me, and sank deep in my seat. The lady beside me said something friendly about almost missing the bus, and I grunted and turned to the window. Laboriously I opened my mouth, just to reassure myself that I still could. There was a slight ache far back in the jaw joint, and I could hear saliva pouring in, collecting in the back of my mouth. I was having a withdrawal into my body; I hadn't slept since Thursday night. I slept and half slept all the way home, sometimes seeing the faces of the Charleston people I'd met, hearing unfinished conversations, sometimes having prophetic dreams about the future.

Once, my eyes were open for a while, and I saw hills with no farms, much steeper and wilder than the hills around home. Another time I woke to see an old coal mining company town of boarded up houses set into a hillside, a one-sided street, and down below, near the creek, the company store, and behind it a broken tipple and a shaft mine entrance. In my near-sleep the town had meaning, about the past, my parents' past, and the names of the towns on signs we passed too: Clendenin, Clay, Sutton, Gassaway. Much later I thought I was dreaming a town that was a skewed version of home. The placement of things was not quite right: the bridge came too soon, the high school was on the wrong side of the river. When I realized I was awake, I was frightened for a few seconds that I had slept through twenty years, been riding this bus all that time, but finally I woke enough to realize that it wasn't home at all, but Weston, an entirely different town. The hills were round topped now, and there were many more farms and cleared fields. Soon I would be in Graysburg and then stopping in front of the Rogers' Rexall at home.

I had one dream, in the final forty-five minutes, of an invented place, a landscape: mountains almost completely encircling a cultivated valley and a dome of violet clouds overhead. Very small, looking down at the earth, were Mother and Daddy, she kneeling at a flower border, he among the vegetables. Both of them faced down and away from the one gap in the mountains, through which could be seen alabaster towers, a castle, or perhaps the skyscrapers of a city. The place where my future was.

By the time I got home, I realized that I had decided to break off with Thad. I would write him an official letter of thank-you and good-bye. His friends had given me a hint of the possibilities in college, of the kinds of people I might meet. I could wait. And at the same time, the future I was preparing myself for precluded Garland even more than Thad. When Garland came to me on Monday, I would say no Garland, we had a wonderful, exciting interlude, but we are too different; we are going in different directions.

But Garland did not appear to be rushing me on Monday. In English class he gave me a chin nod from the back of the room where he and Nathan Critch had their heads together. I thought he might be playing hard to get, so I decided I wouldn't have to be so scrupulous about him. Even if there were no future in our relationship, he probably wouldn't understand if I tried to explain. I could even ride the motorcycle with him if I felt like it—through town or up to the Brazier Burger, just so I didn't get into a situation like last week. There was nothing wrong with Garland except that he didn't have any motivation for making something of himself. He probably had a lot of potential. Think of how he rebuilt that motorcycle. Think of how naturally he wrote the essay last fall, and his famous wit! I played vaguely with the idea of using my last year before college helping Garland.

On Thursday I saw him halfway down the hall, and I paused in plain sight and fooled around in my pocketbook to give him a chance to come over, but he didn't seem to see me, and later, right before lunch, it happened again: I saw him, and walked pointedly into the lunchroom alone assuming he would follow, but he didn't, and I had to hunt up someone else to sit and eat with. I began to wonder what was going on, if I had missed some signal. I went over the details of that afternoon in my mind and couldn't discover what I'd done wrong. I began to get a little frightened that I had been altogether mistaken about Garland. By Friday I was thinking he was a seducer, that he had been making fun of me. His nasty pleasure was to trick girls into believing he liked them, and then to turn around and laugh in their faces. To pretend that nothing had happened at all, and make the girl think she was going crazy. I didn't even want to see him again from a distance, so when the last bell rang, I emptied out my locker to have an excuse for staying late. The other girls with lockers on the landing left, and people tramped down the steps past me.

Gail Gordon came down wearing her new madras sundress with a little jacket to match. The endless parade of her clothes. "Hey, Gail, how come you're not at the ball game?"

She stopped, looked at the gym shorts and sneakers and books strewn all over the floor. Just for an instant, in her still-faced lack of surprise, she reminded me of Bunny. She said, "Do you want a ride home? I have to talk to you about something."

I decided Garland had had plenty of time to leave, so I tossed everything back in the bottom of the locker where it had come from. "Sure. What do you have to talk to me about?" I figured what she wanted was to talk more about Charleston. She had already questioned me in detail about how their prom was, what clothes they wore.

"Listen," she said, "I talked to Stubby Bart about getting us a job at the swimming pool."

"Getting us a job! I didn't know you wanted one!"

"Johnny's going to be gone all summer. This uncle of his is in the construction business in Brooklyn, and he's going up and work the whole summer. He wants to spend his own money, you know. Buy a car or at least buy the gas for my car. Anyhow, I went in and talked to Stubby and it turns out he can hire two lifeguards, and I said well, I know Blair Ellen Morgan has her lifesaving too, and she did some substituting last summer, so he said to come down to the pool next week while he's painting, and he'll set us up."

I took a long look at her. It was her chin you noticed first, that big, fine chin. Everything else seemed to hang from it. "You just walked into his office and asked him?"

"Sure, why not?"

The truth was that I had been working up courage for weeks about how to go down and ask him for a job. "I would have been afraid of bothering him about pool business at school."

"Afraid of bothering Stubby! I've been clomping around in his stupid band for six years, and besides he's a cousin of Johnny's.

And besides that, Daddy's on the board of directors for the swimming pool, so he darn well better listen to me. If I can't ask for a job, who can?"

I had thought of asking *my* father to speak to Stubby for me, but it didn't seem like the right way to do things. I thought that when you wanted to do a thing, you made an application and then waited for weeks, and if you were very meritorious and extremely lucky, you might be selected.

We were going out the main door, and down at the end of the walkway, lounging against one of the pillars with the concrete ball on top, was Garland.

He frowned when he saw us, and stood up, shoved a hand in his pocket and tucked a book under his arm. This must be the next step in his nefarious scheme, I thought, but Garland didn't look nefarious, especially with a schoolbook. His sneer seemed weak, and there was a gray cast to his skin, as if he needed sleep. He seemed small to me, but that may have been because of Gail's mass at my left shoulder. I made my insides cool and gelid and gave him the nicest smile. I even spoke first. "Hello, Garland," I said. "Where have you been keeping yourself?"

He made a gesture with his chin, jerked it up in a short tic. "Come on, Blair Ellen," he said, "I'll give you a ride."

Gail said, "Don't mind me. I'll just toddle home."

"I'm not going anywhere with him." I didn't mean it harshly, I was even still smiling.

He glanced at Gail. "Your parents won't see you. I'll let you off a block from the house like before."

Gail made an O with her mouth. She was having a great time, she loved not being bored. "Like last time?" she said.

The smile had spread all over the front of my face as if it would last forever. I shook my head no.

He took two pinched steps toward me and said, "I've got to talk to you." With Gail, I thought, you knew where you stood, second fiddle to Johnny. She didn't disappear when you expected her to show up.

I could feel the smile pressing in, as if it were a cookie cutter and I were the dough. Mother used to say that if I pouted too long my face would freeze that way, and the idea had always terrified me, but this seemed much worse, to be frozen this way, with this pleasant smile flattening me forever. "No thanks," I said. "Not today." I thought: I was ready to talk to you on Monday and Tuesday and Wednesday and today. What do you think I'm going to do, wait till you're in the right mood?

"Well, goddam you to hell, then," said Garland, and he flung the algebra book as hard as he could over the hedge. The cover ripped off as it flew through the air, and Garland thrashed through the hedge after it, cursing when the heavy branches caught him, then kicking the book when he got free and heading down the side of the steep bank, ignoring the steps, sliding, falling, and cursing.

"Well, for heavensake," said Gail. "You certainly caused a reaction with him."

Gail and I spent a lot of time together that summer, what with working at the pool and Johnny being away. She wanted to hear all about me and Garland, and I was so mad at him that I told about the ring for the first time ever. Then she wanted to hear about why I broke up with Thad, and when she was tired of my old boyfriends, she started making plans for new ones for me. She knew a lot of boys at her country club, she said. She thought it was time for me to meet some of them. She wanted me to go to the club with her, the first day we were off from the pool. She had another project for me too. She wanted us to drive to New York to visit Johnny. He had cousins by the bushel, she told me, all handsome and athletic. You'd love going with a boy from Brooklyn, she said, Think how much farther away that is than Charleston. She was convinced her parents would let her go if my parents would let me go, because everyone knew my parents were moral. I never mentioned the plan to Mother and Daddy because I didn't trust Gail enough to go off with her like that. When I went to the city, I would arrive alone with the riches of possibility spread out before me as if they had tumbled from my lap.

But Gail kept talking about it at the pool: during rest periods, after the pool closed and we were hosing down the sidewalks, and on the phone in the evening. She brought me presents: a roast beef sandwich on homemade wheat bread, a Mexican blouse that made her look too bosomy. She was patient and indefatigable, almost as if she were a boy trying to get me to like him. There was something appropriate about being wooed, something heavy and summerlike.

The pool felt right that summer too. I had always thought of myself as the kind of person who filled her days with reading and generally useful activities, but at the pool I was doing something very useful by simply sitting. My presence up on the high chair kept order and guarded lives of little children. The wonderful thing was that I did nothing, but was in the center. The pool was built at the old water purification plant where Coburn Creek came down out of the hills. The blockhouse was painted bright aqua with the same color inside the dressing rooms and on the poured concrete of the pool itself and its sidewalks and the snack bar—all shocking, vivid aqua. If you had time to kill, or if you were looking for someone, you came down to the pool. If you didn't swim, you stood around outside the cyclone fence and watched. Boys came before and after city league baseball games wearing their gray uniforms, and the girls would get up from their beach towels and go to them. People looked at me too, and I flirted too. My legs were brown and I had three identically styled Jantzen swimsuits, one bronze, one gold, one copper, each with a senior lifesaving patch. That summer, even the stubble on my legs was golden. I would put my ankle on my knee and look at my leg with the bright blue water as a backdrop.

I had to blow the whistle every now and then because the little kids would run on the sidewalks or duck one another, or some nonswimmer would go cling to the ropes that divided the deep end from the shallow. We ran a pretty tight ship, Gail and I, keeping the kids in line, but there were long periods when I could go into a kind of trance of blue sky and blue water and deep green hills. The shrieks of pleasure and heylookame splashes became distant and ran together like the trees along the rim of the hills.

One day I was standing at the edge of the pool trying to decide if I had enough energy to swim laps before we let the kids in. It was a slimy sort of day, overcast, but not enough to keep the heat off, and the water looked greasy, too thick to swim in. Gail came out wearing one of Johnny's number ten varsity tee shirts over an expensive Cole of California.

"Well," she said, "guess who Stubby hired to pass out the baskets." The regular woman had had to quit for a gall bladder operation. "I'll give you a hint. She rode down on the back of Garland Odell's motorcycle."

"India?" I was struck by a hazy guilt, vague like the high, gray cloud cover.

"She's in there now, learning the cash register." Gail gave me an odd look. She said, "Aren't you going to go in and say hello?"

We started toward the dressing room. "How is she going to get here every day?"

"Garland, I guess, and sometimes her friend from Four States that no one knows anything about." In the echoing girls' dressing room she lowered her voice, but not very much. "I heard that guy from Four States is married."

Before I could ask any more about that rumor, we were in the office, Stubby and India behind the counter as Gail had said, but she hadn't said that Garland was still here. He sneered when he saw me. He was terribly dirty: greasy finger wipes on his tee shirt, his hair slick and flopping, his glasses smudged. He launched himself toward the door, but veered briefly to whisper, "I'm sorry I cursed you. I never should have cursed you," and then he was gone, up the walk. There was a moment of suspension before we heard the motorcycle: Stubby pointing at the cash register, Gail smirking at the ceiling, but mostly it was India's smile and a short nod as if to say, there, didn't he do a good job?

I tried to make friends with India during the four weeks she worked for us at the pool. I was tired of Gail's problems with Johnny not writing, and even a little tired of her wide-ranging gossip. So during rest periods I would go help India pass out baskets and check season passes. She was calm and pleasant as you please, and I finally asked about the goat. They got rid of it, she said, when they got rid of all the other animals except the chickens, which was when they moved down off the mountain to Carmell's old house. But I didn't know how to ask more: Were you sad? Were you sad about the dogs? Someone would come in, or I would have to go back to work. We never talked about Garland. I learned she was still poor because she had two outfits for work, a blue checked dress with a white collar and a pink checked camisole top and skirt, both thin and soft with age, always clean and pressed. I imagined her getting up early to iron the dresses before the mist had lifted off Coburn Creek. I noticed that she still wore her remaining charm bracelet, but I never wore mine, although I thought of it once, as a silent message, but I couldn't figure out what the message would be. I began to think she was not as interesting as she used to be. Her mystery seemed to have become stupid and thick.

Garland was around from time to time too, but he never stayed when he saw me. He wore that same tee shirt with the smeared grease hand print and his jeans seemed to get baggier as if he were losing weight. I often found him standing at the counter across from India, but with his head down cradled in his arms.

One day, another one of those iron smelting days when the sun never came through the haze, just after the pool closed, Garland was facing away from me, and I had an impulse, went directly to him and touched his shoulder. "Garland, I've been meaning to tell you, I'm sorry too."

I had more to say; I wanted to be sure he understood exactly what I was sorry for, the pretending, the distant smile, but he jumped when I touched him, and some kind of pain went over his face, a wince that seemed to pass into his neck and shoulders, become a shrug, and give a momentum to his whole body that carried him through a leap sideways and out the door.

I said to India, "What's going on? What's the matter with him? He looks like he hasn't slept in days."

For a second she seemed about to answer me, but then her smile came over her like a perfect small pearl, a smile that made her face as smooth and seamless as the side of a china bowl. "He's always working on that motorcycle," she said. "He never gets clean."

Outside the motorcycle revved and spat off. "What did I say wrong?"

"Nothing. Why nothing, Blair Ellen. Garland likes you." She

got out her white vinyl clutch purse, a lipstick and compact, and began to color her lips. I stood there dissatisfied: waves of Clorox fumes from my mop.

"Isn't he going to take you home?"

She pressed her lips together, spread lipstick off to the corners of her mouth with her little finger. "Not tonight."

At that moment there was another crunch of gravel in the parking lot, and through the evergreen bushes I could see a black fender with a row of old-fashioned silver air vents like smashed wide BBs. India snapped her compact closed and without hurrying, but without wasting a moment, went off.

Gail came running out of the other dressing room, dropping her mop in her haste and running to the doorway to look. "Nope," she said. "I still can't see his face."

I was disgusted. Gail's greediness disgusted me, and India's lipstick smile and Garland's dullness. The summer had started out so well, and everything seemed to have gotten sticky and deeply boring. People running away, no one left but Gail. My eyes seemed glued together, straining to peer through oil.

I went back to mopping. "Why on earth do you care who India goes with?" I said to Gail.

She hiked her weight up onto the counter to avoid my mop and crossed her legs. "I don't care. I just don't like the way she acts like it's such a precious secret. I know they're old friends of yours, Blair Ellen—"

"Not really."

"But you have to admit they're strange. I'd just like to see who her precious big-secret boyfriend is. She's probably ashamed to let anyone see him. That's probably the real reason."

Gail was kicking her crossed leg rhythmically as she talked, and the rhythm of her leg, the continuation of her voice, the endless motion of it, gave me a seasickness. I'm quitting, I thought. I've had it with this place. I've had it with this town, and Gail and India and all of them.

Another car pulled into the lot, and the door slammed at once, feet came running. The man coming down our walk was in a big hurry. He was slightly built and had on loose tan work clothes and a billed hat pulled so low that you couldn't see his face.

Something about him made me shut one of the double doors and call, "Sorry! Pool's closed!"

Under the shadow of the hat his mouth twisted to one side. "I ain't here to swim," he said, never losing a stride, and I had to back away or get knocked down. I wanted to slam the door in his face but you have to have a reason, more of a reason than nausea and distrust. He came barreling in like he owned the place, and I was aware of an odor, and thought, is that alcohol? Is this man drunk? He stopped just inside the door, his arms, long for his size, swinging slightly, and his hands made into fists. "Where's the man?" he said.

I wanted to move near Gail and have the protection of her larger body, and her apparent casualness, but I stood my ground. "Who do you mean?"

"The man that runs this place."

"We're the lifeguards," I said. "We're running the place right now. What can we do for you?" It was his shoulders, I decided, and the way he had his head low, as if he were about to plunge on through you or anything else in his way. He wouldn't hit two teen-age girls, I thought, and then was afraid that was exactly what he would do.

He said, "India Odell works here, don't she?"

Gail stopped banging her heels on the counter. "Say, do you live over at Four States?"

I said, "India works here, but she left a little while ago."

"Who with?" Small bones in his chin, large teeth.

"Listen," I said. "We don't know who you are. We can't go around giving out information about employees without knowing who we're talking to."

The tight white skin turned red. "I'm her goddam father, that's who I am! I'm Elroy Odell, her goddam father."

"*Elroy?*" said Gail, with a particular gurgle in her throat that meant she thought something was funny.

And Elroy Odell never doubted for an instant he was being laughed at: he sprang at her, slammed his large hands on the counter on either side of her and thrust his face up at her. Gail pulled her jaw back as far as she could, and then froze. I got a grip on my mop, ready to attack if I had to. He screamed in her face and pounded the counter on either side of her so hard that she bounced up and down, but he never actually touched her. "That's right!" he screamed. "Elroy Odell! I'm her father and I have a goddam right to know who's goddam taking her home!"

"It was Garland," I said. "He always comes and picks her up on his motorcycle. We heard the motorcycle outside, right, Gail? He's your son, right? Garland is?"

He stared in Gail's face for another couple of seconds as if he hadn't heard, but then he turned to me, doing something ugly with his mouth, sucking his teeth and running his tongue along his gums. I thought he was going to spit, or throw up, but he sneered. "So they tell me," he said.

"He's an awfully good brother to her, isn't he, Gail? He brings her to work and picks her up. Right, Gail?"

Elroy seemed to have swallowed whatever nasty taste had been in his mouth. "The little bastard's as bad as the rest of them," he said. "I should fix him too. Always after her."

Something had happened to me; my nausea was gone. The pool office was its normal color again; the evergreen bushes outside. I felt enormously alive: Garland and India's father! I thought, what a horrible man! Poor Garland and India!

Elroy seemed to recollect himself, and he tipped his hat back to show his eyes, bay brown like Garland's. "Well," he said, "I shouldn't have bothered you young ladies. But you have to understand how a father feels about his daughter." He grinned, or at any rate showed his long, white teeth, and then made a sudden sideways duck like Garland, and left.

Gail and I waited until we heard his car spit gravel and roar out, and then Gail said, "My God, that man was going to hit me." Her cheeks had turned deep red, and she looked at me in a sort of wide-eyed demand for guidance.

I said, "He smelled drunk."

"He's insane, that's what he is. He should be locked up." She slid off the counter and bolted the door.

I said, "Do you suppose we should try and warn India?"

"Tell the police maybe. But I'm not going to get messed up with those people. They all carry squirrel guns in their glove compartments."

"Squirrel guns don't fit in glove compartments," I said.

We drove around town for a while, up to Buddy's, but Garland wasn't there, back down the hill. A sheen of late afternoon lying over town, the steel-bright haze slipping into bronze evening. At first we didn't say much, but moment by moment the shock of fear faded, and I was amazed looking back at that depressed mood I had been in. Action had perked me up. I handled myself pretty well, too, better than Gail, I thought, rather affectionate toward her. "You know," I said, "I met India's grandmother once and she talked about him. She said he was her bad boy. She said she had twins, and Carmell Odell's father was her good one, and India and Garland's dad was her bad one, but she says she gave him the good name."

"*El*roy is the good name? I'm afraid to hear what she called the other one."

We laughed together and I was really liking Gail again. I liked her solidity. I liked it that she didn't fade and re-form and flicker like the Odells. She didn't run off and get married. When Gail gets married, I thought, everyone will be invited.

She wanted me to come to her house for dinner. Her parents were out and she would make me her special baked sandwich.

I called home from the Brazier Burger, and Mother wasn't pleased, but I explained that I wanted to do it because Gail was lonely. "You know how her parents are always out," I said. Mother, who grew up in the 1930s, always sympathized with rich victims like the Lindbergh baby and little Gloria Vanderbilt, so she clicked her tongue and didn't object.

The Gordon house was buff-colored brick with a mansard roof, and a buff brick driveway that made a half circle in front of the house. I hadn't been there often: I remembered a couple of birthday parties and the Christmas party last year. The Gordons owned so many things; their kitchen was huge, and walnut-stained cabinets ran all around the room, more than you'd ever need, and there was a bronze enamel wall oven. It was the first kitchen I'd ever seen with a stainless steel sink. I was especially taken with the floor; real, clicking, red Spanish tile.

Gail got to work at once. "This sandwich is my specialty," she said. "You bake it open faced and the cheese and meat sort of run together down into the bread. It absolutely has to be Italian bread. We'll have a tossed salad with it, and blender shakes. I stick chocolate syrup in the Osterizer and ice cubes instead of ice cream and it comes out almost as good as a real shake, but with less calories."

It didn't seem to bother her that I wasn't answering. My competent, heroic self seemed to have taken a vacation. I was quietly overwhelmed by the bronze oven, the ground round instead of chuck. When she opened a cabinet, I had a glimpse of strange labels on the cans, not Heinz or Del Monte, and she said, "That's the gourmet cabinet. Whenever Mom goes to Pittsburgh she brings back stuff from Kauffman's gourmet shop. I'm putting artichoke hearts in the salad. Do you like them?"

I had to admit I'd never had one, and she brought me one on a fork, dripping oil, holding her cupped palm under it, and slipped it into my mouth the way a mother gives a bite to her baby. It was such a slippery food, and at first I didn't like the direct contact with the olive oil, but then it came over me that Gail was making all these preparations for me, not for Johnny, or for a party, but for me alone, and the artichoke heart left a good taste in my mouth. "You've got wooden salad bowls," I said. "The whole set." At home we had an orange Melmac serving bowl and a spoon; the fork had melted on the stove. Our kitchen was fairly new, and Mother took excellent care of it, but she never would have allowed a double-sized refrigerator or wall oven. She would have given a salesman with imported tiles her look for rowdy boys in the classroom. I had always thought of myself as a spiritual person, not materialistic, but I felt a wave of yearning for these heavy Gordon objects in their browns and bronzes and deep reds. The round table with linen placemats and captain's chairs. I wanted to go in the dining room where I could dimly see wall-to-wall carpeting. How would you clean up the crumbs, I wondered, but the Gordons would have the best system, whatever it was. Built-in vacuum cleaners, maybe. Inside me, a pinched little girl with her hands clasped as for singing said, yes but, are they happy? Don't the Gordons drink cocktails and go out every night? Isn't Gail so lonely she's going to all this trouble just for a girl friend?

"Do your parents go out a lot, Gail?" I said.

She was making a dessert while the sandwiches broiled: pudding and angel cake and fruit assembled individually in tall glasses. "Yeah, I guess so. They have bridge. A lot of meetings."

"I guess that makes it pretty lonely here."

"Are you kidding? That means I get to have Johnny all to myself. I fix his dinner, and then we study. He has to work so hard, with all the sports, but we keep his grades up."

Almost drowsily I watched her drop a maraschino cherry into each dessert. This big, fine, glossy kitchen, and the whole huge house, and Gail and Johnny all alone in it. I wondered if they did it, and if so, where? Lots of beds, and I thought vaguely of the bathtub where I'd hidden at her eleventh birthday party. Or right here in the kitchen. With an apron. I imagined Johnny sitting where I was, on a bar stool, and Gail cooking, as she was now, lifting the salad with wooden utensils, breasts under her tee shirt tossing up and down too. She stops talking, the refrigerator ceases its hum. Johnny, tight, thick Johnny, crosses the Spanish tiles, and lays hands on her from behind.

Gail said, "You don't want to eat in the dining room with the chandelier hanging over your head, do you?" We decided on the captain's chairs and linen placemats in the breakfast area, and we carried over the salads, the blender shakes. And if you don't do it, you and Johnny, I thought, how close do you come?

I said, "I love your house, Gail. Ever since that party you had in fifth grade. Your mother had all kinds of games planned for us, but we played hide-and-seek instead. I think everybody wanted to explore the house."

Gail said, "Why don't you sleep over tonight and I'll make blueberry pancakes for breakfast."

I couldn't believe she was talking about pancakes while we were shoveling down baked sandwich. I said, "If it's okay with your mother, I could call home and ask."

"Mom will never notice," said Gail, and she went in for the dessert. By this time I was so full I had to wait for each bite to slide down before I dared something else, but Gail just kept on spooning it in. She didn't gobble, but she never stopped either. Something confident and ever-rolling about Gail that was just right in her house. Something deep and safe about this house.

We hadn't quite finished dessert when Gail's parents came in. She got up to give them a kiss, and I felt myself cringe; they were such large people. Mr. Gordon splendid in a plaid sports jacket, carrying his tie, Mrs. Gordon in a sleeveless, brown linen dress and huge straw pocketbook. Broad shoulders and hanging jowls and a slow-moving dignity that made me feel in comparison like an antelope with trembling hindquarters.

"We had to come home early," said Mr. Gordon. "Mom had a headache." He winked at me and said, "Is my girl giving you enough to eat? She's usually on a diet and fixes little lettuce salads with lemon juice."

"We had a wonderful dinner," I said.

Mrs. Gordon leaned over the table and squinted. "Oh, baked sandwich. Did you leave it in long enough this time, Gail? I wish I'd stayed home and had it with you, instead of the stuff they served—awful overdone meat. Little thin, gray slices." She shuddered and took off her necklace, kicked off her shoes. Mr. Gordon's jacket was over his shoulder now, and I began to get worried that they were going to strip down to their underwear. But they were backing out. Mrs. Gordon came back for a second. "Gail, honey, have Blair Ellen stay over. We'll make sour cream waffles in the morning when I'm feeling better."

"There," said Gail. "You see? She loves me to have guests."

"I don't have my toothbrush."

"We have a gross of toothbrushes, and I have a dozen nightgowns. Her sour cream waffles are even better than my blueberry pancakes."

There was no refusing the Gordons, I thought, comfortably dialing Mother. Maybe after Gail was asleep I would sneak out of her room and go through the house barefoot, wade my toes in the deep-pile carpet that ran from the dining room another half mile or so through the living room and den.

I told Mother that Mrs. Gordon insisted. "But you've already been there for hours," she said in a strangely thin voice. "What if Mrs. Gordon is tired?"

"Mother!" I was humiliated because Gail was right there in the kitchen with me, putting dishes in the dishwasher. "Mother, she suggested it herself. She already went to bed. It isn't like someone has to take care of us, you know."

"Well," said Mother in this pathetic little voice, "your father and I will still be here when you decide to come home."

Gail had two rooms connected by a bath like a suite in a motel. The larger was her old room where we'd had the party when she was eleven. There was a rocking horse and a reversible blackboard easel, and all her toys and games, everything as it had been when she was a child, as if she could at any moment go back and be a child again if she wanted to. Her new room, her teen-age room, had striped, tailored bedspreads on the twin beds and painted shutters. We went through a large drawer of nightgowns, and I picked out a long yellow one with a shiny stripe running through it.

I said, "Are you going to tell your parents about Elroy Odell?"

Gail looked surprised. "Are you kidding? Are you telling yours?"

"Of course not." I thought it was obvious that my parents would panic, but hers seemed so large and fearless, as if such a skinny little man would never bother them. Gail took pink checked babydoll pajamas, and all that seemed so distant. This place was a fortress; huge supplies of food. You could stay here safely for years.

Gail showed me the toothbrushes in the closet, and there was a lifetime supply of them too. I spent a long time cleaning my teeth, scrubbing my face. The longer I scrubbed, the more everything faded: my parents, Odells.

When I came out, Gail had turned on the air conditioner, and the television with no sound, and she was talking on the telephone. She covered the mouthpiece. "Guess who I called?"

"Johnny?" I was sure it had to be Johnny from the way she was reclining against a pile of pillows with one leg propped up.

She made a face. "I wish. It's Wray. He wants to talk to you. He wants to take you out on a special date, dinner at the General Gray and then a movie. He wants it to be all dress up and formal. And they have a wonderful Saturday night buffet at the General Gray with three separate roast beefs: rare, medium, and well done. My Dad and Mom go all the time."

I made a dramatic, silent NO with my lips.

"Come on, Blair Ellen."

I tried to be mad at her, but it was as if the roast beef at the General Gray and Wray as an escort were just more things she was pressing on me like the yellow nightgown and the chartreuse toothbrush. So I took the phone and said, "Wray, what do you and Gail have cooked up now?"

"Hello, Blair Ellen," said Wray in his artificially deep voice. He'd had a high, rather humorous voice the one time I met him in person, a good voice for satire and mockery. I imagined him doing some kind of throat exercises to get this manly depth. "Have you seen *Dr. Strangelove* yet?"

Wray, it turned out, had seen it twice already and thought it was the greatest movie of the century. I said, "Are you sure you want to see the same movie three times?"

He deepened his voice even further for a whisper that was like a groan of passion: "It won't be the same movie—with you there."

I rolled my eyes, but Gail was concentrating on her rollers. I wanted to gag, but, of course, he was Gail's friend, and she hadn't heard the dripping cavern of a voice. I looked around the room, was reassured by the flickering television, Gail's large haunches spread Indian style on the bed. Something inevitable about Wray. Maybe his voice was just an aberration that came over him when he was on the phone. The movie was a comedy, after all, not a love story. So I let him set up the date for Saturday night, and he was to call Thursday just to be sure everything was okay on my end. I figured I could always get Mother to not let me go if it came to that. "There," I said to Gail, "I did it. I have a date with Wray."

"Good," she said, examining her toenails. "You'll have fun. I wouldn't expect you ever to go steady with him or anything like that. Although he does drive a Firebird. But you should be going out, you know, until you find the right one for you."

"Did you go out when you were waiting to find Johnny?"

"Sure. I went out with Wray."

She was right about that: I didn't want to sit home on Saturday nights anymore. I wanted to be out, in action, good or bad. I crawled under the covers and tried to watch the movie on TV, but it was something strange and foreign and I never did figure out what was happening. Sports cars sped down a little winding road past terraced villas to the ocean. I couldn't tell the beautiful women apart. The bedsheets were tucked in and I usually kicked the sheets loose at once, but it seemed right here at Gail's. Going out with Wray would be tucked too. I would have to be very, very, nice to him. But it would also be pleasant to say, oh yeah, I have a date Saturday night. Some guy from Graysburg; he goes to Woodrow Wilson High School. Yeah, I'm tucked in for Saturday night.

I decided to tell Wray I never kissed on the first date. I would work around to a conversation on morals early in the evening and explain my position. It is a sort of a test, I would say, of the boy and girl both, to see if they like each other as companions. I really believed it, although I had kissed Thad the first time he ever walked to my cabin from vespers, and with Garland there hadn't even been anything so formal as a walk home. I tried to reason out the difference in the cases, but finally decided that it didn't matter. What mattered was that I didn't want to kiss Wray's drippy, fake-sexy voice. And if my principle would protect me, that was just fine. Those other kisses had been phenomena, running their course like flames along a branch.

On Thursday night I was in the kitchen with Mother greasing and flouring pans while she made a cake. The phone rang, and Mother answered, and waved and pointed to me. Slowly I washed my hands, slowly went in to where she was chatting away as if he were a perfectly ordinary person. She even sat down, crossed her legs, and laughed her Blair giggle and touched her hair. I thought well, maybe Wray is different today, Mother seems to like him. But when she finally put me on, it was the same old gasping, slithering-in-your-ear Wray. There was a long pause after my "Hello" and his throaty "How are you?" as if I'd been ill or something. I said, "Fine, thanks but I can't talk"—I turned my back on the kitchen so Mother couldn't hear my lie—"I was just walking out the door with a cake for our next-door neighbor who tragically lost her baby boy." Even Wray had to take the sex out of his voice for a dead baby.

Mother was sifting when I came back. "That was quick."

"Yeah, well. I just had to find out what time he was coming Saturday." I watched Mother's efficient bang on the side of the metal sifter to force the last of the flour through. "How did Wray sound to you?"

"Very polite. So many boys don't know how to talk to adults. Of course, I could tell all the time he wanted to get to you."

"Does he seem like the kind of boy you'd like to kiss if you were on a date with him?"

She stopped banging. "You said he was a humorous boy."

It was hopeless. I could feel her accusing tone. I was asking about something we didn't speak of. She had given me booklets and told me all about menstruation and the development of the fetus, but not a word about pleasure or disgust. I said, "When I met him he was humorous, but something happens on the phone. He starts breathing in my ear—"

"Maybe he's nervous."

I wanted her to see him as I did, the face to match the phone voice, all mouth, with saliva strung across the corners. "He turns slimy, like a jellyfish. If he tried to kiss me, I'd probably throw up."

Mother drew her head back in a way that usually preceded fury, but she spoke calmly, erasing slimy and jellyfish and throw-up. "When I was your age, we were lucky to have enough money to go to the movies."

"I know," I muttered. "It was the Depression."

"It was the Depression, and I think if a boy had ever got together enough money to invite me to dinner *and* a movie, I would have floated on air."

I said, "And if that boy took you out to dinner and the movies, what I want to know is, what did you owe him?"

First she smoothed the measuring cup full of flour with a dinner knife, and then, unexpectedly, caught me with her enormous gray eyes. "If all you can think of is what you owe him, then maybe you shouldn't go out with him at all."

She was absolutely right. It was even what I wanted to say: no thanks, Wray, I don't like your slimy-sexy voice or the way you snort when you laugh. But the instant the words formed in my mind I despaired of ever saying them. The impossibility of saying directly to someone, "I don't like you" emptied me out entirely. I'd have to call his house, I thought. I might have to speak to his father.

I didn't work on Saturday, so I had the whole day to get ready. I washed my hair early in the morning and put it in rollers. I pressed the dress I was going to wear, even going painstakingly over the eight rows of ruffles down the bodice, and I put white polish on my T-straps. I went out on the patio to paint my nails. No book, just me, the nail polish, the heat. The one good thing about the sticky slowness of the afternoon was that it seemed like evening would never come.

Mother had stopped singing in the kitchen and Daddy was down in the garden. I could see his farmboy hat bobbing up and down in the corn. Beyond the corn patch was a stand of old elm and oak with their uppermost branches moving in some breeze that didn't touch me, a short, obsessive wave like church ladies fanning themselves. A redwood fence separated the garden from the fields, and as far as I knew Daddy had never crossed it. He had no desire to hunt, hike, or picnic. He liked yards and vegetable gardens and he wanted a view clear of roofs and washlines. I was the only one who ever crossed the fence, and I hadn't done it since I was so little I had to get special permission. Even the garden had seemed distant then, and of course it had been farther because we were still living in the big house. Mother would make me a thermos bottle of chocolate milk and watch me down the slope through the site of our present house, and I would marvel at how completely alone I was. I made an expedition of it, with the chocolate milk and cheese and crackers. I would climb the fence, skirt the grove of big trees and go straight into the grass, taller by midsummer than I was. In the grass, I was out of sight of Mother, and there were terrifyingly heavy leaps of grasshoppers on my arms and the back of my neck. I might have met mad dogs or snakes, and no one would have known. I ran as fast as I could, twenty yards of terror, to an enormous tree fallen across a stream, a long, black trunk, root-end high in the air. A ship, a city, a whole world. I always climbed to the prow immediately, and waved back up at the house. Part of the thrill was that I could never see her wave back, that I only believed she was there, and at the same time believed that I was all alone out here. I liked to look at the field around me, the houses back on Davis Street, the hills on all sides, dull, tipped waves of cleared fields penetrating into the woods. I always told myself how some day I'd go all the way up on the highest hills, when I was a teen-ager. I had been so sure then that as a teen-ager I would be my same self only stronger and braver. And here was the traitor painting her toenails. Just the kind of toy poodle of a girl I'd had contempt for when I was ten.

Daddy came up the yard with a paper sack. He looked perfectly serene as he sat down in the aluminum chair beside my lounge, lit his pipe, and started shucking corn. "Hey, Sibyl!" he said in his deepest voice.

"Whoo hoo?" said Mother, peering out the kitchen window.

"Boil that water, sweetheart, here comes lunch."

"It's on the way, honey."

I couldn't stand them when they started calling each other sweetheart and honeybunch. I closed my eyes.

Daddy said, "Well, I see you're painting your toes too. Is this fella going to be looking at your feet?"

"I sincerely hope not," I said. "I happen to be working tomorrow, and my feet are at eye level of anybody who comes to the pool."

He shucked an ear, but looked at my feet again, propped against a towel on the lounge chair. "I never thought toes were very pretty myself. I never did understand painting them red."

"It isn't red, it's rose." I started itching when Daddy noticed my clothes or pointed out something about my hair or my body. Some corn silk drifted my way and I picked it off the towel so it wouldn't stick in the polish.

Daddy said, "Well, you may be painting your toes for the pool, but you sure are fixing up the rest of you for that fella."

Freshly shaved armpits started to sting with sweat, rollers pinched my scalp. I looked up over the trees to the hills. I knew why, although I couldn't explain to Daddy. I wanted there to be nothing for Wray to criticize. Not a lank hair, not a chipped nail: no stubble or odor. Nothing to catch hold of and sneer at. Nothing to catch hold of, period.

The dress I wore that evening was a real *Seventeen* magazine Saturday night date dress. It was white with its own robin's egg blue matador jacket. I looked at it a long time in the mirror after I had my lipstick on, my hair brushed and sprayed lightly. Everything was smooth, even the ruffles hiding my bosom. I kept changing the angle and looking until I heard the vacuum cleaner and went out to find Mother going over the couch cushions. I said, "I really wish you wouldn't."

"I was going to anyhow!" I noticed she had put on her cotton sundress that Aunt Pearl brought her from Guatemala.

She finished the couch and started briskly across the floor, so I sat on the couch, figuring it wouldn't soil my dress. Mother turned off the vacuum and disappeared in the closet. "Mother, you're not getting out the camera are you?"

She looked around the closet door and smiled. "What was that, honey?"

"I don't want my picture taken. I don't like Wray and I'm never going to go out with him again and I don't want to remember tonight."

"Just one," she said. "Your hair has the cutest little puff and you look so clean."

"No," I said, but she had the whole set out, the Polaroid, the film, the tube of fixer, and instruction manual. After all, I had worked hard to get myself to look like this. I let her take three pictures, and the one where I threw my head back and kicked one foot up behind me is the one I still have. She has one too, stuck in the corner of my graduation portrait, a demure one, chin down, eyes up. Wray grabbed the third one.

He came early. We had just laid the snapshots out on the coffee table to dry when the Firebird pulled in the driveway, past Hoovers', cautiously easing in behind our Falcon. Mother made a dash for the closet with the vacuum, and then Wray was knocking; he was in the same room with me; at least the dread was over. And he didn't run to my ear and start murmuring. He was wearing a yellow sports jacket and white bucks, and he had a modified rocker's bowl haircut that emphasized the roundness of his baby cheeks. Not a pimple, not a roughness, not a single coarse man's hair. I had forgotten he was so round, a little egg of a person; he's going to be an egg all his life, I thought, feeling despair for him as well as myself.

He squatted down beside the coffee table, bouncing on his thighs and buttocks and said, "Mrs. Morgan, what a photographer you are! Look how you caught that smile!"

Mother squatted down on the floor beside him, and the two of them talked about framing and how to avoid redspot eyes with a flash. I wondered what would happen if I went back to my room and got back into my shorts and ran my puffy bangs under the shower. Would Mother go out to dinner with Wray? She would have a nice time, I thought, and Wray would never humiliate her with his fake sexiness. But Daddy came in behind me, all fresh in a clean shirt. He gave me three pats on the shoulder, so cheerful and calm, and Wray was so silly, trying to flatter Mother. I just drifted to the couch and lit gently in my floating dress and waited.

Mother offered Wray the picture. He said he wanted to pay her for it, and she said of course not, and Daddy said take the money, and she pretended to scold Daddy, and I got so disgusted with the two of them that I was ready to go when Wray slipped the picture in his pocket and hinted about the time of our reservation. Mother and Daddy stood in the driveway and waved us off, and Kim Hoover came out on her back step, hoping to get introduced. I was ashamed of her, and of Mother and Daddy with their arms around one another's waists. For a few seconds the clouds parted and sunshine came across the grass at a low angle, making a broad gold band between the shadows of the two houses, and the sudden beauty made me plunge inside myself. This is not what I want to be doing, I thought very clearly. Gail Gordon notwithstanding, I don't want to be here now with him.

In the car he continued to use a normal voice. He said he liked my parents, even though they were teachers, and I said they seemed to like him. There was a silence and I noticed how he drove forward, and then I scolded myself; my goodness, Blair Ellen Morgan, maybe his eyes are bad. But it *was* his fault that he filled the silence with stories about his teachers who were all queers, and the ones who weren't queers were still pretty weird. I tried to put a look of ironic detachment on my face, to demonstrate subtly that I couldn't approve of these stories, but Wray didn't get it, and he went on systematically telling the quirks and tics of the teaching staff of Woodrow Wilson High School.

By the time we got to the hotel, people were beginning to look misshapen to me. They shrank if they were small and swelled if they were large, and it only became worse when Wray started talking about his favorite sport, professional wrestling. He subscribed to wrestling magazines and watched every match that was televised. Once he even got his father to take him to Pittsburgh to see it live. None of the great stars were there that night, he said, no one of the stature of Gorgeous George or the Executioner, but he had seen dwarfs and two fat women. He knew it was all fixed, but that made it even funnier. What he liked about the wrestlers was that they were even more weird than his high school teachers.

I wonder now if Wray would have talked about something else if I had joined in the conversation. But I was as close to silent as I have ever been. I smiled like the sweetest frozen dessert, and I watched Wray, watched him as you watch a pimple come out in the corner between your cheek and nostril, with horror and intimacy. He sweated and snorted while I ate rare roast beef and fried chicken and roast turkey and no vegetables except mashed potatoes, and a peach Melba. Wray described imaginary wrestling matches between the other diners at the General Gray: a heavyset family man he called the Giant Greaseball versus Grandma Muscles. On and on, through dinner, then past the people in the street, then in the lobby of the movie theatre. I smiled and yearned to be alone with my thoughts in the dark movie theatre, but I should have guessed, Wray's movie was a gross distortion too, just like his wrestlers and queer teachers. It was supposed to be funny, but all I could see were stupid men who repeated the same actions over and over in black and white, and I began to be afraid I would never again be free of the chill heaviness of the air conditioning, or see with my own eyes, in color.

Then Wray started to make noises. It was sighs at first, and I tried to get involved in the movie so I could forget about him, but he lay back on his seat and turned his face toward me. He gazed and sighed so deeply that my cheek started to prickle. After a while his elbow came onto the arm rest and I whisked mine off, but that left me with no place for my arms because the man on the other side was using that arm rest. Wray's face continued to tip toward me, a gray moon, the same colorlessness as the people on the screen. Wray plucked my left hand up out of my lap and pulled it onto his knee and rolled it lightly between his two chubby, damp palms. Up on the screen an insane general was speaking hoarsely about Bodily Fluids, and I had the feeling Wray was leaching out mine, and replacing them with his. Warmth rose and spread from his body, and just behind the warmth would be a soft eggy odor that would make me throw up all that bleeding dinner meat.

I threw myself forward in my seat, and jerked my hand away. Wray yawned enormously and stretched so widely that his arm was behind me, and he let it land on the back of my chair, and then—I couldn't believe he was doing it—he dropped his hand onto my back and began to stroke my spine. At first I tried to lean forward more, but he took that to mean I wanted his hand lower, so he went down to the small of my back and then started up under the matador jacket. I could feel his heat right through the fabric.

I twisted away and half stood, and said somewhat louder than I meant to, "*Please*, Wray! I haven't seen the movie twice like you have!"

He snatched back his hand and looked in the opposite direction, and while I never did relax between the tension and the air conditioning and that mean movie, at least I had full use of my seat.

At the very end of the movie Wray grabbed my hand again and I let him hold it this time for forty-five seconds during the credits, and then I started to get up and he did too. Walking down the street, out in the normal evening warmth and damp, I decided unequivocally that I was not going to let him kiss me at all. I would do anything rather than have his dampness on me.

His fluids. No saliva, no trails of eggy odor. I didn't smile when he pointed out a man getting into a car and said that looked like a real queer if he ever saw one. He asked what I thought of the movie.

I said, "Oh, it was well done, I guess, but I'm just not sophisticated enough to laugh at hydrogen bombs." It was almost the first thing I'd said except please don't, and he became very quiet as we started driving. I figured he was planning his next assault, but I kept on talking. "My idea of a good movie," I said, "is *Exodus* or *Ben-Hur*. And sometimes for fun I watch old cowboy movies on the late show with my father."

Wray said, "The Skyline drive-in shows cowboy pictures every Friday night. I bet you'd like that."

"Cowboy movies at a drive-in doesn't sound quite the same."

"Do you want to do something else Friday night?"

"I have to work at a pool party. Saturday too. And the week after we're having a festival of choirs at church."

"A festival of choirs," muttered Wray. "That sounds real exciting."

In the dark I began to smile. I wasn't afraid anymore. If he was going to be sardonic, I would be pure. "I find church work very rewarding," I said.

Wray didn't say anything as we drove past the glass plants and then on down the road past the huge slag dumps of burnt coal and waste products at the chemical plant. The slag was glowing tonight, burning slowly, spontaneously. I began to feel a little sorry for Wray, now that I was strong. In a way I had tricked him all along by my sweetness and silence. I should have given him a hint, I thought, that he was disgusting me. Just the same, I was not going to let him kiss me. All I wanted was to get home, for this to be over. I'll never go out with someone I don't like again, I thought.

Just beyond the plants was a big parking lot with a single two-story block building and a neon Budweiser sign that said Dew Drop Inn. There were always a lot of cars there, and usually motorcycles too. There was someone sitting on a motorcycle, and, yes, it was Garland Odell, I was sure of it, sitting all by himself on his Harley out there in the parking lot of that crummy old roadhouse.

"Gar-land," I yelled, rolling down the window and waving, but I didn't think he saw me.

"Who's that?"

"Somebody I go to school with." Wray kept glancing at the rear view mirror nervously, so I added, "We have some pretty rough characters down in this neck of the woods."

We drove along a section of the highway with no houses and almost no trees because it was downwind of the chemical plant. Wray said, "Is that your friend coming?"

I looked out the back, and there was a motorcycle behind us. My heart leaped, my heart pounded. To be saved by Garland! I couldn't let it happen of course, I'd come with Wray. I said, "I never could tell one motorcycle from another."

"I think it's him," said Wray, sounding depressed.

He came right up to our tail, and suddenly passed, at very close quarters. "Goddamit," said Wray, "what does that idiot think he's doing?" Garland rode two abreast with us for several seconds, and there was light reflecting from his glasses as he peered in. I looked away. Could he see me? Did I want him to see me? He went on around at last and disappeared down the highway. "That guy's crazy," said Wray. "That guy's a friend of yours?"

"Oh, not really." It was over. Garland hadn't seen me, or he didn't care. "His sister works down at the pool with Gail and me."

"Everybody in town works at that goddam pool," said Wray.

He was so bad-tempered that my spirits rose again. I wasn't about to let someone kiss me who cursed under a little pressure. We were coming up to the Brazier Burger and I said, "This is where we all hang out or get a bite to eat."

He hit the brakes and swung into the lot. "Are you hungry? Do you want a hamburger?"

"I'd take something to drink." I thought I saw the motorcycle parked in the shadows by the garbage cans. There was one man at the service window, a father ordering ice cream for his kids. "I'll go in and get us a table," I said, leaving Wray. It was, of course, completely unnecessary. The picnic tables at the Brazier Burger were always more than ample for the crowds, and this seemed to be an amazingly quiet Saturday night. I couldn't see anyone at all inside, but I went through the glass door anyhow. All the way in the back, by himself with his cowboy boots up on the table and his bench tipped back, was Garland.

He was dressed up in the boots and the red, blue, and black cowboy shirt. He put his feet down and glared at me. Another night I would have turned away, but this time I was both desperate and strong, and I beckoned. Although he continued to glare, he balled up the paper cup he'd been drinking from and tossed it onto the table, and came. "Firebirds, Impalas," he said. "When do you get a Sting Ray?"

At this little distance he was skinny and red, and there were fine lines around his eyes. "I've got to talk to you," I said.

"All right."

"Well, I didn't mean right now. I'm with somebody. Couldn't you come to the pool tomorrow?"

"I'm leaving tomorrow."

"When are you coming back?"

"I'm leaving for good. I'm going in the army."

I had one of my flashes of light, but with no voice, no righteous explanation. Garland revealed in intense colors, deep shadows behind and below him. And off on the periphery, the glass door opening, Wray making his way in slowly with a tray. "The army? You're going to the army just like that?"

"It's not just like that. I said I was going. I even told you."

Wray had two large Cokes on a tray. How stupid, I thought. He wouldn't be having nearly as much trouble balancing if he had just carried one in each hand without the tray.

I said, "It has to be tomorrow?"

Wray said, "Is this your friend with the motorcycle?"

I said, "This is my friend Garland Odell; he's going to the army tomorrow."

Wray gave his snort-laugh. "Changed the uniforms, haven't they? Or is this the country-and-western army?"

You little snot, I thought, beginning a genuine smile. Garland had made a sideways escape twist of his body, but he stopped and waited for me. What I loved about this moment was my certainty about what I was going to do. I didn't know if it was right or wrong, but I knew what I was going to do. Maybe I even loved it more for probably being wrong. I said, "Wray, I hate to do this, but something has come up. Garland is leaving tomorrow and I have to talk to him. Tonight." Garland stopped twisting and pulled his chin up for a grin.

The tray shuddered in Wray's hands. "Wait a minute."

"Thank you for the lovely evening but I'm going to say good-bye now."

"You can't go off with this guy on his motorcycle—"

"Who's going to stop her?" said Garland, and I thought I'd better get out of there before it all started to look sordid.

"You stay out of it!" Wray's voice scrinching high, the Cokes sloshing onto the tray. "That was an expensive dinner, Blair Ellen!"

"Oh, man," said Garland. "Where did you dig up this guy?"

I snapped open my pocketbook, the wallet inside. The five dollar bill was all I had, my mad money, and if I used it I was going to be out with Garland and nothing. I tossed the bill on the tray in a puddle of Coke. "Here's your money," I said. "If I owe you more, let me know."

"That's not what I want! I don't want your money!"

We started for the door. Garland darted in front to open it for me.

"I don't want your money!" shouted Wray. And to prove it, he dropped the tray with the two large Cokes and the five dollar bill where he stood, and Coke splashed all over his white bucks. "So help me God Blair Ellen I'll tell your Mother!"

Garland and I ran, both afraid, I suppose, that I would change my mind. I threw myself on the motorcycle and Garland took my clutch bag, stowed it in the saddlebag. I said, "I wasn't nice to that boy," but Garland only hurried more, kicking the starter twice, rushing the motor and then we spun off in a shower of gravel. I had no scarf this time, and my hair lashed my forehead, and my skirt ballooned. I clasped my hands under Garland's rib cage and closed my eyes. "Garland! Where are we going?"

"Where do you want to go?"

"I don't care, but don't tell me till we get there, I'm closing my eyes."

He said okay I asked for it and took a sharp right that I thought should be Main Street, but might be the alley, then a left over bumps, then an uphill run in low gear. I tried to get confused, rolled my head a little, wanting to know nothing but motion and Garland's bones. To get rid of Wray like that. Very bad, very bad. In the back of my mind was a stable place where I was explaining myself at length to Mother, how it would have been a betrayal of myself to spend any more time with Wray. His dinner and movies and jokes and Firebirds were just currency to buy wet kisses and feels, I told her. She was listening with her wide eyes about to take off in two directions like birds. But, she said, did you have to humiliate Wray? Wouldn't it have been better to go home and explain it to him? (We were going up another steep hill now, and I had to cling to Garland.) But Mother, there was Garland, too. Garland. She grew smaller, you'll be sorry later, she said, you know that.

We stopped; he turned off the engine. I got off the motorcycle, awkward, unsure of how far the ground was. Where we had come was high, with a powerful breeze.

"It sounds like a storm," I said.

Garland put one arm around my shoulder, and with his right hand held my right one and directed me. "Do you want to guess where we are yet?"

"Not yet."

"Duck." He passed me through some narrow opening, I reached out and there was a heavy wire fence he had parted and we walked through. I had been on the verge of knowing; the hill felt like high school hill, but this strange passage made me awkward again and my teeth began to chatter. I wished I had my five dollars back and wondered if Wray had picked it up. Garland had hidden my pocketbook. "Steps," he said.

We were climbing steps in the open, I could feel more wind as we went up. A high place for sacrifices, I was saying to myself. I must know this place, how can there be a place like this ten minutes from the Brazier Burger that I don't know, and then I thought that maybe I had lost track of time and it had actually been hours since we left.

Garland placed my hands on cold metal, made them grip. "Okay, guess," he said, but just as the metal seemed about to tell me, I couldn't stand not being sure and opened my eyes. I was dizzied by great distances, a vast, seemingly skyless darkness and away down below yellow streetlights and windows. Nearby was the darkened high school, of course. We were at the top of the bleachers. "I almost knew," I said.

We kissed a while where we stood, until I started shivering again, and then we sat down to get some protection from the wind. I said, "Why do you want to go and join the army?"

He started to pull away, but I caught him around the waist and he stayed. He said, "You think the army's for dummies. Well, I'll get my high school diploma in the army, and I can take college too if I want to. I can't stay around here anymore."

He said it flatly, but irrevocably, and I thought I knew why. "Your father came to the pool last week."

"Yeah, I heard."

I was hoping he would go on, tell me about Elroy. We were having an adventure; I was ready to sympathize. What had it been like, to have Elroy Odell for a father? To have a father who wouldn't claim you. We had kissed, we were half lying on the bleachers and I was ready to hear everything, but he didn't speak. Instead I began to hear his breathing and to smell a damp sweetness. Above all to feel the contrast between the warmth where he lay against me and the wind on my back.

He came toward me, for a kiss, I thought, but spoke into the corner of my lips. "Listen, I'm going now, I want to know, did you like me? You did like me, didn't you? *She* always said you did and I was too hard-headed to see it. You did like me, didn't you?"

As I nodded yes, of course, he felt the nod with his fingertips, and began kissing again, not waiting for me to say it aloud. As if the little hint of a nod were all he could ask for. He kissed me and stroked my sides, warming my arms and back; I could feel a gift of warmth from him. After a little while our kissing died down, and I found we really were lying down, on our sides, his nose in my hair. Inside me I heard someone arousing herself lazily, yawning and stretching like a cat. She was larger than I was, at least when she stretched like this, moving under the stroke of his hand.

I whispered, "She's the lucky one." And for a second, when he asked me who? I wasn't sure, but I said, "India."

"Why? What do you mean?"

"She's lucky to have had all this time to get to know you. She can spend as much time with you as she wants."

"She doesn't think she's so lucky. She thinks I'm trouble. Ask her. Not as much trouble as Elroy, but trouble."

I said, "Why don't we run off now, on your bike, get away from town and the army and college too. You'd be a fugitive from justice and I'd be a runaway—"

He didn't say anything at first, then, "I'd do it, but you're just playing around, aren't you?"

I knew I was. That long lazy girl who loved sensation was only one of many. I wished she was the main one. Then we'd run off and do what came naturally, but he was right, I was just playing with my mind.

Garland stroked my side some more, but it was cooler and the catstretch girl seemed asleep again. He whispered, "I want to be special for you. I want to do something no one ever did before." It was so calm between us there that I thought he meant do something for the newspapers, a deed of valor, a robbery. "I'm going away to the army," he said, "and Lord knows I don't mean to hurt you, but I want to be the first one to do something to you." I think I must have giggled nervously without knowing it because he said, "I'm serious."

I said, "What do you want to do to me?"

"Don't sound angry, I don't want to do anything you don't want me to. Just something that I'll be the very first. I don't even care if you lie. You can just tell me I'm the first if you want to." He laid a hand on my ruffles and I froze, feeling nothing; a lot of ruffles and a stiff brassiere underneath.

"All right," I said, "I never let anyone do that." He laughed.

"What's so funny?"

"I don't know. The way you said it. You haven't done much, have you?"

"You know what your problem is, Garland? You talk too much. You'd do a lot better if you just kept your mouth shut."

He shut up. He simply lay there with his hand on my chest,

breathing in my hair. First I was aware of the weight of the hand, and then heat in the shape of his spread fingers, penetrating the ruffles, penetrating the nylon and plastic down into my skin and fat. Very slowly the hand encircled that piece of me, made a cup, cupped me. I opened my eyes and looked at his taut cheek. I lifted his hand and unbuttoned the dress myself, unfastened the bra from behind and lay back. Garland pulled the dress aside, pushed the bra out of the way and there were my breasts lifted up in his hands naked, exposed to the storm wind, contracting and undulating as he moved them, monstrously large things. Garland kept murmuring how beautiful they were, but they frightened me, lifted so high. I had never seen them at this angle, and just when I didn't think I could bear to see them any longer, Garland saved me by covering them with his hands and slowly putting his face between them. A sort of bubble passed through me, caused my eyes to open even wider, and I felt the catstretch again, but this time it was not she but me stretching and sighing. Staring at the heavy, wind-shifted clouds that glowed slightly from the town below. Once I thought I saw a spotlight, like an airplane signal or a carnival beacon. I closed my eyes, and when I opened them again, much later, it seemed, there were bright lights coming through the planks of the bleachers, and three harsh blats on a car horn.

I squirmed to get free, panicked over the hook of the bra, I'd never get it together again, never get all that flesh packed back in. Garland tried to slow me down. "Take your hands off me, Garland Odell," I said.

There was a flashlight down below us, under the bleachers, and a man's deep voice calling up, "Odell, is that you up there?"

"Hey," called Garland, also a deep voice. "Who's that down there?"

I didn't understand why all these deep voices, especially Garland's, why this explosion of thick masculinity. I finally had the bra on, but now there were the buttons.

The flashlight wavered. "It's Don Hagen, Odell."

"Hey, Officer Don," said Garland. "Are you looking for someone to arrest?"

"Nope, a missing person."

[226]

"Nobody missing up here."

"How about Blair Ellen Morgan, is she up there?"

My impulse was to flee. Unbuttoned and all, just to get off these bleachers, run up some dark road and hide myself among tree roots and boulders. But Garland whispered, "Go on, tell him you're okay."

Trying to make my voice deep and manly too, I said, "Hi, Don, I'm not missing."

"Your mother wants you, Blair Ellen." He had moved directly under us and was speaking in a more normal voice. I felt my head shooting away into the distance. The little snitch Wray. But how dare Mother call the police?

I managed my voice with care. "I'll be right down."

Garland grabbed my wrist. "Hey, Don, I'm going into the service tomorrow. We were just saying good-bye. We weren't doing any harm."

"Take your time," said Don. "No hurry." His flashlight beam wobbled away, and I felt as still as stone.

"Old Don's okay," said Garland.

I said, "How could she call the police? You'd think there was a crime."

"I guess your little creep of a boyfriend thought there was one. I guess he thought he got robbed."

In my heart I knew Mother thought there was a crime too, that I had broken my word to Wray. And if she knew what had been going on up here on the bleachers, that would be a crime too.

We sat for a little while shoulder to shoulder, then he put his arm around me, and we kissed, but my head was still far away and Garland's kisses weren't nearly enough to reach me when I wasn't really there anymore.

I wondered what Mother and Daddy would do for punishment. Looks, most likely. Brows furrowed, Daddy shaking his head three, four, five times. How can we ever trust you again? We should have nipped it in the bud when you started hanging around with that Hoover girl; she was a bad influence. Well, I thought, whatever it is, I only have one more year. Then there's college. Real life starts.

Garland startled me when he spoke, I'd almost forgotten he

was still with me. He said, "You want to go, don't you? Well, I'll go talk to her with you. Your mother's okay."

I couldn't believe he expected to explain this to Mother. Garland, all red and flickering, in his high-heeled boots. When we got down, I said, "I want to say good-bye here, Garland. I want to remember you up here." It was true enough; he was finer here, taller, with more electricity, although part of me was saying that just to keep him from coming into that other world. We were both reassured when we saw that Don was driving his pickup instead of the police car. Wearing civilian clothes. I gave Garland a kiss right in front of him, too, and I could feel how much he liked that, having Don as a witness. The last I saw of him was from the truck cab, sitting on his motorcycle, in silhouette, one leg cocked up, lighting a cigarette.

Don glanced at me sideways. "Sorry to drag you off like that, but your mother is pretty upset." I didn't say a word. I spread my skirt over my knees, laid my bag in the center of my lap and looked out the window. "Yeah," said Don, "I really hate to do this." He glanced again, then finally gave up talking and whistled instead to fill the five minutes till he could drop me at our driveway. The Falcon wasn't there, so I figured Daddy was out looking for me too. The good news was that Wray wasn't there either. I felt my hem in the back, to make sure it was down, checked that the buttons were in the right buttonholes.

Mother was all by herself standing at the dining room table with one lamp on. "Lloyd?" she said, as I came in. Something strange was going on, she never just stood anywhere without doing something, and she had on a dress and a comb in her hand, but she hadn't been combing. "Oh, Blair Ellen, I'm so glad you're back. Didn't he come in? I didn't hear a car, but I guess it's just as well, I'm not thinking very straight. I didn't even put on any milk for cocoa." She was just talking a blue streak, wearing that church dress and giving little half smiles and the beginnings of giggles. "Did he find you at the Brazier Burger? I thought that's where you might be. I told him what kind of car Wray had—"

"Mother, what's the matter?"

"I was sorry too, as soon as I sent him. But it didn't seem right to call Lloyd out of lodge, they were having some big investiture service. I ran over to Betty Hoover's, and Don Hagen was there and he offered to go get you—"

I had a flash of her breaking down, and me having to stay home next year to take care of her. "I'm sorry, Blair Ellen, honey, but I can't decide whether to take a bus, or there's a train—I don't know what clothes—" her face, which had been darting in all directions, suddenly collapsed to the middle and the weight of it seemed to knock her down into a chair and tears ran down her cheeks. "I talked to Pearl," she said, ."so I think she's okay, but she sounded groggy because they gave her tranquilizers."

"What was it, Mother, what happened?" A good daughter would have run right over and embraced her while she cried, but my body had closed up, and my hands hung at my side.

"It's a heart attack again," she said. "I talked to the doctors too, they say he's going to make it, but that's what they said about Joe Stone too. And Pearl is so doped up she doesn't seem to know if it's Mr. Tobin or Joe she's married to."

"He's not dead?"

"I don't know why it's affecting me like this," she said. "I never even liked the man. It's the way Pearl sounded, she said, 'It's happening again, Sibyl, will it always happen?' "

"I think you'd better take the train," I said. "And you should have called Daddy as soon as it happened." Something took over in me, a part of me like Mother as she was supposed to be. I told her to go into her room and pack five or six sets of underwear and I'd come in to help pick the dresses. I called the lodge, and then I started coffee, thinking how I'd make up a thermos for her to take on the train, and I'd have to make sure she packed her charcoal-colored suit, in case there was a funeral.

As I dialed the phone to check the train schedule, I could see myself doing it in a cone of spotlight; I looked vivid, and this moment seemed important. In another cone of light was me embracing Garland. And I thought I glimpsed a landscape of my life, mostly dim, even murky, but there were these moments of light, precious instants when I had done the best thing, for me and others.

PART
THREE

THEY CALL THE AIRPLANE FROM PITTSBURGH DOWN INTO WEST Virginia a commuter, which is to say that it has no foil packets of almonds, and the propeller vibration is transmitted directly through the fuselage and seats to the thirteen passengers. I am always unnerved by the way the wings of the little plane shudder when we hit a low pressure pocket, but I like the sense of being airborne, of actually flying through thin air in a metal machine. The long ridge of the Allegheny front off to the east never flattens the way even the Rockies do from a jet, and the farther south we fly, the more I can feel the fullness and volume of the hills and I am drawn down, through the dirty glass, past the propeller blur, toward those blunt-topped green hills of home.

That trip I was going down for the tenth anniversary of my high school graduating class. As the hills rose and fell below like waves in the earth, what kept popping to the surface were the faces of those people I hadn't seen for ten years and more. How can I look back ten years and see anything, I thought; I'm too young to think in decades. The faces didn't seem ten years in the past, even though I never saw any of them when I was home. So many of the neighbors, like the Hoovers, had moved away. I never went home for more than a couple of days anyhow. Sometimes Aaron would be with me, sometimes Mother and Daddy come up to visit us, or we meet in some neutral place like Washington or Winchester for a weekend. I like it this way; my work, my friends aren't down here. Only my parents.

But when I began to get mail from the reunion committee, the faces rose before me, and I felt a dissatisfaction with the present, or perhaps with the fact of having chosen this present instead of some other one. I had a hankering for other possibilities, for a life in which I ended up married to someone from my class, a farmer or a miner. No offense to the great state of West Virginia, said Aaron, but I don't want to meet your redneck high school friends. I said nothing, but when by mistake I checked the box in the questionnaire marked "single" instead of "married" I mailed it back without a correction. I suppose I was having a vague fantasy of an interlude with someone from home. Maybe Johnny Bardoline, I thought, gazing down at the brown cow ponds, the little patchy farms. The plane vibrated, and I vibrated, and I thought of all the boys I had been too shy to let know I liked them.

We descended toward the sliced-off hilltop of the Graysburg airport. Too soon, I thought; I wanted to stay in the mood; I wanted to embrace something, the hills maybe. We swung in low over some steers who didn't look up, and we bounced and rattled and the brakes squealed. Thrills over, the plane was merely stuffy and cramped, and the airport didn't look like home; it was too flat, an unfamiliar, hazy hot plateau that took forever to roll across. I wished I had Aaron with me after all; Aaron was my home, not this place.

Mother and Daddy had some people with them, teacher friends, who had waited after seeing their party off just to meet me. New York, they said, how exciting. Social work must be so interesting. Welfare? No, I explained, I work in the rehabilitation of long-term in-patients—paralyzed people, cerebral palsy. The poor things, they said. Actually, I'm rather encouraged, I said. Oh yes, they said, shaking their heads sadly.

"Weren't they nice?" said Mother as we moved through the heat of the parking lot. "I work with her on the county textbook committee. I think you made a good impression."

Daddy said, "What do you think of the Pinto? It's a stripped-down little car, but it goes."

"Most of the time," said Mother.

He always bought Fords. He had been tempted to try one of the Japanese imports, he told me, but he decided to stick with America.

Mother was impatient to get back to the new friends. They taught in Maryland for twenty years, she told me, and then one day they just picked up and came home. They wanted to live in West Virginia.

Something was bothering me: the thinness of the Pinto's metal. Mother's eagerness to talk about strangers. Hot wind filling the car. I tried to grunt politely until they were through with their separate topics; I tried to look at the countryside now that I was down in it, but a rush of anger came over me, shocking and sudden like sheets of rain across a meadow.

"Well," I said, "Aaron is fine, in case anyone's interested."

"Oh," said Mother. "How *is* Aaron?"

"Fine."

"Aaron is a fine young man," said Daddy. "Couldn't ask for a better son-in-law, could we, Sibyl?"

"I wish he could have come down with you."

I was full of suspicion. What did they *really* mean? That they were delighted Aaron hadn't come? That they saw this as a chance to reconstitute our little unit of three as it used to be? That they wanted me to come home like the Maryland teachers, and say I'd been wrong ever to leave? All their questions about Aaron—how was the thesis coming, how was his father—everything had a cheerfulness I didn't trust. And not a word about *my* news that I'd mentioned in my post card. They were interested in Aaron and his life up there, but they didn't want to hear of anything about my life. My real life.

Daddy said, "I bet you've been looking forward to a real West Virginia beefsteak tomato."

I said, "We get good tomatoes, Daddy. There's a greengrocer right around the corner on Broadway. He gets really nice vine-ripened New Jersey tomatoes."

Daddy's chin dropped a couple of centimeters and I felt Mother turn to me, disapproving because I was not being nice to Daddy.

Daddy said, "*Aaron* would know the difference. *He* knows a good tomato when he tastes one."

Inside me a voice exclaimed don't be silly; I know the difference too, don't you think I know that New Jersey tomatoes aren't the same? But this unexpected darkness around me was too heavy, and I didn't speak aloud. I thought I could shake it off if they would just ask the right question, if they would just ask what my big news was. They probably thought I was pregnant, that would be their idea of big news. I really shouldn't come down here by myself, I thought. Something happens; I get moody. So much better when Daddy and Mother visit us. I get tickets to musical shows and make Bisquick crumb cake and Aaron laughs at me for climbing up on a chair to knock down cobwebs from the paint-rounded moldings. Mother and Daddy are worth the effort, though, in New York. They are delightful guests. Mother dances with enthusiasm saying oh yes I'd love to see the Museum of the American Indian, and also the botanic gardens, and a walk through the Village and Soho too and dinner in Chinatown and Little Italy. Yes, please, everything. Daddy sucks his pipe and maintains an ironic distance, collecting freaks and wonders to tell his buddies down at the lodge: the mountain of garbage bags in front of my apartment house, the classical string trio playing on the church steps, and above all, winos and transvestites.

My head had begun to hurt, a straight band of pressure across my eyebrows. "It's so hot," I said. "The plane was stuffy, and I've got an awful headache."

"I'll carry your suitcase," said Daddy.

"Well, go lie down," said Mother. "I'll get a cold washcloth."

The easiest thing was to let them do it. They were going to take care of me. Mother put my blinds down, got the washcloth; Daddy set the suitcase on the chair, and opened it, like a bellboy. They tiptoed and whispered, and I drifted back behind the headache and anger, and a half-dream, half-fantasy came to me. I've been so ill, I dreamed. I've had amnesia. The cool oblong over my forehead released a drip of cold water that ran down my temple, tickled my ear. I've been partially paralyzed, I thought; I've been lost for ten years, and they just found me and brought me here to convalesce. My legs have atrophied; they're skinny and yellow, but I will soon walk again. Little by little they will give me simple exercises, to walk to the garden, to dry dishes. Mostly the sleep cure, to forget all intervening events.

At dinner Mother filled my plate herself: huge slices of tomato, pork chop, applesauce. "How's your headache, honey?"

"Oh, it's gone," I said. There was a certain pressure remaining, but I was ready to take care of myself. I put a little more applesauce on my plate just so she'd know. I said, "It may have been the altitude change. You know my sinuses." They still furrowed their foreheads, worrying, worrying.

Mother said, "Lloyd, do you remember the fit Blair Ellen threw when we had to move out of the old house into this one?"

"Sure do," said Daddy.

"Sure do," I said.

Mother said, "Blair Ellen was right, we should never have moved in the first place, and we shouldn't have sold it."

Daddy said, "Sibyl threw the fit this time, even though it was her idea to sell it."

I said, "It looks like they're fixing it up nicely."

"That's the point. You can fix up a good old house, but these new ones are cheap. The tiles in the bathroom are falling off. We should have bought ceramic tile in the first place instead of that horrible marbleized plastic that turned yellow and fell off."

"But, Sibyl," said Daddy. "The tile didn't go bad, it was the grout."

"I say we were penny wise and pound foolish. We should have invested in the real thing in the first place."

"Then we'd have broken ceramic all over the bathtub," said Daddy.

"It's a new house," said Mother. "Things shouldn't be breaking so soon."

"It's not a new house; it's a fifteen-year-old house."

This, I thought, was something new. My father and mother never argued. Other people argued, but not them. I said, "The house must be going through adolescence. I thought I would fall apart in my adolescence too."

They both stared at me, and Mother said, "You didn't have a hard adolescence. You had an easy adolescence."

"Mother! I was terribly unhappy!"

Daddy started winking at me, and Mother said, "You were so busy with school, and all your girl friends and boyfriends. I never saw anyone with so many interests and places to go and things to do and always laughing—"

"That must have been some other daughter you had, because I was lonely and miserable."

Mother's eyes became huge. "Pearl and I knew something about trouble, but *you* just sailed along."

My vision was beginning to cloud over again. Duskily I could see Daddy winking at me. The phone rang; she went to get it, and he whispered, "It's the change. Very moody. They all get moody when they go through the change."

I was about to tell him that I seemed to be going through the change too, because I was moody, and everything they did irritated and confused me, and I didn't know how to be with the two of them anymore, but Mother came back, fastening on her denim wraparound skirt. She was perfectly calm and cheerful again. "I have to go down to church," she said. "Blair Ellen, can you make Daddy's coffee?"

"You didn't finish eating," I said. "You hardly took two bites."

Daddy said, "What is it this time? You'd think that church could get through one night without you."

She fluffed her hair and smiled benignly down on the two of us. "They're making centerpieces for the father-son banquet and Betty Hagen says they need something; they don't look right. I'll only be half an hour."

I said, "Why aren't the sons and fathers making the centerpieces?"

But Mother laughed as if I'd made a joke and left Daddy and me staring at each other over the puddles of tomato seeds.

"Spends half her time down at that church," he said, as if he never went himself. "And if it's not the church it's some old lady who can't drive herself to the doctor, or the woman's club *has* to have her on a committee. Those other women don't have the responsibilities she does. But they can't do anything without her." He muttered and filled his pipe.

I cleared the table and said, "I doubt she'd do it if she didn't enjoy it."

He said, "Mostly I'm sick of that holier-than-thou Betty Hagen. She got herself born again and now she thinks she runs that church."

"Who's Betty Hagen?"

"You know, she's the one that married her daughter's boyfriend. Your mother practically gave her that house to live in for free—"

"Betty Hoover?" I said. "Betty Hoover married Don Hagen?"

"That's right, you've got it. They come back nice and married and he's decided he's a lay preacher and suddenly she's trying to run our church—and the two of them never saw the inside of a church till last year."

"Well, for heavensakes," I said. "What do you know." I could hardly wait for Mother to get back so I could find out about Betty and Don. Betty and Don, and whatever happened to Bunny and Kim. Maybe Bunny would come to the reunion. I felt a rush of energy, started the coffee and went to unpack. So things happened here too: Mother and Daddy argue, Don Hagen becomes a preacher, and Betty Hoover marries him. This is real life, I thought, maybe even my life.

I had brought with me a certain empire-waisted blue dress in case I chickened out about wearing the dress I really preferred. Something long and violet, cut like a slip. I put it on without a brassiere, sashed it with an antique scarf, put on the gold slippers, the velvet choker and five strands of blue and purple beads. A dress that made me think of Bunny and now her mother too—free, colorful, overflowing. I went out to show Daddy.

I stood in the angle of the L for a couple of seconds, where every corner of the house was visible. Daddy was in his recliner reading the paper with the television on. I had seen Mother serve tea in the armchair and loveseat while Daddy was two feet away smoking and listening to the television through a little plastic earplug, and no one seemed to notice anything strange about the invisible barrier. Where did I sit in those days? Often in the wing chair that faced out the window. I would read there, or, in the old days, pretend to read and watch the Hoovers. I was always looking for something, I thought, I was always thinking there was some person I could learn what I needed from.

I turned on the overhead light. "How do you like my outfit, Daddy?" I took a whirl; I jangled and swished. I knew he would hate it. "It's school colors, for the reunion."

"You're going to the reunion in *that*? You look like a gypsy in a nightgown."

It could have been worse. He had decided to be humorous. Maybe considering an anecdote for the fellows at lodge: my own daughter, a married woman, but that's the way they dress in New York!

I said, "I figure since I live in New York people will expect me to look exotic, right?"

He turned his face away from me, exposed to the blue and yellow television light as if he were taking the sun. "You never had to go up there in the first place," he said softly. "West Virginia may not be the biggest, but it's got a little of everything."

"I never said anything against West Virginia. I love West Virginia."

"Coal is coming back too. You wait. They're going to be on their hands and knees begging for coal. And that means your environmentalist friends too."

We always had one political discussion. They were usually good-humored because Daddy didn't care all that much, but wanted me to know where he stood. I settled on the hassock, and said, "Well, if we burn too much coal and turn the rain acid, we may all be begging for trees."

Daddy smiled. "There has to be progress, Blair Ellen. That's one thing I'm sure about. This country was founded on progress."

The phone rang and as I ran for it I called to Daddy, "That's General Electric, Daddy, not America."

The voice on the phone was Aaron. Very short, dry, and distant. Oh, no, I thought, it's his father's heart, and the apartment's been robbed. "What's the matter?" I said. "Are you all right?"

"Oh, yeah." He sounded slow and pathetic, sorry for himself.

A thick silence, and this time I just waited till he went on. "Shelley is coming in. She's coming this weekend. Tomorrow."

"Tell her to stay around till I get back."

"How soon can you come?"

"Maybe Wednesday."

Silence again. Then, "Well, what am I supposed to do with her?"

"She's your cousin, Aaron, for heavensake."

"She's your friend. You know I can't get along with her. She'll want to drink wine and smoke dope all night and I have to work."

"Oh, Aaron, she's a vegetarian now."

"Wine and grass are vegetables. Can't you come back sooner?"

"I just got here, Aaron!" I had no patience with him when he started sounding mournful. Daddy came by, went to the kitchen. I wanted to get back to our discussion. Aaron seemed far away, Shelley at an infinite distance. Daddy was putting out a bag of Oreos, pouring milk. I wanted to say, the truth of the matter is, Aaron, that I just found out about Betty Hoover and Don Hagen. And Daddy and I were about to do corporations and Nixon. I can't think about Shelley.

I changed after I got off the phone and went in the kitchen and watched Daddy sipping milk and coffee alternately as he ate cookies. I said, "That was Aaron. His cousin Shelley is coming to visit. Do you remember Shelley, my old roommate?"

"The girl with the big mouth?" He glanced at me sideways. "No offense to Aaron. You know we think the world of Aaron."

"She does have a big mouth. Aaron hates it more than you do. I always wanted to be like her."

Daddy rolled his eyes. "Have a cookie," he said. "Sit down and tell me how glad you are that the president is going to have to resign."

I did sit down. I didn't want to talk about Shelley either. She was from a dark period of my life. I had wanted to be like her because I had no models of how to be in a city. I ate an Oreo and said, "As a matter of fact, I don't want him to resign at all. I'd prefer an impeachment and trial."

Daddy stopped chewing for a brief moment, then swallowed

and settled himself to go at it seriously, but we were interrupted again. This time it was Mother, bursting in with her face young, her arms full of bundles. "Don't eat those old cookies!" she cried, dancing around us, grabbing bowls and spoons. "I bought soft ice cream and hot fudge!"

Just to prove he didn't take orders, Daddy ate two more Oreos, and then he folded his hands in his lap while she made him an enormous sundae and told us about the centerpieces she had thrown together out of nothing. I made my own sundae, trying to keep it small, but the soft ice cream seemed to slide so easily into the bowl that I added more and more, and heavy spoonfuls of hot fudge.

There was something so satisfying about the sundaes. Something about all the other times we three had sat around the table slathering our mouths with sweets: after school, after dinner, late at night before going to bed. I said, "Aren't you two ever going to ask me what my news is?"

They looked at each other. Mother said, "We figured it was something that didn't work out or else you would have mentioned it."

I dipped my spoon into the ice cream again, and took a little hot fudge, and told them I was quitting work now that Aaron had a real tenure-track teaching job. I was going to get my MSW. They were delighted. I told them all about it. Then Mother told about how Betty Hagen had gone to visit Bunny in Newport News, Virginia, and Don followed one or both of them, but stayed with Betty. Then Daddy told about how Thorny Thornton had been passed over again for assistant superintendent of schools, and eventually we got back to the president's resignation and whether or not it was good to wash the country's laundry in public. Talking and talking. Daddy sleek and solid, but with the softness of humor in the corners of his mouth and eyes. Mother flashing enthusiasm and sternness over the rights and wrongs of issues. The three of us, eating ice cream and talking, in perfect balance.

The VFW sat in the middle of the parking lot, windowless as a pillbox, a neon sign on top and a flagpole in front. There weren't many cars yet, and I wondered if I had the wrong night, or if most of the people in my class had decided in mysterious accord to ignore the reunion.

"Do you want me to walk you in?" said Daddy.

He didn't like the idea of a female person, all dressed up, going into the VFW alone. "Thanks, Daddy," I said. "I'll be okay. I'll probably get a ride home with somebody so you won't have to come out again."

"I'd better come for you. They allow liquor in there, you know."

I gave him a kiss on the cheek, his cool, flat cheek, sweet-smelling, last contact with home. I went into a vestibule with a coat rack and doors, and I straight-armed the big double ones and sprang all the way inside, quickly scanning the place where I'd landed: a wide, bland hall where someone was testing the lights, turning them high and low; a stage to my right with a band's amplifying equipment; tables filling all of the floor space except one small area near the band; a few couples scattered around the tables; and loops of yellow and purple crepe paper louring over-head.

Was this it? I thought. This is the famous drunken VFW? This is the Tenth Reunion of the Class of 1964? Everything was so stark; I looked for something lovely and found a corsage of roses moving toward me on a broad, green bosom. The woman seemed to be too old to be in my class; an auburn bullet of hair thrust high and back. In a dry but authoritative voice, she said, "Blair Ellen Morgan."

Some gear caught in me, and I started smiling before I recognized her face, and when I did, I was so delighted that I almost hugged her. "Carmell!" I said. She drew back, and I remembered they don't give so many hugs and kisses down here.

She folded her hands under her bosom. "You aren't all that different," she said. "I'd say you picked up a little weight, maybe, but it don't spoil your figure. You walked right by Teresa." She gestured economically with her chin toward a table by the door. I had plunged in without looking to the side; there was a card table set up there with rows of name tags and stacks of programs, and Teresa Spinett in red, frowning her enormous dark eyes slightly.

I gave my biggest smile but Teresa didn't even move her chin in response. Both of them, she and Carmell, seemed suspicious of me. I began to wonder if I was doing something else wrong, even though I had controlled my aggressive hugging.

Teresa said, "You live in New York City and you don't have any kids." I nodded, waiting. "I'm the one who went over all the information sheets and made up the name tags."

"She's on my committee," said Carmell. "I'm the head of the party arrangements. Some people didn't like the VFW and thought it wasn't fancy enough."

"It looks nice to me."

"Some people," said Teresa, "means Gail Bardoline."

Carmell said, "Well, *I'm* not the one naming names, but I said to Gail no sir *you* may have the money to rent the Hotel General Gray but I don't have that kind of money and I don't think most of the people in our class do either. We'll have a good time at the VFW; you don't need the fanciest place in the country to have a good time."

"This looks just lovely, really," I said, eager to convince and not offend.

Someone else was coming up, a lovely slim woman in a flowing yellow dress. "Linda!" I said, "Linda!" and she did give me a hug, a great big one, smelling of the woods and the Orient. She looked wonderful, in fact I thought all four of us looked wonderful. I felt a surge of enthusiasm for how Carmell had turned solid in her hugeness, and Teresa had stayed snappy, and Linda grown sophisticated with her hair long. They told me how many children they had, how Linda was teaching at Woodrow Wilson High School, and I told them how much I liked living in New York and invited them all to come and visit me, and everything was fine until I asked Linda about her cousin Johnny, and that got Carmell and Teresa sour again over Gail, and Linda apparently didn't want to be involved in that wrangle, so she drifted off.

Carmell was saying, "Gail and Johnny may not come. Gail isn't so sure she wants to rub shoulders with the rest of us." Out of the corner of my eye I was recognizing other people now; I wanted to move on the way Linda had. "Well, Gail always was like that," said Carmell, "nice as you please until something didn't go her way and then she'd rather pull the whole thing down." In exactly the same tone she added, "Here comes my husband. Dwayne, come over here and meet Blair Ellen Morgan, she's the one from New York."

Dwayne was tall, bony in the neck and square in the shoulders, not altogether comfortable in his plaid sports jacket, I thought, but he had deep grin lines in his face, and he wore his hair in the old rockabilly style. I used to be fascinated by boys who looked like that, so free and easy in their joints. He let Carmell do the talking and he swayed from side to side slightly, rhythmically. Carmell had plenty to say, mostly about how hard she worked on this party. Dwayne and I watched each other.

"You were the hardest one to seat, Blair Ellen," she said. "All the tables seemed to come out even, and I still had you."

"Am I the only person who isn't coming in a couple?"

"Well, they're some divorced boys, but that didn't seem right to put you with, so I finally put you with Garland, he never has been married, or never told me anyhow. But who knows if he'll show up. India says he's coming, but I don't know. Well, if you end up at the dance without a partner, I'll make Dwayne come over."

Dwayne's long body seemed to catch itself swaying and straighten up. "I'd volunteer to do that."

Between Dwayne's compliment and knowing I was going to sit with Garland, I felt a flush of attractiveness. It ran through my body, powerful enough to start me off on my own around the room. More were arriving now, although they were still sitting in static little clumps, too far away from each other. I knew how they should be, closer, standing, backing up and bumping each other, then making the air crackle with laughs. They would pick up energy from each other, bounce. I started bouncing myself, meeting husbands and wives, meeting Linda's husband, and when I turned again, it had begun to happen—the band testing microphones, someone had put out bowls of ice and little squat restaurant glasses, and on all the tables bottles of Scotch and bourbon sprouting like mushrooms. As I went from table to table, I made the same joke to everyone about how I'm so stupid I forgot it was always BYO in this county, and of course everyone tried to give me a drink, so I carried a glass with four ice cubes and a little Scotch from table to table. I barely sipped it, but I hadn't eaten all day in order to sash up tightly, and my head got light. That was a great advantage because the drooping streamers became graceful; I saw them as a lowered ceiling of flowers. People bloomed too, the women's dresses, of course, but the men as well. All sorts of graceful tall and low people, even the ones who sat awkwardly at the tables without mixing seemed to be waiting for me to come and liberate them. People who had been fat became slim, and people who had become fat seemed to deserve the extra weight. Girls had let their hair grow, and boys had developed dignified high foreheads. In my delight with everyone I whirled like a petal in the wind until I recognized my table by India Odell's red hair, and I approached slowly, getting a good look at her before she saw me. She was wearing a pale green costume somehow medieval: tight-sleeved coat open over a high-waisted dress that lifted her breasts.

When she noticed me, she got to her feet, and I was impressed by some change in her face, more than not wearing glasses, an openness, something solved triumphantly. We hugged, and her arms were as strong as cable.

I was struck as always by the bay eyes. "You don't wear glasses anymore," I said.

She shrugged. "Contacts. But *you* haven't changed at all."

"I've tried to!"

She laughed, "No, just the same Blair Ellen."

"Is it the bangs? I just can't cut off my bangs."

"No, it's all of you." For some reason I found myself believing whatever she said; one who used to be silent was speaking; she must have the truth. I was afraid my purple dress and antique scarves were shabby beside her, but she seemed proud of me, held onto my arm, wanted me to meet her husband. "Duke," she said, "this is Blair Ellen Morgan. She was just about the smartest person in our class, a class officer and everything."

I said, "But I was never queen, India was our queen."

Duke liked that. He had a big throw-back-the-head laugh. He was much older than we were, near fifty I would guess, a big-chested man of many textures: curly gray sideburns, rough skin, a gold chain in the chest curls at his throat. "Hey," he said, enclosing my hand, a real square dealer handshake, "Hey, nice to meet you, Blair Ellen Morgan, I mean it. What are you drinking? Scotch? But not that stuff, let me get you some real Scotch." Continuing to hold my elbow after the handshake, taking me out of India's hands, he directed me into a chair, took my glass, and eased India down beside me. Very paternal, I thought; cute. Just what you'd want from a man old enough to be your father. Under the table he had a leather case, a complete traveling bar with little chromium shot glasses and three brands of Scotch. The ice in the bowl had melted too much to suit him, so he went off to the kitchen telling me and India to have Old Home Week while he was gone.

"He's really terrific, India," I said. I never felt so sincere in my life. I thought I had never liked so many people so much. Our whole class, big successes! Wonderful choice of husbands! I said, "Do you have kids?"

She said, "No, no kids." Then, "We haven't been married very long. Duke's my third husband."

"Your *third* husband?" I was stunned. Three of them? It seemed a little risqué, somehow. People I knew lived with one another for a while and if it didn't work out broke up, but they didn't have three husbands. People from a different generation did: Aunt Pearl or Elizabeth Taylor, but not us!

"Well, the first one doesn't count for much. That was my last year in high school—"

"You were married in high school? Come on India! I was worrying about French kissing, and you were married? Was it the guy with the black Buick?" Dimples appeared in her cheeks. I remembered India in her little, faded, cotton skirts and the cheap ballet flats and seams in her stockings, and I used to think she was deprived, and all the time she had a husband. I said, "Sometimes my ignorance when I was sixteen just makes me sick." She was laughing at me, but I didn't mind India laughing. "I mean it, I was naive in the worst way. I walked around with some kind of a hood on my head, I had no idea what was going on around me."

From way down in her throat, a laugh. "That marriage was the worst mistake of my life. The second one was better, but Duke is the best of all. The real thing."

He was back, pouring me Johnnie Walker Black Label. I insisted on mostly ice and India didn't want to have her drink freshened. "Sit down now, Duke," she said. "Blair Ellen is fine and I'm fine. You relax now. She wants to know if we have any kids."

"Lord have mercy, Miss Blair Ellen!" said Duke. "We've only been married three months." He leaned toward me, over her, his chin two inches from her chest. "She made me wait. Two long years of waiting."

"Well, tell her why, Duke. You make me sound awful."

"I ask you, Blair Ellen Morgan, I ask you, what is wrong with serving in the armed forces of your country?"

If he'd been twenty-four or thirty, and if I hadn't been feeling so delighted with the reunion, I might have told him, but I wanted to love everyone, and I just opened my eyes wide.

"Tell it right, Duke."

"She wouldn't marry me as long as I was in the service. It was my career. I was a sergeant major in the U.S. Army and she outright refused to marry me until I retired. Now what do you think about that?"

"They drink too much in the service," she said. "He has a real good job now, Blair Ellen. He's a personnel executive with the hospital."

He gave her neck a nuzzle and more or less kept his face out of her bosom. "Yeah, it's a good job. I like it. India got it for me."

"No, I didn't, you got it for yourself."

"Hell, India, you did it. She can do anything in that hospital she wants to. She practically runs it already, she's the head nurse in the cardiac unit."

Duke and I together gazed proudly at India. How wonderful, I thought, sipping the Scotch, not thinned by melting ice cubes yet. So all along India had been the kind who knew what she wanted. She would never just sort of move in with someone, I thought, not book by typewriter by guitar the way Aaron and I had sidled upon one another. She would never sneak down to city hall one Monday afternoon and get married mostly because she heard her mother and father were coming to visit Aunt Pearl in New Jersey.

"India," I said, "you have always been pretty, but now, even your smile is bigger."

"Teeth," she said, drawing her lips back and tapping her luminous front teeth with a fingernail. "I never used to open my mouth when I smiled because there was decay all along here."

"No one told her about dentists," said Duke. "Ain't that a sight? You'd think that somewhere along the line, some teacher or somebody, would have figured out to send her to a dentist."

I was conscience struck. My parents were the teachers, and I had thought India was going around with her mouth shut because she was shy or maybe not as bright as she could be.

"It wasn't anybody's fault," she said. "I just thought that's the way the world was. Garland had perfect teeth and I had rotten ones. I would have died if anyone guessed."

The microphones were clicking, Carmell telling everyone to sit down. "All right, everyone," said Carmell. "The ladies of the VFW want to get home sometime tonight. We can visit all we want after we eat." She welcomed us, then introduced Linda, and Linda welcomed us. I began to drift, as if I were in church or at an eight A.M. lecture. Duke was holding India's hand on top of the table, everyone in couples but me. Even Aaron, I thought. I figured Shelley must be there by now; they would be eating pot roast, the only main course Aaron could make, or else, if Shelley didn't eat meat, out at Chuan Yuan. Someone had died, said Linda, and she wanted to light a candle and have a minute of silence. A boy and girl I hardly knew: the girl in childbirth; the boy in Vietnam. I tried to feel grief but wanted to get back to excitement.

As soon as Linda said amen, the women came bursting out of the kitchen with soup bowls full of salad greens and plates of brown 'n serve rolls. The VFW lady for our table said, "There's three places here with nobody at them."

"One's my brother," said India. "He's coming."

I said, "Do you suppose Gail and Johnny are the other two? They just walked in."

There had been a disturbance near the door, a couple of former football players on their feet, reaching to shake hands with Johnny Bardoline. Gail was behind him, wearing black. It took them a long time to cross the room because so many people wanted to speak to him. He looked thinner than in high school, but his hair was the same, dense and shiny like black cat fur, with the whimsical hairline, the swoop in the middle. Everyone still loved Johnny.

When they got to us, he made his slow grin and shook hands all around, accepted seats and a drink from Duke. Gail's face looked exactly as it always had, good make-up, soft hairstyle from a good beauty parlor. She was frowning, though, and she sank heavily in a chair and pointed at her voluminous tunic. "Can't drink. I'm pregnant." We congratulated her, Duke made a toast, Johnny said they were hoping for a boy, they already had two great little girls. Gail said, "But even when I'm drinking I can't stand Johnnie Walker Black. Dewar's White Label is okay, or even Teacher's, but that stuff will burn your tongue off."

I let Duke fill me up again, with Johnnie Walker Black. "I like it," I said. "It puts hair on your chest."

She stared at me in utterly bad humor, and said, "Cheap."

I thought she meant me, my little joke, my clothes, but she waved a hand at the ceiling. "I knew it would look like this. Yellow crepe paper. I quit their committee, you know. I can't stand people who think of the cost before anything else."

"Come on, Gail," said Johnny, waving at somebody across the room.

"I don't mind cutting costs if you have to, but you can't start cheap, you can't think cheap. You'd think we were all on relief down here. We could have done better for the same money. Maybe not what Blair Ellen is used to in New York City, but we could have done better than this."

"It looks good to me," I said.

"I knew you'd be polite. Didn't I say Blair Ellen would be polite, Johnny?"

"Nothing wrong with being polite," said Johnny.

"Hey," said Duke. "It's the liquor, not the bottle, that's what I always say. The company, not the house."

The VFW lady put the first two plates down—meatloaf and mashed potatoes, green beans, a sprig of parsley.

"All I wanted," said Gail, "was flowers on the table, some inexpensive champagne. Or just red wine. Broiled steaks would have been simple enough. Baked potatoes and sour cream. But not meatloaf."

"Salisbury steak," said our VFW lady, letting Gail's plate fall to the table from a somewhat greater height than anyone else's, but Gail didn't seem to notice; she started right in eating.

She said, "Well, they made fresh potatoes anyhow. You have to give them that much credit."

Johnny gave me a quick, flirtatious grin. "I bet Blair Ellen enjoys home cooking after all that fancy stuff."

"I don't eat in restaurants, Johnny. I have a kitchen in my house."

"I'm going to have you all to my house for dinner," said Gail. "I'll show you we can do things right around here."

"Hey, that's real nice," said Duke. "These are good people, right, India honey?"

But India had her hand up in the air waving. There was another commotion from the football boys near the door. I saw someone there with light hair, Tommy Tucker? and behind him, staying close to the wall, in a white denim suit and tinted glasses, was Garland. He strolled in our direction, very casual, lighting a cigarette as he came. Trying to look like he just blew in from the Coast, I thought, with that open-throated flowered shirt, and a little fringe of hair on his forehead like the bust of a Roman senator. Too stylish for my taste. He stopped behind the empty chair, shook hands when the men offered, nodded to Gail and me and ignored India.

"Take a load off, Gar," said Duke.

"Dinner isn't as bad as it looks," said Gail.

Of all these people, I thought, Garland is the only stranger. He had the same small-boned chin and the same red fox color, but that was all I recognized. "Stop standing there like a fool, Garland," said India in a voice like cutting wire, and I had to look at her, because I didn't recognize that voice either. Something wasn't right, I thought. Something at once complicated and coldly stark. I had been so much happier in the threesome—India, Duke, and me. Garland was a cool spot on my right. When Johnny asked what he was doing these days, India answered for him. Starting a course in computer programing, she said. Living in Silver Spring with her and Duke. I was suspicious. What had he been doing all these years if he was just starting training in something now?

I decided I'd rather talk to Johnny. He was directly across from me, and he reminded me of Aaron in a comfortable, dark-eyed way. He talked about coaching. He liked it even better than playing sports himself, he said. He never would have guessed that. He worked out with his teams to keep in shape a little, but the main thing, what he loved, was working with the boys. Seeing them get strong, develop their skills, put it all together as a team.

I began to feel loving again. That was the kind of thing I wanted to hear. Let Garland Odell sit as lightly as a piece of ash; Johnny Bardoline was a real person, a man of flesh.

I said, "Johnny, remember when you were class president and I was vice-president? Whenever someone brought you some work to do you would hand it to me."

"I wouldn't do that to you," grinned Johnny.

"Oh, yes, you would," said Gail. "A lot of people wanted him to run for city council last year, but he didn't think he wanted to sit through all the meetings. Johnny's basically lazy."

Johnny made a silly face that nobody saw but me.

I was beginning to think that maybe he was the one I had been wanting. He had a sweetness, impossible to pass up. But Carmell was calling us to order again and Johnny, as our last president, had to go up and give out door prizes, and Gail went along with him. When they announced the next prize was for shortest time married, I said, "That'll be you, India."

But she shook her head and pointed. It was Teresa Spinett in her brilliant red dress, with a short, wide-shouldered man who looked enough like her to have been one of her brothers. As they stood shoulder to shoulder, very serious, accepting a foil-wrapped gift box, there was a long explosive holler.

"Oh, Lord," said India.

I couldn't see. "Who is it?"

"Tommy Tucker. They used to be married. Didn't you know?"

The noise came again, and this time Tommy half rose so that I saw his face, an extraordinary red color. Tommy said, "But he's such a *little* squirt. He's like one of those fellas that rides the horses."

Voices speaking to Tommy, and he was subsiding, OK OK. Teresa tossed her thick hair and her new husband lowered his head and clenched his fists.

"How did Tommy get in here anyhow?" said India. "He never graduated with the class. Did you bring him, Garland?"

Garland yawned. "I never graduated with the class either."

"Tommy Tucker would never have thought to come if you didn't bring him."

"I beg your pardon; he was on his way up here in a muscle shirt and motorcycle boots. I got him to put on a suit." Garland grinned, a hint of his old expressiveness, but malicious, I thought, with the eyes hidden.

"You keep hanging out with trash," whispered India. "You just go ahead and hang out with your drunks and drug addicts."

I leaned toward India just a little, wanting to hear. Interested in spite of myself in Garland's ten years. But India said nothing more, and Tommy Tucker stayed out of sight and the band played a blast of imitation Rolling Stones, and there was a general plunge to the dance floor, as if everyone had tired of talking.

"Hey, Gar," said Duke. "When are you going to ask her to dance?"

I thought he meant me. Well, I thought, that would be an acceptable thing to happen next. I wouldn't mind dancing with him. But Garland said, "India knows I'll dance with her anytime."

"Ask her like a gent, Gar," said Duke.

"India, you want to dance?"

She slipped out of her puff-sleeved coat and let it crumple behind her on the chair and went toward the dance floor without looking back. Garland followed.

"Ain't she something else?" said Duke. Tenderly he folded her coat. I was clinging to the rim of a hole; the music had started and I had been passed over. All the rest of them were paired off for the evening, for the duration of the world. I watched Duke's hands smooth the coat, thinking they would be nice hands to hold in a slow dance, but he said, "I'm always glad when we go out with old Garland; it gives her someone to dance with. I have a bad knee myself."

"Listen, Duke," I said. "I hope you'll excuse me, but there are some people I haven't talked to yet."

He got up and patted my elbow. "Hey, it's your party, go talk to your friends."

But I didn't really want to talk; I wanted to go and do what I would have been afraid to do when I was sixteen, what I still had to do quickly, without thinking, or I would never have courage. I was going to stand near the dancing and look like I wanted to be asked. I placed myself where I could see Garland and India. He was the only man in a light suit, and between the suit and her arms and neck and bosom, they seemed to be their own source of illumination, and at the same time, with their calm faces, like molded people. They danced the lindy, that old dance that had passed out of fashion when they were barely old enough to walk. Everyone else was doing looser, no-contact dances, but Garland and India with their distant, serene faces went under one another's arms and twirled to the back, and back again. They unraveled a dozen variations before they ever approximated the same one again.

And then the voice said, "Hey, Blair Ellen, wanna dance?" And I moved toward the man and the music before I ever guessed who it was. In fact, even as I extended my arms and looked, I still didn't recognize him: puffy eyes, large-pored red nose, a sweating forehead deep-ridged and wrinkled. Then I realized it was Tommy Tucker, his beauty long since ground away, and so drunk that he was nowhere near the beat of the song. I didn't care, though, I danced on my own and waved to people and thought about how Tommy was one of the ones I wanted so much when I was sixteen, and how he never asked.

The band bridged to a low song, and Tommy's long arms came at me with sticky hands to reel me in. I hadn't danced with a tall man in a long time, and I had forgotten how he can wrap almost double around you like a strait jacket. Tommy rested his chin on the top of my head, using me for balance, breathing all over me. I pulled my head out from under him. "So, what have you been doing with yourself, Tommy?"

He dropped his face onto my neck and groaned, "So soft." He was making me damp, surrounding me with a steam bath of whisky vapor. I wiggled to get away, but he settled around me more firmly. "Women are so soft," he said. "Little women are the softest."

"Not me," I said. "I'm as hard as nails, Tommy." Nothing to panic about, I told myself, this is just big old Tommy Tucker; the only danger is suffocation. My face had got mashed into his sleeve and I had begun to concentrate seriously on getting free when I was released all at once into air.

"Hey, Tommy, what do you say, can I have this dance?" Johnny Bardoline had pulled him off.

"Sure man, hey," Tommy gave Johnny an off-target punch in the bicep. "I need to take a piss anyhow."

Johnny was much more my size and willing to leave an air space between us. "Sorry about him."

"I was going to get loose eventually," I said, "but this way I don't have to work up a sweat."

"Poor old Tommy's drunk all the time now. It's a real shame."

I'm not so sober myself, I thought, not when I'm dancing with you, Johnny. The music rolled us together from time to time. I was aware of his thick, square hands. I moved a little closer, and he was there to meet me, no more air space, a solid block of chest.

The slow song ended and Johnny looked around, checking to see if Gail was watching, I expected. I wondered if he would have asked me to dance if I hadn't needed help. When the fast music started, he stayed with me, and I felt a wonderful settling inside. I said, "You know, Johnny, I don't believe we ever danced together before. You were always so faithful to Gail."

"You never went to dances."

"Yes, I did."

"We all figured you were too good, I guess, with your parents being teachers and all."

I felt pity for poor Blair Ellen at sixteen wanting so badly. Wanting to be a cheerleader, wanting Johnny Bardoline or some other boyfriend. Poor Tommy Tucker. Poor sixteen-year-old Blair Ellen.

"That's why it seems so funny," said Johnny, glancing at me

through his eyelashes. "It's so funny that you're a big city swinger now."

I didn't get it at first. I wasn't even sure I heard right. "Nobody believes me," I said. "I live the world's dullest life. I go to work and come home and cook dinner."

"Sure," said Johnny.

"Honest! This reunion is the biggest excitement I've had in months."

Johnny kept laughing at whatever I said, and I laughed too, and we kept dancing and then, after a while, Carmell's husband Dwayne came up and wanted to dance with me. Johnny kept a hand on my shoulder and said he didn't know about that, and he really did seem sorry to give me up. They're going to do this all night, I thought, all the men want to dance with me. They think I'm exciting. I felt exciting. I felt an energy moving all through me, coming out my fingertips.

It was after I had danced a little while with Dwayne that someone screamed. A short scream that demanded notice, followed by Carmell bellowing for Dwayne. Dwayne turned from me and joined the surge toward the source of the disturbance. A microphone fell over and the music stopped. Efficiently, the lead singer of the band carried his guitar and an amplifier to the back of the stage. In the space he had cleared Teresa Spinett climbed up and uttered two more piercing screams. It was a fight, a real fight. I saw Tommy Tucker's pale hair flopping in the center of the crowd, and I found a chair, which wasn't high enough, so I stood on the nearest table. Me and Teresa on opposite banks of the roiling crowd.

They pulled the fighters apart, Tommy cursing and making a windmill, Teresa's new husband straining against the ones holding him, but not hard enough to break loose. You couldn't tell if Tommy wanted to get loose or was just trying to find his center of gravity. He blubbered curses without any consonants, and then his knees seemed to buckle, and the dead weight launched him forward, free before he knew it himself, and Teresa's husband broke loose easily and came at him throwing effective little piston punches. Tommy, drunk as he was, had no chance at all. He took punches in the belly as he fell and in the face as he tried to get up. The crowd closed in again, and finally Johnny Bardo-line got Teresa's husband off Tommy, and Dwayne and some other people took Tommy in sort of a cross-chest carry and headed him for the door. His head was lolling, his eyes rolling ceilingward as if he couldn't find anything worth focusing on. But he seemed to smile or else it was that his mouth and nose had all run together with brilliant, thick blood.

I sat down at the edge of the table. I had thought it was going to be fun, a fight to tell Aaron about, but Tommy's face emptied something out of me. He used to be so handsome, and he had said, you're soft. He wanted something soft, I thought, and it seemed so pathetic I could have cried. I'm coming down, I thought, I was high and I'm coming down.

"You're sitting on the table," said a voice, and I turned to see the light reflected in Garland Odell's glasses. The music was start-ing again, Teresa and her new husband dancing. Garland came closer, a straight shaft of a man with enormous, reflective, fly eyes.

"What's the matter with Tommy?" I said.

Garland shrugged. "He's a drunk," but I must have made a gesture of impatience at such a simple-minded answer, because Garland went on. "It isn't like it's something new, you know. He was always that way. I remember the first game after he got kicked off the team, he'd been drinking all day and we were standing around under the bleachers with this mayonnaise jar full of whisky and old Tommy started cursing about the tackle from Buckhannon that used to knee him in the groin, and he got him-self worked up to the point that when the Buckhannon guys came off the field at half time, he threw the mayonnaise jar at the tackle, and everybody, their whole team, piled on top of Tommy. He got his ass kicked good that time. Me and Nathan Critch climbed up through the bleachers like monkeys till it was all over."

"Some friends," I said.

Garland grinned with his long, stunning, white teeth showing, and I wished that India had gotten the good teeth in the first place. "Come for a walk with me," he said. "I'll show you some-thing." He inclined his head toward the door. I would rather have danced, but I didn't want to be left out again, even for a moment. We went through the double doors, but instead of going on outside, he took the door in the vestibule opposite the coat rack and let me pass down while he snapped the button lock and put on the lights. Downstairs was the recreation hall: a pool table with a sheet over it, a Ping-pong set, a fireplace with a grouping of red leatherette couch and chairs. I stood near the couch while Garland made a nervous circuit of the room, trying lights, finding the switch that turned on the electric logs. He dragged a pedestal ash tray to the couch and sat down. Upstairs the percussion beat went on and on. Garland had a foil packet in his coat that he opened to reveal five thick joints. "I'm going to smoke some dope," he said. "I thought you might want to join me. Being from New York and all."

I said, "You know, I'm getting tired of assumptions being made about me because I live in New York."

He took a deep drag and passed it to me, laid his head back on the couch. He was too skinny, too slick. With hidden eyes and a chin like a red fox. And I didn't trust people who went around with their joints already rolled. I stood there holding it and wasting smoke, and then thought, well, I drank Duke's Scotch, why not smoke with Garland.

The smoke came in a soft flow of air, thick as a wrist. "Are you going to stand?" said Garland as I passed it back to him. I felt foolish; I sat as far from him as possible.

I said, "Garland, I should tell you, I'm married."

He burst out laughing, choked on his smoke. "For Chrissake, Blair Ellen, what do you think I'm going to do?"

I am an absurdity, I thought. It's always like this in public, I get scared over something stupid and make a fool of myself. "I didn't mean you were going to do something to me, I just wanted that straight because everyone is assuming things about me. I'm not some kind of exotic person, I'm married and I live a quiet life." I felt the pressure of the words coming out of me, like a rupturing sack of marbles. I sucked doubly deep on my next turn, a wonderful smoke that didn't burn anything and stayed in easily. It quieted me; a definite resettling of my point of view. Several shifts in succession, in fact, and Garland said something and I missed it. The vinyl of the couch crackled and the back of my arms seemed to be sticking. Surreptitiously I lifted a finger, and the couch made a complaining noise. I was spread all over the couch like peanut butter, and with no more center. I had a sudden flash of insight that if you felt like this long enough you could very easily want to get beat up, to have pain pummel you back into shape. I closed my eyes and tried hard to find my shape. There did seem to be one, when I concentrated. It seemed that I had been for a long time without knowing it a hollow mountain with cold caverns inside. Sometimes I was not the mountain but huddling inside it, maybe sealed up forever.

From a distance he said, "Blair Ellen, are you all right?"

I knew I hadn't talked for a long time. Everything was preternaturally silent and some feet were walking around upstairs. I had lost the beat. "It's cold," I said, and my mouth stuck together.

He was all the way at the other end of the couch, but he swam over, tried to cross the distance. "What do you want? Are you cold? Do you want me to sit closer? What do you want?"

I was amazed; he had asked the one question that seemed important, the one that I despaired of answering, and then I thought, he didn't mean it profoundly, he just meant what do I want at this moment. The distance between us iced over like a lake, thick and blue gray. Garland's face hanging low over the horizon, pulsating from ghostly to darkly outlined. My teeth chattered and I closed my eyes. I opened one eye and saw that fake log that glowed without flames. "I see it," I said. "I see the fire, thanks."

"Jesus," said Garland. "Are you always like this when you smoke?"

The stupid repeating roll of the red log light. "The band stopped for a while, didn't it? I think it was too quiet, and I got cold in the spaces. I'm not making any sense."

Garland left his arm behind me, but leaned his head back. "You make as much sense as anyone else."

I said, "I wish you'd stop hiding your eyes."

He took the glasses off, and I was surprised that he would do what I wanted for no reason except that I asked. I looked for a long time at his face, at the dark marks under his eyes, at his eyes themselves, which seemed blacker than I remembered. He made me sad, the same sadness I had felt when I looked down at Tommy Tucker. He started kissing me, and that was sad too because I thought he was still trying to do what I wanted, and this time he got it wrong. Dry, smoky kisses that left me lonely, so I thought of Aaron. I saw him on a couch in the distance, on our couch at home, kissing someone, kissing Shelley. It made my kissing Garland seem fair, but it didn't make the kisses less dry and grating. After a while I pulled away, got back from him.

"I know," said Garland. "You're married."

I let him think that; it was easier than trying to explain the dryness, which made no more sense than coldness. I said, "I should never smoke when I've been drinking. It's just too much for me. All I hear are those drums pounding."

He said, "Do you want to get out of here? I'll get Duke's car."

I wondered if Garland would drive me to New York. There was something so adrift about him, and so willing, that I thought he might do it. I imagined arriving home around eight or nine A.M. and finding Shelley in our bed. Aaron's shame, Garland's amusement. It was no joke, I shouldn't have hollowed myself out by smoking. "Garland," I said, "what I really wanted was, would you go up and dance with me?"

He put his glasses back on; he turned off the logs.

I said, "If you don't want to—"

"It don't matter," he said. "Believe me, Blair Ellen, I'm glad to. It's no big thing one way or the other."

When we were up with the music and it was impossible to have a conversation anymore, I had a blast of intense curiosity about Garland's life: all the things I hadn't asked him. Over a fast song I shouted, "Garland, where have you been? What have you been doing for the last ten years?"

He inclined his head to me, not hearing, and at that moment India floated up smiling, green and pink and gold, and Duke holding her hand. "I was hoping you two would get together," she said. "I really was." And before I could explain anything she had drifted away.

The band played old songs and I expected Garland to disappear after a while, to drift off as India had. I couldn't imagine what he was waiting around for; I hadn't given him anything. Once I shouted, "Wouldn't you rather be dancing with India?"

I don't know what he thought I said, but he moved us nearer India and Duke, who seemed to have decided to dance after all, and we danced for a while as a foursome. Then the band started playing the song about the West Virginia mountain mama and it was as if there had been a general wordless agreement that this song would be the thing that pulled us all together, the moment of actual reunion. We formed a big circle, four, six, ten, twenty of us, firmly insisting on including everyone, even the people who were still sitting at the tables. The song wasn't even written by a West Virginian! I thought, but it didn't matter. Nothing uncomfortable mattered, not Garland's dryness or the things gone flat or Johnny Bardoline all the way on the other side of the circle from me. I felt the change, and I knew that ten years from now, when I looked back, this would be the moment that we would remember, when we thought of the reunion, the moment when we were all singing, "Take me home, country roads." Tears came to my eyes as the band ran through the verse again, and once more, and then the music was over, the reunion was over, and people were saying good-bye. They'd been leaving couple by couple for an hour. Garland said they'd drive me home, but he had to go somewhere first, he'd be back. I figured he was going off to smoke another joint, to miss the nostalgia. India came running over, worried about where he'd gone, and I said I hoped it was okay with her, he'd offered me a ride. She was relieved; she was delighted. I went back to bouncing around with good-byes, some reserve of energy, enjoying all the offers for a ride home, an offer to go to a little after-party. No, no, I said, no thanks, I'm set. I felt warmly regarded, even beloved. Garland came back again, and at my shoulder he was very still, cooled off, rid of any sentimental feelings. I went looking for my shawl, found it under the table, feeling high again for a moment, then feeling a fineness of irritation at the end of my nerves as the high fled.

The parking lot was muffled and smeared with a high mist; the pole light was the only thing to see except for other subdued people getting into cars like images of us. The mist was closing in fast, and I had a feeling that if I didn't get home soon I would fall asleep wherever I was, quietly engulfed. Duke's car was gray too, gray velours upholstery and quilted gray vinyl on the doors and ceiling. In the back seat Garland put his arm around me, and India and Duke turned and looked at us. "Where are we going?" said Duke.

I pulled myself out of the softness. "I don't want to spoil the party, but I think I really have to go home."

"You don't want to go home!" said Duke. "What's the matter with this younger generation?"

Garland put his face on my neck, but I only felt it as more gray velours. I appealed to India. "I don't know when I've been so tired."

The finely molded disk nodded. "I expect it's the nerves. I was so nervous about tonight I almost didn't come."

"You were?" I said. "But you looked so calm."

"And Garland," she said. "Garland was so nervous he couldn't show up without being on something."

A long, gentle chuckle from Garland and he rolled back to his side of the back seat. Out of the grayness and weariness something forming for me, something I wanted. "Listen, India, I want to say, I'm so glad you came. For some reason—we weren't best friends in high school or anything—but for some reason I always think of you. I used to think of you up on the mountain, even after you moved down. It was so wonderful up there."

India's face, calm center in all this gray. "Do you want to go up there, Blair Ellen? I haven't been up there in years. We could walk up tomorrow if you wanted to."

I hadn't expected such a simple response: I thought I was expressing something difficult and vague. "I have to go to church," I said. "And we always go out to dinner on Sunday—"

India said, "Garland, you'll still be around on Monday won't you? We can do it on Monday."

"Sure," said Duke. "Let's have a cookout. We can try the new grill we bought Grandma. You kids can take a hike and then we'll have a cookout."

It sounded too easy; I tried to make sure I wasn't just wishing it, to spend another day with them. Think it over, I insisted, call me tomorrow if it's okay, or Monday. If you still want to do it, just let me know.

All afternoon Sunday I waited on the patio for them to call. A headache had slowed me during the morning, and at the Hotel General Gray buffet I had disappointed Mother, I knew, by my laconic reunion anecdotes. Yes, I said, Gail and Johnny were there. Yes, they were going to have another baby. Yes? she said. Yes? Who else? I didn't even mention India and Garland, or the wreck of Tommy Tucker. When I was a child, too, I thought, I never told her about the most important ones.

The afternoon stretched ahead, long and hot with purple clouds trying to build into thunderheads, and I wondered whether or not they would really call. What did I know about them at all? Were they people who meant what they said, would do what they promised? I lay on my lounge secretly terrified that I had been mistaken, had misjudged, would be disappointed. India will call, I told myself. She thinks I'm still out. Evening is a much more sensible time for making calls about plans for the next day.

But that evening they didn't call either, and after a few television shows with Daddy I went to bed. Lay in bed awake thinking they still might call. Who cares? I thought. What happened to the wonderful feeling from the reunion? What are Garland and India to you? Didn't you get over them years ago?

Monday morning was beautiful: blue and clear with a wind, chilly under my sheet, and for a full half-minute I was cheerful and forgot I was waiting. But by the time I was dressed, it had come back, and all I could think to do was to make potato salad in case they did call, so I would have something to take, and if not, we could eat it for dinner. Late in the morning Mother and Daddy went to town; while the potatoes took their two hours of marinating in oil and vinegar, I sat, and waited in earnest. I sat in the dining room, all the house visible, and really gave myself over to it. Didn't castigate myself for acting like a teen-ager, didn't pretend the call meant nothing to me. I never sit in stillness at home; there is always something to do, cooking, rearranging, reading, the guitar. But that morning I did nothing, marinated in my waiting like the potatoes. After a while the air took on a dark gelidity, as if space had solidified, as if everything around me—table and chairs, lamps, loveseat, blue and gold day outside—as if all had been frozen in gemstone.

When the phone rang, I knew it would be India. She had, on the phone, a small, precise voice.

"Blair Ellen?" she said. "We wanted to know what time you were coming, or did you want Garland to come and pick you up?" This is her business voice, I thought, her nurse voice, kind and calm but no nonsense. What happened, I wondered. There had been no question in her mind; she thought we had made a firm date. Why had I been waiting? For proof they were serious people? I felt a flush of activity. I ran and opened all the windows, even the ones in the living room that Mother always kept shut. Breezes came through, curtains wafted. I ran to the kitchen and chopped onion and Spanish olives, tossed them with the potatoes, added Mother's cheap salad dressing. I would have made real mayonnaise if I'd known they would call. I ran to the shower and planned what to wear, jeans of course, it was to be a hike. The jeans with the matching vest and the bandana blouse.

When I came out, Mother and Daddy were both back, and Daddy was sitting at the table while she made a sandwich. "Listen," I said, "I'm going on a picnic. I made potato salad to take, but there's plenty for you to have some too."

Mother peeled plastic off a slice of cheese.

"Do you want to drive?" said Daddy.

"It seems a little at the last minute," said Mother. "Are you going to tell us where you're going?"

"There was a misunderstanding," I said, finding myself reluctant to explain. I wasn't sure myself what I'd been paralyzed by. Daddy nodded and Mother narrowed her eyes by an eyelash. Always attuned to the tiniest dissimulation on my part. I said, "It's Garland and India Odell. Or rather she's not an Odell anymore, she's on her third husband." I couldn't believe I was spewing that out in my first breath about them. Mother's eagle eye and crossed arms, causing me to confess where there was only confusion.

She said, "You never mentioned they were at the reunion."

"Who?" said Daddy. "Who are these people?"

"Oh, come on, Daddy, you remember. India was our prom queen when we were juniors and our homecoming queen when we were seniors, and just everything. She has red hair—"

"With the troublemaker brother, I remember. Didn't we finally have to throw him out of school?"

"No, you did not throw him out of school. He dropped out and joined the army. Nobody threw him out."

"There was something," said Daddy. "I know we almost threw him out."

"But why," said Mother, genuinely puzzled. "Why do you want to spend a whole afternoon with them of all people?"

A strange little settling of reality: a disappointment in me that she had never guessed, never had any idea that they were important to me. She never knew about them, that summer with Aunt Pearl, never knew about Garland the night Aunt Pearl's husband got sick. I kept them a secret, and she had no idea.

"It's funny," I said. "I was put at their table Saturday night, and I started talking to India and her husband, and we got along so well." I told them about her nursing career, and Duke, and even how everyone seemed a little worried about Garland's future. Daddy snorted that Garland should have worried about his future in high school, and Mother insisted on slicing some pimentos to decorate my potato salad. Mother recalled how nice India had been, and Garland too, very polite, and I wondered if I would ever tell her the rest of it. Probably not, I thought sadly. I was probably still afraid she could take something from me. The precious secrets of my adolescence.

I drove slowly up Coburn Creek Road, a hardtop with no shoulder, a sort of causeway into the hills. I was dazzled by the white and yellow sunlight, and the intensity of the greens, the redness of the banks where the road carved through the hill. The car moved too fast, though. I would just begin to see the low meadow where the creek looped around some white-faced steers, and then there'd be a curve and I'd be climbing through the woods again. So many moves and small decisions in driving. I wanted to be in a back seat letting my eyes roam lazily with the creek, to feel the car vibrate in my jaw and hear grown-ups talking in the front.

The road went up the last hill before Odells', and for a moment, as I delighted in the green tunnel of trees, I didn't recognize the stone house in the clearing. It was some distance above the road, and a little girl was carrying a puppy to a woman hanging out sheets. Woods closer in to the house now, no more flower gardens, but no rusty chassis and engine blocks either. Clean people, but not really Stone Paradise anymore.

Odells' farmhouse, on the other hand, looked just the same, maybe even better because I had more appreciation of a solidly built house now: a steep pitch to the roof, the broad front porch and brick pillars. I coasted down the driveway toward the barn: the back was all business, screened porch with washing machine, the vegetable garden. We used to play wide-ranging games down there bounded by the garden, the barn and the creek: red rover, all the kinds of tag. There was a picnic table set up in the yard now, covered with flowered plastic. Duke was lugging a grill with an orange hood out from under the back porch.

He put it down when he saw me and came and opened my car door, smelling of aftershave, immaculate in a green polo shirt, white pants, and white loafers. "Come and see Grandma's grill," he said. "Just the same as the one at our house, except at home we have the gas starter."

I sat at the table with the potato salad beside me while Duke set up the grill and talked. His and India's house, he said, came with a built-in barbeque pit; all the houses were built with them fifteen years ago. They threw one party where they had the pit going and the gas starter grill, and two large-size hibachis.

Garland came down the steps then, moving quietly, wearing city clothes, wheat jeans and a pale shirt woven through with a shiny stripe.

"Hey Gar," said Duke. "You remember the party at my house last summer when I had all those grills going? We baked potatoes and corn in the big pit."

"Steamers," said Garland. Standing by my bench.

"Yup, steamers too, all before the steaks. I had better than a hundred people over that day."

"It looked like they were all sleeping over too. They were too drunk to leave."

"Hey," said Duke, "don't give Miss Blair Ellen the wrong idea." But then he went ahead to tell how many cases of beer they knocked back, and how much gin and Scotch. "What I like," Duke said, "is an open house. That's the one thing in the world I want besides India: to be able to say to people, come over when you feel like it, eat and drink all you want, and stay as long as you can."

"People will make a fool of you too," said Garland.

"Garland, let me tell you something. All you get out of life is to choose what kind of fool you'll be, and that's the kind of fool I want to be." Then he grinned. "Besides, I've got India to keep me from going overboard."

Garland made a face, maybe he'd heard all this wisdom before. He seemed to be looking at the sky, but he said, "Do you want that stuff put in the refrigerator?"

He was so quick, one moment standing five feet away, the next springing up the porch stairs with the potato salad. At the same time India and their grandmother coming down the driveway, India dressed in green and white to match Duke, their grandmother lurching heavily, hanging on India's arm.

I remembered the old woman as large but ancient, and I was somewhat surprised to see her still alive, still moving, even in this shrunken and bent form. Her eyes were sunken deep in her head and she made sucking noises as they eased her into a chair. Teeth, I thought. She didn't used to have teeth. They must have all gone to the dentist when they came down off the mountain.

India smoothed the hair over her grandmother's temples and said, "Do you remember Blair Ellen Morgan, Grandma? She came up to visit us on Odell Mountain one time."

Grandma checked that her dress covered her knees. "Was she the one that owned that house?"

"That was my Aunt Pearl," I said. "I was just a little girl."

"They had to sell that place, didn't they?"

"My aunt couldn't keep it up after my uncle died."

"I knew they wouldn't keep that place." They had gathered

[267]

around her, India kneeling, Duke hovering, Garland returning with a six-pack of beer and sitting on the ground beside her.

I said, "Well, I certainly never forgot you, Mrs. Odell. I thought you lived in heaven."

"Heaven!" she sucked her teeth, worked her lips over them, perfectly white teeth, perfectly even, with pink plastic gums. "Well, law, I sure hope heaven picks up some before I get there because that old house seemed like the other place to me."

I said, "I was just a little girl, but I thought it was wonderful up there. I liked all the animals."

"We had animals all right. Pigs and chickens and dogs. I don't know what all. You liked that place? Do you want to buy it? I'd sell it to you."

Garland laughed, "You tell 'em, Grandma."

"It's mine, ain't it? I can sell it, can't I? Or maybe Otis or one of you children did something behind my back so I can't sell it anymore."

India's cheeks spotted a deep magenta, and she got up. "You know we wouldn't do anything behind your back, Grandma. Why do you talk like that?"

"I'm not just talking. I mean it. If that girl wants to buy that place, I'll sell it to her in a minute."

India made a little flap with her hands and turned her back on us. "I can't stand it when she gets suspicious. You sit with her, Duke."

"I don't need nobody to sit with me," she said. "I can't go nowhere, I'm just a sick old lady."

Garland said, "Have a beer, Grandma."

"Keep that stuff away from me," she said, but she made another funny noise with her lips, and Garland laughed. It seemed to be a joke between them.

I said, "Garland, were you happy to move off the mountain too?"

"Oh, I guess so. I didn't mind it as much as they did."

The old woman said, "*He's* the one that should have stayed up there. Then he would have stayed out of trouble."

India, with her back to us said, "He's not in trouble. Garland is fine. You have him mixed up with Elroy."

"I don't either. Garland's just like Elroy, but I don't get them mixed up."

They had changed on me again; India who was perfect in her calmness had colored with fury, and Garland was sitting peacefully, joking with the old woman. I thought I had everything backwards.

Duke said, "Hey, are you people going to go up to that old place or just talk about it? Grandma and I are going to get hungry pretty soon."

India turned around, the splotches gone from her cheeks. "Do you still want to, Blair Ellen?"

"I do, but I wasn't sure you did."

"Garland said he'd drive us as far as the truck will go."

He got up and stretched, picked up the rest of the six-pack by its plastic ring. "You won't catch me climbing all that way to see an old house with the roof caved in."

Grandma said, "The roof's not caved in. That roof will outlast the walls. I don't know why anybody would want to go up there, but as long as you're going, bring me down a bag of green apples from my apple tree. Just enough for a pie."

India said, "We don't know if it bears anymore, Grandma. It's been a long time."

"I'll lay my money on that old tree. It's the one good thing up there. That tree and the roof."

She told India where to find a burlap bag for the apples, and Garland went and warmed up the blunt-nosed truck, so old it had running boards. I felt the way I did when I was little and eager to leave while the adults went about the endless details of getting ready. Excitement in the back of my throat, a vibration, an ululation almost. Let's go, let's go, I thought, as India stopped for a kiss from Duke. I climbed in first, she climbed in after me, we finally rumbled off.

The wind blew in and swept the hair off Garland's forehead; he drove with his right arm draped over the wheel, his left one out the window, clamped on the door. I moved toward India so I wouldn't crowd him, and her leg was warm and resilient. She said something to Garland, so quick and low that I couldn't make out what it was. Garland only shrugged for an answer, and wrenched the wheel, took us across the rattling bridge, headed up Odell Mountain. The truck lurched, and I bounced and slid from one to the other of them.

India said, "You don't have to drive so fast." Garland just grinned, looking young, younger, too young for us. "I think you want Blair Ellen in your lap."

"I wouldn't mind," he said.

It seemed safe to touch them both; bouncing onto his lap didn't sound bad at all. In flashes, as we jerked, I saw parts of them: India's engagement ring, a real hunk of ice. Peach-colored freckles on her shoulder, Garland's forearm on the wheel, tendons moving at his wrist. The taut fabric over his knee. I asked them questions, just to hear their voices, whose truck was this, who took care of their grandmother, who kept the garden, who took in the hay. Everyone's truck, said Garland. Aunt Dora and Carmell, said India. The garden was Otis's and Dwayne shared the hay.

We passed a clearing where grass was growing over the blackened foundations of a house. I said, "Wasn't that the Crains'? Isn't that where Evalina used to live?"

"It burned down," said India. "Now all those Crains live with Evalina and Joe."

At the turnaround, a little field with some mattress springs and an ice box, Garland accelerated, then braked and swung around backwards into the weeds. "That's it," he said. "All out for the hike." He kicked open his door and ripped a beer out of the six-pack.

India said, "Walking's safer than riding with him," and started up the road.

Garland stuck his legs out on the running board and lay back on the front seat with his beer on his chest, looking like he belonged there, in a truck, on the mountain with a beer. I ran to catch up with India. "I guess he really isn't coming," I said. She made a noise, but seemed wrapped up in her own thoughts, or perhaps she was only wrapped in the act of trudging. I thought that this may have been the way she walked to and from the school bus, not looking at anything, putting one foot in front of the other. After a while it seemed to me, too, that the weeds weren't that interesting, and I fell in and trudged too.

She said, after a while, "Do you believe people cause other people to do things?"

It was such a serious question. The wrong kind of serious for walking up Odell Mountain, I thought. "What do you mean? Do you mean are people responsible for what other people do?"

"Yes, that's it. Are people responsible for each other. I mean, Garland got sent over there to the war, and I think I could have stopped him from joining up if I'd wanted to."

"He would have been drafted anyhow."

"He might not have. His eyes are pretty bad, if he hadn't been trying to get in. I'll tell you what I know for certain, though. What I know for certain is that something wasn't good for him over there. He *saw* some things. I know he wouldn't have *done* anything, but he saw things. I used to know everything about him, but not since he came back. I wish to hell he'd never gone." She gave a little laugh. "I don't mean to sound like a protester."

"I was a protester," I said. "I mean, I worked against the war. I was pretty active too."

She was looking down, so I only saw her cheek, and it was still. "That's funny. I never would have thought you were. I would have thought—" I waited, eager to know what *she* had imagined for my life. But she said, "That really is funny. It seems like all my life you were the one I wanted to be like. That time you came up here, when we were little, when I saw you coming, I thought I would die because I didn't have any of the toys I thought you'd be used to."

"We were all messed up, weren't we?" I said. "You thought I wanted toys, I didn't know what it was I wanted, but I thought you had it."

She stopped walking and looked me directly in the face. "Do you know what I wish now? I wish you and Garland would get married and come and live with me and Duke in Silver Spring. That would be a real reunion."

And then she disappeared. Almost before she finished speaking, she gave her body a twist toward some waist-high weeds and disappeared from sight.

"India!" It seemed like magic, I didn't want to be left behind, and I needed to confess to her, that I wasn't available to be part of her plans. "India!"

She reappeared ten feet up the bank, clinging with both hands. "Step over that ditch," she said. "The rope's mostly gone but you can still find some steps." She was pulling herself up, half crawling, half climbing hand over hand. I was going to have to plunge in too or else be left behind. I sprang desperately, landed out of the weeds in a dirt slide that filled my sandals, but I ignored discomfort and set my eyes on her bottom working its way above me. The first step was a loose stone, and the next one, dirt shaped by a rotten board. Then I found an upright pipe in the middle of the weeds, and I crashed through boldly, breaking one of my greatest childhood taboos, never to go where the poisons live: copperheads, the ivy, black widow spiders.

The next time India disappeared she went over the top, and I scrambled after her. Onto a pine-wooded slope almost bare of undergrowth. India started to run over the swell, and I took my time, enjoying the gradual opening-up, and the wind. Things came into sight beyond the pines, the tall grass, the flat-topped boulders: I stepped up on one and saw the house, and India leaping for it, forgetting me entirely, springing over the grass, plunging to embrace the house. It made me sad, or perhaps envious, that the house was India's, and also that she was rushing to it, and away from me. I stayed on the boulder until she had gone around to the back, and then I followed, watching the barn come into sight, the woods behind it, and behind them, hills rising, irregular ridges, bright deciduous trees, firs almost black, one hill laid against another as if we were at the end of civilization.

The good tar paper roof of the house was firmly in place except for one corner of the porch where a support had fallen away. No rocking chair, though, and a paper-pale hornet's nest seemed to have been deserted too. I looked in a window and was disturbed by how barren the room was, especially how the walls were unfinished horizontal laths, never plastered. Never covered. Had India and Garland lived without real walls? No paint, no wallpaper? That's such a small thing, I thought. But it frightened me, the difference. The distance. I walked to the back, passing the well, found the back door open and India standing inside by a pile of brown leaves on old linoleum.

"Kitchen?" I said.

She nodded, hugging herself as if she were cold, staring at the wall, or rather, at a metal collar around a hole in the wall. "That was the cookstove," she said.

"You didn't leave much when you left."

"We left the stove, but we told the Crains they could take things that weren't nailed down, so they took out the nails and carried off the stove." A door led to a small leanto of a room with a sloping roof. She went in, and I followed. It had a cupboard with some canned food and a mattress laid on a homemade plywood and block bed. "Some of the old men come up here in the fall to hunt," she said. "They just lie here and listen to their dogs run. Pop used to run coon hounds too, only he never did it from the house, he had a little shanty out in the woods." She sat on the bed; she got up again. "We had a real bed, at least. This was my room. This was where I was afraid you'd see I didn't have a dollhouse."

"I liked the goat better than a dollhouse."

"Actually," she said, looking out the window, "it wasn't just my room, it was Garland's and mine."

I nodded; she was telling me something important, but I didn't quite get it. I said, "And your grandparents slept in the front room?"

"Yes, they had the big bed in there, and the sofa and whatever else we owned. And our little bed was in here." She looked me in the face again, no dimples, her oval white face and bay eyes. "We slept together in a little tiny bed in here."

Pairs, I thought, everyone always in pairs. And at that moment, for some reason, I thought, everyone but me in pairs. Mother and Daddy, Aaron and Shelley, Garland and India.

"Garland and I didn't know any better," she said, "and I doubt Pop did either, he was just an ignorant old man who didn't want anyone bothering him. He didn't want to know how the rest of the people did anything. Grandma knew better, but she was slow getting used to the idea that we were growing up. When we were little, we were just like a pile of puppies, it didn't matter, but when we got big, it wasn't right."

I tried to remember them as they were then, if this explained anything, and what I remembered was India's silence, and some

[273]

tremor, perhaps of knowledge, perhaps only a toothache. I re-membered Garland burning with his strange energy. I made an effort and thought of Aaron, and how our bed is in some way the center of our lives, and how he tells me his dreams and it turns out the same figure was in my dream too, or else by the time he finishes telling me I have forgotten mine and taken over part of his. "At least you weren't alone, India."

She said, "Carmell was the first one who found out. I don't even remember what I said that let it out, but all of a sudden she was covering up her mouth and squealing like a little stuck pig, and the next thing I knew Aunt Dora was starting in on me, but by that time I figured out what was going on and said Carmell didn't understand, she got it wrong."

I touched her shoulder. I would only be hearing this once. I said, "But India, you and Garland were as innocent as Adam and Eve in the Garden."

"Garland was," she said, "but I wasn't ever innocent. I figured everything out. I figured that Garland was the one who'd have to sleep on the floor. He couldn't understand what was wrong. He's just like Pop that way, never understands what the rest of the people have to do with anything. 'Tell Aunt Dora to mind her own business,' he said, 'I'll fix Carmell myself.' And all the time I was laying down quilts on the floor. I explained that he was the one who had to sleep on the floor because that's the way men are, so he slept down there with the drafts and whatever crawled through the chinks in the wall until we moved. And I lay up in the bed thinking I was doing things the way normal people do."

"I guess you were," I said. "For better or worse."

"I should have let him stay in the bed."

I thought so too. I thought that whatever they were doing together in the bed it was better than trying to do what you only guessed you were supposed to.

She turned her face from the window, back to me, and gave me a smile, as if that were the end of it. She had said what she was going to say. I was ashamed of my greediness, but I couldn't help wondering what it had been like, they two in the tiny bed for years, whispering, touching. She laughed. "You look like you lost your best friend, Blair Ellen. I'm the one with the sad story." And she reached out and put her arm around my shoulder, drew me to her for a hug. "It wasn't so bad, most of it. We were lucky, really. I never even think about all that, except for coming up here, I would never have thought about it at all." She had a smell of fresh baking. "Look," she said, "I knew he'd come."

Garland striding out of the woods with his shirt off. Moving his head from side to side making sure no one was sneaking up on him. "He should have been born in time to be a pioneer," I said. "With Daniel Boone. He looks like he's discovering the Cumberland Gap."

"Him and Pop both," said India. "All the men in my family."

She let go of me and tapped on the window, and Garland changed directions, and we went out on the back porch to meet him.

"You forgot the apple bag," he said. He was on the ground, we were looking down at him. "What were you two doing in that hot little hole?"

"Talking," said India. "Talking about being kids."

There was a vein pulsing at the base of Garland's neck. India touched it, and he closed his eyes. She said, "Why don't you and Blair Ellen get married?"

Garland opened his eyes, made a sour mouth. "Don't be dumb, India. She's already married."

India looked at me, but I didn't have to say anything. "We'll have to find him someone else then," she said.

We walked away from the house singly, to pick apples, the wind holding us at a certain distance from one another. I thought: why, I have the whole rest of the day with them. I'll have a conversation with India about hospitals and talk about the war with Duke and Garland. I'd find out what happened to Elroy. I might ask Grandma Odell what it was like to be married to a pioneer. The world expanded as we walked, the sky and land opened. In this direction you could see fields and farmhouses; the town would be over that gap, just out of sight, near the steam columns from the power plant. Mother and Daddy down there somewhere, busy with the garden, the neighbors, church, and school. Somewhere farther, Pittsburgh and the broad, rich, dairy flank of Pennsylvania. Beyond that, in the towers, Aaron writing lectures, writing poems.

Nothing finished.

About the Author

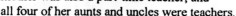

MEREDITH SUE WILLIS was raised in Shinnston, West Virginia. She grew up in an atmosphere of storytelling, preaching, and radio melodramas. She published her first story when she was fifteen years old. Educated in the public schools of Shinnston, West Virginia, she had her father as her teacher for Biology, Chemistry, and Physics. Her mother was also a part-time teacher, and all four of her aunts and uncles were teachers. Her paternal grandparents operated a country store; her maternal grandfather was a coal miner who witnessed the Great Monongah mine disaster of 1907; and her maternal grandmother was a mining camp midwife.

She dropped out of college to become a VISTA volunteer in Norfolk, Virginia, then returned to college. She earned a Bachelor's degree from Barnard College and a Master of Fine Arts from Columbia University. She then began to work as a writer-in-the-schools with Teachers & Writers Collaborative, one of the earliest of the arts-in-education organizations. Teachers & Writers publishes her books on creative writing: Personal Fiction Writing, Blazing Pencils, and Deep Revision. Her other published work includes A Space Apart, Only Great Changes, Quilt Pieces, In the Mountains of America, and two novels for children, The Secret Super Powers of Marco and Marco's Monster.

She lives in South Orange, New Jersey with her husband Andrew B. Weinberger and their son Joel.

LaVergne, TN USA
11 November 2009

163801LV00003B/141/A